# THE

# INNOCENCE

# OF

# WESTBURY

# BOOKS BY FREDERIC MARTIN

**The Vox Oculis Series**

Not Alone

The Innocence of Westbury

Forest

# THE INNOCENCE OF WESTBURY

## A VOX OCULIS NOVEL: BOOK TWO

### FREDERIC MARTIN

NTHSENSE BOOKS

Published by NthSense Books
Richmond, Vermont
www.nthsensebooks.com

NthSense, NthSense Books, and the NthSense Books logo are trademarks of NthSense, LLC.



ISBN: 978-1-7340240-7-4 (hardcover)
ISBN: 978-1-7340240-2-9 (paperback)
ISBN: 978-1-7340240-3-6 (ebook)

*To Elizabeth Cady Martin*
*for being a delightful and dedicated spouse,*
*not to mention a ferocious proofreader.*

*;^)*

# AUTHOR'S NOTE

Welcome to *The Innocence of Westbury,* the second book of the "Vox Oculis" series. In the first book, *Not Alone,* you met our heroes Will Woods and Blue DuBois. Before you begin reading *Innocence of Westbury,* I feel a quick lesson on French pronunciation is required as most of you are probably not from Vermont or France or Quebec or the host of other French speaking countries. Blue's last name is French in origin and pronounced natively as "doo-bwah" and that is Blue's strongly preferred pronunciation. Vermonters are very accustomed to native French pronunciations as our northern border is shared with Quebec, the province in Canada that is most rigorous about preserving its French heritage, to the point of requiring all outdoor signage to be in French with the option of having English translation in smaller font below the French. In fact, many visitors to Quebec would be shocked to find that there is a small, but significant, portion of its residents who do not know a scrap of English. Quebec is so emphatic about its French heritage that it has gone as far as having several referendums on seceding from Canada and getting darn close to actually succeeding (in seceding . . . ;^).

Being adjacent to Quebec means Vermont gets a lot of visitors from Quebec (and vice-versa) and a lot of those visitors find a nice

Vermont boy or girl and fall in love and wind up settling in Vermont. As you might guess (as this has been going on for generations and generations) there are a lot of French surnames, business names, road names, even town names here in Vermont. And yet, Americans being Americans, and even Vermonters, some of these names eventually wind up being pronounced in literal American-ish. For example, the name "Charlebois" (shar-luh-bwah) gets Americanized to "charley-boys" and "LaVerdière" (la-ver-dee-air) becomes "luh-ver-dee-ur". As you can imagine, Blue's surname often gets pronounced "dew-boys." Many folk go along with the American pronunciation (even some in the Charlebois family go along with "charley-boys") but Blue is fairly insistent on the native pronunciation. In fact, she would be disappointed if, as you read this book, in your head you pronounced her name *"dew-boys"* instead of *"doo-bwah"* and furthermore, she would probably know if you did, if you are a leaker, as I imagine many of you are, though you may not yourself know it. Yet.

Also another minor tidbit, something that might be more familiar to many of you, is that there are several different ways of writing those six characters which include: "Du Bois", "Dubois", and of course "DuBois." My own given name is realized in all of the following forms: "Fredrick", "Frederick", "Fredrich", "Fredric", Frédéric, and of course the *correct* English version (ahem) which is "Frederic." You get the idea and probably many of you have names that face the same nightmare of misspellings and mispronunciations and are familiar with having to live with it your entire lives. If you do, I hope you have sympathy for the suffering that Blue and I go through almost every day.

So with that explanation, you may do as you please, but both Blue and myself would be most appreciative if you adopt our preferred pronunciations and spellings as you engross yourself in the pages that follow. And, by the way, I pronounce my name "fred-rick", not "fred-e-rick". Go figure.

   *-fm*

# AUGUST, 2031

*"In my talk I have mentioned 'perception of reality' several times and I will mention it many times more because that is what this talk is really about. Yes, we have seen that people with vox oculis can communicate verbally with their eyes. Yes, we have explored the physiology of that sensory capability. Yes, we have found that many of us have vestigial vox oculis tissue and yes, that tissue can functionally leak some of our thoughts to those that have true vox oculis.*

*All of this is very challenging to comprehend and for many, astonishing. But we have only scratched the surface of the implications of this ability because it is not necessarily this extra sensory perception alone that alters the reality for a person with vox oculis, it is the neurobiology that we all are blessed with that can take this extra sense and integrate it with our entire neural-chemical system that includes not only our five basic senses, but our gut-brain axis, reflexes, adrenal glands, logical centers, emotional centers, memory, and even technological advances such as AR implants and simstim.*

*What happens when we put all these together? What is the*

*reality? Is it just what you see? Is it just what you hear? Is it just what you ate? No, of course not. It is not 'just' any one of these things, it is all of them blended together to give you the experience you are having right now. Maybe your eyes are closed and you are picturing something in your head that is a synthesis of what you are hearing. Maybe you are half asleep and daydreaming something totally bizarre yet totally realistic. Maybe you have to pee and are trying to get the image of a waterfall out of your head.*

*Now imagine you had one additional neural input that could eavesdrop on not just the verbal thoughts, but the fully processed reality—images, emotions, physical comfort—experienced by the people sitting around you now. What images would be forming in your head? What would your internal dialog be? What would your emotional state be? And the most interesting question of all: exactly how much of their reality becomes part of your reality?"*

— FROM THE INTERNATIONAL SYMPOSIUM
ON GENETIC VARIANCE, CASTLETON
UNIVERSITY, AUGUST 14TH, 2031

AUGUST, 2011

# PROLOGUE

NYPD Detective Rodney James contemplated the abstract nature of his half-eaten sausage and cheese breakfast sandwich as it sat nestled in the oddly symmetrical folds of the grease-stained foil paper. He imagined it as a bloom cut from some alien tree that grew breakfast sandwiches, hanging like foil coated fruit from steely branches in the streets of Manhattan, plucked by herds of trendily-dressed creatures whose faces were permanently set in an expression that could only be defined as "out-of-my-way-I'm-on-my-way-somewhere-exceedingly-important."

His musings were interrupted with the slap of a case folder flopping on the only clear spot of his overly cluttered cubicle desk. He had plenty of lukewarm cold-case folders skewed about already, but a new one was always a bit of a thrill. Each one held the potential of an exciting discovery leading to resolution of some decades-old mystery. It was a treasure hunt. Gambling, really. Frustrating 99.9 percent of the time, but with that intoxicating 0.1 percent possibility of hitting the jackpot. One in a thousand. To some, those were terrible odds. Not to him.

"Are you going to eat the rest of that? If not, I'm starving."

Rodney looked up into the face of Chief Detective Daniels and said, "You shall starve, then. What's in here?"

"Well, depends on how you look at it. Ice cold case if you look at it like a normal detective, but glowing warm if you knew who it came from."

"Harris?"

"You know," the chief grabbed the breakfast sandwich and took a large bite out of it but kept on talking while he chewed, "Harris pointed this one at you very particularly. You should be flattered."

Rodney picked up the folder and thumbed through the contents. "WITSEC[1]? Witness protection? Why isn't this going to the U.S. Marshals?"

"It came *from* the Marshals, you idiot. Read it but remember you have to keep it very tight. They don't let this info out unless it is a very good reason. Look at the other files."

Rodney flicked through until he came to one labeled "Babineau."

"That fucker, Babineau." He looked up at the chief. The chief nodded. "How did Harris get all this? I thought he was retired."

"He's retired *and* he's a legend. He gets info he wants. You don't stop being a detective just because you retire. The last piece you need to look at is this." The chief pulled a newspaper clipping out of the folder. It was from yesterday's New York Times. A drug related kidnapping in Vermont. He read it and as he did, he felt a tiny rush of adrenaline. It was a stretch, but if it came from Harris, it probably wasn't. Harris had uncanny instincts about these things. He looked back up at the chief, who nodded.

"This is to be kept between you and me and Harris *only*. You got that?"

He nodded. He didn't have to be told. Witness protection was taken extremely seriously—not even to be shared with colleagues. A leak could kill someone. Did kill someone. More than one. This was his case five years ago when he worked on it in cooperation with the State Police. It was Harris's case twelve years ago when it was a sting, code named "Gambrel."

He looked back at the article and stared at the one name that, along with the name "Babineau" was the axis that this whole case turned around, the one that Harris spotted out of the avalanche of information that poured out of every outlet, every hour, every day. Harris had sussed out that name and made the connection and pulled together the file that he was looking at now. The notion that this one article could revive such a dead dog as Gambrel was intoxicating. All it took was that one name.

DuBois.

1

———

## NEW NORMAL

Will's eyes were closed. He had closed them so he could enjoy the sensation of the intense morning sun that streamed through his window and pressed his body into the soft folds of his comforter like a big warm hand. A late-summer breeze sifted through the window screen and danced lightly up his legs, skipping over his bare torso to his face, where it brushed lightly across his eyebrows and forehead. He took in a long, slow breath, feeling his chest expand and stretch, pulling his skin tight, causing it to tug on the crisscross of still-fresh scars, reminding him that if he moved too much, too fast, the confusion of damaged tissue in his upper left chest would protest. But if he didn't move, just breathed slowly in . . . then slowly out . . . he could pretend he was the same undamaged boy that he was at the beginning of the summer. Care-free, pain-free, fame-free, guilt free.

It was nice.

His mind felt free, too. It was quiet and relaxed for the first time in weeks. And exhausted. It had been so clenched up from the non-stop barrage of interviews, phone calls, text messages, emails, and snail mails that his brain cells felt like they had been balled up like a knotted snarl of tangled Christmas tree lights. And there were the follow-up appointments at the hospital and the tense day when he woke up with a headache and a teeny-tiny fever and his mom freaked out and rushed him to the emergency room terrified that it was an infection in his wound. It wasn't, of course, it was just another sideshow in this crazy circus of the past couple of weeks.

But now, it was a beautiful morning, he was alone in his bedroom, it was quiet in the house, and he had the whole day to himself. For the first time, he felt like he could finally turn the page on this chapter of his life. It had certainly been an exciting chapter. The climax was, of course, two weeks ago. He had been shot. With a handgun. Point blank. The bullet had entered his body at terrific speed, careening off a rib, causing it to miss his vagus nerve (thank God, now that he knew what that was) and taking an alternate route through the tip of his left lung (thanks a lot), causing the lung to collapse (gradually–a little bit more with each breath). Somewhere along that path, the bullet managed to clip a small artery before it bounced off his scapula and made a tumbling exit out his back, tearing a hole in his muscle and skin as it went. It had finally clattered to the floor somewhere in the room behind him, deformed and spent, all of its energy having been used to create havoc inside his body.

The clipped artery had refused to stop bleeding, probably because he refused to stop trying to rescue his friend, Blue. Instead, a steady flow of his blood, and life, seeped through the exit wound onto the floor behind him. Blood loss is what almost killed him. Dead. Gone. The tragic death of a teen not yet even fully grown into manhood. Never to excel in college and grad school and realize his dream of becoming a preeminent scientist. Never to experience the euphoria of falling in love. His only lasting legacy being the heroic rescue of a helpless orphan girl from clutches of a cold-blooded drug dealer. Will Woods—dead teen hero. Mourned by a grieved community. Memorialized with a giant statue in Jefford's Park.

Yeah, right—get a grip, Woods, he thought. A bag of ashes in a brass urn and an obituary in the Westbury News-Press was the best he could expect.

But he wasn't a bag of ashes. He was still a very live bag of living, breathing bone and protoplasm. He took in another deep breath and let it out slowly, enjoying the sensation of air going in .. . and then out. He thought about how billions of humans around the globe were doing the exact same thing. Air going in . . . and then out . . . and then in . . . and then out. He wondered how many of those people had read about him or seen the news clips. Thousands? Hundreds of thousands? Millions? How many times had the story been posted and shared and tweeted and retweeted? That was one of the weirdest parts of the whole thing—his story going global —now a permanent part of his electronic legacy. Wherever he went from now on it would be, "Oh yeah, I remember that story. That was *you*!?" It was already weird enough just around town. Even strangers would walk up to him. "Hey, Will, how are you doing? Did it hurt, getting shot?" Did it hurt. What do you think? Of course it frigging hurt! Here, let me demonstrate (pulls out a gun, shoots the questioner in the shoulder). There! How are you doing? Did that hurt?

The funny thing was that some people acted almost jealous. He remembered being jealous of kids in casts who had broken an arm or leg. Why was that? Who would ever be jealous of someone going through so much pain? It was weird. He figured it was all the attention. People are so kind to you and generous, even the annoying strangers. And in the beginning, all that attention felt really great, but after about a week, it started to get a little tiring, and then it got really annoying, and now he'd reached the point where he just wanted to lock the door and tell them all to kindly fuck off. He had never really appreciated being a nobody before, but now he did. Now there was no more anonymity. Everyone knows you. People who had never given you the time of day before suddenly start acting like they're your best friend.

And then there was this whole "hero" thing. They kept calling him a hero. Somehow being shot made him the hero. How did they figure that? Blue was the real hero. She'd been the one with the courage to go after the drug dealer (and single-handed at that, thanks to Will's cowardice). It was because of her that their town was now rid of that psychopath. And she was the one who'd suffered the most, enduring twenty-four hours of captivity, beaten, bound, gagged, isolated, and alone, sure she was going to die. And now, instead of her being the hero, people were treating her like she was the victim—damaged goods. Even worse were the idiots on Facebook that were pushing complete lies; that she was an addict, that she was the dealer's lover, that it wasn't an abduction it was part of some S&M thing. What the hell was wrong with those people? He'd blasted them back but instead of listening to the truth, these morons wove him into their whole alternate narrative. They were so wrapped up in their own non-reality that it was impossible to talk any sense into them. He had finally given up and just thanked God that Blue didn't do FB and didn't see all this crap. Nobody needed to see that, especially her. Jesus, after what she'd been through she needed everyone's support instead of being beaten-up even more. And the way she had been acting lately, it seemed like she could use a lot of support. He thought a therapist like his mom could help, if only Blue didn't have a pathological hatred of therapists or anyone with a "Dr." in front of their name. In fact, Will wasn't sure there was anyone she trusted enough to let them inside her head. On the other hand, she *had* reached out to him at the homecoming party.

Will sighed. His whole body had tensed up and now his shoulder was hurting again. Damn. Why did he care so much anyway? Yeah, she was the first person he had met outside of his family that shared their secret special ability, vox oculis, and maybe that accounted for some of it, but it wasn't all of it. It wasn't physical attraction, though she was lithe and graceful and had a classic profile that had the potential for great beauty if she ever relaxed her semi-permanent state of grim seriousness. No, she was still more of a tom-boy than a teenage girl, at least in Will's mind. Hard to imagine a romantic relationship developing there. As for her volatile personality, it wasn't exactly what you'd call "sparkling," though there was an undeniable quality of honesty and camaraderie about her when they were together.

Nope, he had no idea why he did, but there it was. He cared about her. And was amazed by her. Blue, the survivor. Her whole family gone and yet here she was, still plugging away, tough as nails and brittle as glass.

He took one more deep breath and let it out like a deflating balloon. So much for the brief delusion of peace and normalcy. He wondered if he could ever just relax and not worry anymore. Blue, reporters, physical therapy, nosey well-wishers, trolls . . . and on top of that, the coming onslaught of sophomore year. He was hoping to fly under the radar at high school, for a while at least, but that was probably just a pipe dream.

He closed his eyes and tried to refocus on the sensation of the warm sun and recapture that feeling of being at peace, but the sun had moved on and he was too wound up now. Just get up, Woods, he told himself. His body stubbornly refused. It wanted to stay on the bed, sun or no sun, but now even the bed refused to cooperate. It tried to eject him with a sudden giant bounce. He opened his eyes and found himself staring directly at an upside-down face.

"*HEY THERE, BIG UGLY BROTHER.*"

"*HEY THERE, DEMENTED LITTLE SISTER.*"

His sister's *vox* flowed through her eyes into his and her words rang in his head with the most irritating tone Rose could muster, but to Will they had a comforting familiarity.

Rose looked at his shoulder. "*UGH! WHAT A MESS! WHY'D YOU TAKE THE BANDAGE OFF?*" She scooted around so that she was lying next to him and leaned her head on his good shoulder. "Does it hurt much?" she said out-loud.

"Nah, not anymore. Just kind of tight and achy."

She reached her arm across and hugged him. "I'm just glad you're still here."

"Aww, you're so sentimental."

"I'm just practical," she said. "If you were gone, I'd have to do the dishes every single night."

"Very funny. You're asking for a tickle attack."

She sat up suddenly, "No, don't! I don't want you to hurt yourself!" She wasn't laughing. "*WILLY! DON'T! PLEASE!*"

A tiny surge of anxiety tickled his stomach like a frantic butterfly. That feeling wasn't coming from him. He looked her in the eye. "*I WON'T. DON'T WORRY, LITTLE MEERKAT.*"

She stared at him, but her expression relaxed. "*YOU BETTER NOT!*" She slumped back down next to him.

That tickle of anxiety he felt from Rose—those sensations had been happening more and more lately—ever since the night he'd been shot. His mom in the hospital, Blue at the homecoming party, and now Rose. When he brought it up with his mom, she told him he should ask his dad about it when he was ready. He'd been puzzling about that one for a while. Why his dad and not his mom? Was this some kind of birds and bees talk? A little late for that, it seemed.

"Willy! Talk to me."

"Blah de blah blah blah blah. And don't call me Willy."

"Don't make fun."

He gave her a little squeeze. "I'm okay, really. I'll be one-hundred percent soon."

"You'd better be. Blue better be, too. Sam said she's acting more like she did at the beginning of the summer. She even skipped dinner once."

Sam was Blue's younger foster brother. What Sam said to Rose just reinforced what Will had been thinking.

"Do you think she's okay?" Rose asked.

"Hey, don't worry, you. Blue is made of tougher stuff than us. She just needs a little more time."

"You really think so?"

"Yeah, I do."

Rose sighed and tucked her head under his chin, "I hope so. I like Blue a lot."

"Yeah. You and me both."

That's all Blue needed was a little time, he thought. A little time and . . . a little help. If he could *just* get her to talk to his mom. Right. Like that worked out spectacularly last time he tried. It was easier rescuing her from being kidnapped than talking her into seeing a therapist—maybe because she was tied up and unconscious when she was captive. Maybe that's what he should do—knock her out and tie her to a chair in his mom's office.

Rose lifted her head and looked at Will. "What are you laughing about?"

He smiled at her. "Nothing. Don't you worry about Blue."

"Why not? You are!"

"Am not!"

"Are too!"

"All right, maybe a little," he said and gave her another squeeze. Yeah, maybe a little, he thought. Maybe a lot.

**2**

---

## BLUE'S BATTLE

Her breath was coming in short gasps, but they were steady at last, and she could exhale without feeling like she might explode. Quick breath, exhale. Quick breath, exhale. Slow it down. A little deeper now, longer exhale. Deep breath, long exhale, repeat. She could feel her pulse calming down. Her face felt warm, as of course it would the way it was pressed into her knees which she had hugged tightly to her chest. She rocked back and forth to the rhythm of her breathing, her bed creaking slightly from the motion. Her brain started to engage again, now that it was no longer focused solely on suppressing the volcano that threatened to overcome her with an eruption of tears and hysteria. And the question her brain asked was the same one it had been asking for over a week, "Why? Why does this keep happening? When will it stop?" That last question was growing more and more ominous. She kept expecting each episode to be the last and that made the next episode even more excruciating.

Her rocking settled into a slow sway, and she kept it going because it was comforting. She was breathing steadily now, with just an occasional sniffle. She had settled enough that she could think clearly again. She went over in her mind everything that had happened since the kidnapping, looking for a reason, a solution, anything that she could cling to that would help her make sense of what was going on. Right after she returned from the hospital, things had seemed to return to a nice norm. There had been some media attention early on, but recently it had swung away from her, and now most of the focus was on Will, and that was fine with her. She was fed up with answering annoying questions like, "How did you feel? Were you scared?" God, how are you supposed to answer that? "Oh yes, I was a terrified, helpless, pathetic, weak little girl!" And then their answer would be, "Oh you poor dear sweet innocent little damsel!" Screw you. Leave me alone. Let me go back to my house, back to my room, back to what was starting to be the first period of peace and stability I have felt in almost five years.

Thankfully, they did. With most of the attention on Will, Blue was free to settle back into the comfort and security of the O'Day household. And that was great, except for one thing.

*This* started happening.

The first hint of it was at the homecoming party when the Woods family and the O'Days were getting ready to watch the interview about the kidnapping on TV. She had felt the inklings of it coming on, but she had instinctively moved next to Will and grabbed his hand. It was a little awkward, holding his hand, but he didn't let go, and it had worked. It quelled the panic. And it felt good . . . holding someone's hand. Will's hand. Anyway, that time it didn't erupt into a full blown episode and she figured it was a one-time thing.

But it was just getting started.

The first full blown attack, Will wasn't around. Neither was the only other person who might have helped, her older foster brother, Wu. The cause was the armchair in the dining room. She had sat down to start reading a book, and as soon as her arms touched the chair, her body jumped reflexively straight up, and she nearly screamed. The sensation of being bound to a chair, helpless, hope-less . . . it returned like a lightning bolt. She nearly lost it. Sobs erupted so hard that she had to hold her breath to keep them from exploding into cries. She squeezed her eyes shut to keep the tears back while she gasped for breath. She managed to hold it in and slip up to her room unnoticed until she recovered.

Since then, the episodes became frighteningly frequent and familiar. They started as a flutter in the middle of her diaphragm. The flutter crawled up into her chest, and once there, it formed a surge of pressure that rose quickly up her neck to her face and, like a volcano, threatened to erupt through her eyes in a massive flow of tears. She felt like she would come apart at the seams. She had to fight like the devil to keep that from happening. So far she had managed, but just barely.

She had tried different strategies to stop it. She stayed away from the armchair, but then other things would trigger it. Surprising things. A noise, or a smell, or the sound of a car going by. She had no idea what triggered this latest one. It had come completely out of the blue. It was so frustrating! Ridiculous! Childish! It pissed her off because she couldn't seem to make it go away. She was also getting exhausted with being constantly on guard, not knowing when it would happen again. Even worse, she was sure Ma Beth had started to notice.

She finally stopped rocking, lifted her head, and took a deep almost-normal breath. It seemed the worst had passed, and she was almost fully recovered, but she knew she would have to wait at least half an hour before she could go out of her room again. That would allow time for the redness and wateriness in her eyes to subside and for the rest of her to calm down enough so she could venture back out and pretend like nothing was wrong. But before even ten minutes had passed, she heard the sound of footsteps coming up her stairs. It was too soon! She sat frozen on the bed. Please don't knock, please don't knock, please don't knock . . .

There was a knock on her door.

"Blue? Are you okay?"

"I'm fine," she replied, too quickly. Ma Beth's voice was usually a welcome comforting sound, but now Blue was terrified that she would come in and see her in this state. She could sense Ma Beth's hesitation on the other side of the door. The seed of panic started to flutter in her chest, but she battled it back down. The door didn't open, but the footsteps didn't retreat down the stairs either.

"Blue, I have to go out and run an errand. I will be gone for about an hour, but Wu is here, downstairs in his room. Will you be okay?"

She wasn't sure she'd be okay. She knew no one else was home except Ma Beth and Wu. Deep down inside a part of her craved to tell Ma Beth to please not leave her, but a larger part of her got angry. She shouldn't be afraid to be alone! She had never been afraid to be by herself. Ever. This feeling was stupid. She could handle it. She'd be fine.

"Blue?"

"Don't worry, I'll be fine." She said it firmly and with conviction. Her anger at herself was giving her confidence again.

"All right," said Ma Beth after another moment of hesitation. "I'll be back soon."

Blue heard Ma Beth slowly descend the stairs. After a few moments, the front door opened and closed. Then car doors opened and closed. Doors? Plural? Wasn't Ma Beth going alone? Blue dashed to the window and looked down to the driveway to catch a glimpse of what—an arm resting on passenger door? Had Wu decided to go with her at the last minute?

Before she knew what she was doing she flung herself downstairs to the second floor and flew down the hallway to look through the bathroom window for a better view of the driveway. She was breathing fast, and she felt the dreaded flutter in her chest start to creep up again. She was wrong! She did not want to be alone! She got to the window. The car was starting to pull away and Blue couldn't see if anyone was inside with Ma Beth.

"No no no no, don't go!" She turned and bolted for the stairs and ran smack into Wu.

"Oooff! Whoa there, Little Fox!" said Wu. He had been working on his computer but heard the footsteps on Blue's stairs and then her rapid footsteps in the hall. He had stepped out of his room to see what the commotion was and ended up right in her path.

Blue acted stunned for a second, but then she looked up at him. He looked back at her half amused, and half concerned. Then his face turned to all concern.

"Hey, hey, hey, it's okay. I'm here! Are you okay?" asked Wu.

Blue just grabbed him and hugged him.

Wu put an arm around her. After a minute he said, "You want to stay with me here while I do my summer book report?"

He felt her head nod, so he guided her into his room.

"You can sit on the bed, or you can use Sam's computer. Here let me log you in." He went over and typed a few characters on Sam's computer and turned around. "There you go. You can just . . ." he stopped. Blue was curled up with her eyes closed at the foot of his bed.

Wu scratched his head, put a pillow next to her, and covered her with a corner of the comforter. She didn't even stir. Wow, thought Wu. She's exhausted. Not only that, her hair was matted and she smelled like she needed a bath. He turned back to his work.

After a while, Wu turned to check on her, but she was gone. Despite his concern, he couldn't help grinning a little and wondering out loud, "How does she do that?"

He went upstairs to make sure she was okay. Her door was closed. Wu knocked and said, "Blue, are you okay?"

Blue, as usual, said, "I'm fine."

To Wu she didn't sound usual or fine. He decided he was going to talk to Ma Beth as soon as she got back.

## 3

## INEVITABLE

"Blue, we need to talk."

Ma Beth had knocked on Blue's door and by the sound of it, Blue could tell that this was all business. It wasn't unexpected. She knew she couldn't keep hiding the fact that something was wrong. And now Wu knew. She probably freaked him out enough that he would've said something to Ma Beth. And Blue was starting to admit to herself for the first time that maybe she needed help. And she didn't like it. She had to let Ma Beth in, but some remnant of stubbornness was trying to convince her that she could handle this on her own.

"May I come in?"

Blue's stubbornness gave way. "Yes," she said.

Ma Beth opened the door and stepped in. The look on her face was calm and resolute but still kind. It was as if nothing in the world could erase the background of kindness in her expressions.

"Blue, I think it is time for you to talk with someone. I have a very good friend coming by today who is well-regarded and highly recommended."

Blue swallowed. The friend was no doubt a therapist, or something worse. She knew this was coming, and, for Ma Beth's sake, she was not going to freak out about it.

Ma Beth continued, "She is a doctor. An M.D. Her degree is in psychiatry, but she is also a psychotherapist. Goodness, there are so many terms for it."

Blue knew all the terms intimately. They were all "psychos." Psychologist, psychiatrist, psychotherapist, psychoanalyst, even psycho-pharmacologist! From crystals and yoga and aromatherapy to full-bore shrink. She had not met one of them that she didn't loathe. And psychiatrists were the worst. They were the ones that could prescribe drugs. Blue wasn't sure she could take this, even from Ma Beth, but before that thought could get a good hold, Ma Beth spoke again.

"I know you don't like therapists and you don't trust doctors, but I want you to give her a chance. Don't turn her off." She gave Blue a moment to process this and then said, "Look at me, Blue."

Blue raised her eyes.

"Please do this for me? Give her a chance. Will you do that for me?"

"*Oh, Blue.*"

A jolt of sorrow passed from Ma Beth's eyes into Blue's and nearly caused her to gasp. She felt a little dizzy. She wasn't quite sure what had just happened. She had never felt someone's *chiss* do that to her before. Maybe I am going crazy, she thought.

"Blue? Will you give her a chance?" repeated Ma Beth

Blue looked at Ma Beth. She felt her will crumbling. Her head started nodding before she even realized she was doing it. It was as if her head knew better than her mind what was right for her. And right now, her mind was reeling from the confusion of emotions that filled it. Maybe someone else could fill it with something better.

It was afternoon. After her exchange with Ma Beth that morning, Blue had spent the entire time sitting cross-legged on her bed, staring out the window. She scanned the view inch-by-inch, concentrating on little details. Each one was a little distraction—a desperate little diversion to keep her brain occupied and her panic at bay.

There was a streetlamp down the block, one of the old-fashioned kind. The frosted glass dome, covered with bird droppings, reminded her of a white rock covered with lichen. The dark green lamp post leaned ever so slightly from being perfectly vertical. The base of the lamp post was ornate and looked freshly painted. It made her wonder—who paints lamp posts? Maybe invisible little men that come out at night, like leprechauns?

The sound of footsteps on the stairway snapped her out of her reverie. There was a knock and then a voice. "Blue?"

Blue was confused. It wasn't Ma Beth, but it was an oddly familiar voice. Ma Beth had said the psychiatrist was a very good friend, but it couldn't be . . .

The knock came again, "Blue, may I come in?"

"Okay . . . I mean, yeah. Sure."

The door opened and in stepped Will's mom.

Blue's confusion turned to shock. She stared at her, open-mouthed.

Mrs. Woods smiled back reassuringly and began, "Hello Blue. I can see Ma Beth didn't tell you it was me that she wanted you to talk to. You probably didn't know that I am a Doctor of Psychiatry, as well as the school counselor. Not many people do. I try to keep a low profile. Is it okay if I sit?"

Blue managed to croak out an "um . . . sure . . . I guess."

As she watched Mrs. Woods—Dr. Woods—sit down on the desk chair, she realized her mouth was hanging open. She snapped it shut. Her defense mechanisms were caught off guard. She didn't like that. She didn't like feeling that she was out of control.

Dr. Woods continued, "Blue, have you experienced sudden

attacks of intense crying or sobbing that seem to come out of nowhere?"

She felt her mouth drop open for the second time. "How could you know?" she whispered.

"Blue, you were a hostage, and hostages often suffer from a condition called PTSD. Have you learned any biology in school?"

Blue thought for a minute, still confused. "PTSD?"

"PTSD," said Dr. Woods, "Post Traumatic Stress Disorder. It is a psychological and physiological reaction to a traumatic experience. The reason I am telling you this is that it is important for you to know that this is your body's reaction to a terrifying experience. The terrifying experience is the 'traumatic stress' and the body's reaction to being over-stressed is the 'disorder.' It is a disorder that we don't fully understand." She paused and then continued, "Your body and your mind were traumatized, and they are reacting to it. I can help you heal that trauma."

Blue started to realize where this was going—some kind of drug therapy, and she was not going down that road again. She started to shake her head, but before she could protest, Dr. Woods made an unexpected statement.

"Blue, next time it happens—the impulse to cry your eyes out—don't fight it. Let it happen. Give in to it completely. It will keep happening until you stop fighting it."

Now Blue was totally off balance. This was not at all what she was expecting. The last thing she wanted to do was to not fight it. That was giving in to it—losing control. Giving up. She started shaking her head again, ready to say something, but she wasn't sure what.

Dr. Woods reached into her bag and pulled out some bottled water and a couple of other items and put them on Blue's desk. She turned back to Blue, looked directly in her eyes and voxed, "YOU CAN'T CONTROL IT, JUST LIKE YOU CAN'T CONTROL WHO YOU ARE. YOUR BODY NEEDS FOR YOU TO STOP FIGHTING IT. DON'T FIGHT IT. YOUR BODY

WILL LET YOU KNOW WHAT TO DO. LISTEN TO IT, AND LET IT DO WHAT IT NEEDS TO DO. WILL YOU DO THAT?"

Blue looked back. Dr. Woods had that same look as Ma Beth. You just couldn't resist. It demolished her defensive armor like the blast from a magic ray-gun. She found herself nodding again. "OKAY," she replied.

Dr. Woods nodded and as she stood up she gave Blue one last significant look, "AND YOU COULD USE A SHOWER!" She smiled and then as promptly as she came in, she was gone. The door was closed, and Blue was alone again.

Dr. Woods hadn't even been there for five minutes. Blue sat there for . . . for who knows how long. She was still shaken slightly by the whole incident. It was taking her a while to process everything. Dr. Woods said that Blue had no control over something her body was trying to do. Blue considered herself a master of control, yet she had found her head nodding in response, almost on its own. And then there were the other times her body had reacted without thinking. It seemed like it knew what to do every time. It was always trying to rescue her, and now it was trying to heal itself. And Dr. Woods said she should let it.

She also said that Blue needed a shower.

Blue dug out a mirror that was buried in the mess on top of her dresser and the face she saw staring back at her nearly caused her to drop it. Hair tangled and matted, shirt wrinkled (when was the last time she had changed it?), and her face still had the pale remnants of a bruise from where Bronco had smacked her. A small scab still adorned a corner of her nose. There were even a couple of very faint hints of red where the duct tape had been across her mouth.

The duct tape. Blue stared at the marks with their oddly straight edges and uniform color. The tape had made it hard to breathe through her bloodied nose, and she hadn't been able to cry out for help. She looked down at her wrists where the zip ties had dug in that first night. There had been bruises there, though now they had faded into barely discernible purplish-yellow shadows. The memory of the room and the chair, and the terror after blurting out her captor's secret, a secret that had been projected, unbidden, into her brain when she stared into his eyes, and the ache from being bound and motionless for hours and hours, a helpless animal, unable to hide, to escape, to control the situation—it all came back to her with way too much reality. The emotion drove over her like a hot wave, an uncontrollable wave, too much like the hot wave she had felt when she thought she was dying. She *had* been dying! She had let that wave carry her away. She looked back in the mirror and saw tears glistening in the corners of her eyes. Don't fight it, Dr. Woods had said. Don't fight it. Let your body do what it needs to do.

So she did.

***

Dr. Woods had warned everyone in the O'Day's house that at some point Blue might fall apart, and that it would be a good thing, but when it actually happened, everyone stopped what they were doing. The house was old and its solid beams, plaster walls, and hardwood floors allowed sounds to echo throughout. And now it reverberated with the sound of Blue's heart-wrenching cries. Even though Dr. Woods had prepared them, no one was untouched by the pain and sorrow embedded in those rhythmic, involuntary wails of anguish.

Blue's storm of emotions peaked and then gradually subsided, finally settling into a muffled, sobbing punctuated with a small hiccup from time to time. After a solid ten minutes, it became quiet again. Ma Beth climbed the two stories and quietly opened Blue's door. She was lying on her bed, hiccupping but asleep. Ma Beth touched Blue's head tenderly and gently covered her with a light blanket and then closed the door before quietly walking back downstairs.

Blue opened her eyes. She looked out her window. It was dusk. She wondered how long she had been lying there. Her covers were over her, so Ma Beth must have come in. Blue felt warm, but there was a cool spot on her cheek. Her pillow was still wet from where she had been sobbing into it, trying to muffle her crying earlier. It was more than wet, it was soaked.

God, how she had cried. She had never felt anything like that in her life. It wasn't the same as the crying she had experienced when she was captive. That was crying from fear and despair. This was the crying of letting go. It was a purging, a release of all the collected pieces of grief and sorrow that had built up for . . . for who knows how long? She had always hated how girls bawled in the movies, how they would lose control of themselves. And yet now she had done it herself. But she wasn't ashamed. All she felt was relief.

And thirst.

In fact, she was completely parched. She remembered the bottled water that Dr. Woods had left. She got up and went over to her desk, grabbed it, and drank it down. The water felt so fresh. Then she noticed what was next to the water bottle—two Snickers bars. Man, they looked good. She opened the first one and wolfed it down, and then she ate the second one only slightly slower. She gulped more water and was amazed that she hardly noticed the Snickers bars. She could usually barely eat one, and now after two she felt like she hadn't eaten a thing. She looked for more food and noticed a towel Dr. Woods had left. Suddenly she felt she couldn't wait another second to get in a nice hot shower.

She froze. Dr. Woods had anticipated everything—the breakdown, the thirst, the hunger, the shower. Blue felt she should be angry. She didn't like therapists messing with her. Instead, she was impressed. Even grateful, maybe. She might have to make some adjustments to her feelings about therapists. No, she reconsidered, not all therapists. Only Dr. Woods.

It sounded like the family was eating dinner downstairs, so Blue slipped down to the bathroom, closed the door, and took a long hot shower. She was amazed at how it felt. She must have taken hundreds of showers in her life, but this was the first where she noticed the individual streams of water hitting her scalp and shoulders and running down her skin. She could feel them shifting randomly as they sought the most efficient route down the curves of her body to her feet. Blue stayed in that warm rain until she felt thoroughly purged of any remnant of anything that had come before, leaving nothing but a fresh, new skin.

She dried and dressed and even ran a brush through her hair. She took a satisfied look at herself in her mirror and as she did, she noticed her wrists again. Hmm, she thought. She rummaged around in her dresser drawer and dug out some of her long neglected bling. She held up her decorated wrists and turned them back and forth. There, that's a damn sight better than staring at bruises all the time, she thought. She finally felt she was ready. She walked as nonchalantly as possible down the stairs and into the family room.

Nate, her oldest foster brother, was watching television, Wu was reading, and Sam was on the computer. Pa Bill was reading the paper, but looked up and said, "You hungry? There's still some lasagna in the kitchen."

Lasagna! She went to the kitchen, where Ma Beth was cleaning up. As Blue walked in, Ma Beth paused from her cleaning and pulled out a hot plate of lasagna and green beans from the toaster oven. She slid it onto the kitchen table and said, "Careful, the plate is hot. Dig in, girl. You look famished!"

Blue looked at Ma Beth's broad smile and said, "Thanks. I am, and . . . and thanks." She looked down at the food and then couldn't think of anything else. It may have been the best lasagna she had ever tasted.

A half-hour later, Ma Beth poked her head into the family room. "Nate, could you take this girl up to her room?" Blue had fallen fast asleep at the kitchen table. Her head was on her arm next to her plate. She was breathing evenly and didn't even flinch as Nate slung her arms around his muscular shoulders, scooped her up, and gently carried her up to her room.

## 4

## LAST RENDEZVOUS

"*S*O *WHAT SHOULD WE DO?*"

Will sat side-by-side with Blue on the grass. There was no moon. The only source of light was a window shining faintly from a house nearby. Other than the normal night noises, it was a very still and peaceful evening. It was their first nighttime rendezvous since before "that" night—the night that nearly became the last night on earth for both of them. They hadn't really talked about it much since then. In fact, Will realized that this was the first time they had even had a chance to be alone since then. And it looked like it might be their last, since school was starting next week, and because they were under a very tight rein. No chance of a secret rendezvous. If they had even tried that and gotten caught, it would've probably resulted in grounding for life. Even to get this one sanctioned night had been a tough time convincing parents. They only agreed under strict conditions. They were to stay in the neighborhood, the park was out of the question, and they had a curfew of 10 pm. It was tame compared to their secret excursions earlier that summer which at times went until two in the morning, but he was more than content to have any time at all.

"*I* DON'T KNOW," replied Blue. "*I*T JUST FEELS SO GREAT TO BE OUT OF THE HOUSE."

"*Y*EAH, AND ALONE FOR ONCE," replied Will. No reporters, no officials, no parents, no sibs, he thought. Just the two of them. Neither of them said anything for a while. Blue sat and picked at the grass, deep in thought.

After a while, Will broke the silence. "So, how are you? Are you doing okay?" he asked.

She didn't look at him as she replied. "I'm fine . . . I mean, I'm okay." It seemed like she wanted to say more, but she was silent.

"That's good to hear, because you had me . . . well, you had all of us worried for a while. You seemed kind of 'off' since the party. You seem a lot better now."

"You know your mother came to see me." She looked up at him and voxed, "*S*O NOW ARE YOU GOING TO SAY, '*I* TOLD YOU SO?'"

"*M*Y MOTHER CAME TO SEE YOU? *Y*OU MEAN LIKE FOR THERAPY? *S*HE DIDN'T TELL ME."

"*I*F YOU SAY SO." She looked away.

"Hey, I'm telling the truth. My mom can't tell us about what she does. She has to keep everything confidential. She's probably being extra careful because of . . . well because of you and me." Blue just kept looking away. He wanted her to look at him. He reached out and touched her shoulder. "Hey." She turned. "*I*'LL NEVER LIE TO YOU ABOUT THIS. *I* REALLY DIDN'T KNOW. *R*EALLY. *A*ND *I*'LL NEVER TELL ANYONE."

She looked down again. After a moment she said, "Well, you *were* right. Your mom is good. She helped a lot. I . . . I think I'd like to see her . . . to talk to her again."

"Hey, that's great," he replied. He debated a moment before going on. "You know, you can talk to me, too, if you need to . . . that is, if you think it would help . . ."

"I don't *need* anyone," she said with a flash of annoyance. "I just said she helped! That doesn't mean I asked for the cavalry to come charging in."

Will sighed. He was hoping that tonight could be a night that revived the good times they had on their night rendezvous earlier that summer. Now he wasn't sure.

"Look, I'm sorry. I know you don't *need* help," he said, while in his head he was thinking, "You don't seem to need or want anybody." What he said out loud next, though, was, "I was just trying to be a friend and offer an ear if you needed it." Now he turned away and started picking at the grass. "Maybe we should just go back inside." Even though he said it, he didn't move.

Blue didn't move either. They both sat there uncomfortably while the wind rustled through the branches above them. A mockingbird went through a noisy medley somewhere nearby.

Will felt an elbow jab him and he looked over at Blue.

"Look, I don't *need* your help. That doesn't mean I don't want to talk to you. Just don't try to be Mr. Fix-It-Man."

"I'm not trying to be Mr. Fix-It Man. All right, maybe a little, but Jesus, Blue, I still don't know squat about you. After all we've been through, you'd think I'd know something. I don't know where you were born, where you grew up, who your parents were, how many brothers and sisters you had. And what about the fire? Every time we get even close to talking about that stuff you become Miss Stone-Faced-Silent Girl. Are you going to be this way the rest of your life?"

Blue glared at him. "It's easy for YOU to be Mr. Happy-Chatty-Good-Listener Guy. Look at the life you have! Just for once imagine that Rose was dead! Your mom and dad are dead! And every other kid you know has a nice happy family. They don't know what it's like, but they nod their sympathetic faces and say, 'you poor girl,' and, 'I understand.' They don't understand a thing!" She paused. "Look, I didn't mean you're the same as them. You're not. It's just that I get so fucking tired of people trying to help me when they don't have a clue."

They sat there in an awkward silence. Even the mockingbird

had given up. Will didn't know what to say. Blue's words had left him a little dazed. They both seemed a little dazed. Neither of them said anything for a while.

Finally Blue spoke, "There, I talked to you. Happy now?" She didn't say it in anger. She actually sounded a little relieved.

"Did you just call me Mr. Happy-Chatty-Good-Listener Guy? God, Blue, that's harsh."

A little "ka-huh" sound came from her and she gave him a shove. "VERY FUNNY." But through the darkness, he thought he could see the corner of her mouth twitch up ever so slightly.

He went on. "LOOK, I DIDN'T MEAN TO PUSH IT. IT WOULD JUST BE NICE TO KNOW YOU BETTER." There was something more that he wanted to say, but he wasn't sure how she would react. The way things were going tonight, it could be anything. What the hell, it may as well be the night of confessions. "HEY, I'VE NEVER SAID THIS TO YOU, BUT I'VE WANTED TO: I'M REALLY SORRY ABOUT YOUR FAMILY." He paused and looked down at the ground, "You're right. I don't know what it's like. I don't know what I'd do if I lost my parents. Or Rosie. Especially Rosie. I'd probably go insane."

Another long period of silence went by. It ended when she bopped her shoulder against his. "You wouldn't go insane. You've got me to talk to."

He looked at her in amazement. Had she really just said that?

"Look, let's change the subject," she said. "We're in danger of getting sappy here. There is something else I wanted to ask you about." She looked at him, "I WANTED TO ASK YOUR DAD FOR SOME-THING, BUT I ALREADY LOST HIS NIGHT VISION CAMERA, AND I DON'T HAVE ANY WAY OF REPLACING IT."

Will smiled, "JEEZ, DON'T WORRY ABOUT THAT! AFTER WHAT HAPPENED? REALLY, NO ONE CARES ABOUT THE CAMERA. MY DAD CAN GET ANOTHER ONE, IT'S NO BIG DEAL. IT'S WATER UNDER THE BRIDGE."

Blue jumped.

"What was that? What did I say?"

"Nothing, nothing, sorry, I just . . . nothing, I just . . ." she looked a little rattled, but she recovered and went on, "*I WAS WONDERING IF HE COULD MAKE ME SOME GLASSES. THE SPECIALLY COATED KIND.*"

Ah, that was all, Will thought. She wanted some coated glasses for school, like the ones he and Rose had, to filter out the buzz of the *chiss,* the thought 'leaks' that came from normal people. He didn't know how she had survived this long without glasses. "*GEEZ, BLUE, I THOUGHT YOU WERE GOING DROP SOMETHING REALLY HEAVY ON ME. I'M POSITIVE HE WOULD MAKE SOME GLASSES FOR YOU, OR YOU COULD PROBABLY USE A PAIR OF MINE OR ROSIE'S. HE MADE A BUNCH OF THEM BECAUSE THEY'RE ALL JUST PLAIN—NO PRESCRIPTION. ANY OF US COULD WEAR THEM. I SHOULD HAVE PROBABLY OFFERED THEM TO YOU SOONER. THEY REALLY HELP AT SCHOOL, ESPECIALLY HIGH SCHOOL. GOD! YOU THINK KIDS HAVE WEIRD THOUGHTS IN MIDDLE SCHOOL, JUST WAIT UNTIL HIGH SCHOOL.*" Will shook his head just thinking about it.

"*THANKS. I MEAN THANKS FOR EVERYTHING.*"

"*HEY, WHAT ARE FRIENDS FOR?*"

They sat silent again, listening to the late summer sounds. Now that the tension had cleared, it was easy sitting there with her, at least that hadn't changed. He always felt comfortable with her. Even when things got awkward or tense, it was just blowing off tension, for both of them. Then it resolved into just an easy companionship. That wasn't true of many people, he realized. He wondered what it was, this quiet companionship.

He felt a light touch on his shoulder. "Your . . . wound . . . how is it healing?" There was a tinge of guilt in her voice.

"It's going to be fine. Really. I hardly notice it now except when I stretch my arm way out," he said.

"*CAN . . . CAN I SEE YOUR SCAR?*"

"*WHY NOT? EVERYONE ELSE ON THE PLANET HAS SEEN IT.*" He tugged at his collar to try and pull it down to show her his shoulder, but he was covered in too many layers. He finally gave up and pulled his T-shirt, sweater, and jacket over his head in one big wad and sat there bare-chested in the chilly night. There was a time he would have felt self-conscious about sitting there half naked in front of a girl, but after his hospital stay, he had few remaining inhibitions. It seemed like his whole body was on public display when he was there. He looked down at the pink fleshy lump where the bullet had entered. It looked so small. It was hard to believe something so small could cause so much damage. The incision line from his operation was still highlighted with bits of scab and little pin holes like snake bites where the stitches had been, and his skin was adorned with purple-blue swirls of bruises. Blue reached out and touched the scars gently.

"*Does that hurt?*"

"*Nah. It is just a little tingly when you touch it, but it doesn't hurt.*"

She put her whole hand on his shoulder. It felt warm against his skin. It felt healing.

"*I . . . I . . .*" she faltered. She looked down.

"Hey," he said. "Hey, look at me."

She turned back, a guilty look on her face.

"*It wasn't your fault. It was my fault. If I'd come with you that night none of this would have happened and Bronco would probably be in jail. I was a coward.*"

"*That's NOT true! You were NOT a coward!*" Her expression had turned from guilty to stern. "*It IS my fault! This shit just happens around me all the time. I don't know why. Wherever I go, just when it looks like life is finally going to be normal again . . . Why? Why do bad things keep happening around me?*" She turned away. "Don't bother trying to tell me it isn't true. You don't know what happened at the other places I've been."

"Well, I won't try and change your mind, but don't bother trying to tell me I'm not a coward either. Deal?"

In answer, she just huffed.

He kept going, "Just answer this one question. In the wake of this horrible wreckage you've left behind you, does anyone have a cooler scar than this?" He gestured to his shoulder.

She turned to him, her face struggling to convey annoyance before it finally gave in to her half smile. "*Okay, then I guess you owe me for that.*"

Will laughed. He rocked sideways and nudged her with his shoulder. She nudged back.

"Hey, we've got a half an hour left. The park's not an option. We should do something." As he said this he struggled back into his clothes.

Blue was quiet for a moment. "How about we do something completely different?" she said. "What if we just went for a walk. Like normal people. No stalking, just walking?"

"You mean, just walk down the street? Talk out loud like normal people? Talk about normal stuff?"

"Yeah, but how about we don't even talk? At all. Just . . . walk."

"*No vox?*"

"*No vox.*"

He considered this for a moment, then gave her a thumbs up. Then he made a zipper motion across his mouth. She smiled. A real smile this time. Rare. He motioned for her to lead on. They both got up and started down the sidewalk side-by-side.

The mockingbird had resumed, but there were other night noises, too. Some of them were natural—the rustling of the leaves, the *cht cht cht* of squirrels, the chirps of the robins and thrushes. Some of them were manmade—the rush of a distant car, a door shutting somewhere, faint music from some open window, a conversation from a couple sitting on their porch. And there was the sound of their footsteps—quieter than most people's, but loud enough to let them know that they were two people walking easily next to each other.

They filled the full time left to them walking down familiar streets in the crisp air of the early-autumn night, moving in and out of the shadows and light, occasionally bumping shoulders or brushing arms. Each contact might have lingered longer than might have been accidental, long enough that Will could feel the warmth and presence of the girl walking beside him.

Neither of them seemed to mind.

5

———

## SUMMER'S SUMMER END

Westbury Police Chief Summer Hannah sat at her beat-up desk munching on a roast beef sandwich. The horseradish mustard was trying to get her attention, but she was so distracted by what she was reading that she didn't even notice the burning rush climbing up her sinuses. That was how a lot of her lunches had been lately. Eating like a robot while she pored over the file on the DuBois abduction.

The State Police had pretty much hit a dead end. Kidnapping with safe recovery and cold trail of the suspect. Those cases tended to slip into the murky depths of obscurity until some random bit of coincidence turned up a new clue. That clue would then have to make its way through the various agencies and into the head of someone who could recollect the case and had the motivation to dive down and revive it. Chief Hannah was determined to be that person.

The horseradish finally got her attention. She glanced up from the file and looked at her sandwich. It was one of her favorites. She'd eaten almost the whole thing and not taken a moment to enjoy it. C'mon, Summer, it's okay to take a break, she thought to herself. She took another bite, closed her eyes, and let her mouth absorb the savory saltiness of the beef and the crunch of lettuce and zing of horseradish.

It made her think about the other things in life she hadn't had time to enjoy. Like love. How long had it been since she went out on a date? Months? Years? Too long, that's for sure. It's not like she didn't have her share of romantic interludes and eager suitors (a female in police uniform being a brazen seductress in the eyes of certain men), and she did yearn for a more permanent companion, but she had a certain standard that made for a much smaller fishpond. More like a fish puddle. In a desert. Sometimes she wished men were more like sandwiches. You could make your own and put in it just the right amounts of the stuff you liked.

She was envious of her college friend April Chastain, now Dr. April Woods, who had managed to snag Ash Woods. Summer was one of the only people who knew about the Woods' secret trait. She was glad to help them keep it secret. It was clear that they were in love, and who would want to spoil that for them? What luck, falling in love with one of your own rare kind. What are the chances of that these days? Pretty long odds for Summer Hannah, now thirty-eight. And the likelihood of generating progeny? Even more iffy.

But Ash and April had children, and one of them was on her mind every time she looked at this case. Their son Will had almost died. And though no one faulted her, Chief Hannah felt responsible. It was her job to protect the people of the town and she let them down. And she felt a special need to be protective of that family, and of Blue DuBois.

These thoughts danced around her head as she chomped steadily on the remains of her sandwich. She swallowed the last bite, sighed, and turned back to the file for the umpteenth time. The suspect had vanished, and his only known identity, 'Bronco' Bob Kelly, had evaporated with him. She had since discovered it was fake, and that he had used it to register a car, rent an apartment, and open a bank account. All without raising a single red flag. The account was now empty, the apartment abandoned, and the car had vanished.

The detectives had found some DNA and partial prints, but no matches turned up in any database. No facial recognition from the police sketches or the ones Blue had made. Chief Hannah assumed he had probably shaved his beard to alter his identity, and he probably had plenty of cash to get transportation. That meant no electronic payment trail to follow.

The guy had slipped through the system and out into the world. That did mean they had gotten rid of a dangerous drug dealer, but it had left behind a vacuum in the drug community that was surely being filled by the next 'Bronco,' the next heroin dealer. Or meth dealer. Or crack dealer. Or prescription opioid fence. Or all of the above. She was as frustrated with what Bronco represented as she was with the fact that he had escaped and that drugs were flowing almost unimpeded through her town. Why was this quiet little town—a town filled with prosperous common-sense people, and a nationally ranked college for God's sake—a place where people felt like they needed to turn to these deadly drugs? It just did not make sense to her. There had already been two overdose deaths in Westbury, and they were sensible people! One had been a father of two high school kids and a respected carpenter. The other was a college athlete. An athlete. Unbelievable. And how were they getting these drugs?

She knew very well how, she thought. She had barely enough people on her staff for 24-7 single coverage, and just two beat-up cruisers. Her only hope was input from public sources, people coming forward voluntarily. Even then, unless the police had enough information for a warrant, they weren't going to get any help from any other agency.

What was really pathetic was that her best public source so far was one obsessed fourteen-year-old that nearly got herself killed. Why was it that the only helpful people were the ones who were the most innocent and most vulnerable? It seemed like she was always picking up the pieces after some good-hearted person did something that put themselves in harm's way. She was supposed to be preventing that from happening, not cleaning up afterward.

The Chief let out a long slow sigh and took a bite of carrot. Her brain kept going despite the loud crunching. One thing is clear, she thought. Bronco was out there, waiting to be caught. Maybe, if she could just find one damn decent lead, she could get him. And maybe, on the way, she would find something that would help rid the infestation in her town.

**6**

---

# SILENT WORLD

The imposing bulk of the high school loomed through the sentinels of oak and maple that surrounded it as Blue approached down the sidewalk. She stopped outside the entrance and watched the mob of teenagers lurching and loping past like a motley herd of young Neanderthals as they crowded through the glass doors of the brick and granite entrance of Westbury High. Well, here it goes, she thought. Unto the breach. Into the crowd. Time to see how bad it is in there.

The glasses that Mr. Woods had given her were sitting in her backpack, just in case. She had almost put them on but then thought she should at least feel out the crowd first—see if she could cope. She had done it in middle school all the way up to the end of eighth grade. Almost. Not quite to the end. One too many crude, cruel observations leaked from one too many stuck-up daddy's-girls, and before she knew it, she was on probation, missing eighth-grade graduation and being uninvited to her third family in four years. She left behind some very bruised bodies and egos, so it wasn't an entirely unsuccessful eighth grade, all things considered, but everything was different now. Uninvited was not what she wanted this time around. She hesitated and reconsidered the glasses. How bad can it be without them? She might as well find out now. She took a breath and then plunged into the fray and was instantly awash in a flood of *chiss.*

"*Why is he looking at me like that . . .*"

"*Oooh! Camel toe . . .*"

"*God, he smells gross . . .*"

"*. . . Nice tits . . .*"

"*. . . Plaid with stripes? Really? . . .*"

The tsunami of teenage hormones poured down the entrance hall and nearly stopped her in her tracks. Will was not kidding. It was unbelievable! Middle school was bad, but it was way more innocent than the surge of teen brain angst washing over her now.

"*. . . Dammit! The cell coverage here sucks! . . .*"

"*. . . Mike's pants are sooo tight . . . nice package . . .*"

"*. . . Gawd! Brenda's dressed like a slut . . .*"

"*. . . I definitely should've gotten stoned before I walked in* here . . . :

All right, maybe this is too much, too soon, she thought. She yanked off her backpack and dug the glasses out and put them on. The silence was so sudden and dramatic, she almost gasped out loud.

That must have been what drowning felt like, she thought. She didn't know why the onslaught of thoughts caught her off guard. She knew it was coming, but the intensity of it was crazy! And it wasn't that it was that loud—non-vox were never very loud—but it was so pervasive! And the content was so . . . so raw! She was used to personal stuff, of course; no one was very discreet when they thought no one could hear, but this! Wow.

She took a minute to stand in a corner and experiment. Looking out on the busy entrance hall with traffic going everywhere, she lifted her glasses . . .

"*. . . Ugh, spaghetti for lunch . . .*"

"*. . . Oh God, there's Sean. Look at me, Sean, look at me . . .*"

"*. . . I think I'm going to puke. Don't puke, don't puke, don't . .
.*"

"*. . . His eyes are so amazing . . . and that grin! . . .*"
And then she lowered the glasses back onto her nose.
"Sarah, what do you have first period?"
"History. Bor-ing"
"Couldn't be worse than English first period."
"Is there any class that's good first period?"
Glasses up . . .
"*. . . God, her skirt is sooo short . . .*"
"*. . . Why can't you look me in the face, dweeb, I've got more
than breasts . . .*"
"*. . . Oh shit, I forgot my lunch . . .*"
"*. . . Damn, I'm out of tampons . . .*"
Glasses down . . .
"Hey, David, how was your summer?"
"Great, how 'bout yours?"
"A month in Colorado!"
"Awesome!"

Thank you, Mr. Woods, Blue thought. She wondered how long
she could have survived without the glasses. She finally lifted up
her bag and started walking down the corridor, picking her way
through the halls and upperclassmen as she headed to her home-
room. She realized that for the first time ever she could walk with
her head up and her eyes wide open. Her strategy before was to
keep eyes down and halfway closed. It was the only way she could
avoid the fog of *chiss* and concentrate on anything.

Now, as she walked, she noticed something else strange and
new. The *chiss* silence made everyone seem like animated
mannequins. There were mannequins before, of course, people
that didn't *chiss*, people whose thoughts were hidden from her. But
those were a minority, like silent extras in her life-movie. The real
actors were, and always had been, the ones that *chissed*. Their
thoughts painted a rich and complex picture of the person behind

them. Anyone else who didn't *chiss* or didn't talk was just a body moving around. Some smelled of too much perfume, some not enough, and some were in bad need of a shower. But now, with the glasses, they were all extras. Even the talkers were only half as interesting. She got the initial inklings of a feeling like she couldn't trust people as much, like they were hiding things from her that they hadn't before.

She also noticed that although it was quieter, it was noisier, too, in a different way. In place of the brain chatter, the background noises that had been obscured now asserted themselves with a new prominence. The slamming lockers, the rustling papers, zipping book bags, shuffling feet. They created a new backdrop, like a change of scenery in a stage drama.

The overall sensation made her feel a little unsteady. It was like she was missing an extra sense to help her keep her balance. But it was also kind of fun. She imagined that this was what it was like to be drunk or stoned. Of course, she could take the glasses off whenever she wanted. She could also sneak a peek over the top of the glasses. Will said he often took his off between classes. He warned that if you do, you have to remember to put them on in class. He said kids are experts at spotting fakes (like she didn't know), so you have to be diligent. Not a problem for her. She was an expert at faking a lot of stuff. She faked being "fine" all the time. But for now, having the glasses on was kind of mind-bendingly cool.

---

"So how was the first day at WWHS?" asked Wu. They were walking home together, Wu, Will, Blue, and a couple other kids from the neighborhood.

"WWHS? Don't you mean WHS?" replied Blue.

One of the other girls said, "No. We like to use the real name: Wacky Westbury High School."

"Or you could use 'weird' or 'wild' or . . . 'weediculous'," said one of the other kids.

"Yeah," said Wu. "You can fill it in with almost anything. Except 'wonderful.'"

They all laughed. A group of them broke off and turned down a side street leaving just Wu, Will, and Blue walking by themselves the rest of the way home.

"So how was it?" asked Will.

"I survived," she replied.

"Obviously," said Wu. "But how was . . . you know," he looked cautiously left and right and then dropped to a whisper, "It? Vox? With the new glasses and everything?"

She looked at Wu over the top of her glasses. Then she looked at Will. "*You explained this to him?*"

"*Yeah,*" replied Will. He had taken his glasses off already. "*He knows all about the special coating and everything. Plus I've been helping him learn to control his chiss.*"

Blue looked back at Wu, who had been studying them both while they voxed. "It was quiet. It was weird," she said.

"Wow," said Wu. "You thought it was quiet? That mad house between classes?"

"Just take that mad house and turn it up a notch, and then imagine it following you into the classroom even after class starts. Without our glasses, it's non-stop," said Will.

"Wow. I mean yeah, that could drive you bananas."

"Aaaannnd . . . yeah," said Blue.

Will knew what she was talking about. She had confided in him about her stint in a psych ward, so he quickly steered the subject away from that. "Hey, Wu, show her how you can control your leaks."

"Don't you mean *chiss*? When you say 'leaks,' it makes it sound like I piss myself.

"Sorry, force of habit. My dad calls it 'crepantis' sometimes, but we usually say leaks or *chiss*."

"What does *crepantis* mean? It sounds like an insect . . . or crapping your pants. All your names sound like pissing or crapping," said Wu.

Will heard a "kah-huh" and looked at Blue. She had her hand over her mouth and looked like she was going to choke. Will wondered if she was actually laughing.

"No! Nothing bad. It's Latin and it means 'rustling' like rustling leaves." As he said it, he kicked at a small pile of golden and red leaves that had collected on the sidewalk from some early turning tree.

"It's perfect," said Blue. "Rustling. Falling leaves. That's it exactly. It's like rustling leaves. All the time." She walked into the pile of leaves and tromped around. The leaves were dry and rattled and rasped as her feet thrust through them. "And then you close your eyes, or put these glasses on and . . ." she stopped tromping. The rustling stopped. The ensuing silence was dramatic.

"Wow. It's really like that? All the time?"

"Any time we're around a lot of people," said Will.

Wu was quiet as they reached the house. He stopped and then said, "So what is it. Am I voxing, leaking, chissing, or crepantising?"

Will, tilting his head back and forth thoughtfully. "Well, you're not really voxing like we do, but if you can control it, you're not leaking . . ."

Blue snorted and started convulsing.

"What? What did I say?"

"Nothing!" Then she lost it and started laughing hysterically. She gasped and said, "Thank God you're not leaking anymore, Wu!" She started laughing so hard that tears started coming out of her eyes.

"Wow, you're in rare form today!" said Will. He looked at Wu, who just shrugged.

"So, when you are done with your seizure, Wu can try it out on you. Controlling his *chiss*, that is."

"Yeah, okay. Sorry, just a second . . ." and then off she went again.

Wow, thought Will. I have never seen her like this before. A giggle fit? Maybe she is getting better. Or she's gone insane.

Wu looked at Blue, who was calming down again, and said, "Are you ready now?"

She nodded, wiping her eyes. "Yeah, sorry Wu. I really do want to hear you control your *chiss*. Can you, for real?"

"Yeah. Will taught me a real useful exercise. Let me try it and tell me what you can hear and what you can't. Ready?"

"Okay, I'm ready, really, Wu."

"Okay. Here it goes. He looked at Blue. "ONE . . . THREE . . . FIVE . . . SEVEN . . . NINE . . ."

"You're reciting odd numbers from one to nine," said Blue, looking slightly puzzled. "And you paused between each one."

"All right, Wu! That was great!" said Will.

Wu was pumping his fist saying, "Yessss!"

Blue said, "Why do I feel like you're screwing with me?"

"No, not at all!" said Wu. "Will came up with this brilliant exercise. I count from one to ten in my head, but I only *chiss* the odd number and then I *think* the even number to myself, but keep them buried, not on the top of my head. Will said *chiss* is only the thoughts you almost say out loud, but don't. That really helped. I just counted to ten in my head, but I only *chissed* the odd numbers! It was really hard when I first tried it, but I think I'm getting the hang of it!"

"Really good actually." Blue looked at Will in a way that seemed like she saw something for the first time.

Will turned to Wu. "Yeah, really good. It's a relief, really. It's hard to not pay attention to people's *chiss*, especially your friends. It'll kind of be nice not having to ignore your *chiss* anymore. Do you find it weird that I've been hearing you all this time?"

"Nah, you're my best friend. Whatever you heard, you sure

managed to keep to yourself. Though there are some things I sure hope ..."

"Ahh, yeah. Let's not get into detail. And don't worry about it. You never even came close to leaking some of the crap I've heard from other people."

"Wow. Yeah. I mean ... whoa, I sure hope you didn't catch—"

"So are we going to just stand here worrying about who leaked what, and who heard what, or are we going to go inside, so I can get some homework done?" interrupted Blue.

"Yeah, I've got a crap-ton to do." Will pushed the gate open.

"Got that right," said Wu. "*Later?*" He held up a fist.

Will smiled. "Nice *chiss.*" He bumped Wu's fist. Wu turned his fist to Blue and so did Will. She gave them both a wry look and then reached out and fist bumped them both, bop-bop. She glanced at Will. "*I'm glad you did this for Wu.*" And then she turned and vanished up the walk and into the house. Will felt a smile come to his face. He turned to Wu, who was staring at him.

"It's kinda weird watching you two. She voxed you just now?"

"Yeah," said Will. "Sorry, it's rude."

"I suppose it would be rude to ask what she said, too," said Wu.

Will looked at his friend, "Let's just say that you lucked into a good foster sister."

Wu looked up the walk toward the house. "Yeah, I agree with that. It's just going to be interesting trying to adjust to this." He turned to Will and gave him a last fist bump and headed up the walk and into the house.

Will turned and headed home thinking, yeah, this is going to be interesting.

7

———

## JORDY

Will crammed his gym stuff into the bottom of his locker and pulled out books for his after-lunch classes. Pretty convenient having a locker right across from the lunchroom, he thought. On the other hand, it was noisy, and the busiest part of the hallway. Not a lot of privacy. He looked over the heads of the packed lunch crowd and spotted Wu who waved. It looked like he had saved a seat for him.

A sudden bang close-by turned Will's attention. About ten feet away he saw a kid leaned up against the lockers rubbing his shoulder. He looked like a freshman. A couple of guys were walking away down the hall, laughing. One of them said, "Good to have you back Georgie-boy."

Will recognized the freshman. It was Jordy Willis, a kid he'd known since grade school.

"Hey, you okay?" he asked.

Jordy looked over at him shyly. "Yeah, I guess."

"Those guys are jerks. Don't let them get to you."

Jordy turned back to his locker and a pile of books fell out. He kicked one of the books.

Will watched him. He looked like he needed a friendly gesture.

"Freshman year will kind of suck, especially the beginning, but it'll get better."

Jordy crammed the books back in the locker and slammed it before they could fall out again and then walked over to Will. Without looking up, he muttered, "Thanks."

"Hey, no problem. Welcome to high school."

"Did it hurt? When you were shot?" Jordy blurted out.

There was that question again. Why was that always the first thing people asked? During the first few days of school it seemed like every kid in school wanted to know. He had tried to answer seriously at first but after a while, answering again and again got exhausting and then irritating and eventually he came up with a variety of one-line answers that varied from a smart-ass, "no, it tickled," to the final, most effective one-liner: "yes." He looked at Jordy and opted out of the one-liner.

"Not at first," he said. "It felt more like a punch. Then it started burning, and then it hurt like hell until it kind of settled into a constant pain. I was sure glad when the medics got there and gave me some pain meds."

"It was a .22, wasn't it?" asked Jordy.

"Yeah, it was." Will always felt defensive about that fact. A .22 was an unimpressive looking bullet. "But it was high velocity and almost point blank. The doctor said it's not the size, but how fast it's going and what it hits."

"Point blank. You're lucky it wasn't a nine-milli. My dad has one. I've shot it before, and it's got a real kick. You really have to hang on to it," Jordy said.

"Yeah, I guess that's something to be happy about. If a .22 almost killed me, a 9mm . . . well, we probably wouldn't be talking now." Will was anxious to end the conversation. He'd had too many like it over the last few weeks. "Hey Jordy, I gotta go. I can talk to you more some other time. It's good to see you, man. Hang in there and don't worry about those jerks."

"Yeah. Thanks. Guess I'll see you around."

"Cool."

Will wove his way through the sea of lunch-eaters to Wu's table.

"Hey, man, was that Jordy Willis?" asked Wu through a mouthful of sandwich.

"Yeah, he got pushed into his locker by a couple of jackasses."

"Yeah, I saw it. Mike and Pike."

"Mike and Pike?"

"Yeah, you don't know those guys? I used to play basketball with Mike, but then he took up with Pike and now all he does is hang with a bunch of stoners."

"Well, it seems that they have some history with Jordy. Sucks for him. Hard way to start out freshman year."

They both sat thoughtfully while they munched on their food.

"What kind of name is Pike?" asked Will. "That can't be his real name. It sounds like something Blue would make up." Will was referring to how Blue had nick-named Bronco "Gronk" and Jack "Greazal" last summer.

"It's Peter Ketcham. His middle initial is "I" and we just started calling him 'Pike' back in middle school. You know, P-I-K, Pike"

"Hmm. I don't remember that. I never saw him much in middle school, though. Maybe it should be 'Prick' instead of 'Pike.'"

Wu laughed and said, "Yeah, he was kind of a jerk back then, too." Wu took his last bite of sandwich. After he swallowed he changed the subject. "So how was gym? How does the arm feel? You think you'll be able to try out by November?"

"Well, it wasn't great. I'm still weak and I can't stretch my arm all the way out yet. My shooting sucks. Coach Ryan says not to worry and just take my time and make sure it heals right. Easy for him to say. I guess I'll just keep working at it. What about you? Have you talked to him yet?"

Wu looked down at the table. He seemed reluctant to say anything.

"He wants you to try out for varsity, doesn't he! Right? Right?"

"Yeah," said Wu, still looking down.

"Wu, that is so totally awesome! Of course he does! You're going to do it, right?"

"Well, what about you? What if you're on JV?"

"C'mon, I'll be lucky to make JV this year. You have to go for varsity. Say you'll do it, or I'm going to stuff this banana peel down your shorts!"

"All right, all right. Keep your banana peel. I just felt bad about the whole deal with you and your shoulder and all."

"C'mon. It is what it is. It's a shame though . . ." he said, holding up the banana peel. "I don't know what to do with this now."

A girl from the table next to theirs said, "Hey, Will, your banana looks a little limp there." Her whole table exploded into high-pitched laughter.

"Heh. Heh. Very clever." He looked over at Wu, whose hand was up to his mouth in a lame attempt to conceal his very obvious convulsions.

Will just rolled his eyes. High school was definitely in full swing again.

**8**

———

# ANNA

Only two weeks into high school and Blue was convinced more and more each day that the glasses were a game changer. In her head she said another silent thank-you to Will's dad.

She also said a silent thank-you to the fates that the legacy of "that" night hadn't followed her to school. At least not yet. Either everyone was giving her space, or the story had gone stale. Easy to see how it would go stale with all the fresh drama that accompanied the beginning of the school year. That suited her just fine. Flying under the radar was a nice comfortable place to be. She just hoped it would last.

She got to her locker and dialed in the combination. Pretty nifty upgrade, she thought, having locking storage at school. No such luxury in middle school. Then again, they didn't give you a whole lot of time to get to it between classes in high school, and with her locker way off in the boonies it was even tighter getting between classes.

Blue lifted her book bag to hook it inside, and as she did, she felt her gut clench. She set the book bag back down. Had she pulled a muscle or something? The book bag was pretty hefty with all the textbooks. A lot more hefty than middle school. She picked up her bag again and managed to hook it inside her locker even though she felt a pulling in her abdomen. Maybe she had eaten something bad. She winced a little as she pulled out the books for her next class. As she did she realized someone was standing next to her. It was a girl with long straw-blonde hair and a wide and friendly face. She looked older. Definitely not a freshman.

"Hi there! I'm Anna. I'm a friend of Will's. My locker is right there," she said, pointing to a locker about ten feet away. "You're Blue, right? Nice to meet you!"

Blue was a little surprised by the girl's forwardness. She was instinctively wary of someone just walking right up to her like that. But there was something about this girl. Something that exuded trustworthiness. She found herself saying, "Hi . . . nice to meet you, too."

Anna leaned toward Blue and whispered, "Do you need anything?"

Blue wasn't quite sure what she meant. "Do I *need* anything?"

"You know . . . supplies?"

"Supplies?"

Anna stared at her intently for a moment, and a then a knowing look came to her face. "Ah! I bet this is your first time."

"What? What are you talking about?"

Anna got a motherly look on her face and said quietly, "Don't worry, I have seen this a million times." She opened her purse and rummaged around in it. "It happened to me when I was eleven and it totally freaked me out." She glanced up and down the hall and then said, "Do you have a purse?"

"Umm . . . no. I don't use a purse." Why would she be asking if she had a purse, and why was this damn stomach cramp not going away?

"That's what they all say. But trust me, you'll want one pretty soon. Is this your book for next class?" She slipped something out of her purse and put it inside the cover of Blue's book and then whispered, "Go to the bathroom, and put this on right now, even if you have to be late for class. Trust me. It will feel weird, but you will thank me later!" She looked at Blue and laughed. It was a disarmingly cheerful laugh. "I love the look on your face right now. Don't worry, you'll figure it out. You better hurry! There isn't much time left before class. Meet me back here after class and I'll set you up with everything else you need. Bye!" She added one more loud whisper as she left, "Welcome to the sisterhood!"

Blue stood there briefly as it finally dawned on her. Another little cramp acknowledged it. Her body was once again telling her what she needed to know. And right now it was telling her to get moving.

---

She was late to Miss Kendrick's algebra class. All the kids were already head-down working on what looked like a quiz. A quiz so soon? Blue slipped down the row to her seat. Miss Kendrick came over and plopped the quiz in front of her. Blue looked up. Miss Kendrick gave her a disapproving, yet knowing look and Blue heard her *chiss* as it snuck around the corner of her glasses, "You get a break this time, dear . . ." and then Miss Kendrick went to the front of the class and sat down behind her desk. That was it. Miss Kendrick knew. Anna knew. It *was* a sisterhood. How had she not noticed this before?

She looked down at the quiz. Easy. But it took her longer than it should have. For some reason, gut cramps and the strange foreign sensation of sitting on a crinkly wad of panty liner was not conducive to concentration. She had been expecting this for a long time. Almost too long of a time. She was nearly fifteen for god's sake. She was beginning to think it would never come, but now that it was here, it was kind of a relief. She wasn't quite sure how she would get through the day, but all the other girls seemed to manage so she damn well would, too. Plus, she had Anna.

Blue tapped her pencil on her desktop, absent-mindedly making little dots on her completed quiz paper. She wasn't quite sure what it was about Anna that made her feel instantly comfortable with her, but there it was. Something about her expression, her way of holding herself, how she had cared enough to come over and help. It was that "care" thing again. Like Wu, like Will, like Ma Beth. And then she realized that was exactly it—Anna was like a walking, talking teenage version of Ma Beth. She smiled to herself at that thought.

"Something amusing about the quiz, Miss DuBois?" Blue looked up. Miss Kendrick was looking sternly at her and holding out her hand for the quiz paper.

"No, not at all." She handed her the quiz and realized she was looking forward to seeing Anna again after class.

## 9

## ALEX

Jack sniffed the zippered fabric pouch. He caught just the slightest lemony tang over a skunky, spicy aroma. He didn't know why he brought it with him to school—habit perhaps. He hadn't smoked in weeks. Part of the promise to his mother. Funny thing was, he didn't really want it anymore anyway. He thought it was going to be hard, like quitting cigarettes or alcohol, but when the first week went by with no craving, no side-effects, no interest at all, he was surprised. Maybe he was immune to addiction. Not likely, he thought, not with a dad like his, locked up for at least seven years and suffering through detox.

Suffer away, you bastard, he thought. Seven years hardly makes up for the seventeen years of shit he and his mother had put up with. And now they had to pick up the wreckage he left behind. It wasn't easy. They had normalized him for so long, they were both still in a daze trying to figure out how to do even the most mundane things—get up, eat breakfast, do chores, even talk. Every second they were waiting for the judgmental jackass to pick apart everything they did, but instead there was only silence. He had left a vacuum that they weren't quite sure how to fill.

There were two things, though, that his mom had jumped on

right away and made no bones about. Jack was to finish high school and stop dealing dope, period, end of sentence. And he was fine with that. He'd only been doing it for the money anyway, and now that his mother's paycheck wasn't going down the alcoholic toilet that was his dad, they suddenly had enough to actually pay bills on time and a little extra afterward. In fact, considering how things could have gone, life was pretty good right now. He suspected that it was due in part to Chief Hannah. He was pretty sure that she and his mom had cut a deal and that was the reason his part in the whole kidnapping saga was never revealed and why his mom was on his case about finishing high-school and getting clean. Those were the unspoken deal-breakers. He could deal with that.

He realized that he was still standing in front of his locker and holding the pouch. It felt like a relic. He tossed it deep into the locker. He'd take it home at the end of the day and leave it there. As he slammed his locker shut and turned to go he found himself facing a kid that was no taller than half of a locker door. He had short hair and horn-rimmed glasses which sat too low on his nose so that when he looked up at Jack, he had to tilt his head way back.

"You're Jack, aren't you?" he said.

"Who wants to know?" replied Jack.

"Name's Alex. I'm a freshman, obviously. I want to talk business with you."

"Don't know what you're talking about, kid." Jack turned and started to walk away.

"What was in that pouch?" said the kid, and then he took a long, deliberate sniff.

Jack stopped and gave the kid the kind of harsh gaze that should have made it crystal clear that he was treading in dangerous territory, but the kid just kept talking.

"Look, I've got some stuff I need to sell but I'm new here and I don't know who might be a customer." He opened the top of his backpack and held it up to Jack, revealing about a dozen prescription bottles.

Jack jumped. He quickly grabbed the top of the backpack squeezing it shut. "Jesus Christ, kid!" he hissed in a loud whisper. "What the hell do you think you're doing? Are you crazy? Get that out of here! I don't ever want to see it again! Scram!" He let go of the backpack, turned his back on the kid and hurried down the hall, thankful that no one seemed to notice Alex's indiscretion. Alex didn't seem deterred, however. He kept pace with Jack and kept talking.

"C'mon, all I need is the names of a couple of kids. I'll never bug you again. It's not like I'm the only one trying to sell stuff, right?"

Jack stopped short and gave the kid his sternest look. "Don't go down that road, kid. And don't talk to me *ever* again!"

"Just a coupla names. Just two! That's all I need," said Alex.

"Jesus, kid, you must annoy the hell out of your parents."

"Two names! Two names, two names . . ."

Jack turned away and walked into his next class, leaving Alex standing in the doorway. He found a desk as far away from the door as possible and sat. He looked back at the door. Alex was still standing there, holding up two fingers and mouthing "Two names," and then he disappeared just as the bell went off.

Jack stared out the window feeling like he had just met a terrier that had bit into his pant leg and was determined to drag him back into a world he thought he had just escaped.

## 10

## THERAPY

The office door was slightly open. Blue stood in front of it, not sure whether to step through. The only reason she had come was because she had promised Ma Beth. At least, that is what she tried to tell herself, but it wasn't the only reason. Dr. Woods had helped her—genuinely helped her. But was she still unwell? *"Yes,"* said a voice deep inside her. But I feel fine right now, she thought. *"For now, but what about not now?"* replied the voice. She hesitated, she still wasn't sure. *"You promised Ma Beth!"* God, that inner voice could be annoying. And persistent. And right. She pushed the door open and walked in.

Dr. Woods looked up and smiled. It was a nice smile. Not condescending. Not artificial.

"Hello, Blue, I'm glad to see you."

"Hi." Blue didn't return the compliment. She wanted to, but she couldn't. Not yet.

"Go ahead and have a seat. Make yourself comfortable."

Blue looked at the small couch that sat opposite Dr. Woods' desk. She glanced warily at the arms of the couch. She sat herself cross-legged, indian-style, right in the middle, as far away from the arms as she could. She looked at Dr. Woods, hoping she hadn't noticed. Fortunately, she was head-down, writing something. Blue noticed Dr. Woods wasn't wearing any glasses, so she pushed her own up and out of the way, on top of her head.

Dr. Woods finished writing in her notebook and then put her pen down and looked up earnestly at Blue. "I want you to know you may get up and leave at any time you want. You don't have to give me any reason, okay?"

Wow. No one had said anything like that to her in her life. Ever. Not a therapist, not a teacher, not a doctor, not even a foster parent.

"Really?"

"Really."

"So I could just get up right now and leave. You wouldn't tell Ma Beth?"

"That's right. You are free to go. I would not tell Ma Beth. I would not tell anyone. Everything in this room is strictly between you and me."

Blue sat thoughtfully for a moment. She looked at Dr. Woods. "*What if I don't believe you?*" she voxed.

"*That's a fair question. Let me just say that it is my job to earn your trust and respect. I hope that I can, but may I ask you to just give me a chance?*"

Blue remembered the Snickers bars, the water, and the towel. Dr. Woods deserved a chance.

"*Yes, I will.*"

"*Thank you, Blue.*" Dr. Woods leaned forward in her chair. "After this session, you don't have to see me again if you don't want. At the same time, you may come to see me anytime you want. Deal?"

"Yeah, I guess. You're telling me I can basically do whatever I want, right?"

"Right. Just let me ask this one thing and then we'll see where it goes, okay?"

"Okay."

Dr. Woods creased her forehead and looked at Blue. She rested her chin in her hand and then said, "Have you ever told your story, your *whole* story, to anyone?"

Wow, Blue thought. Start out with the big one, why don't you? She looked down at her hands. Her thoughts flashed back to her very first therapist. She had told him the whole story. Blue was ten at the time. She was desperate to tell someone, to find someone to comfort her, tell her everything was going to be all right. But she had babbled in a mix of voice and vox that must have sounded like complete nonsense to the therapist, who couldn't vox, of course, but Blue assumed he could. So instead of her complete story, the therapist heard a staccato mash of nonsense. The vox part was lost to him. He treated her like she was learning disabled, delusional, and a liar. A delusional lying retard. That's how her new life started out. That's when she started to realize that no one knew her or understood her. That started the first chain of panic, anger, and hysteria. That feeling echoed inside her now.

Her reply was flat. "I tried."

"And?"

"And he didn't believe me." All the anger and frustration at how she had been treated cried out to be released in a foul-mouthed screaming diatribe, but she held back. She had tried that before with the others, but it had led to bad things. Instead, she just sat there, recalling her sessions with the other doctors. She knew what they did believe. Their *chiss* revealed everything. It was completely wrong, but what could she do? It was the worst feeling in the world, people thinking that you are lying to them and drawing their own damn conclusions, including that you're a liar when you're not!

"What *did* he believe?" asked Dr. Woods.

Now Blue couldn't hold back her bitterness, even with Dr. Woods. "You already know! It's all right there in those files in front of you! None of the doctors knew I could *hear* their *chiss* when they wrote! I know what's in there! Delusional! Schizophrenic! Clozapine! Zyprexa! Counseling! Therapy! All for a problem I didn't have!

They thought I was lying to them, lying to myself!" She looked hard at Dr. Woods. "*Do you know what that's like?*"

"*I don't.*"

"*It's like a nightmare and you can't wake up.*"

A look of anguish flashed across Dr. Woods' face, like a passing shadow. She looked down, only for a moment, and then looked back up at Blue. "*But you did wake up?*"

Blue looked back down at her hands. "I did wake up. I learned how to tell them what they wanted to hear. I learned to close my eyes, so I wouldn't hear their *chiss*, so I wouldn't get hysterical. I learned to act like a normal kid, even though I didn't know what that was."

"So no one has ever really heard your story."

Blue shook her head. She didn't look up at Dr. Woods. She knew what the next question was going to be, and she was ready to get up and leave.

"I'm not going to ask you for your story, if that's what you're thinking."

That was exactly what she was thinking. Blue looked at Dr. Woods. If not that, what *would* she ask?

"I'll never ask you. I mean that. What I will tell you is this," and she paused, looking Blue in the eye. "*Find someone you trust and respect and tell them. The whole story. If that is me, fine. If it is someone else, that is fine, too, but it is important that you not carry this story around alone anymore.*"

Blue looked back down. She wasn't sure what to do now. This was new territory. No one had ever said anything like that to her before. She decided to go at least a little further. "There was someone I trusted. But I couldn't tell them everything. How can you tell someone about vox? They don't understand. I always had to make something up. It wasn't the same." She looked up. "*You can't make up something for this.*"

Dr. Woods sat thoughtfully for a while. Finally, she said, "You will find people you can trust and will understand. It may take a while, but it is worth the effort and patience. I hope that one day you will be able to trust me, but I am not asking you to do that now, I am just asking for the opportunity to earn your trust. That's all." Dr. Woods leaned back in her chair. "And that's all for this session. Whether or not you return for another is totally up to you."

"I can go now?"

"Yes, of course. Like I said, you can leave anytime."

Blue unfolded her legs and sat on the edge of the couch, preparing to stand up. She hesitated. She wasn't sure she wanted to go, but if she stayed, she wasn't sure what Dr. Woods would do next, or what she herself would do next, for that matter. "If you're not going to ask me to tell you my whole story, what would you ask instead?"

Dr. Woods replied cheerfully and without hesitation. "I think I would ask you what your favorite thing to do is!"

"It's not in those papers you have?"

"No, believe it or not. Apparently, no one ever asked you that. And you know what? I've read through your file and to me it's like they are talking about someone else, someone that doesn't exist, so I am taking this file and putting it away. I am not going to look at it again. I am going to start fresh. And my first question is going to be exactly that. What is your favorite thing to do?"

---

"So what did you tell her?" asked Wu as they walked home from school. It was cold and getting dark already with the shortest of winter days only weeks away. The trees rattled with the few leftover dead leaves clinging to the stark branches. A lot of kids were giving up on walking and taking the bus instead. Wu and Blue had missed the bus, but it wasn't a long walk for them. They were walking briskly to keep warm. "You must have told her drawing! And read-ing! And destroying remote controls!"

Blue gave Wu a shove in response. "Yes, I told her drawing and reading and my favorite authors, but I did NOT say destroying remote controls!"

Blue didn't tell Wu about some of the other things she told Dr. Woods. Some of the things she came up with surprised even herself. She told Dr. Woods how she loved to close her eyes and listen to sounds—just sounds, without the vox background. Another was sitting in the family room after dinner and watching and listening to Sam, Wu, Nate, Ma Beth, and Pa Bill, and talking to them about simple everyday things. They talked and thought about everything, good and bad. And they listened to her. They treated her with respect and dignity. It always felt good to sit there and soak it all up and know that she was a part of that family.

And she had reveled in the night excursions with Will. Given that she and Will had broken rules and done it without permission, and it had led to the night they both nearly died, she wasn't sure how Dr. Woods would react to that one. But it didn't seem to faze her at all. Blue wasn't sure what to make of that yet. This was one of the most private things she had shared with anyone other than Will. It was also one that could still cause trouble. It surely would have resulted in major repercussions in prior foster situations. Maybe it was because Will was involved that there was no fallout. She didn't know. She had to admit that it had felt good to share that, and the other things, with Dr. Woods, but she was still wary and not quite ready to open up completely.

"Earth to Blue. Earth to Blue. Are you there, Blue?" Wu had been walking patiently beside her.

"I'm here," she said. A pang of guilt hit her, though, something that had been coming more frequently lately. This was Wu. She owed him more. "Sorry, I was just thinking."

"No worries. Good thoughts, I hope."

Blue took a moment before she replied and then said honestly, "Yeah, good thoughts." She decided she was going to go back to Dr. Woods.

# 11

## THE GRIND

It was 10 pm, and Will still wasn't done with his homework. It was dark, and he was tired. He just wanted to friggin' go to bed! Six weeks of school without a break was starting to wear him down. He stared at the math book in front of him, trying to muster the will to grind through the last problems and get it over with. The last problems were always the hardest, and sometimes the last one was impossible. Half the time he just skipped the last problem and went to bed frustrated. Teachers were sadists. And this year all the teachers seemed determined to break the students, at least in Will's mind. They were obsessed with making sure the school met "The New Standard." What was this all-important new standard—a plot to make every kid a robot? A zombie? A pile of exhausted anxiety?

A buzzing interrupted his grousing. He didn't know whether to be annoyed or overjoyed at the distraction. While it broke the drudgery, it also prolonged it. Thankfully, it was a text from Blue.

Getting a text from any of the O'Days was evidence of a new era in the O'Day household. Because of what had happened over the summer, Pa Bill had finally relented and decided that each of the kids should have their own cell phone. The cheapest flip phones, maybe, but at least cell phones. This was probably only the third text Will had gotten from Blue and it was exactly the same as the first two:

"email"

He smiled. She hated texting on the flip-phone. She much preferred email, but he'd been keeping his email app shut off most of the time. Somehow his email address had gotten out and he was getting queries from everywhere about "that" night. It wasn't just the U.S., it was Europe, Japan, Russia, Australia. And recently the traffic had bumped up—most likely because it was mid fall—term paper season. He was getting tons of kids asking questions, since he was the topic of their term papers. So on top of the pile of home-work, he was trying to keep up with all the queries. The constant blooping of the incoming email had been driving him nuts, so he only opened the app a couple of times a day. At one point he was going to change his email address and avoid the whole mess, but for some reason, he kept it open. Most of the time, at his mom's suggestion, he just sent a form letter in reply, but he also tried to add a personal note from time to time, especially if it was a girl. Somehow Blue had managed to keep her email address out of the public eye, so she didn't get any of these emails.

He launched the mail app and found the message from Blue. It read:

"Is Baxter a grammar Nazi?"

Ah yes, Baxter. Will's freshman English teacher. He typed out a reply:

"Not first quarter. He is definitely a full-
time typo Nazi though. So watch owt."

He smiled at the thought of Blue sitting through Baxter's

classes. Baxter was a pretty cool guy and had some off-the-wall ways of lecturing. Will figured it was a perfect fit for Blue.

He stared at the deluge of unread email and sighed. He wasn't sure how much longer he could keep up with it. Fortunately, the email barrage was the only thing out-of-the ordinary now. Everything else had fallen into a normal rhythm again. School had kind of forced that on everyone. It didn't matter how crazy the events of the summer were, the memory of them was set aside once the social and academic demands of high-school kicked-in. He didn't have too much trouble with the social side. He had a small but tight group of friends. He, Anna, and Wu were the core of that group, but they each had other friends they pulled in from time to time. He felt lucky. He saw a lot of awkward kids adrift in the stormy social sea, looking for an anchorage somewhere. The lucky ones would eventually gravitate toward music, or theater, or sports, or something like that. The unlucky few got sucked into drugs.

Then there were some who just drifted in limbo. Jordy was one of those, Will thought. Will had chatted with him a little at the beginning of the quarter but since then, Jordy had seemed withdrawn—just kind of existing. Will never saw him with any friends except maybe that scrawny scrapper, a kid named Alex. And those a-holes Mike and Pike seemed inordinately bent on persecuting Jordy. He thought they would have given up by now. Will had told them to back off a couple of times, but that seemed to fuel them rather than quench them. Will figured it would be best to stay out of it, or else it would just make it worse for Jordy.

Anna was the opposite. She had this positive aura about her that just radiated good will. Nothing seemed to get her down. You could be in the bleakest mood and with just a brief dose of Anna, you walked away standing a little taller, a little lighter.

She had made friends with Blue, which was awesome. Blue needed a friend like that. Will hardly ever saw Blue during the school day except at one study hall on Wednesdays. They never got much done at those study halls. They would just vox back and forth the entire time, and no one else in the room had a clue. It was glorious. When they ran out of things to say, they would come up with bizarre topics for no other reason than to keep the vox conversation going just because they could. It was fun, it was secret, it was so cool. It revived a little bit of the aura of their summer rendezvous. Will looked forward to Wednesdays.

He smiled as he reminisced about the second or third Wednesday they were in study hall together. That was the day when hell froze over, pigs flew, and fish danced the Macarena, as his mother would say. That was the Wednesday that Blue walked into study hall wearing . . . a skirt! Will couldn't believe his eyes! He had grown so accustomed to seeing her in jeans, he just assumed she'd be a tomboy forever. When she spotted him staring at her she scowled and spat daggers out her eyes, *"NOT. ONE. FUCKING. WORD!"* God, he couldn't believe it. The tomboy in a skirt. He really had to restrain himself from making a smart comment—it was sooo tempting. Thing was, she looked pretty good in a skirt. In fact, shockingly good. He wondered if this was the same kid he had gone through so many adventures with last summer. This was a completely different creature, at least on the outside. She avoided his eyes that study hall, but he managed to catch her glance at one point and vox, *"HEY, YOU LOOK GOOD! I MEAN IT!"* She had looked away quickly, but he thought he caught a tiny smile. Kind of a tortured smile. It was like she was happy with the compliment but angry that she should be happy.

Anyway, that had been a month ago, and after getting over the initial shock, seeing her in a skirt didn't seem that surprising anymore. In fact seeing her in jeans or skirt, either way, she was definitely looking more like a girl. An attractive girl.

A buzzing knocked him out of his reverie. It was a text from Wu. He looked at the clock. Damn, it was 10:30, and he hadn't finished his trig problems.

"what u get for 12? 30 deg?"

That was the last problem in the set. Will was only on problem 9. He groaned. Trig mid-term next Wednesday and an interview for the school newspaper tomorrow during study hall. Patty Smith had been bugging him from the beginning of the school year for an interview. He had put her off because he had been so sick and tired of interviews and questions. He had given her his 'form reply'—the same one he was sending to all his term paper groupies—but she took one look at it and said, "Everyone knows that stuff. I want to dig *deeper*. I want the *inside* story!" Whatever that was.

He knew Patty had tried Blue, too, but Blue had put the kibosh on that right away. Patty had backed off both of them for a while, but with Thanksgiving coming up in a month, she was putting the pressure on Will again; she wanted a splashy article for the holiday. He had finally relented, figuring the sooner he got her off his back, the better, especially with all the end-of-quarter projects coming due soon. He had asked Patty if she was going to try to interview Blue again, too, but she was coy about it.

"Maybe, if I can ever corner her. She seems to have an instinct for avoiding me," Patty had said.

Will grinned. Yeah, maybe if you weren't broadcasting your *chiss* non-stop you could sneak up on her, he thought. Patty had the loudest *chiss* of any non-vox that he had ever heard. He could hear her right through his glasses sometimes. He wondered if she might be able to hear, even a little bit. Of course, her mouth leaked a lot, too, and her pen. He wasn't looking forward to what she might ask or write.

Screw it. Life was too complicated. His brain was fried for the night. He slapped the book shut, turned off the light, and rolled onto his back. He texted Wu back:


"dk cu tmrw"


Trig was going to have to wait for study hall. And Patty was going to have to wait for her interview, again. Maybe forever.

**12**

———

## COLD CASE

"*N*YPD, *Detective Rodney James speaking.*"

The voice coming out of the phone had a languid yet business-like timbre, a quality Chief Hannah was accustomed to hearing when talking to people involved in law enforcement. She wondered if she sounded that way to them.

"Detective James, this is Chief Summer Hannah of the Westbury Police Department. I'm responding to the email you sent me."

"*Chief Hannah. I really appreciate your calling me back.*"

"How can I help you, Detective?" she replied.

"*As I mentioned in my email, I'm in the Cold Case Squad here in New York. The reason I contacted you is that the kidnapping and shooting in Westbury caught the eye of a colleague of mine. He has a hunch that it might be connected with one of our cold cases.*"

Chief Hannah sat up at this, a flutter of excitement in her chest. "It wouldn't surprise me," said Chief Hannah. "We were suspicious that the drug dealer, the man who referred to himself as Bronco, was likely getting supplied from a metropolitan area. If you have something on him, it would be a huge break for us."

There was a pause before Detective James replied. "*Um, we actually weren't looking at Bronco, though it wouldn't surprise me if the*

*Narcotics Unit might be interested. With regards to this cold case, however, we were only interested in Blue DuBois."*

"Blue?" Chief Hannah tried to keep the surprise out of her voice.

*"Yes. I know how surprising that may sound and I am sorry that I can't get into too much detail about how this came about, at least not at this stage of the game. Like I said, it is just a hunch on the part of a colleague, albeit a very well respected colleague. It may not go anywhere, but we're giving it some due diligence to see if it has legs. To that end, I was hoping you would be willing to answer a few questions that might help us figure out if we're completely full of shh . . . um . . . shoe polish or not."*

Chief Hannah nearly laughed out loud. "You kind of caught me off guard, Detective. Honestly, I don't know much about Blue's background other than the common knowledge, but I'll try to answer your questions. If I can't, I know other people that can give you more in-depth answers."

*"Thank you, Chief Hannah. I really appreciate that. I'll try not to take too much of your time. We may not need anything more than common knowledge at this point. My first question is this: We understand that Blue is an orphan. Do you happen to know how she became an orphan?"*

"Well, we know that she was the only survivor of a home fire."

There was a pause before Detective James replied. *"Interesting."* It sounded like he was typing some notes. He continued, *"Do you happen to know the names of her parents? Her biological parents?"*

"I don't know. We do know that she has no living relatives and has been through several foster home situations before she landed here. I didn't see any relevance to the kidnapping, so I didn't dig any deeper."

*"Sisters? Brothers?"*

"She had one younger sister that died in the fire. Her name was, um, Heather, I think. I can check on that for you."

*"Heather? Hmm. Interesting."* More typing. *"Do you happen to know where her home was—the home that the fire occurred in?"*

"I don't. However, I do know someone that has access to more information that may include that—a medical professional that Blue sees. She happens to be a personal friend of mine. I could ask her and get back to you. She's a psychiatrist." Chief Hannah wasn't sure she should have mentioned the last bit, but she had a good feeling about Detective James so far.

*"That would be very helpful,"* said Detective James. He typed a little more and then paused before continuing. *"It seems this girl has been through a lot."*

"Yes, she has. You could even call that an understatement," said Chief Hannah.

*"I hear you,"* he said. There was another pause before he added, *"Fourteen. Damn. You remember being fourteen? It was hard enough just surviving the social scene back then. Look, I don't want this to be the source of more stress for her. I think it would be best if we kept this just between you, me, and sources that wouldn't leak back to the family. Like I said, I don't know that it's going to go anywhere at this point."*

And yet every instinct was telling Chief Hannah that her answers had all been winners so far. You're not fooling me, Detective James, she thought. At the same time another set of instincts was telling her that this was a genuinely good guy. But good guy or not, she needed more than she'd heard so far. "Detective James, you can't leave me totally hanging here. What kind of cold case in New York would involve a fourteen-year-old kid in Vermont?"

There was yet another pause on the other end of the line, and she was ready for a stonewall, but what Detective James offered her almost made her regret the question. *"Okay, I'll give you what I can, which isn't much. Let me ask a question and maybe you can infer from that. When you talk to your friend, could you look for information that might indicate whether or not Blue's birth parents were involved in horticulture? In particular, indoor horticulture. Were they gardeners or landscapers or involved in that type of business?"*

"Horticulture," replied Chief Hannah. The only indoor horticulture that police would be interested in would be clandestine grow houses. Marijuana most likely. He's trying to connect an illicit grow house operation in New York with Blue's parents. Her parents involved with illicit drugs? Jesus.

*"Yes. Horticulture. I'm guessing you figured it out already. All the more reason to be discreet about this information. Look, I don't want you to get too excited. There are some interesting coincidences here, but there are also some very big contradictions that you are unaware of and they are likely to turn this into a dead-end. And that's about all I can say right now."*

"Okay," said Chief Hannah, "I can live with that. For now."

A laugh came out of the phone, *"Thanks. I'm sorry. I hope that I'll be able to make this all a little clearer at some point. I do appreciate your help. I look forward to hearing what you find out."*

"Me, too," said Chief Hannah.

*"Until then,"* said Detective James.

"Until then," replied Chief Hannah.

Detective James hung up, but Chief Hannah sat there with the phone hovering in the air. Blue's parents involved with illicit drugs? Jesus. It wasn't hard to imagine, just shocking. There is no way Blue could have suspected that, is there? It seems that if she knew, she wouldn't be so obsessed with her anti-drug crusade. But maybe just the opposite. She sighed. Don't get obsessed with this, Summer, she told herself. Like he said, this was probably all a coincidence.

A sudden bleeping made her realize the phone was still in her hand and off-hook. She cradled the phone and grabbed her hat. She needed to at least follow through with Dr. Woods. Maybe a few answers from her would make this go away, and in her heart she hoped that would be the case, but her cop-brain was telling her that Detective James' hunch had just gained momentum, like a train getting up a head of steam, and was heading straight toward a fourteen-year-old who loathed drug dealers so much she nearly died trying to take one down.

## 13

## LOOSE ENDS

An icy October gust stabbed Bronco's bare neck, sending a sharp chill down his back. He felt the hairs of his arm stiffen and lift against the chill, pressing against the nylon fabric of the bulky parka as he reached up with one hand to pull the collar tighter and close the offending gap. The other hand was still gripping the corner of a slimy, soggy backpack that sat slumped in the bottom of the dented aluminum rowboat which was rocking uneasily in the chop of the little mountain lake. A ragged gash of torn red fabric on the side of the pack mirrored the grim, resigned look on his stubble-strewn face. It figures, he thought. When things start to go wrong they continue to go wrong until the story ends. That's what his miserable son-of-a-bitch father might have said if he was here now. He wasn't here now, of course. Bronco had taken care of that.

His father's remains had been flushed down the toilet of the men's restroom at the mortuary just after the solemn funeral director, who stood with just the right amount of well-practiced sympathy, had handed him the cheap, garishly decorated tin urn which contained a bag holding his father's ashes. Bronco had promptly gone to the restroom, pulled the bag of ashes out of the urn, slashed it with his pocketknife, dumped the contents into the toilet, and pissed on the dusty pile as it sank into the bowl. When he flushed, he watched without emotion as the whole mess swirled into a dirty grey vortex and vanished down the porcelain gullet with a gurgling glug. Goodbye, you miserable bastard, he had thought then. And many times since then.

That was years ago. The slashed bag that was staring at him now had dumped something that was actually precious to him— six pounds of gold coins worth $80,000. They were resting some- where in the dense mat of weeds on the bottom of this frigid lake. When things start to go wrong they continue to go wrong. Great. If only that little witch, the mind-reader, that girl, hadn't started this whole shit show, he wouldn't be sitting here freezing his ass off trying to pick up all the pieces of his life that blew up that August night. Instead, he would have been safely out of the country and relaxing on a nice warm Central American beach.

Another icy gust slipped into an unguarded gap in his jacket. He wasn't sure if it was the gust or the memory of that girl that caused the spastic shiver that suddenly seized him. He still couldn't believe it—that she had actually read his mind. Yet, every time he went over what happened that night, he came to the same conclu- sion: there was no other way she could have known that his Dad had killed Ethan, his little brother, the smart one, the stubborn one. And who knows what else she had learned in the time he was in that room with her? Some of the things he thought were safely secreted in his head now seemed vulnerable. And dangerous. Not knowing what she knew had been eating away at him ever since that night.

What really irritated him was that she should have been dead from the horse-sized dose of heroin he'd given her. But she wasn't, all because of that boy showing up and then Jack and then the cops. It all went to hell from there—a bullet in his butt causing him to lose control of the Camaro and launch it into the lake and then the confrontation with the NY State Police who had responded to the accident and their huge fine on top of the bill for the extraction of the totaled Camaro from the lake and then the disappointing discovery that the backpack wasn't in the car. And there was that fucking surgeon in New York who extorted a ridiculous fee for patching him up and staying quiet about it. That surgeon was going to get some payback. But it all hit bottom when he found out that this girl, who was turning out to be some sort of immortal savant, was also a mini-Rembrandt, producing a ridiculously accurate portrait of him for the police. Fortunately, it showed him with a beard, now gone, but he was considering the extra precaution of a little appearance altering surgery. That would mean another chunk of cash down the drain.

God damn it. He really needed that gold back.

He let go of the backpack and it sagged into a scummy puddle in the bottom of the boat. Three miserable freezing hours with a boat hook to find and fish that friggin' thing out of the lake, but not before he had pulled up a bicycle wheel, a disgusting bag of decayed dead something, a pair of camo-patterned panties, a fishing rod, and a baseball cap that had "I'd rather be F---ing!" embroidered on it. And then the initial elation of finding his Glock, his Browning, and his wad of about $6,000 of soggy twenty dollar bills intact had evaporated the instant he discovered the ragged hole and the missing pouch of gold.

A bong rang out, amplified by the cold air hovering over the lake. Another bong as he slammed his fist in frustration a second time into the side of the aluminum hull. Dammit. There was no way he was going to find and fish that small pouch out of the weedy, murky water with just a boat hook. It was too late in the day to even try. With the sun going down and his soaking jacket sleeves, he had to get off that lake. He was not going to add hypothermia to the long list of things-gone-wrong. He pulled his gloves off and stuffed his hands under his jacket and into his armpits. He waited for the tingle that let him know they were warmed enough to work again. Then he pulled out his phone and took pictures of the shore so he could triangulate where he was when he came back. He warmed his hands one more time before tugging on his cold wet gloves and digging the oars into the water for the quarter-mile pull back to the dock.

The question of exactly when he could come back kept his mind occupied as he overcame his combination of irritation and shivering and settled into a steady rhythm with the oars. He would need to find an underwater metal detector. And he was going to have to dive. It was probably ten or twelve feet deep based on the length of the extendable boat hook he had used. He could do that, but he would need a mask, snorkel, and fins. It was far too late in the season for him to do it now. He didn't have the equipment or skill to dive in water when it was that cold and he certainly wasn't going to trust anyone else to do it. He had to face the fact that it wasn't going to happen until spring.

So what to do until spring? He'd been toying with the idea of picking up a gig he'd heard about—a summer camp not far from here, about an hour's drive. Some NYC businessman needed a caretaker for his camp for the winter. It might be an ideal situation. It would get him out of the city. He didn't exactly feel secure that they wouldn't track him down there eventually. Coming up here would be another way to erase a trail. It would also put him right near Vermont. There was a loose end in Westbury. The girl. He didn't know what to do about it, it wasn't like there was a handbook on mind-readers, but not doing anything seemed like a bad idea. Being closer to Westbury while at the same time disappearing from NYC seemed like a good way to keep out of trouble and keep track of the situation in case anything developed.

By the time he approached the dock, he had stopped shivering. In fact, he was actually warm and a lot more relaxed. He realized the gold wasn't going anywhere, and in a way, it was a blessing the backpack had flown out of the Camaro when it smashed through the guardrail and flipped into the lake. There might have been some very uncomfortable questions from the State Police about its contents when the car was pulled out. Fortunately, the car wasn't the issue, no one was looking for a Camaro, they were looking for a Toyota, but his red backpack had been flagged by the Westbury PD on the news. The NY State Police weren't stupid—they surely would have been monitoring any alerts. They could've easily detained him if they'd seen the backpack and its contents. Instead, all they did was ask some stern questions, have him take a sobriety test, which he passed, gave him a hefty ticket, and released him. Miraculously, the whole time, his bullet wound hadn't bled and given him away. All-in-all, he had escaped all the worst case scenarios.

He suddenly stopped rowing in mid-stroke. The boat coasted slowly to a stop as it dawned on him. Even though some things went wrong, most of it had all gone right. He was still free. He had most of his stuff back, and he had the start of a solid new plan to lay low and get his gold back. He just had to be patient. Okay, old man fate, he thought, you threw a few curveballs at me. Nice try. Here I am, still kicking like mad. I can take it. End of story. Time to start the next story and if I have to stay a few months in the Adirondacks to make it work, so be it.

He smiled for what was probably the first time that day, or even the first time in weeks. It took him only two strong strokes to close the remaining distance to the dock. Anyone observing from the shore would have seen nothing unusual, just one of those crazy, scruffy, late-season Adirondack fishermen tying his boat to the dock on a bone-chilling fall afternoon with a look on his face like he had just won a fishing derby.

14

DINNER AT THE WOODS'

Blue walked up the sidewalk to the front door of the Woods' house. At the end of their last therapy session, Dr. Woods had invited Blue to come to the Woods' house for dinner, and now here she was. She tried to remember the last time she was invited to someone's house to dinner. Just her. She couldn't remember, of course, because it had never happened. This was a first, she realized, and yet it seemed oddly comfortable. Maybe it was because of her friendship with Will or his sweet little sister, Rose. Or maybe it was because of Dr. Woods.

Her sessions with Dr. Woods had been like none she'd had before. They were supposed to be therapy sessions, or counseling, or whatever, so she was expecting the same kind of bullshit she'd gone through with all the other so-called therapists. But these seemed more like just good conversations. At first she had tried hard to determine when Dr. Woods was just being a nice person and when she was doing something as a therapist, but at some point she had stopped worrying about it. And when that happened she started to relax. In fact, after the last session, as she got up from the couch, she realized that she had been slouched casually in one corner, her back nestled right in the crook of the back with her elbow resting on the arm of the seat. No panic, no fear.

A little icy gust brought Blue's mind back to the present, and she realized that she was still standing in front of the Woods' door. She reached her gloved finger out to push the doorbell but hesitated. Tonight was the fifth anniversary. She had told no one but it was likely Dr. Woods knew. Had she invited her on this night on purpose? It didn't matter. It was time to put it behind her. She mashed the doorbell button before she could think about it too much. There was a cheerful "bing-bong" sound inside. Damn, this is beginning to feel like an episode of *Modern Family,* she thought. As she stood waiting she took note of the fact that this was one of the few times she had ever entered this house through the front door. Funny. And not only that, this would be the first time since she was ten that she would be with a whole family that could vox. And vox freely. She wasn't sure quite what to expect. It had been so long she didn't even know quite how she should act or what the etiquette was. Not that it really mattered. What mattered was that she was about to finally be back with her people. Her people. She realized there really was such a thing as "her people."

What was taking so long? The night air was actually colder than she expected, and she was starting to shiver a little. Just as she reached out to push the bell again, the door burst open.

"*Hey, Blue!*"

"Happy birthday!"

"*Whoo hoo!*"

"Welcome to Woods Hole!"

"*Woods Hole? What are you talking about?*"

"*That's what we call our house.*"

"Come in, Blue, it's freezing out there!"

This all came in a jumble of voice and vox from the four Woods family members who were crowded around the door.

Blue was taken off guard but managed to say, "Thanks, but my birthday isn't until next week."

"Yes, we know," said Mrs. Woods, "But since Rosie's is in two days, and yours is so close, we decided to make this a dinner celebration for both of you. Please, come inside!"

"Rosie, you're turning ten?" said Blue turning to look at Rosie as she stepped in.

"That's right, but you're turning fifteen! You're going to be an old maid!"

"Rosie! Be polite."

"That's okay Mrs. W." "ROSIE, YOU'RE GOING TO BE A BIG BRAT," voxed Blue.

"She's already a big brat," said Will.

Rose giggled, "I know . . . right?" She stuck her tongue out at Will and seized Blue's hand, pulling her down the hall. She voxed, "C'MON TO MY ROOM. WE'RE GONNA HAVE GIRL TALK UNTIL DINNER!"

The feeling of a small hand grabbing hers and tugging at her arm pulled at something deep inside. It almost made Blue gasp out loud. A tingle ran across her skin as she felt this energetic free spirit. It revived a long neglected sensation of peace and innocence. She had forgotten what that was like.

"Rosie, be polite. Blue is the guest of the whole family!"

"It's okay, Mrs. Woods," said Blue. "I'd like to spend some time with Rosie. Is it okay if I call you Rosie, Rose?"

"Yes, just not Rosemary!"

"Is Rosemary your full name?"

"It is, and it's one of my favorite spices!" said Mrs. Woods, "But Rosemary is not very fond of it."

"IT MAKES IT SOUND LIKE I'M A GRANDMA," voxed Rose to Blue.

"WELL, MAYBE YOU'LL BE A GRANDMA SOMEDAY," REPLIED BLUE. "I HAVE A SECRET I'LL TELL YOU THAT MIGHT MAKE YOU FEEL BETTER ABOUT IT . . ."

"Just be ready to eat in twenty minutes!" Mrs. Woods said behind them as they headed down the hall.

They sat down to dinner and Will's mom put a full plate in front of Blue. On it was a huge salad and a slice of lasagna ("*MA BETH TOLD ME IT WAS YOUR FAVORITE!*"). Both the salad and the lasagna were not quite like anything she'd had before. The salad had nuts and tiny orange wedges in it and the greens were dark. The lasagna looked right but had a much different smell.

Will's dad cleared his throat and raised his water glass and said, "To this momentous occasion of Blue and Rose's birthdays and to Blue's first *official* . . . ahem . . . visit to our house. I say cheers!"

Blue felt her ears redden and hoped no one noticed, but she needn't have worried. As soon as Will's dad set his glass down, eating commenced and all attention was on food. Well, they get right down to business here, she thought. She picked up her fork and carved out a small bite of the slightly foreign looking lasagna, but as soon as it hit her tongue, a little moan escaped her eyes, "*OH MY GOD.*"

Will's mom looked at her with a crease in her brow. "*IS SOMETHING WRONG?*"

Blue chewed slowly, entranced by the richness of the new flavors she was experiencing, and replied, "*No, NOT AT ALL! THIS IS FUCKING AMAZING . . .*" Oh shit. She looked around. Everyone had stopped eating and was looking at her. Rose had her hand up to her mouth.

"Shit! I am so sorry . . . I mean . . ." "*SHIT!*" She dropped her fork and covered her mouth and her eyes before she could do any more damage. Her ears were broadcasting, though, and they felt like they were going to burst into flames at any moment. Dammit! She'd blown it already. Not two minutes into dinner. She started hearing strange sounds and she ventured a peek between her fingers. She didn't see Rose but heard giggling coming from under the table. Will's face was red—at least the part that was showing from behind the napkin clamped over his mouth. He was making small explosion sounds behind the napkin. Will's dad had his head down, but his shoulders were shaking up and down like he had a high-speed case of hiccups. Blue looked at Will's mom, who seemed to be the only one not reacting. Her mouth was twisted up in the strangest way, though. Blue wasn't quite sure what to make of it.

"I am SOOO sorry!" she said.

"Well," started Will's mom, "I think we can forgive you. I am sure it's been a long while." Will's mom's mouth slowly returned to somewhat normal, which allowed her grin to show through. "Rosemary Woods, stop giggling and sit up at the table! And Will, you can straighten up, too."

Rose reappeared above the table and it looked as if her laughter was mostly spent, but an occasional giggle kept popping out.

Will put his napkin down and said, "We *never* hear language like that at this table."

"Will, that's enough," said his mom. "And, Ash, you can just stop now, too."

Mr. Woods had started his head-down quaking again. Finally, he looked up, somewhat composed. "Yes, you're right, dear. And you're right, too, Will. I guess none of us are saints here." "YOU ARE QUITE FORGIVEN, BLUE. JUST . . . TRY AND TAMP IT DOWN A LITTLE."

"I am really, truly, so, so sorry," said Blue.

"Apology accepted," said Will's mom. And that was that. Blue felt a rush of relief.

Will's mom worked on getting the conversation going in another direction. "How was school today, Rose?"

Rose got in one final half-giggle that was quenched with a stern look from Will's mom. "It was fine. Billy mashed his finger in gym." "PASS THE BREAD AND BUTTER, PLEASE?"

"DON'T FILL UP ON BREAD, PLEASE." "Did he break his finger?"

"I think so. He came back from the nurse's office with a splint on it."

"Isn't Billy the same kid that fell off the swings and broke his ankle?" asked Will.

"Yep, the very same one. We call him 'Broken Bone Billy'." "WILL, PASS THE BREAD!"

*"MOM SAID NOT TO FILL UP!"*

"I don't think it is polite to make fun of someone with names like that," said Will's mom.

"Oh, he doesn't care. He actually likes it," said Rose. She gave Will the stink eye for refusing to pass the bread.

"I'd like some bread, too, please," said Blue.

Will rolled his eyes and passed the bread to Blue. Blue took a slice and then passed the bread to Rose, giving Will a look and then glancing at Will's mom, who pretended not to notice.

"And you, Will? How was school?" asked Will's mom.

"Pretty much the usual insanity."

"Do you suppose you could elaborate on that for us?" asked Will's dad. "We like to hear some of the day-to-day drama of high school in detail. It makes us nostalgic."

Will was chewing thoughtfully on his lasagna. He swallowed and then said, "Well, Mike and Pike harassed Jordy Willis again, and I went over and told them off and then they mocked me because I was only shot with a .22 which they called a pea-shooter and I said, 'So what have you been shot with?' and that shut them up. Other than that, we had a trig quiz and a fire drill when some-body pulled the fire alarm." *"LIKE I SAID, JUST A NORMAL DAY . . ."*

"So does that subject come up a lot at school?" asked Will's dad.

"You mean fire alarms?"

Rose snorted. Will's mom gave Will a stern glance.

"Oh, you mean getting shot!" Will said, flashing half a grin that Blue suspected only she and Rose could see. "No, not that much. Everyone's too wrapped up in their own social drama at school. Except for Patty Smith who wants to make a splash in the school newspaper." *"SHE'S BEING A PAIN ABOUT WANTING AN EXCLUSIVE 'IN DEPTH' INTERVIEW."*

"Do you think there is something wrong with that?" asked Will's dad.

"Well, it's not like the story isn't out there. And I don't know what she means about digging deeper." "*I think she just wants to put a warped perspective on it.*"

"She wants to interview me, too," said Blue.

"You told her no, though, right?" asked Will.

"I told her yes," said Blue, and she looked down and took another bite of that amazing lasagna.

"What? Blue, she is just going to stir the high school rumor pot, and we will be dealing with it the rest of the year!"

She looked back up and saw that everyone had stopped eating and were looking to her for a reply. She finished her bite of lasagna and said, "Bronco is still out there. And somebody must have taken his place by now." "*Nobody seems to care. People need to worry about it.*"

The table was silent for a while. Finally, Will's mom said, "I think there is something to be said for that."

Will just grumbled, which disappointed Blue. She was hoping for a little support from him.

"*Yeah, so just man-up and deal with it, Will!*" voxed Rose, glancing at Blue with a smile.

"Rosemary!" said Will's mom.

"Well he should," said Rose looking down.

Will played with some food on his plate but then looked up and said, "Okay, if you are willing to do it, then I will, too." "*She should get it from both of us.*"

"*It's settled then!*" Rose voxed with finality. Mrs. Woods gave Rose a stern glance this time.

"Well, this has been a very interesting conversation, and you two have reached a very important decision, and I think it is time to change the subject. We have many things to celebrate tonight. And once everyone is finished with dinner, we have my favorite dessert to celebrate with!" said Will's dad.

The dessert was as new and fresh as the rest of the meal. It was a spicy chocolate pudding with a graham cracker crust. It tasted rich but wasn't heavy on Blue's stomach.

"It's made with tofu, believe it or not." said Will's mom.

Tofu! She never in her life thought she'd ever like tofu.

Rose jumped up with her empty dessert dish and reached over and grabbed Blue's. "You're our guest, and it's almost your birthday, so you sit, and I'll help with clean up." She grabbed a couple of other plates. "And then we should play a game. Like Rummikub or Settlers!"

"It's closer to *your* birthday, so I should help . . ." Blue started to stand up.

"*SIT!*" commanded Rose. "*I'll get them! It's my turn anyway.*" She grabbed more plates and headed toward the kitchen.

"*Brat!*" retorted Blue.

Rose replied by looking over her shoulder and sticking out her tongue just as she disappeared into the kitchen.

There was something in that image—Rose with her head turned and tongue sticking out—that caught Blue off guard. It sat shimmering in her mind like a ghost, just for a moment, but long enough to penetrate into a corner of her memory where it reached out and unlocked something before she could stop it, something that had been locked up for a long time . . .

"Since Blue is here, maybe we should play a vox game like 'Zoom' or 'Find the Fox,' like we did in the old days," suggested Will. He turned to Blue and voxed, "*What do you think?*"

Blue suddenly felt like she had stood up too fast. The room was spinning, and the voices around her sounded like swirling echoes. She could just make out what they were saying. They were asking her something. ". . . Blue, are you okay?" They kept repeating it, but she couldn't answer. She realized she couldn't breathe. Heather couldn't breathe. She had to get Heather. She felt herself standing up and lunging toward the kitchen where she ran straight into Rose. Rose staggered back and looked up into Blue's face.

"*Blue! What's wrong?*" Rose had a worried and frightened look.

Blue felt a hand on her shoulder and Mrs. Woods voice, "Blue, it's okay. You are safe!"

Blue shrugged the hand off her shoulder and pushed her way back into the dining room. She was still dizzy. And hot. She had to get out of there. She had to get out of the house. She staggered to the front door and stumbled out into the cold. The icy air slapped her in the face and bare arms and legs. She grabbed the rail of the porch and sat down slowly, taking deep gasping breaths. She could breathe. But each breath was punctuated with a sob. She sat there, her mind completely numb—the only sensation being the cold night air and the sparkle of moonlight refracting off the unbroken frosting of fresh snow.

She was aware of feeling warmer—that someone had put a coat over her shoulders. And then there was warmth next to her as someone sat down by her side. And then there was an arm around her shoulders. She leaned into the arm and body next to her. It was comforting, and it helped bring the spinning to a stop. Her hearing started to return to normal. She could hear the sharp crackle of the noises that a freezing night makes. She could hear the breathing of Mrs. Woods next to her. Then she heard words. They were her own words, and they were flowing out of her mouth, making smoky clouds in the air in front of her.

"I saw Heather. I thought Rose was Heather. Heather couldn't breathe. I tried to save her. But I couldn't. I couldn't breathe either." She stopped and sniffed at her running nose. She realized her hand was wet from tears rolling off her cheeks. "This keeps happening! I try and stop it, and it stops for a while. But I can't forget it! I can't let go of it! I don't want to forget my family, my mom, my dad, my sister!" She paused to dry her face on her sleeve. "I wanted to die. I was ready to die. When Bronco gave me that heroin—I was ready for this to stop. I wanted to join my family. I was hoping I'd feel like I was home again here. It feels like home with the O'Days. But then things like this just keep happening! I just want it to stop!"

Mrs. Woods didn't reply. She just sat holding her and rocking very gently. It felt good. It felt peaceful. The next words just tumbled out by themselves. "I don't want to die now. I just want the sadness to go away."

"I think it has already started to," said Mrs. Woods.

Blue looked up at Mrs. Woods. "*You mean because I just told you something? Something about my story?*"

Mrs. Woods nodded and voxed, "*I think so.*"

Another icy gust sent a tingle across her face. She sighed and rubbed the wetness off her cheeks. She knew Mrs. Woods was right, yet she didn't quite believe she could ever be completely free of this. For the moment, though, she could close her eyes and lean her head into the soft, warm sweater worn by the only doctor she had ever felt she could trust.

* * *

The snowy sidewalk flowed underneath her like a sparkling, frosty river. She watched as one boot came into view and planted itself with a creaky plopping sound, and then it disappeared behind her as it moved with the current of the sidewalk. And the next boot came up and took its place. Left boot, right boot, left boot. Plop, creak, plop, creak, plop, creak. Every now and then her breath spawned a wisp of cloud that drifted over the scene, making her feel like she was floating high above the ground. Another set of boots plodded alongside of hers, keeping them company. They were good company. They made their own rhythm—clump, squeak, clump, squeak, clump, squeak. The syncopated beat of their boots sounded crisp and magnified in the deep cold of the night. Plop, creak, clump, squeak, plop, creak, clump, squeak. At some point, she became aware that her gloved hand was in his. She didn't know how it got there. It didn't matter. She didn't let go.

They reached the gate to the O'Day house and stopped together wordlessly. The glowing white framed windows were nestled in the gray shingles and surrounded with stark, bare lilac branches. The light beckoned her to come inside, but she wasn't ready to go in yet.

She looked up at Will's face. It shone faintly in the combined light of the glistening snow, the sliver of a moon, and the bright windows. He was looking at the house, studying it as an outsider would, knowing he was welcome but knowing that it was not his home. It was a steady, resigned look. She noticed how his eyelashes stood out, black yet iridescent. It was a beautiful face. He looked down at her, and she quickly looked away.

"Hey. You okay?"

How many times had he said that to her since she'd known him? Never complaining himself, always making sure she was okay. Even insisting on walking her home tonight, of all nights. A night when she exposed her inner-most private closet full of very live and active skeletons. He didn't press her for details. He didn't act embarrassed or awkward. He was just there, like a big brother. His presence calmed her down. She owed him for that. She owed him something that he wanted, and she needed. She needed to open up.

She looked up at him. "HEY, I'M OKAY. REALLY. THANKS FOR WALKING WITH ME. IT WAS . . ." she paused and looked away again. Was she ready to cross this bridge?

"It was what?"

She turned back to him. "LOOK, YOU TOLD ME THAT YOU WANTED TO KNOW MORE ABOUT WHAT HAPPENED. YOU TOLD ME YOU WOULD NEVER TELL ANYONE ELSE."

"I PROMISE. I WOULD BE A CRAP FRIEND IF YOU COULDN'T TRUST ME. I DON'T WANT TO BE A CRAP FRIEND."

"YOU'RE NOT A CRAP FRIEND, YOU IDIOT." She smiled. It was a forced smile. "SORRY, YOU'RE NOT AN IDIOT EITHER. IT'S JUST THAT THIS IS REALLY TOUGH FOR ME." She hesitated. Why was this so hard? Why did she feel like she was about to jump in front of a bus whenever she got to the point of sharing this secret demon she carried around inside her? She looked at his face again. Damn. There it was. She was surrounded by them. People who were accepting and kind and not condescending.

Screw it, she thought. It's now or never. "I'VE NEVER TOLD ANYONE THIS. TONIGHT WAS . . . IT WAS A BIG DEAL FOR ME. THIS DATE EVERY YEAR HAS BEEN A BIG DEAL. AND NOT IN A GOOD WAY. IT WAS FIVE YEARS AGO TONIGHT THAT I LOST MY FAMILY, ALMOST THIS VERY HOUR. EVERY YEAR I FALL APART. I FREAK OUT. I THOUGHT THIS YEAR MIGHT BE DIFFERENT."

Will's eyes were steady. His face looked like his hand felt—reassuring. It kept her going. "LOOK, I'M NOT READY TO TELL YOU EVERYTHING, BUT I NEED TO TELL YOU THIS. THEN MAYBE YOU WON'T THINK I AM SO BAT-SHIT CRAZY. THE FIRE THAT KILLED MY FAMILY—IT WAS DRUG RELATED—SOME SORT OF RETRIBUTION. MY DAD DID SOMETHING THAT LANDED A BUNCH OF BIG DRUG KINGPINS IN JAIL. WE HAD TO MOVE AND CHANGE OUR NAME. WITNESS PROTECTION. BUT THEY FOUND US. THEY CAME AT NIGHT, TWO OF THEM. MY DAD AND I WERE OUTSIDE. HE TOLD ME TO STAY OUTSIDE AND HIDE. HE AND THE MEN WENT INSIDE. MOM AND HEATHER WERE ALREADY INSIDE . . ." She could feel the tears welling up. That was enough. Enough for now. She leaned her forehead into Will's chest. "That's why I had to go after Bronco. I don't know why this drives me so hard. It just does. I can't let them get away with it. I just can't." She stopped and waited for Will's reaction. Please don't let this be a mistake, she said to herself. Will didn't reply right away. That was okay. It gave her time to let the tears slow down. She watched them fall from her eyes and make little gray holes in the carpet of snow at their feet.

Finally, he spoke. "And that's why you want to do the interview with Patty. You want to save everyone from the next drug dealer."

She let out a long sigh and looked back up into his eyes. "YES."

"I GUESS THAT MAKES YOU A BIT LIKE YOUR DAD, THEN."

She had to lean her forehead into his chest again. More gray holes. She gripped his jacket with both hands while he held her by her shaking shoulders.

They stood there together a long time as a light snow began to fall, very slowly. Eventually, the tears stopped falling. They were replaced with a feeling of peace. She was warm and comfortable standing there. The world felt solid under her feet, and with Will to lean on, it felt like nothing could knock them over. Their shoulders had collected a frosting of snow by the time Will finally broke the silence. "God, Blue, I wish I knew what more to do or say. This exact moment five years ago. I don't know how you can stand it."

"I can't sometimes."

"Jesus."

She lifted her head and looked at him. "*I DON'T KNOW WHAT TO TELL YOU THAT COULD HELP ME, BUT THIS ANNIVERSARY NIGHT HAS BEEN BETTER THAN ANY OF THE OTHERS. SO WHATEVER YOU'RE DOING, JUST KEEP DOING IT, OKAY?*"

"*OKAY.*"

Snow was on his eyelashes now. They sparkled and danced as he blinked. The smile on his face made her own face glow and she felt one corner of her mouth curl upward. A glow came from inside her, too, making her jacket suddenly feel like she was overdressed. He was there. Like a big brother. But not like a big brother. A big brother would not be making her feel this warm.

## 15

## REVELATIONS

Will sat alone at the beat-up graffiti-engraved oak library table, his usual Wednesday study hall perch. He gazed vacantly at the elaborate diagrams speckling the pages of his open trig book. His pencil wandered aimlessly around on his paper making random arrows instead of solving problems. His eyes kept drifting to the envelope that lay face down on the table just under the cover of his book. It was just a simple birthday card and yet he had agonized for hours over what to write inside. Ever since last Friday night it didn't matter what he was doing or where he was, he found himself thinking about that night—how Blue had opened up about her past, how her head pressed against his chest and her hands gripped his jacket while he held her, how warm it felt just having her there leaning against him. He suddenly saw a different Blue and now he found himself at a loss for what to say to her.

He looked at the vacant seat across from him that should have a girl sitting in it. She'd taken the study hall to interview with Patty. He pushed his pencil around some more and then suddenly threw it down and slapped his book shut. There was no way he was getting any work done. She could be distracting when she was there, but her not being there was even more distracting. He sighed and closed his eyes, leaning back in his chair so that his face was pointing at the ceiling. He thought maybe that would cause gravity to pull these thoughts into the back of his mind. It just made it worse. He sighed again and sat up straight and nearly fell out of his seat.

Blue was sitting there—book open as if she'd been sitting there the whole time. God, how does she do that, he thought, a smile rising in the corner of his mouth.

"*That was a quick interview,*" he voxed.

She voxed back, "*Yeah. She's a fast talker.*"

"*Well, how'd it go?*" he asked.

She looked up thoughtfully. "*It went okay. I really think she's on board with getting the drug issue out in the open, but she also asked a couple of questions I wasn't keen on.*"

"*Like what?*" asked Will.

"*Like about the crap talk that was going around for a while.*"

"*You mean . . .*"

"*Yeah, that Bronco was my boyfriend, you know. I told her it was bullshit,*" voxed Blue.

"*Is she going to print that?*" he asked.

"*Probably. Maybe. I don't know. Doesn't really matter. It's crap.*" She grabbed her pencil and looked down at her homework. "*I gotta get this Algebra done or Kendrick will kill me.*"

Will watched her as she turned all her focus on her book. Her behavior made it clear that it did matter. He looked down at the envelope. He slid it out from under his book and pushed it across the table and whispered, "Happy birthday."

She glanced at him and then stared at the envelope. He tried to act nonchalant by re-opening his trig book and pretending to concentrate on his homework. But he watched from the corner of his eye as she opened the envelope and pulled out the card. She contemplated the front for a moment and then opened the card. He watched as her eyes scanned the words. She didn't move. Ten seconds, twenty seconds . . . damn, he thought, it was the wrong thing. He looked away but caught a *"Hey."* He turned back to her. She was looking at him with an apologetic expression, like someone who just realized they had forgotten to take a dog out for a promised walk. *"Look, the other night, I'm sorry—"*

He stopped her, *"Hey, you've got nothing to apologize for."*

*"You're wrong, I do. I'm sorry for not telling you more about me earlier. After the other night, it felt . . . well . . . it just really helped. And your card . . . I mean . . . well thanks. You are a really good friend."* She looked down, embarrassed.

A wave of relief flowed through Will. He had been half-expecting the Blue that would scowl and shut him down. But that Blue seemed to have been fading away over the last several weeks, like a shed skin.

*"You know, it was fun walking with you that last night before school,"* he voxed.

*"Yeah,"* agreed Blue.

*"And it was nice to walk you home last week, too. I mean, I'm really sorry about your family, but I'm really glad to know what happened, and it just felt nice to talk to you, and walk with you."* And hold you, he thought. An impulse came over him, *"Do you want to do something? I mean not a dance or a date or anything, I mean just like . . . I don't know . . ."* Shit. He realized he *was* asking her on a date.

Blue sat tapping her paper with her pencil, making little dots all over it. *"Umm . . .Westbury Public Library maybe? We could do homework together, just like here,"* she voxed.

*"And no Tarkenton. I like it. Let's do it,"* replied Will, relieved. A study date wasn't a real date, was it?

*"Next Wednesday at 7?"* Blue voxed still tapping her pencil.

*"Yeah. Cool. And we can walk. I'll come by your house."*

*"Cool."*

And like that, everything felt right again. They both turned to their books and dug into the logical world of math for the rest of the study hall, but Will could feel her presence across from him. If he had tried to describe it in words, he would have said it was like the soft crackle of a campfire. But no one asked him to describe it, and there was no need to anyway.

---

Blue stayed at the oak table through the next period. Will had gone to his next class. She stared at the card. It was a simple card, just a flower on the front and the words "Happy 15th !" But the flower was a bluebell. It had to be a coincidence, there is no way he could have known. And inside it had one word "Hey."

"Hey you." Anna plunked herself down across from Blue where Will had been sitting. Her presence felt almost as comforting as Will's.

"Hey you, too," replied Blue. She wasn't sure she was going to get her algebra done now. Half the time they shared an amiable and quiet companionship, but when Anna was in a chatty mood, she was a complete, unrepentant note-passer. Texting was out of the question—not only because Blue's lame flip-phone sucked for texting, but confiscation was almost guaranteed. Notes were the ancient, proven method, and she suspected the teachers turned a blind eye to it. It seemed sacred. And Anna never got caught. Her notes seemed to magically appear at strategic moments. Even on the days that she really wanted to study, Blue still found herself choking down a laugh at the stuff that Anna passed her.

Today was a little different, though. Anna slid a note across the table with her pencil eraser. Instead of the usual broad smile, she had an almost reverential look on her face. Blue checked on Tarkenton and then unfolded and read the note.

*Will worries about you. I asked why and he said it would break a trust between you two. Do you realize how amazing that is? You two have something special going.*

Blue felt a flush rise up from her neck to the top of her head. She glanced at Anna and saw that her look had changed to a soft, admiring, knowing smile. Blue looked down quickly. Damn! Anna had it all wrong. She didn't know about vox. Maybe she was mistaking their voxing for something else. To Anna it probably looked like they were staring at each other a lot. It's not like they were boyfriend-girlfriend. How could she explain this to her without writing a two-page note? Sometimes she wished she could magically make her friend into a vox. It would be so much easier. She glanced at Anna, who had a smug look on her face. Anna mouthed silently "You're blushing!" while her mind leaked, "*I KNEW IT!*"

Arrgh! Blue flipped over the note and scribbled down a reply and pushed it back to Anna.

*It's not what you think ! ! ! ! ! ! !*

Anna read it and got a little guilty look on her face. The note slid back.

*I'm sorry. Really. I just think you two are perfect together.*

Dammit, Anna. Why do you have to be so nice and so reasonable? She realized she owed Anna more, too. God, the way it was going, she was going to start spilling her guts to everyone. What was happening to her? Was this what normal kids did? She sighed and put the words down, paused, and then pushed the note back over.

## We need to talk.

Anna read it quickly and smiled as she expertly slipped the note into a pile of her homework papers and pulled out what looked like an essay, just as Tarkenton slithered up and leered over Blue's shoulder with a look of anticipated victory. His face collapsed instantly into a perturbed expression of disappointment as all he could see was legitimate schoolwork. It gave Blue a little thrill. They had won this little skirmish, and it was such a normal-kid way of doing it.

---

"Okay, Miss Hot Stuff, what's this big mysterious thing you have to talk to me about?"

Blue and Anna met in a band practice room, the one private place where you could legitimately get a pass if you were buddies with the band teacher. Of course Anna could get a pass to just about anywhere—the teachers loved her.

"Look, the thing between me and Will . . ."

"So there *is* a thing between you and Will!"

"No wait, please." The look on her face must have gotten Anna's attention.

"Hey, hey. I'm sorry," said Anna. "I just so want there to be a thing. But that's me. It's not fair to you. I'm all ears now."

Blue hesitated, not so sure she wanted to tell this to anyone anymore.

Once again Anna seemed to sense how she felt. "Hey, Ms.

DuBois. I may talk a lot, but I would never tell anyone anything you didn't want me to. I mean that."

The look on Anna's face was as serious and sober as Blue had ever seen it. It was the look that gave Blue confidence to take this step. "It's because we share a genetic trait. He's kind of like a brother. Not directly related!" She added this last part when she saw Anna's face bloom into surprise.

"Related! Genetic trait? Oh my God, you guys don't have . . ."

"No! We don't have leukemia or anything like that! It's something you would never guess. You could never guess. You have to keep it secret. I mean that. When I tell you, you'll see why. Look, I'm almost even sorry I told you we had a secret, because . . ." She paused for a moment. Why *did* she feel like she had to tell someone? Dr. Woods said she should share with someone she trusted.

Anna pretty much pulled the trigger herself, "I am an *expert* secret keeper. That's why everyone talks to me. Go ahead, lay it on me. That's what I am here for, to soak up your troubles."

God, Anna was a piece of work. Her upbeat attitude was contagious, even to Blue. "Okay, Miss Cocky Secret-Keeper, this one is going to test your abilities then. Are you ready?"

"Do your worst, kiddo."

"All right. Here it goes, Will and I have vox oculis."

"Vox oculis?! What the *hell* is vox oculis? I thought you said it wasn't a disease! That sure sounds like *something* disease related. Please don't tell me it's something bad."

"No! No—relax, it's okay. Believe me, sometimes we think it's a disease, but it's not. It is genetic, though. It's our eyes. We have a special tissue in our eyes. Will and I, we can talk to each other with our eyes."

The room was deadly silent for a moment, perhaps because of the sound absorbing tiles or perhaps because Anna had stopped breathing. It all ended when Anna suddenly sucked in a lung full of air and exploded.

"WHAT!!?"

They had to make up a believable excuse in hurried whispers as they walked to the principal's office. Not even Anna's good graces with the band teacher prevented them from getting sent there after Anna's very loud and animated reaction to Blue's revelation. Blue never regretted it though. There were just some people in this world that you knew you needed on your side.

## 16

## TWO CASES, TWO CLUES

"Wow." Officer Ed Simmons sat on a stool at the high reception desk at the entrance to the police station. There was an open folder on the desk, and he was flipping through the pile of documents that it contained. "So these are all from Detective James?"

"Some are from Dr. Woods," said Chief Hannah, tapping her pencil on her open notebook.

"This is crazy. Three different identities, and your Detective James thinks all three are the same person—Blue DuBois. What the hell?"

"Yeah, pretty crazy."

"What do you make of it?" asked Ed.

"Well, part of it is certain. The victim in Detective James's case, a girl named *Belle* DuBois, was part of the family that was put into WITSEC. Witness Protection. The family's WITSEC name was Stanton. Belle DuBois became Blue Stanton. So, Belle DuBois and Blue Stanton are definitely the same person. The thing that caught Detective James' eye was the article in the New York Times about our kidnapping. Blue's name popped out. That is our Blue DuBois. That's why he decided to give us a call last month."

"So Belle DuBois, Blue Stanton. Subtract 'Belle' and 'Stanton' and you get Blue DuBois," said Ed. "Yeah, I can see how making that association could be compelling."

"Yeah, exactly. And some of the other information is eerily similar, too. They are the same age, and they have the same hair color and eye color. All three birthdays are within days of each other and they were born in adjacent states. And, critically, both families died in home fires."

"So really compelling."

"Yeah, until you start looking closer."

"You mean the birth certificates," said Ed as he gestured at the folder.

"Right. In spite of the coincidences, as far as a court is concerned the birth certificates prove that these are three different people. It doesn't matter if their names or hair or eyes or location are similar. It wouldn't even matter if they were identical. Three birth certificates, three social security numbers, means three distinct individuals. The exception is that Belle DuBois and Blue Stanton would be confirmed as the same person by the U.S. Marshalls. They're the only ones that a judge would believe."

"Because the Marshalls administer WITSEC."

"Right. And that's where this whole idea dead ends. Literally."

"You mean this." Ed held up a sheet of paper. The words "Death Certificate" in bold, gothic lettering transformed the otherwise ordinary sheet of paper into a bleak and tragic testimony of the fate of Blue Elizabeth Stanton. "Proof that Belle DuBois, aka Blue Stanton, is deceased."

"Exactly," said Chief Hannah.

"Unless WITSEC faked her death," said Ed.

"Now that's the Ed Simmons I've come to know, coming up with the wildcards. I think you'll like Rodney."

One of Ed's eyebrows rose. "On a first name basis now, are you?"

"Hey—strictly professional. But he's a nice guy and he told me to call him Rodney. Look, I call you Ed."

"Yeah, but we're practically married. I spend more time with you than my wife," Ed smirked.

Chief Hannah rolled her eyes, "Don't I know it."

"See, we even talk like a married couple."

"Ed! Let's be professional here."

"Whatever you say, honey."

Chief Hannah thought it would be pointless to roll her eyes yet again. "As to your suggestion, *Officer Simmons,* apparently faking death is the one thing WITSEC doesn't do to protect identity."

"You got that directly from WITSEC?" asked Ed.

"Not me, they won't give a small town cop like me the time of day. But Rodney has connections. Being a member of the NYPD Cold Case Squad opens a lot of doors for him. He got confirmation that they did not generate that death certificate. The hospital where she died issued it. The hospital confirmed it."

Ed scratched his chin, "But WITSEC didn't say they weren't involved in some other way, they just said they didn't generate the death certificate. What about Blue's birth certificate, our Blue? Says here that her parents are 'unknown.' That sounds like something WITSEC would generate."

"Like I said. I think you'll like Rodney. You two think alike. That's what's keeping him going right now. He's pursuing a couple of scenarios."

"So maybe I'm missing something," said Ed, "but it occurs to me that we could put an end to this all right now if we just asked Blue. 'Hey, Blue, were you ever Blue Stanton?' Pretty much a yes or WTF answer. That would kind of settle things either way, right?"

"Yeah, you'd think it would be that easy, but it's complicated. She's a minor and to question her, we need to get the guardian's permission and right now, the guardian is the state—the Department of Families and Children."

"The DFC[1]? I thought the O'Days would be the guardians."

"They have applied, but it's delayed. Probably held up by the court because of Blue's kidnapping."

"Well, what about Mr. and Mrs. O'Day? Surely she would've mentioned something about this to them."

"Yeah, you'd think, but apparently Blue hasn't told anyone much about her past and they don't push her on it. You have to remember, Blue has been through a lot. I talked to April—Dr. Woods—about it and she advocates not pushing Blue on questions about her past. She didn't get into detail because of patient confidentiality but I'm pretty sure it has to do with PTSD. It's like war veterans—they pack away their traumatic war experience and don't want to revisit it, but it eats away at them anyway. So even if we had permission from the DFC, unless there was a slam dunk case or there was some threatening situation, Dr. Woods wants to stay the course and avoid any interview. So unless something more credible comes along, Blue DuBois is Blue DuBois and the names Belle DuBois and Blue Stanton never leave this room."

"Yeah, I get that," said Ed. "Kind of frustrating though. It seems a key part of this is just dangling there—low hanging fruit."

"Watch out for low hanging fruit," said Chief Hannah, "it's often baiting a trap, as they say."

"Yeah, I suppose. There is still one other thing that is bothering me though. Why is Rod so fired up about making this connection with Blue?"

"It's *Rodney,* not Rod, and it's because if Blue was really Blue Stanton, and she survived the fire, she might be able to identify who killed her family."

"Meaning it was a murder."

"They never determined it, but yes, Rodney is pretty convinced it was murder. A drug related murder."

"Meaning, Blue could be a witness in his case."

Chief Hannah nodded.

"So drug related but Bronco is not involved?"

"Rodney said there was no link. Bronco's only involvement was his role in getting Blue's name into the national news."

Ed was thoughtful for a moment, "As a potential murder witness, you think Blue could be in danger?"

"I think Detective James would let us know if that became the case."

They were both quiet for a while.

"So what do we do now?" asked Ed.

"What can we do? I think we help Detective James do his job. That means keeping quiet and take our cues from him. And meanwhile, we keep doing our job which is to keep everyone safe, including Blue."

"And look for Bronco," added Ed.

"Yeah, let's not lose focus on our own case."

The phone rang and Ed reached for it. "And answer phones," he said. "Westbury Police Department, Officer Ed Simmons speaking."

"Yeah, and answer phones," said Chief Hannah under her breath. She realized that Rodney James's cold case had distracted her from their own work. She tried to clear her head and get back on track to the kidnapping and Bronco and drugs and kids and high school and wishing there was a magic wand to take the whole town back to a simpler day when the worst problem kids got into was getting drunk and stealing road signs. Her thoughts were interrupted by Ed, who was holding up the receiver and pointing it at her.

"I think you need to take this call. It's Silas Farr. You know, Simon's brother?" said Ed.

"The one who took over the Farr family farm? I thought he passed away."

"No, he gave up farming but he's still hanging in there, living in the old family farmhouse by himself. Says he has a renter who hasn't paid in months."

"Tell him to come in and file a complaint, Ed. You don't need me to help with that."

"The rent was for a garage. The deadbeat left a car behind. A silver Toyota with license 725 8115. Left taillight is smashed."

"Jesus!" She grabbed the phone. "Silas, is that you? This is Chief Hannah. Are you at home now?"

The reply that came out of the phone had a heavy Vermont accent, *"Where else would I be? Can' hardly walk anywhere anymore."*

"Stay there! We'll be there in ten minutes!"

She slammed the phone down and grabbed her coat and hat all in one motion. Ed was already heading for the door. They exchanged an excited glance as they jumped in the cruiser and only felt a little bad about cutting someone off as they fishtailed it out of the parking lot and pushed the aging vehicle to its limit.

Chief Hannah gazed curiously at the shreds of metal that were the remains of the left taillight on the silver Toyota that crouched in the corner of Silas's equipment shed. They curved in gently like the inverse petals of a flower, contrasting brightly against the dark interior of the trunk. It amazed her to think that it was her bullet that had hit this mark and started a chain of havoc inside the car, punching through several layers of seat backs and ultimately embedding itself in the flesh of her fugitive. He had left behind a smudge of blood but not enough that the injury looked life-threatening. The bullet had escaped along with Bronco. It was nowhere to be found.

"This guy is unreal, Ed." She cast these words over her shoulder at Ed who was standing behind her. "He keeps this completely separate identity of Bob Kelly, right down to his own car and registration, and then he keeps a second car completely secret as his getaway car. What's your bet that the other car is under another fake name?"

"I have no idea, I'm not betting. If he was this good at false identity, who's to say he didn't have several. Who would go to this much trouble to hide his identity anyway? And if he was this smart, why would he be a low-level drug dealer?"

"I dunno. It may not be so stupid. He may have been getting $20 a bag, twice what it's selling for down south."

"You mean New York?"

"Yeah, or Philly or Boston or Newark."

"Geez, you'd think that wouldn't last long. Wouldn't more dealers want in on a market like that, like ours?"

"It's gotta be happening already, Ed. People are still getting it, even with Bronco gone. He can't be the only one."

"We're not set up for handling this." Ed looked down at his shoes and dug his toe into the gravel thoughtfully.

"I agree, but we have to get ready somehow. It's our job." She stood up. "Tape this off and get a detective down here. I'm going to talk to Silas for a minute."

She weaved her way through a chaos of rusty old farm equipment and collapsing sheds to the main house which was still standing fairly firm, though sagging a bit. Silas was standing in the front doorway. He had clearly been watching their activity from his house. It was also clear he wasn't going to invite her in.

"Hi Silas, how they goin'?" she started.

"Been better toyms, but I'm gettin' boey. Whatcha make of that car anyway?"

"Looks like the one I shot at. Can't find my bullet though."

"Your no' gonna foynd it. It's buried in his hoynd quarters boey the look of it. Unless he dug it ow' and plopped it in the fron' sea'." Silas lapsed into a rhythmic wheeze that resembled a rusty starter motor on an old tractor. Chief Hannah realized that this ghastly sound was Silas laughing.

"Yeah, I think that is pretty unlikely. Shame, though, I miss my bullet. I'd really like it back. You know they only issue us one bullet. We have to just keep re-using it."

Silas sounded like he was going to expire on the spot. She had second thoughts about joking with the crusty old guy. She wanted to soften him up, but she didn't want him to die on her. "So, I guess I've got to find this guy then."

"Yeah, I suppose you do." Silas appeared to have recovered quickly from his fit and he looked more relaxed.

"So can you tell me about his other car?"

"No' much. I never wen' down there. I don' nose into other people's business. He rented the shed from me and so long as he don' burn it down, what he does with it is his business."

"I don't suppose you kept records."

"Wha' for?"

Chief Hannah wanted to roll her eyes, but she refrained. Cash economy was pretty rampant in rural Vermont. Silas probably just took the cash and didn't report it, so he didn't have to pay the taxes.

"For the rental. You charged for it didn't you? You must know something about this guy."

"You ain' gonna arrest me neow are you?"

"I'm not the IRS, Silas, and all I want is to find this guy. I'm not much interested in how you do business. Just tell me what you know about him."

"Wha' I know is that he paid cash money on the firs' of every month, and if that ain' all I need to know, then I don' know nothin'. He told me his name was Bob somebody and I said I didn' care. As long as he wasn' doing nothing but parking those cars there and bringing me my ren' each month, I don' care. But I made clear to him that if I din' get my ren', I'm calling a tow truck."

"But you didn't call a tow truck, you called us."

"I wasn' coun'in' on finding a car with a patch of dried blood and a bulle' hole. I ain' stupid. Of course, I called you. And besides, his other car wasn' there. That one was worth something"

"So can you tell me about the other car? What was the make and model? Did you get a license number?"

"No, like I told you. I never wen' down there. Tha' was his business, and I don' nose into other people's business. I saw it when he drove it in a coupla times. It was a black monster. Lotta power, and aluminum wheels. A spor's car if ever I saw one. Never saw the license plate though. No' my business."

"Chevy? Ford? Toyota?"

"Nah, I don' know. Sure wasn' a foreign job though. Looked like Dee-troi' iron to me."

"Okay, Silas, thanks this is helpful, but not as much as it could be. I sure wish you'd at least get a name and address if you rent that shed out again, and maybe some license numbers. It's perfectly okay to ask that stuff from a renter. How else are you going to track them down if they skip the rent?"

"Yeah, I suppose you're righ'. I'd like ta think you could trus' people these days, but maybe you can' always. You ain' goin to tell the IRS neow are you?"

"No, Silas, I told you I wasn't and I ain't . . . I'm not. That doesn't mean they won't track you down themselves someday and demand back taxes."

"Yeah, I'll be dead by then." Silas was silent for a moment. She could sense he was holding something back. Finally, he volunteered. "Well, I'm pretty sure the license pla'e was New York. But that's all I know. Good luck finding tha' fellah. I hope you get your bulle' back. I don' suppose I'll get my missing three months ren' out of this?"

Chief Hannah shook her head and said, "No, I don't suppose. See you around, Silas. Don't skip town." She ended the interview by turning and walking back toward the shed. Behind her, she heard the rhythmic wheezing sound again.

She walked back to the shed, her mind going a thousand miles an hour. New York plates. That would definitely narrow the search, but only to one of the most populous states in the country. Still, it led somewhere. And a bullet wound to the right buttock. That certainly narrows it down. He would have had to go to someone to get that taken care of. Emergency room records were a good first place to start. The car description was vague, but she could come back with her laptop and show him some black sports car images to try and narrow it down. Silas was sure to be able to pick one or two matches. And she was sure to find some more clues in the car.

And she just might be able to leverage her new acquaintance in the NYPD.

She stepped over a rusty piece of random farm equipment and rounded the corner to the shed. The trunk of the Toyota was open, and Ed stood behind it with three items in his blue-gloved hands. A shovel, a pick-axe, and a fist full of extra heavy duty black garbage bags. Ed looked grimly at her.

"I'm thinking we keep this quiet," he said. "I don't mean hide it. I mean, this part does not get in the press release . . ." Ed paused a good long time.

"I'm with you. It goes into evidence, but that's it. Those kids have been through enough." The thought of just how close those bags came to being used, and the thought of what kind of sorry piece of humanity could even conceive of, let alone go through with, killing two kids and bagging them and burying them like garbage . . .

"God, Chief. I want to nail this sonovabitch so badly."

"You and me both." And that meant being smart about this new clue. "Look, Ed, we keep this out of the news. Need-to-know basis only. I'll talk to Silas and hold the IRS over his head. He'll keep quiet. And Ed," she turned to look him in the eye, "this puts us back on the hunt. State and Feds can't ignore this."

17

-----

# CARETAKER

Bronco watched the little wisps of steam rise off his pants and socks as he stood as close as he dared to the spitting, hissing fireplace. The pin-pricking tingling sensation in his toes told him that they were finally regaining sensation. He was beginning to wonder exactly what he had taken on by agreeing to this caretaker job. The first storm of the season came out of nowhere and dumped more snow than he had seen in an entire winter in less than twelve hours. Even using the camp's diesel tractor and its monster sixty inch snowblower attachment it had taken him two hours to clear the quarter-mile long driveway and now it looked like he would have to do it again pretty soon. Christ, if it keeps up like this the whole winter, he thought, I'd better find some better boots.

He turned around to warm up his back side and as he did, he caught the enticing scent of fresh ground espresso as the Jura finished his latte with a *fwoosh*. Well, he thought, if I have to tough it out, this isn't a bad place to do it. Even though the owner called it a "camp" it seemed as far from a camp as you could imagine, save for the log construction and the rough-hewn, rugged décor and massive stone fireplaces. Contained inside the Adirondack-style architectural monster was a jacuzzi, a sauna, a game room with pool table, a gourmet-equipped kitchen, a giant living room with a cathedral ceiling and bona-fide full size Steinway grand piano, and five bedrooms, each with its own private bathroom. He couldn't believe it when he first stepped into the place a month ago. By the time he had found it, about five miles from the last sign of civilization and after a wrong turn down a rutted dead-end logging road, he was expecting a squat mud-chinked hovel straight out of a Grizzly Adams tale. Instead, he stepped into a New York tycoon's fortune-fueled ideal of an Adirondack hunting paradise.

He took a sip of his latte and surveyed the living room with its lavish furnishings contrasting sharply against the brilliant whiteness of the snowstorm raging silently outside the massive picture window. Yeah, he thought, not a bad place to be holed up, but that was just the problem. He felt holed up. He needed people. He needed a crowd. He needed to get out and about. It was forty-five minutes to Lake Placid and its resorts, on a good day, but today, who knows. He might not even make it. He should have listened to the previous caretaker who took one look at the tires on his car and said, "I'd get a set of Hakkapelittas if I were you." He hadn't because he'd had enough of unexpected expenses already. After today, however, he was having second thoughts. The whole idea that he could be trapped here with one lousy snowstorm made him very uncomfortable.

It wasn't just the idea of being trapped, it was being trapped in this place. There was something sinister about it. It was remote, it was isolated, and it actually got dark out here—so dark that on a moonless night you couldn't see your hand in front of your face. He'd never been any place where it could get that dark. He felt safer on the bright streets of New York than he did stepping out the door of this place at night. But it didn't feel right inside, either. He'd tried relaxing in the Jacuzzi with a glass of wine the other night but after five minutes he couldn't stand it anymore. It was as if the complete void of any humanity near him was causing the noise of his own brain to drown him. His thoughts kept going off into the weeds making up bizarre house-in-the-woods horror scenarios, like a Stephen King novel. Probably because he'd been reading them lately. Those and a stack of books on ESP. All because of that damn girl.

Well, horror scenario or not, he knew he made the right decision coming here. It was better than the sure horror scenario that would've nailed him sooner or later if he'd hung around the city. His instinct had told him that it was only a matter of time until that Westbury cop would glom on to a thread, with or without the girl's ESP help, that would lead her to his Camaro and then to his address in New York, which is why he had already taken the step of erasing himself from that place.

Screw it, he thought, if he was going to be here for the winter, he was going to make it tolerable. He drained the latte and programmed the Jura for a second cup and then stepped over to his laptop to type in a search. Miraculously, this place had land-line high-speed internet which partly made up for the fact that it was in an absolute cell phone dead zone. He found a site where he could get some Hakkapelittas, an outdoor store for some boots, and a couple of promising bars in Lake Placid. Showing off a few pictures of this place should make it trivial to attract some quality companionship for his Jacuzzi and bedroom. Maybe all five bedrooms. That should make it pretty tolerable—that along with a nice roaring fireplace fed by those damned Stephen King novels.

## 18

## THANKSGIVING EDITION

Blue sat in the girls' room stall mulling over everything that had happened in the last couple of weeks—the dinner at the Woods', the anniversary of her family's tragedy, her fifteenth birthday, and then what Dr. Woods had said at their last session. She had explained to Blue that sharing thoughts and concerns was a way of diffusing them. Sharing could be talking to someone, or it could be as simple as writing it down. She said Blue's drawings had served that purpose. Even her freak-out at the dinner was sharing. By verbalizing or visualizing those thoughts, you move the weight of those thoughts out of your head and onto paper or to a sympathetic listener.

"But doesn't a listener get burdened by them?" she had asked.

"No," Dr. Woods had said, "because the listener is *detached*. Your thoughts and concerns don't affect them the same way they affect you. They're personal for you."

A sudden banging on the stall door interrupted Blue's thoughts.

"Hey, you going to take all day in there? Haven't you ever changed a plug before?"

A cruel tittering followed the loud comment. As Blue stood up and pulled up her jeans, the banging resumed with a rhythmic beat. Great. Just grab your stuff and get out of there, she thought to herself. She flushed the toilet and stepped out of the stall, planning to exit the bathroom as quickly as possible, but blocking her way was a sturdy, tough-looking girl about two inches taller than her. Two other girls were there, clearly part of her posse.

"Well now, look who it is. The famous hostage. Hiding out in a bathroom stall, are we?"

Damn. The *Monitor* must be out, she thought. No more flying under the radar. Blue studied the girl and recognized her as a loud, tough kid that everyone tended to steer clear of. Blue was familiar with the type. Loud, brash, bullying, and usually with a weaker follower or two. These types also usually leaked *chiss* like sieves. Because of that, Blue usually wasn't afraid of them. She could anticipate trouble and steer clear of it. But this girl caught her off guard.

Why her mind worked this way, Blue had no idea, but right now it felt the need to create a handle for this tough girl. Sheeba. That's the name that just materialized in her brain. Blue was going to label this girl Sheeba. At the very same moment she christened Sheeba, she made her move. She slid as quickly as she could sideways along the bathroom wall, hoping to slip through to the exit.

Sheeba wasn't done with Blue, though. She grabbed her arm with a tough grip and stopped her cold. "Hey there, little rodeo queen, looks like you're late for class. You could get in trouble."

Rodeo queen? What was she talking about? "You're late for class, too, then. You'll get in just as much trouble," Blue said.

Sheeba gave a short, coarse laugh and her posse echoed it in a poor imitation. "Not for us, little saddle warmer, we're just headin' to lunch. Nobody get's in trouble for being late to lunch. This is much more fun than lunch, anyway. We get to interview the great bronco buster, Miss Blue-Balls Do-Boys!"

This time Sheeba and her posse burst out in unfeigned cruel laughter. They were clearly quite pleased with the cleverness of their name-calling. Blue was not. "It's pronounced 'doo-bwah'," she said, "and I don't ride horses." She tried to twist away, but Sheeba had a vice-like grip.

Now the girls really started laughing. Blue tried to stay cool, but she was annoyed. She had known that as soon as the article was published, there would be fallout. But "rodeo queen?" "Saddle warmer?" Where the hell did those come from?

Sheeba recovered from laughing first. "Oh I just bet you don't ride horses. You just ride broncos! I bet you had quite a ride in that saddle! Did he buck you hard, that big old Bronco? How was the saddle? I bet it had a nice big saddle horn!" She ground her hips as she said it.

The girls were laughing uncontrollably now. Blue felt her face getting hot and red, and it just made them laugh harder. She had to get out of there. They were bigger, but she knew she was quick. Blue yanked her arm hard, got out of Sheeba's iron grip, and then ducked between the two posse girls and took one running step out the door. She thought she was clear when she was suddenly yanked backward by her backpack strap. Sheeba had clamped on to her backpack before she could get clear. Her feet, in mid-stride, walked right out from under her and she landed flat on her backside.

"There she is girls," said Sheeba, "On her back. Her favorite position with her feet spread wide!" Sheeba kicked Blue in her thigh, hard, and then leaned down close to her face and hissed, "Watch yourself, Little Miss Do-Boys."

Blue stared defiantly at Sheeba's face. Her glasses had been knocked off, and now she could read her *chiss* crystal clear.

"CUT OFF THE BEST SUPPLY OF SMACK IN TOWN. THANKS A LOT YOU LITTLE BITCH!"

Blue glanced at Sheeba's arm. She had long, loose sleeves and from where Blue was on the floor, she could look right up one sleeve and see needle marks. She looked back at Sheeba who had noticed Blue's glance. Sheeba quickly stood up and backed away.

Blue heard the hard, crude *chiss* coming from Sheeba, "CUNT!"

Sheeba turned to the posse and said, "Fuck it, let's get some lunch."

The girls scattered. Blue was left alone on the bathroom floor with no witness or excuse, and she would be late. Again. Great. The little bubble of peace she had was over. At least this sort of torment was familiar enough that she could deal with it. And there was no doubt in her mind now that the interview for the *Monitor* was the right thing to do. Dealers were still in town. Sheeba was still getting heroin. Those needle marks weren't fresh, but they couldn't be very old, either. But bronco buster? Time to get a copy of the *Monitor* and see what she was up against. She picked up her backpack, got off the floor, and limped as quickly as she could to her next class.

---

Will stared at the fresh copy of the *WHS Monitor*. His eyes scanned over the last lines of Blue's interview and a wry smile came to his face:

**WHS Monitor:** Why did you go out that night?
**Ms. DuBois:** I just couldn't sleep. My bedroom is on the third floor and it can get really hot.
**WHS Monitor:** So you just went out without anyone knowing? Didn't you think that could be dangerous?
**Ms. DuBois:** Obviously, I didn't think this was going to happen.
**WHS Monitor:** Some people are saying that the reason you went out was that you knew Bronco already and were going out to meet him in secret.
**Ms. DuBois:** Well, some people are full of <expletive>

So Patty *did* print that part of Blue's interview. Blue gave a perfect response, but it was bound to flare up the rumor mill again. He shook his head.

Wu sat with him at the lunch table, fidgeting with a pencil. "So, did you read that part about the rumors about Blue? That she might have been Bronco's girlfriend? That is complete bullshit!"

"Yeah, and I'm pretty sure that's the word that was 'expletive,'" replied Will.

"I don't think Patty should have been allowed to print that. Doesn't Baxter screen the paper before it goes to print? He can censor that stuff."

"Yeah, I don't think Baxter's the type that would go overboard censoring," said Will.

"Hey, Wu. Hey, Will. Can I sit with you guys?" Anna didn't wait for an answer. She just plunked her lunch bag down and dragged a chair over. "What's with the long face, Wu?"

"Haven't you read the *Monitor*?" asked Will.

"You mean the 'Bronco boyfriend' theory? Peh—that's old news, nobody really believes that stuff. Patty just wants to keep it alive to keep the gossip group gabbling."

"Yeah, well, I think it's pretty crappy to keep a rumor like that going, repeating made-up stuff that isn't true just because it sells papers," said Will. "Even with my interview, Patty kept pushing me on who it was that Bronco chased outside, like I haven't answered that a million times—I don't know, I didn't even see a face. Honestly, it's like no one believes us, almost like *we* were the bad guys.

"Will, *everyone* knows you're the good guys. Really, you worry too much." Anna opened her bag, like it was just another day, took out her sandwich, and took a big bite. "Gawd, I just love hummus, tomato, and avocado sandwiches!" She said this with remarkable elocution, considering her mouth was crammed full.

"Somehow, that doesn't reassure me all that much," said Will.

Anna leaned over, still chewing and kissed him on the cheek, leaving behind a little smear of hummus. "Mr. Woods, you are the sweetest guy in this school, and every girl would kill to go out with you. Just relax! Ride this out. Don't get your knickers in a twist about it. Really. That article is pretty benign compared to half the stuff I hear every single day in the halls and bathrooms. You boys just live a sheltered life, poor babies." She took another bite of her sandwich and gave a little moan of pleasure.

Will shook his head while wiping off the hummus. "Well, that makes me feel a little better for some weird reason. All right, I'll try and let it go. A little. I just hope it doesn't send Blue off into a funk."

"You don't have to worry about Blue. I've got that covered. And she is waaayyy tougher than you two. That's for *sure!*"

Will didn't say anything. Blue actually *was* tougher than the rest of them together. But the rest of them didn't know some of the things he knew about Blue. He was going to make sure that Blue had more than just Anna covering her back.

---

"Hey, it looks like you have a little hitch in your git-along," said Nate.

Blue was walking home with Wu, Nate, and Will. Will and Wu looked at her, and she stopped walking.

Wu said, "Hey, anything wrong? Did you twist an ankle or something?"

Blue did not want to tell them about the encounter with Sheeba and her crew. Unlike her mental demons, Sheeba was flesh and blood, a type of demon she could handle on her own. No use in getting the boys involved. "Yeah, or something. In Gym. I'm okay."

Wu seemed satisfied and they resumed their walk.

"*Bullshit!*"

Blue looked to the left. Will was looking at her with a scowl on his face. His glasses were off. He had slipped his *vox* in by reflecting it off the inside of her glasses.

She looked over the top of her glasses at him. "*Mind your own business,*" she voxed, but for once, she was kinda glad he knew she was lying.

Jack shivered a little as he mashed out the stub of his cigarette in the overfull ashtray on the dash. He reached down and turned the heat on full, impatient for the slow warming blast from the aging Buick to make some progress at melting away the sparkly crust of frost on the windshield. As he waited, he turned his attention back to the paper that was sitting in his lap, rereading the section that had engraved furrows of puzzlement and concern on his face.

**WHS Monitor:** The person who came in and knocked Bronco down and then ran—you weren't able to identify this person?

**Mr. Woods:** No. You see, I was a tiny bit distracted—getting shot in the chest kind of does that to you.

**WHS Monitor:** Sorry, I understand you were probably in shock, but you can't remember anything about the person? Long hair, short hair, dark hair, beard?

**Mr. Woods:** Look, all I remember is Bronco standing there and suddenly a guy—or maybe a tall girl, I don't know, someone—was there in the room and pushed Bronco onto the floor. They were wearing pants and a hoodie, and I didn't see any hair or face—it was covered by the hoodie.

**WHS Monitor:** Jeans? Cords? Tennis shoes? Boots?

**Mr. Woods:** It was dark, it was a blur, it could have been any of those. About all I can tell you is their clothes weren't bright colors—grays and black if anything. I can tell you for certain that they weren't wearing pink My Little Pony sneakers.

**WHS Monitor:** Do you think there is a possibility the person was a student at WHS?

**Mr. Woods:** Sure, why not? Or Justin Beiber or Noomi Rapace for that matter. Maybe it was you. Has anybody asked if it was you?

Jack had to smile a little at Will's snarkiness. That kid had some gumption. His smile didn't last long, though. The article had dragged up a subject he had been happy to forget and put behind him, but in reality he couldn't forget. There had been too many questions left hanging and never resolved and they had been quietly dogging him ever since that night. Now they sat staring at him from the newspaper like an overdue notice. The police had to know what his role was that night. Sure, his mom probably made a deal with them to keep it quiet, but why had Will never said anything? There was no doubt Will had recognized him. And Jack had run like a scared rabbit rather than stay and try and help Will and Blue. If he were Will, he'd never forgive him for that. Instead, Will had covered for him. Why would he do that? They didn't even know each other except by name and maybe a nod as they passed in the hallways. Will had never even tried to talk to him, let alone broach the subject, and that had fit just fine with Jack's little bubble of denial. And for his part, he had subconsciously been avoiding Will like the plague anyway.

But now the subject was out there. People were going to be talking about it. He couldn't ignore it anymore. He felt like he should at least thank Will, but just the thought of facing him conjured a cloud of guilt.

Jack lit another cigarette and jammed the shifter into reverse. Screw it, he thought. I don't have to worry about it until tomorrow. Right now, I'm just going to pick up Mom and head home for a nice warm meal in a nice warm house that has no demons lurking in it. At least that problem had been put to rest for a long time in a prison that wasn't even in Vermont anymore. His dad had been transferred to a prison nice and far away in Massachusetts.

**19**

---

# DINNER AT THE WILLIS' HOUSE

Jordy sat as motionless as possible. He felt that if he moved even the tiniest bit, the bomb sitting at the head of the table would explode. His dad was radiating anger like a hot teakettle. Jordy never knew exactly what the problem was. All he knew was that his dad had come home like this more and more over the past year, ever since he had started his new business. When his dad was like this, getting through dinner without setting him off could be tricky. For Jordy, skipping dinner or excusing himself early wasn't an option. That would definitely detonate the bomb. He had to, at very least, go through the minimum prescribed dinner-eating routine before he could excuse himself and escape to his room, his sanctuary. So until then, he concentrated on moving the food from his plate to his mouth, making himself as small as possible.

Jordy's brain wouldn't leave him alone, though. It wanted to torture him on its own by replaying the disaster-of-the-day. The pathetic thing was that just thinking about that was more appealing than dealing with the dinner-table reality. He decided the disaster-of-the-day was better than the torture of dinner. At least it had a little glimmer of upside to it.

It had started as he was walking down the hall toward his locker near the back entrance of school. He had to quickly duck out of the way when Wilma Watkins and her gaggle of sidekicks had popped suddenly out of the girls' room and swept by. He did not want to cross with that crowd. They were part of the Mike and Pike mob. Wilma had a grim look on her face, but her attention had seemed to be focused on something else, and she hadn't even taken a second look at him.

Then, just as he had started to head back down the hall, Blue DuBois came out of the same girls' room. As soon as he saw her, his heart skipped a beat, and his grim mood lightened a little. This was the little glimmer, and he dwelled on it for a moment. He'd had a terrible crush on Blue ever since she showed up in his math class the first week of school. She was one of the few people who didn't seem to level any judgment on him. She was just a classmate who understood math like he did. They had a friendly competition for who got the best grades and had even exchanged jokes from time to time. Once, when she laughed at one of his jokes, he nearly fainted with joy. When she returned with her own joke, he overreacted, laughing hysterically. It was embarrassing, but she didn't seem to take notice, or if she did, she took care not to show it. He didn't remember any girl treating him like that, ever.

But today, he noticed that there was something different about her —she wasn't wearing her glasses. He'd never seen her without her glasses on. Her face was flushed and so pretty that it was nearly heart-stopping. Jordy had always thought she was attractive, but at that moment . . . well, he couldn't even think straight. She seemed distracted, with her thoughts a million miles away, which made her not only beautiful, but mysterious. He noticed she was limping. He felt like he should say something sympathetic. It was a rare opportunity, but what could he say? His brain was stumbling over itself trying to search for something caring or clever or chummy or cool, but it was failing him. It was a jumble of joking, caring, sexual, shy, nervous notions all bouncing around at the same time trying to form into something coherent. He had no time, and she would be gone in an instant. At the last second he just blurted out, "Hey Blue, I saw you were in the *Monitor* today." It seemed innocent enough.

She turned to look at him, and her features turned from a million-miles-away to a right-here-and-now withering gaze. It devastated him. She didn't say anything. She didn't have to. What had come out of his mouth seemed to be the very last thing she wanted to hear. She swept past him and left him in the dust. He felt like he wanted to throw up and then find a hole to hide in so he could throw up again.

Later, when he actually read the article in the paper, he felt like an ass. All afternoon he had thought about it, and he kept coming to the same conclusion: any chances he might have had with her were gone now.

Jordy stared at the lumps of food on his plate. He couldn't even identify what it was he was eating.

"Did you get the commission?" His dad's voice broke the silence. The question was directed at his mother. She was a real estate agent and had been on the verge of her first sale. It was supposed to close today. Jordy realized he had forgotten completely about it.

There was a long pause. "It fell through. The building inspector found something."

His father let out a heavy sigh. It came out like a thick, cold fog, sucking the warmth out of everything as it flowed over the table. It was palpable, like a pillow smothering your happiness. Both his parent's faces were taught. The food in Jordy's mouth was tasteless. He chewed it out of duty to his body. He prayed that the conversation wouldn't escalate, like it had so many nights before.

"How about you, sport? Did you manage to accomplish anything today?" His father's sarcasm may have been directed at him, but it was another swipe at his mother, too. His heart sank. It was going to be one of those nights. Again.

"I got 100 percent on my algebra quiz." He said it hopefully, even though he knew it was hopeless.

"What about history?"

Jordy's heart didn't have much room to fall any farther, but somehow it did. He dug, once again, for some answer that wouldn't disappoint his dad. "We haven't had any grades for a while, but I think I'm doing pretty good."

"Pretty good? Like the C you got on the last history test? Is that pretty good?"

"No." The food in front of Jordy sat there like a paste, waiting to get stuck in his throat. He couldn't look up. All he could do was push some more whatever-it-was on his fork and place it in his mouth. It felt like a wad of wet paper and tasted about the same. He chewed it anyway because it gave him an excuse to not say anything. How his father could make him feel worse than he made himself feel after today, he didn't know.

"Well," said his dad, "so much for everyone pulling their weight around here. I expected you to do better, Jordan."

His mom didn't say anything. She was probably feeling the same as him, but if she was, she never shared it with him. She was her own island, defending her own shores. No help coming from that direction. Jordy was on his own. He ached to get away from the dinner table, get back to his room, close the door, and get on his computer to escape.

"What are you going to do tonight after dinner?" asked his father. It was directed at him.

"Study." The answer came out of him like a reflex. It was the only correct answer.

"Study what?"

"History."

His father was silent. It wasn't the best reaction from him, but it was far from the worst. Jordy took another bite of what he finally recognized as squash. He couldn't wait to get finished but each bite was taking forever to get down. His dad was staring down at his own plate while his jaw moved up and down, up and down, chewing, chewing, and swallowing. Another bite. Chewing, chewing, swallowing. His dad ate like a machine. Jordy wondered if his dad was from another planet—a robot placed on earth just to keep a teenager in a cage and prepare him for harvesting when he was old enough.

"I'm done. May I be excused, please?"

His dad just waved his fork.

Jordy took his dishes into the kitchen, carefully rinsed them, and put everything in the dishwasher, making sure they were put in just so. If he didn't he would be hearing about that for sure. He just wanted to get out of there without any mistakes and get to his room.

Why the hell his father never bothered him in his room, Jordy didn't know, but it was his one decent feature. Once Jordy was safely in there, he could be on his computer, with the back of the screen to his door. His father would come to the door but never enter. It was like there was an invisible barrier there. More evidence that his dad was an alien. Jordy could be playing *Warcraft* or looking at porn, and his dad would never take notice—never even step in to look at the screen.

Tonight he felt a need to log into *Revenger: Apocalypse*. He knew it was lame to get his thrills from massacring a bunch of lunatic green giants who were bent on enslaving humans and herding them for meat. But the music was awesome, and the act of nailing the giants with a nail gun was satisfying. His favorite ploy was to nail them to a wall and let the wild hoar-crusters chew them up. The graphics were pretty spectacular, and they kept the game interesting. Sometimes he would log on after lights-out with his earbuds in and crank it. But for right now, he kept the music off and the earbuds out. He knew that at any minute . . .

"What are you working on?" His dad made his regular appearance in his bedroom doorway right on schedule.

"My next history report. American Revolution."

His father stood on the threshold but didn't move an inch past it. He didn't even listen to Jordy's reply. Just a robot, asking the questions his 'dad' programming told him to ask. "Good." Then he was gone. Jordy knew that later, on nights like this, it would get loud in his parent's bedroom. There would be sounds that should not be heard by anyone, sounds that he should tell someone about. Sounds that turned to carefully covered bruises on his mother the next morning. Sounds that, if he acknowledged them, could wind up as bruises on him.

It was time to stick in the earbuds. He put them snugly in his ears and turned up the volume. He nailed away, managing to catch an extra ugly two-headed green giant. It yelled curses and insults at him and almost pulled out all the nails and got free, but Jordy kept nailing and nailing and nailing until the giant was completely immobile. It roared for the other giants to help him, but they were too far away, and Jordy just kept nailing and nailing and nailing, not even waiting for the hoar-crusters. He wanted to finish this two-headed asshole himself. The giant finally died and disappeared in a cloud of green smoke. Jordy's reward was a pot of gold and an ax.

He sat back, strangely unsatisfied. He didn't get his usual victory "high." He felt just as depressed as before, and now he could hear the voices starting to rise outside his bedroom. He pushed the earbuds in farther and queued up his go-to playlist. He slid his desk drawer open, reached all the way to the back, and felt around for his little mint tin. He pulled it out, opened the lid, and studied the little yellow octagons inside. Gifts from Alex.

Alex was a scrawny loner, and a bit weird, but at least he was someone Jordy could talk to and commiserate with. Alex would have been a school punching bag, too, but he managed to avoid all that by raiding his mom's prescriptions and making would-be tormentors into customers instead. Drugs for deference, he called it. Drugs for defense. Drugs for pretty good cash return, though, too. In an act of camaraderie, Alex had given Jordy a couple of Oxymorphone—"O-Bombs", "Octagons." Jordy was hesitant at first. He wasn't an idiot. He knew they were risky, but he took them from Alex anyway. Whether he chose to try them sometime or not, just having them there in his drawer felt reassuring. They were an emergency backup plan. It was a Plan B when his Plan A's ran out.

He felt, more than heard, the sudden banging and shouting happening on the other side of his earbuds. Before he knew it, one of the yellow pills was in his mouth. He hesitated only a second before swallowing it. Time for Plan B. This was such a fucked up day, he deserved an escape. He cracked open a Coke from his stash, took a long swig, and cranked the music higher. Then he turned out his light and shut his bedroom door. The first tendrils of numbness mixed with euphoria started to seep through his capillaries. This was good. The music was good. The shouting and crying in the background were washed out by the rhythms pulsing into his ears. He flopped back on his bed, closed his eyes, and let Nirvana, Pearl Jam, Green Day, and a little yellow stop sign rock the pain out of his head.

## 20

# RE-VISION

Blue had her homework open in front of her, but she was looking at Will. "Anna is awesome. I totally trust her," she voxed.

"Me, too," voxed Will. They were sitting in the town library, studying together. It wasn't really a date, Will told himself, but they weren't really studying either. "I don't think I've heard you use the word 'awesome' before. Ever. I think Anna is rubbing off on you a little," he voxed, with a smirk.

She gave him a very subtle but unmistakable stink-eye.

"Now *that* I've seen before. A lot," he whispered.

And yet, Will thought, she'd come a long way. He tried to imagine having a normal conversation with Blue back at the beginning of the school year. Ever since the night of her meltdown at their house, it had been like night and day. She had relaxed. Even in the wake of the *Monitor* article. In fact, she was more open than ever talking about it.

"Look, I want to talk to you about something serious. I know you're going to think I'm crazy, but please hear me out," she voxed.

"*Going to think?*" he voxed. Another stink-eye from Blue. "*Okay okay, I'm listening. Seriously.*"

Blue continued. "*Patty's article didn't exactly work out the way we thought, but it did stir things up. Now we need to do something more than just talking, we need to act. Don't say anything yet.*"

Her last words were clearly a reaction to his rolling eyes. "*Go on,*" he voxed.

"*I don't mean any more 'super-hero' stuff. But I don't mean all the feel-good-but-totally-lame stuff either,*" she voxed.

"*You mean like 'Just Say No' posters and rallies.*"

"*Exactly. 'Hugs Not Drugs'. Gaaahh! I'd rather poke a stick in my eye than do that righteous crap.*"

Will smiled. "*'Just say Nope to Dope!' Yeah, I'm not sure they get it. But you have to give them credit. At least they're trying.*"

Blue frowned. "*All right, Mr. Happy-Chatty-Good-Listener-Guy, I'll give them that. They're trying. But that's not what I want to do. I want to find a way to end it. Slogan shmogan. I want to do something real, not just talk.*"

"*Hey,*" he voxed, "*running Bronco out of town was pretty real.*"

"*But we don't even know if he's gone for good.*" She stared at him intently, "*What if he came back? What if he is running the drugs nearby and getting other people to deal them in town? That's just what he did with Jack.*"

Will shook his head. "*He's not coming back. Why would he take that chance? They found his car! They have his DNA from the blood! He'd get nailed in a second. He'll just find another small town somewhere else.*"

"*Don't you see? That's just it. He. Is. Still. Out there.*" Blue punctuated her words by rapping her pen on her paper, making little blue dots on her homework. "*We didn't stop him from dealing drugs, we just moved him—either outside of town or to*

ANOTHER TOWN. THAT'S WHAT PISSES ME OFF. WE WENT THROUGH ALL . . . THAT . . . AND IT DIDN'T ACCOMPLISH A DAMN THING."

Will tilted his head back and forth thoughtfully. "WELL, AT LEAST HE GOT SHOT IN THE ASS. AND MAYBE WE SLOWED DOWN THE HEROIN TRADE FOR A WHILE."

"YEAH, MAYBE, BUT IT'S STILL GOING, FOR SURE. I SAW NEEDLE MARKS ON WILMA WATKINS ARM."

"WILMA WATKINS? ISN'T SHE THAT GIRL-RILLA THAT HAS A LAUGH THAT SOUNDS LIKE A HYENA?"

Blue snorted. "GIRL-RILLA. THAT'S PERFECT."

He knew better by now than to ask how she saw the needle marks or if she was sure they were needle marks. He had no doubt that it was true. "OKAY, SO IT'S BACK OR NEVER WENT AWAY, BUT I REALLY DOUBT THAT IT'S BRONCO BEHIND IT. WHY WOULD HE COME BACK SO SOON OR AT ALL? WHY RISK IT?"

"HE'D COME BACK TO GET ME," voxed Blue.

"What!" hissed Will.

A voice came from the front of the room. "Quiet please." The librarian peered at them from his desk, with a lifted eyebrow.

Will said softly, "Sorry!" He turned back to Blue, "BLUE THAT'S JUST CRAZY TALK. HE IS NOT COMING BACK FOR YOU! HE HAS ABSOLUTELY NO REASON TO! THERE ARE SO MANY PEOPLE THAT COULD IDENTIFY HIM, AND HE'D BE ARRESTED ON THE SPOT! WHY WOULD YOU SAY SOMETHING LIKE THAT?"

He was truly puzzled. It was such an off-the-wall notion that Bronco would be on a Blue-hunt. He was also puzzled by Blue's face. It was calm. It had that same look she had when she revealed Bronco to him last summer, only it lacked the look of impatience she had with him then. "IF YOU KNOW SOMETHING I DON'T, I THINK I HAVE A RIGHT TO KNOW."

"YOU DO HAVE A RIGHT TO KNOW," she voxed. "BUT IT'S GOING TO BE HARD TO EXPLAIN."

"DON'T WORRY, I'M THE HAPPY-CHATTY-GOOD-LISTENER-GUY."

She did that stifled laugh thing again, "ka-huh," and her mouth twisted into a suppressed grin. She looked to her left and then to her right, like she was about to reveal a secret, even though nobody could possibly have overheard. "AFTER BRONCO HIT ME, I FOUND OUT SOMETHING EVEN MORE INCRIMINATING ABOUT HIM. I MEAN LIFETIME-IN-JAIL INCRIMINATING. AND HE FOUND OUT SOMETHING ABOUT ME."

She stared at him, apparently waiting for him to fill in the blank.

"ARE YOU TELLING ME THAT BRONCO IS A VOX?"

She shook her head and waited again.

"HE LEAKED SOMETHING?"

Her expression turned apprehensive. She nodded.

"AND THEN . . . OH SHIT. HE CAUGHT YOU READING HIS CHISS."

She looked down at the table.

"WHAT DID YOU SAY THAT GAVE IT AWAY? LIKE HOW SERIOUS WAS IT?"

Blue looked back up at him. "I'M PRETTY SURE HE WAS GETTING READY TO LET ME GO. BUT AFTER THAT, THERE WAS NO WAY. THAT'S HOW SERIOUS IT WAS. IT WAS MY OWN FAULT. I FUCKED UP."

Will could see tears forming in her eyes. "HEY, YOU WERE KIDNAPPED! TIED UP! YOU PROBABLY STILL HAD A CONCUSSION! DON'T YOU DARE BLAME YOURSELF! AND DON'T YOU DARE TELL ME I'M WRONG BECAUSE I'M NOT!"

She looked down again. Will glanced at the librarian, who quickly looked back at what he was reading. It was clear that he had been watching them, but the look on his face had been curiosity, not scolding. Will looked back at Blue who had raised her face again. She looked composed and also had a new expression. New for Blue anyway. It was almost grateful.

"THANKS FOR THAT, BUT YOU MIGHT CHANGE YOUR MIND. BRONCO LEAKED THAT HE MURDERED HIS FATHER. AND THAT HE GOT AWAY WITH IT."

Will sat in stunned silence.

"THERE'S MORE," Blue continued. "A LOT MORE. HE KILLED HIS FATHER BECAUSE HIS FATHER HAD MURDERED HIS BROTHER. BRONCO'S FATHER PUSHED HIS BROTHER DOWN THE STAIRS IN A DRUNKEN RAGE, AND

*BRONCO NEVER FORGAVE HIM. SO ONE NIGHT, HE SUFFOCATED HIS FATHER WHEN HE WAS PASSED OUT DRUNK."*

This blast of information was even more unexpected than the first. *"HOW COULD YOU POSSIBLY FIND OUT THAT MUCH? ARE YOU TELLING ME HE JUST DECIDED TO CONFESS TO YOU IN ONE EPIC LONG CHISS?"* Maybe she could have pieced it together, he thought. She was captive a long time.

*"AND THIS IS WHERE IT GETS REALLY CRAZY. I DIDN'T HEAR ALL THIS, I SAW IT,"* she voxed.

*"WHAT?"*

*"I KNOW. CRAZY, RIGHT? IT WAS LIKE A VIVID DAYDREAM. I SAW HIS FATHER PUSHING HIS BROTHER DOWN THE STAIRS—I SAW BRONCO CRYING OVER HIS DEAD BROTHER—I SAW BRONCO LEANING OVER HIS FATHER'S HEAD AND HIS FATHER STRUGGLING AND THEN STOPPING. IT HAPPENED RIGHT AFTER I SAID SOMETHING TO BRONCO THAT REALLY PISSED HIM OFF. THAT'S WHEN HE HIT ME AND THEN GOT HIS FACE REAL CLOSE TO MINE. I WAS SCARED SHITLESS. HE LOOKED AT ME EYE-TO-EYE AND SAID, 'PEOPLE DIE ALL THE TIME FOR ALL KINDS OF STUPID REASONS' AND THEN THESE VISIONS FLASHED THROUGH MY HEAD. I WAS SO SHOCKED I JUST BLURTED OUT WHAT I WAS SEEING WITHOUT THINKING. I SAID, 'YOUR FATHER KILLED YOUR BROTHER!' I MIGHT HAVE SAID MORE. I DON'T KNOW. ALL I KNOW IS THAT HE TOTALLY FREAKED OUT, AND I KNEW THEN THAT I WAS DEAD."*

Will's mind was whirling trying to process all this, but his eyes managed to blurt out two words, *"PARTICIPATIO VISIO."* It was something he knew about but had never experienced. His dad had tried explaining it to Will, but he had never been able to say why or when it would happen. *"JESUS, BLUE."*

*"PARTICIPATIO VISIO? IT'S REAL THEN? I WASN'T JUST DREAMING IT?"*

*"YEAH, IT'S REAL. AT LEAST I THINK IT'S REAL. DAD TOLD ME ABOUT IT. HE HAS A FEW THEORIES ON HOW IT WORKS. JESUS, BLUE, WHY HAVE YOU BEEN CARRYING THIS AROUND ALL THIS TIME? YOU COULD HAVE TOLD ME. AND CHIEF HANNAH SHOULD HEAR THIS."*

*"YEAH, RIGHT. TRY AND EXPLAIN HOW I LEARNED ALL THIS TO A NON-*

VOX. *LIKE I'D LIKE TO GO DOWN THAT ROAD AGAIN. DID YOU COMPLETELY FORGET THAT I GOT THROWN INTO A PSYCH WARD FOR THAT?"*

Of course, thought Will. He realized that she didn't know about Chief Hannah. He looked at her with just the slightest raised eyebrow.

"WHAT?" Blue asked.

"*SOOOO . . . I TOLD WU ABOUT US, AND YOU TOLD ANNA ABOUT US . . .*" He left the rest for her to fill in.

"*YOU TOLD CHIEF HANNAH ABOUT US?*"

He shook his head. "*MY MOTHER DID. THEY WERE BEST FRIENDS BACK IN COLLEGE. MOM TOTALLY TRUSTS HER. CHIEF HANNAH ASKED ME NOT TO SHARE IT WITH YOU UNLESS IT WAS REALLY IMPORTANT. I THINK THIS IS PRETTY IMPORTANT.*"

"*FUCKING-A THIS IS IMPORTANT! THIS CHANGES EVERYTHING!*"

"*YEAH, BUT THIS COULD NEVER BE USED IN COURT! 'WILL THE WITNESS PLEASE DESCRIBE THE VISIONS THAT THE ACCUSED BROADCAST TO THEIR BRAIN!'*" Will shook his head.

"*NO, OF COURSE NOT,*" voxed Blue, "*BUT CHIEF HANNAH COULD USE THIS INFORMATION TO TRACK DOWN BRONCO'S REAL IDENTITY. THOSE TWO EVENTS—THERE MUST BE A RECORD OF THEM.*"

"*WHY NOT US? WE COULD USE THIS INFORMATION TO TRACK DOWN BRONCO'S IDENTITY,*" voxed Will.

"*YOU THINK I HAVEN'T TRIED ALREADY?*"

Of course, thought Will. Blue wouldn't have sat on this information. "*DID YOU FIND ANYTHING?*"

"*NOT REALLY,*" voxed Blue. "*THE ONLY FALLING-DOWN-STAIRS DEATHS I COULD FIND WERE A LITTLE KID AND SOMEONE IN A WHEEL-CHAIR. BRONCO'S BROTHER WAS NEITHER. AND AS FOR OLD MEN DYING PEACEFULLY IN THEIR SLEEP? YEAH, ABOUT A JILLION OF THOSE.*"

"*WHAT ABOUT SUFFOCATION DEATHS?*" asked Will.

"*GOD, IT'S DEPRESSING TO RESEARCH THAT. DID YOU KNOW THAT 4000 BABIES DIE EACH YEAR FROM SUFFOCATION! BABIES! THAT DRIVES ME INSANE. AND GET THIS, THERE ARE LIKE, 10,000 SUFFOCATION DEATHS OF REALLY OLD PEOPLE AND HALF OF THOSE ARE WHILE THEY ARE IN THE*

HOSPITAL!" She went on, "AND DID YOU KNOW THAT THERE ARE OVER 7000 SUICIDES A YEAR FROM SUFFOCATION?" She reached her hand over her head and pulled on an imaginary rope while she lolled her head and stuck her tongue out.

"HANGING?"

She nodded.

"THERE ARE THAT MANY SUICIDES? IS THIS THE WHOLE WORLD OR JUST THE U.S.?"

"ARE YOU KIDDING? THIS IS JUST THE U.S. AND THAT IS JUST THE NUMBER OF SUICIDES FROM SUFFOCATION!"

"THEN WHAT, THERE ARE 10,000 OR SO TOTAL SUICIDES A YEAR?"

"HA! NOT EVEN CLOSE. THERE ARE 17,000 SUICIDES JUST FROM GUNS! SEVENTEEN THOUSAND! JUST FROM GUNS!"

"JESUS."

"THAT'S LIKE . . ." her eyes looked down and moved side to side very briefly, then she looked up again, "A GUN SUICIDE EVERY THIRTY MINUTES, JUST IN THIS COUNTRY!"

"DID YOU JUST DO THAT IN YOUR HEAD?"

"WELL, YEAH."

He pulled out his calculator. 17000 divided by 365 divided by 24 equaled 1.94. She was right. About two an hour. "HOW DID YOU DO THAT SO FAST?"

"WELL—HALF OF 365 IS ABOUT 182 WHICH IS CLOSE ENOUGH TO 170 WHICH IS ONE HUNDREDTH OF 17000, SO TAKE HALF THAT WHICH IS ABOUT 50 A DAY, MAYBE LESS BECAUSE 170 IS LESS THAN 182 SO LET'S SAY 48ISH BECAUSE IT'S EASY AND DIVIDE THAT BY 24 AND YOU GET TWO. ABOUT TWO AN HOUR, OR ABOUT EVERY THIRTY MINUTES."

He shook his head. Was this girl going to ever stop surprising him? "WHAT'S YOUR GRADE IN ALGEBRA?"

"IT DOESN'T MATTER. WHAT'S IMPORTANT IS THAT WHEN YOU ADD IT ALL UP THERE IS A SUICIDE EVERY THIRTY MINUTES! JUST IN THIS COUNTRY! JUST. FROM. GUNS. THERE HAVE BEEN TWO GUN SUICIDES IN THIS COUNTRY JUST WHILE WE'VE BEEN SITTING HERE!"

They were both silent for a while. It *was* depressing, thought

Will. He forgot completely about Bronco and just dwelled on those statistics for a while. It was Blue who finally pulled the conversation back on track.

"*WE MIGHT FIND SOME SUFFOCATION DEATHS THAT MATCH IF WE KEEP LOOKING, BUT CHIEF HANNAH MUST HAVE ACCESS TO THINGS LIKE MORTUARY REPORTS AND POLICE REPORTS AND NEWS WIRES. THEY DO THIS KIND OF RESEARCH ALL THE TIME,*" she voxed.

"*WELL, IT'S YOUR CALL. IT WAS YOUR VISION,*" voxed Will. "*YOU HAVE TO DECIDE IF YOU WANT TO GO THERE OR NOT. I WON'T TELL ANYONE, EVER. I PROMISE, UNLESS YOU TELL ME IT'S OKAY.*"

She was quiet for a moment and then she looked at him with an odd intensity. "*WILL YOU GO WITH ME?*"

It was odd because it sounded almost pleading with a note of apprehension, emotions he had never heard from Blue. He didn't hesitate. "*OF COURSE! DO YOU THINK I'D MISS WATCHING CHIEF HANNAH'S REACTION WHEN YOU TELL HER? AND I CAN BACK YOUR STORY UP, TOO. YOU KNOW IF WE HAD TO, I THINK DAD WOULD EVEN BACK YOU UP. HE'S HAD PARTICIPATIO VISIO BEFORE.*"

Blue's pleading look melted away. What replaced it was a look of puzzled surprise, like she had picked up a colorful stone and the stone suddenly came to life. She looked down.

He did his vox click to get her attention. "<*CLICK, CLICK, CLICK*>, *HEY YOU. YOU LOOK LIKE YOU JUST SWALLOWED A FROG.*"

She looked up at him. "*NO, IT'S JUST THAT . . .*"

She stopped and looked down again. Will watched her. He'd never seen her act quite like this before. When she finally raised her head, she voxed, "*I'VE NEVER HAD ANYONE TO BACK ME UP BEFORE.*"

**21**

---

## THE CLENCH

Jordy stared at the paper on the desk in front of him. He wondered if he was breathing. His chest was paralyzed, not moving and yet the atmosphere was sustaining him, keeping him alive. Air was somehow eddying in and out of his lungs without his assistance. For what reason, he wasn't sure, because his life had just ended.

D.

He had never seen a D in his life, and now it sat there staring him in the face like a demented sideways laugh. Ha ha! You're dead.

>:D

A sick feeling in the pit of his stomach surged for a moment, just to remind him that it was there. Again. He tried to remember when he first noticed it. Maybe last summer. Maybe back when his dad started coming home from work in darker and darker moods. He didn't know. It crept up on him over weeks until the day he got his first grades and he felt like he was going to puke. It was like a little demon sitting inside him, never letting him feel like he was completely healthy. He had even given it a name. The Clench. Each little setback piled it on a little more, and there had been so many setbacks. It was relentless. A bad grade here. Mike and Pike taunting him there. Going home to an impossible-to-please father who spewed his failure from his train wreck of a business directly on to him.

And now this. He didn't know why he was shocked. He hadn't done squat for this history report, putting it off and putting it off, hoping it would go away, until the day before it was due. "Half your grade this quarter," the teacher had said. "Hope you worked hard on it. If not, it's a little late now," he had said.

Shut up, Jordy had said in his head. Just shut up.

That night Jordy had crammed, trying to throw something together. It was hopeless. In the end, he had written a bunch of junk and then thrown it in a nice report sleeve and chucked it in his backpack. It had sat in there, lurking like a bag of rotten tomatoes threatening to burst until he finally dropped it on McCarthy's desk. Jordy knew it was a disaster, but there was just a little bit of hope that somehow he would slide through. He'd get a C or maybe a C+. Just enough to keep his dad from crucifying him. Ha ha ha. Dream on, Jordy boy. Here's your ass handed back to you on a silver platter. D, you Dumbass. D for Disaster. D for Dead as a Doornail. The final Damnation.

Jordy looked at the door. He was half tempted to just get up and leave school right then. Just walk right out—keep on going. But where? Where did he have to go? Home was the last place he wanted to be, at least around dinnertime, when the inevitable question would come up. How long could he stall? Until grades came out at the end of second quarter? Maybe. His dad knew about the history paper. Jordy had told him he was working on it. But he didn't know when they would be graded. He had some time. Not much, but some time. Maybe some extra work, an extra project to make up for it . . .

Blue tapped her pencil on her notebook. She was finding it hard to concentrate. She and Will had agreed to meet later this afternoon and go talk with Chief Hannah. The secret that had seemed doomed to wither away from neglect in the dark recesses of her memory was now clamoring to get out, now that it found there was an audience that would listen to it—*really* listen to it. It was sort of like a dog the minute you say, "Go for a walk?" Boom, there was no containing its enthusiasm. Maybe, just maybe, they could still get this guy.

As Miss Kendrick was scribbling assignments on the whiteboard, Blue couldn't help but feel like there was something wrong to the right of her. She looked over to the next desk and Jordy Willis was sitting there with his head planted face down on the backpack parked on his desktop. His arms were wrapped around it like it was a life preserver.

Blue glanced at the front of the room. Miss Kendrick's back was still turned. The other kids in class were just beginning to settle down, and she knew the bell would go off any minute. "Hey, Jordy, are you okay?"

He didn't answer. Instead, he just lifted his head with his eyes closed and leaned back, tilting his face to the ceiling. He breathed in and then let the air out slowly, like the hissing brakes on a tractor-trailer. This behavior had many familiar signs to it. Blue was a veteran of them all. Being on the other side of it, however, she wasn't quite sure what to do.

She wasn't exactly buddies with Jordy, but he was good at math and seemed to take joy in it. It was fun working on problems with him sometimes. When they weren't working on math, it could get a little awkward. He wasn't exactly a social genius, but neither was she, so together they made kind of a mess of it, but they managed to maintain a level of friendly camaraderie.

Right now, though, there was none of that. He was completely distracted by something else. Something not good.

All through class, Jordy did nothing but keep his eyes closed.

Sometimes with his head tilted back, sometimes on the backpack. She couldn't help but let it distract her a little. Miss Kendrick had noticed, too, she could tell, but she didn't bring attention to it. When the bell finally released them, he got straight up and hurried out of the classroom with his head down. Blue packed up her stuff as quickly as she could and went after him.

She caught sight of him heading toward the main hall, and she pushed her way through the crowd and caught up to him. It looked like he was headed for the front entrance. It was only fourth period. The only people heading outside at this time of day were the serious stoners.

"Hey! Jordy!"

He stopped and turned toward her. He had a dead look on his face. Now she was really concerned.

"What's going on?"

His eyes came to life with the slightest glimmer. He started to say something when a voice came booming through the crowd.

"Hey, Blue!" It was Will. The little glimmer in Jordy's eyes went out, and he looked over at Will. He looked back at Blue and then turned and slipped out the front entrance so quickly, she didn't have time to react.

Will came over to Blue and she scowled at him.

"Hey, what's that all about?"

She pulled her glasses off. Will followed suit. *"SOMETHING'S WRONG WITH JORDY, AND HE WAS JUST ABOUT TO TELL ME WHEN YOU CAME BUMBLING OVER."*

*"WELL, SORRY. HOW WAS I SUPPOSED TO KNOW?"* He looked out the wide array of glass doors that made up the main entrance. She followed his glance and saw that Jordy had headed purposefully down the sidewalk.

"Do you suppose he's skipping the rest of school? Pretty early in the day," said Will.

"I'm guessing yes. He was pretty weird all during algebra," replied Blue.

"Yeah, well he's having a pretty rough year. Mike and Pike have been harassing him most of the year, especially since the *Monitor* article came out."

"Why the *Monitor* article?"

Will gave her quizzical look. "You do know Jordy has a terrible crush on you, right?"

She felt uncomfortable all of the sudden. Yeah, she sort of suspected, but . . . "How do you know?"

"Because he asks me about you all the time lately. You know our lockers are almost next to each other. Somehow Mike and Pike caught wind of it and now they tease him all the time. It's because . . . well . . . it's because of . . . never mind."

"Bronco-buster. Yeah, I know."

Will continued out loud, "Hey, look, I'm sorry I interrupted. It would have been good if you could've talked to Jordy. He needs a friend." "But what I wanted to tell you is that Chief Hannah texted me back, and we're on for 3:30."

"That's great," she voxed. But the encounter with Jordy had certainly calmed down that rambunctious puppy dog that had been so anxious to get out of her head.

"Okay, then we'll meet here after school and walk over?"

"Okay."

"Cool. See you later." He turned and headed down his hall, and she turned and headed down hers, but her brain was now trying to figure out what it was about Jordy that made her feel off-balance. There was something there, and if she had a chance, she would figure it out, but school wasn't leaving her much time. She sighed and put it aside for now. It would just have to wait until tonight. Right now she had to switch into English-class mode.

---

The world was turned upside down. His bedroom ceiling seemed more like a floor. Jordy felt like he was attached to his bed magically. The reverse gravity was pulling him toward the ceiling, but his bed was holding on to him. The speckled texture of the plaster seemed like a sea of cottage cheese, and he wanted to fall into it. Anything to obliterate the hot panic that was surging to get out of his gut.

McCarthy hadn't let him off the hook. No make-up work. No leniency. Jordy's only remaining opportunity was the final exam—a pathetic 20 percent of his final grade.

When would his dad find out? What would he do? The thought of it cranked up the Clench so hard, it was making him sick. Staring at his ceiling was his only distraction. That and the music blasting into his skull. Even video games had lost their distraction power. Porn had done nothing for him. He considered the last oxy sitting in his desk drawer. He had tried to get more from Alex but even that was a dead end. "My mom's waiting for her refill," Alex had said. "Besides, there are kids in line ahead of you, and they have a certain kind of leverage—like they are bigger and stronger than me and ride my bus. And they are assholes." He couldn't fault Alex for that, but that left him with just one oxy and he didn't want to waste it. Right now he was relatively safe. That would change around 5:30 when his dad got home. That's when he might need it. But he still needed something else now—something to stop his brain from going into a death spin.

There was one thing. He'd promised his mom he wouldn't. But that was a year ago and things were very different now. The mere thought of it started a warm glow of craving that was already distracting him from the Clench. He pulled his earbuds out, jumped out of bed and the next thing he knew he was staring at a glittering array of sculpted bottles filled with every shade of honey-colored fermented bliss, all nestled comfortably in his parents very well stocked liquor cabinet.

It was a short walk from WHS to the police department, taking Blue and Will right through the small downtown. Westbury had a quirky ritual of hanging wooden, painted turkey figures from every lamp post in the weeks before Thanksgiving. The lamp posts themselves were seasonal enough—ornate cast iron painted green with a frosty globe on top of each one. It was an old town, and the buildings in it were old and made of brick and granite and fieldstone. Winter scenes from downtown Westbury had made it into probably every picture book about New England ever printed. Hollywood had even used the town as a setting for a few movies.

And now that scene included two backpacked teenagers. Like most New England teens, this pair was underdressed for the weather but didn't seem to notice or care.

"So are you good friends with Jordy?" asked Blue.

"We were kind of friends in grade school. Back then, there was a big difference between fourth and fifth grades, so it's not like we were best buddies. But I played basketball with him at recess, and we had an advanced math class together. He was much better at it than me. Like you."

"I doubt that I'm any better than you. It's not like algebra is *that* hard."

"It is for most kids. Just because you find it easy doesn't mean it *is* easy."

"Yeah, well, Jordy is as good at it as me. Probably better. But not today. Today he was in his own private little hell."

"I had a couple of days like that last year. Basketball rescued me, though." Will stretched his left arm reflexively.

Blue noticed. "Can you play this year?"

"We'll see. Probably. Coach said I could be on JV no problem, but there's no chance at varsity. My shooting is getting better now, but I think everyone is being over-protective. Maybe I can at least be the star of JV, with Wu on varsity."

"Wu is totally psyched. You should see him at home. He carries his basketball everywhere. Sam said he even sleeps with it."

Will laughed. "That's just like Wu. It's pretty cool, though. I'm happy for him."

"It's really important to have an anchor like that. Something you're good at."

"Like drawing for you?" he asked

"Yeah, maybe. People can be anchors, too," Blue said, turning her head to look at Will.

"You mean like friends? Yeah, having good friends helps a lot."

"I mean you. You're a good anchor. You're friendly to everyone. You're friends with Jordy. He doesn't have many friends."

Will blushed. He never thought of himself as someone's anchor.

"Yeah, well, I see him every morning between classes. I'll talk to him tomorrow morning, maybe I can find out if anything is wrong."

"Thanks." She nudged him. "See. You just volunteered to do that without being asked. Face it, Mr. Good-Listener-Guy, you're an anchor."

He blushed even more. As they climbed the steps of Westbury P.D. he hoped Chief Hannah wouldn't notice. He'd blame it on the cold air.

———

Jordy couldn't believe he'd made it through dinner. Apparently, no one at school reported him missing. Either that or his mother just didn't say anything about it to his dad. She was the one they'd call, thank God. His dad was in an extra-dark mood, but it was actually better than his usual sarcastic, ultra-critical cross-examinations. This mood was quiet. Whatever he was stewing about, it must have had little to do with home. Either that or it had everything to do with home, and his dad just didn't want to talk about it with them. That was just fine. Between his dad's silence and the nice buzz he still had from his parents stash, Jordy almost found dinner pleasant. He excused himself, cleaned up his dish and slipped into his room.

Now it was a waiting game. So far, so good. His dad was probably working his way through a couple of stiff ones, and his mom was probably just trying to stay out of his way. If he could just make it through to bedtime, he'd be safe at least until the morning. What he was going to do tomorrow, he wasn't sure. Sooner or later his dad would find out about the D. But when? When? When? He felt a slight urge to run into the living room and blurt out everything just to get it over with. He couldn't do it, though. He'd just as soon step in front of a bus.

No, he would wait it out. Hell, maybe his dad would have a heart-attack tonight or drive off and leave them for good. God, if I knew how to drive a car, I'd just go myself, Jordy thought. Drive away from this fucked up life.

These thoughts pounded through his brain as he stuffed his earbuds in and the rhythm of the music thumped away, throbbing relentlessly—*when, when, when would he find out?*—and with each *when,* his stomach squeezed like it was milking him of his sanity. Then there was a scream, a scream that didn't belong to the music. The rhythm in his earbuds morphed into a knocking sound that didn't belong. The knocking was arrhythmic. It was someone knocking insistently on his locked bedroom door. He sat bolt upright. Had his dad found out? Shit! The pathetic lock on his door was far from parent proof. His dad could get through it any time he wanted. Jordy was trapped. The knocking stopped. Jordy reluctantly unlocked the door. His father was standing there and the look on his face made Jordy pull out his earbuds.

"I have to take your mother to the hospital. She . . . she had a . . . an accident. She fell." His words were slurred.

"What? Is she okay?" Jordy started to walk around his dad to go find her.

"She's okay," his dad said, ferociously, holding out an arm to block Jordy. "She just might need some stitches and . . . well we just need to go. Now. I'm just letting you know. Go back to whatever you were doing. Studying. Or whatever."

And with that, his dad shut the door.

What. The. Fuck? That's all his brain could produce. Over and over again, like a chant. "What the fuck? What the fuck? What the fuck?" It went on for some time. Deep inside he realized his brain had gone into some emergency safe boot. "Your brain didn't shut down properly, would you like to startup in what-the-fuck mode?" It went on and on while his latent processes tried to figure out what the expression on his dad's face was. It was foreign. It was something that didn't belong on a dad-robot face. It was . . . it was . . .

It was guilt.

Jesus Christ. It hit him like a freight train. His dad had just crossed a line, the track of civility, the track of what can be tolerated. His mother didn't just fall.

What the fuck. What the fuck. What the fuck . . .

Jordy found himself getting up. He paced back and forth. Go back to what you were doing, his dad said. Yeah, right, robot-dad. Trade one nightmare for another. He stumbled out of his room and down to the living room. He could see through the picture window that they'd gotten in the car and were just backing out of the driveway. Jordy watched as the glow from the car's headlights swept through the living room, flashing on him as they went. He thought he caught a glimpse of blood on his mom's face through the windshield. Then the car disappeared down the street.

Jordy paced around the living room and then found himself moving down the deserted hallway to his parent's bedroom. There were drops of blood on the carpet. He gazed around until his eyes landed on a Plexiglas trophy—something his father had gotten somewhere along the line for some stupid sales record. It was lying on its side, drops of blood, still wet, glimmering on one edge.

What the fuck. What the fuck. What the fuck.

His legs carried him back out of the bedroom. He paced up and down the hall. Up and down. Up and down. And finally stopped. He was in front of the door to his dad's home office. He pushed the door open, walked in and stopped in front of his dad's safe.

His dad's safe used to be like a treasure cave to Jordy. He had been drawn to it ever since he first saw the shiny gold coins stored there. Since then, he had memorized everything inside it. He had known the combination since he was twelve. It was a delicious secret, like his mint tin. Whenever he was home alone he used to open the safe and meticulously catalog everything that was inside. There was his dad's Glock and boxes of ammo. He never dared touch those, convinced that if he as much as touched the harsh looking weapon, his dad would know through some cosmic connection. But everything else in the safe was fair game. He would carefully remove and study each item and then carefully put it back in exactly the same place.

There was money. A stack of 100 crisp new twenty-dollar bills— all with Andrew Jackson's face staring in the same direction— neatly stored in an old cedar cigar box. Then there was the box with the sixteen glittering one-ounce golden eagle coins, each inside their own clear hard plastic sleeve. There was his grandfather's beautiful Omega pocket watch with its luminous art-deco hands; he used to take that watch into the closet and shut the door so he could see the glowing green 12, 3, 6, 9, and the snake-like hands moving slowly from green dot to green dot, hovering in the darkness like they were held by a ghostly grim reaper. Then there was his mother's gold link necklace with the iridescent pearl surrounded by tiny diamonds. That was one of his favorite treasures. Something about that precious metal chain slinking silkily through his fingers and the depth of the glistening creamy pearl made him feel secure.

Jordy had been thinking about that money and the gold coins. With the two thousand dollars and those coins, which were worth about ten thousand, he could last a long time on his own. If he got a job, he could make it on his own. There was just the little problem of stealing. If he was caught, he'd be sent to juvie. Was that so bad? Better than here. But he'd be leaving his mother behind. She'd have to make it on her own. On the other hand, what good was he doing her? And she was an adult, she could leave at any time. He wondered why she hadn't already taken the money and run. And the necklace. It was her necklace. Did she stay because of him?

Before tonight, Jordy felt guilty about having these thoughts. But tonight, it seemed almost a foregone conclusion. Get the hell out of here. He reached forward and tapped the familiar code on the lock keypad. It made its usual idiotic happy tone followed by the confident snick of the lock as it disengaged. He turned a handle and felt it slide the big bolts out of their slots. The heavy door swung open silently as he pulled on the handle.

And then a remarkable thing happened. The Clench relaxed. The weight of the door tugging at his arm pulled the knot right out of his gut. Jordy wondered if he closed the door if the Clench would come back. He wasn't about to try. Instead, he reached in and lifted out the cedar box. He opened its lid and—

Nothing. It was empty.

Jordy let the box slip out of his hands and onto the floor, and then he looked frantically for the case with the gold coins. It was still there, but the minute he touched it, he knew it was empty. The heft of sixteen ounces of solid gold was easy to detect when it was gone. He slid the empty case aside and as he did, the light from the hallway slanted across his shoulder and landed on a sparkling golden chain. It was still there. He could also see the luminous dots of the Omega hovering in the shadows. The bastard hadn't hocked them. Yet.

Jordy pulled at the delicate links of the gold chain, and as they slid into the light they revealed a twinkling miniature oval constellation of diamonds. In the middle of the diamonds was the luminescent pearl that glowed like a pale moon.

And on the shelf in the shadows behind the moon lurked the glistening black slab of high-tech reinforced nylon polymer that formed the sinuous hand grip of a 9mm Glock G17.

**22**

———

# YIN YANG

Chief Hannah leaned in closer to her computer screen, carefully re-reading each word of the five-year-old newspaper article she had found online, making sure she wasn't just imagining what was written there. She wasn't.

*Weldkill Courier*
Weldkill, New York.
November 9, 2006

Tragic Accidental Death of Local Teen

Last night a student from Weldkill High School died from injuries sustained from a fall at his home. Justin Farrell said he found his youngest son, Ethan, age 18, at the foot of their second-floor stairway at about midnight after hearing a loud noise. The Weldkill Volunteer Rescue squad responded and took Ethan to the Nyack Hospital Emergency Room, but they were unable to revive him and he was declared dead at 1 a.m. this morning. His father reported that his son "Must have just gotten up to get a drink of water and tripped. He's fallen down those stairs so many times and never been hurt before." Authorities have ruled it an accidental death. Ethan is survived by his father, Justin, and his older brother, William. A memorial service is planned for this Sunday.

Justin and Ethan Farrell. Five years ago. And an older brother, William A. Farrell. It didn't take long to find the obituary for the father, Justin. Passed away in his sleep six months later. Ruled a natural death. No police report, just an obit.

This was it. A break. Finally. It was like a fresh spring breeze after a long month of stagnation. Chief Hannah and Ed had managed to get the State to reopen the investigation after the discovery of the Toyota at Farr's farm but even though they had discovered a lot of evidence, it painted a picture of nothing. Nothing they didn't already know. Even the discovery that the Chief's bullet had injured Bronco didn't lead to anything. No emergency room records. No DNA hits. There was a possibility that he was dead, his body undiscovered, but it wasn't likely. There hadn't been enough blood in the car. The Chief concluded that the most probable scenario was that he found a mob doctor to treat him.

There had always been hope of another break in the case—a chance sighting of Bronco in his American sports car with aluminum wheels and New York plates. A drug arrest in another town that would lead to a DNA match or fingerprint match. But there had been nothing. Dead silence. Until the article on the screen in front of her.

She wasn't exactly sure what to do with this information yet. There was no way she could explain away how she had made the connection between Bronco and the Farrell deaths. There would be thorough questioning about the source of the connection, but she could never reveal the truth about the source—a kid that could literally read minds. That was a confidence that went beyond the laws of normal society. She was going to have to come up with an alternative explanation.

Will and Blue had come to the station the day before, after school. Blue was clearly apprehensive about being there, but as soon as Will explained what was going on to Chief Hannah, she had turned to Blue and looked her in the eye. She used her *chiss*, "I'M ON YOUR SIDE. ANYTHING YOU TELL ME IS COMPLETELY CONFIDEN-TIAL. I MEAN THAT. YOU CAN ASK WILL'S MOM IF YOU'RE UNSURE."

After that, the dam burst and the whole story came out. It was unbelievable. The Chief had to look to Will for confirmation. He nodded. "It's called participatio visio. You can check with my dad if you want and he'll explain it."

She didn't need to. She knew that Ash would back Will up. And if everything that Blue revealed with her story were true, the Chief would be able to find corroborating evidence. And here it was.

As pleased as she was, though, there wasn't anything in the article that could be used against Bronco. His father's death was ruled natural with no indication of foul play. But she had a name. William Farrell. She couldn't help a small smile as she turned to look out the large window next to her desk. I'm coming for you William. You better believe I'm coming for you.

Her thoughts were interrupted by Ed's footsteps in the hall.

"Hey, Chief! Here it is a Friday and not even a rush hour speeding ticket this morning. I'm beginning to wonder if this town even—"

Ed was interrupted by the phone. She held up her finger to pause Ed while she answered. "Westbury Police Department, Chief Hannah speaking."

From all the way across the room Ed could hear frantic yelling erupting out of the phone and within seconds they were in their cruiser, running blues and twos toward Westbury High.

**23**

---

# BLACK FRIDAY, NOVEMBER 18, 2011

**11:30 am**

Will stared at the *WHS Monitor* that was folded and stuffed in the top shelf of his locker. The rumor mill was still grinding along. He didn't even need to take his glasses off to hear the *chiss* of what people were thinking as they glanced and whispered in the halls when he walked by. Was Will hiding something about the mysterious extra man? Was Blue really Bronco's secret lover? It was the sort of garbage he was expecting so he really didn't pay much attention to it.

He had a lot more pressing things to think about now—Blue's participatio visio, their visit to the police station, the enticing possibility that they might actually catch Bronco. The meeting with Chief Hannah in itself was a revelation. She had reacted with almost childlike giddiness when she heard Blue's story. Seeing her reaction opened his eyes to the realization that the police really cared deeply about this case and that they had been frustrated by the lack of leads. They had been working the problem for all these weeks and he had been completely oblivious to it, living entirely inside the isolation of the high-school babble bubble. Now that he had seen what was happening on the outside, he was anxious to get through the school day and get back to the police station to see if they had uncovered anything with the new information.

He finished pulling his English stuff out of his locker, swung the door closed and laughed. Blue had been standing behind his open locker door.

"Very sneaky," he said.

"It was easy. You were deep in thought," said Blue.

"There's a lot to think about. It's been a weird year and now it's like we're about to start season two of 'The Hunt for Bronco.'"

She gave a wry smile. "Yeah, that's one way of looking at it." She pulled her glasses down on her nose and looked up at him.

He took her cue and pushed his glasses to the top of his head.

"*Hey,*" she voxed, "*I just want to say thanks for the library date. I wouldn't have gone to Chief Hannah if it weren't for that. I'm pretty sure something good is going to come from this.*"

She called it a date. So I guess it was a date, he thought.

"*Yeah, me, too. Hey, I was going to go over to the station to check after school. Do you want to come with?*"

"*Yeah. I'd like that. And the library after school . . . let's keep doing that. Maybe even do other stuff.*"

Will felt his ears get warm. He wasn't sure what she meant by other stuff. "*Uh, yeah, sure.*"

She pushed her glasses back up. "I gotta go—I've got to get to class early." She started to turn to leave and then stopped, stepped over to him and gave him a shoulder bump. She glanced up at him with a hint of a smile and then headed down the hall.

He watched her walk away. Her smooth dark hair flowed through a silver barrette and down her slim back halfway to her hips, which danced smoothly as they made their way through the forest of kids in the hallway. He watched her until all he could see was the glistening hair on the top of her head, and then even that last bit disappeared as she turned a corner and was gone. Just like that, it didn't feel like a weird year anymore. It felt like a wonderful year.

And then with a bang, he was jolted back to the weird reality by an all-too-familiar sound—one he was starting to get pretty sick of. Mike and Pike were at it again, shoving Jordy into his locker, he was sure. He glanced toward Jordy's locker and saw him swaying unsteadily next to it. That was it. Will had had enough. He dropped his backpack and turned just as Mike and Pike brushed past him, intentionally close. Thanks guys, he thought, and he grabbed Pike, who was closest, by the shirt and swung him around hard, right into a locker. BANG! It was a satisfying impact. Will had caught him totally off guard.

Pike stood there in what looked to be a confused fog. He seemed amazed at what happened, or perhaps just stoned, or both.

Mike stared at them both for a moment and then looked at Will. "Oh, what have we here? Mr. Feisty! Protector of Georgie, the little rodeo clown. Thinks he's tough stuff!" Mike shoved Will back against his locker. Will banged hard against it, but that was okay. Mike had pushed Will into a perfectly leveraged position. Will lifted his leg and with his back firmly against the lockers, planted his foot in the center of Mike's chest and launched him into a cafeteria table. It was just like something out of an action movie. Mike plowed across the top of the table, scattering food and trays. Pike just watched in continued astonishment. So did Will. He wasn't sure he believed what he had just done, but a rush of adrenaline made him not care.

Mike jumped up out of the tangle of cafeteria furniture and was winding up to charge. Pike was winding up, too. He was just a bit slower. Will braced for their attack. Somewhere someone started to shout, "Fight! Fight! Fight!" and then "POW!"

There are times when a sound is so shocking that the world comes to a halt. Just for a moment. And in that moment the silence is complete until the smallest sound breaks it. That sound in this case was a metallic tinkle on the hall floor. It was as if that sound was the signal for the world to start up again.

Will was looking directly at Mike who had put his hand to his side. Slowly he lifted it and looked at the red blotch in his palm. Another POW! Another clink, tinkle, tinkle. Mike's head jerked sideways, his eyes closed, and he slumped back onto the table he had just climbed off of.

Another POW! Another metallic tinkle, and Pike stumbled backward. Will turned toward the source of the deadly sounds, fully expecting to see a crazy guy with an AR-15 pointed directly at him.

What he saw instead was a kid with a languid look of surprise and bemusement on his face. His hands were clasped together in front of him, his arms relaxed and pointing down, forming a V. At the bottom of the V was a handgun with just a wisp of smoke coming out the tip like a smudged out cigarette.

"Jordy, what are you doing?"

Jordy looked at Will. His expression didn't change, and it was then that Will noticed how his features looked melted, like Jordy had aged ten years.

"Killing people . . . I guess." He spoke haltingly, like the words were heavy and hard to push out. He started looking around him and the V in front of him rose up, the tip of the V searching for a target. Will became aware of a strange rumble, like the thunder of an avalanche of chairs and tables and feet. He realized kids had been tumbling out of the cafeteria and pushing everything and everyone out of the way. There were no screams, just short urgent exclamations: "look out!" "get down!" "gun!" "go go go!" goading the herd into a muted panic.

POW! Will saw Jordy's arms bucking, fighting the kick of the dark, lethal mechanism as a short flash spit out from its mouth, the tinkle of the shell hitting the floor ringing out over the clatter of the stampede. Several kids dropped to the floor before getting back up and scrambling away. One didn't get up.

Will was frozen to the floor in front of his open locker door. He felt like an invisible disembodied observer. The V of Jordy's arms was panning across the room left to right, its deadly point facing away from Will. Then it stopped. A teacher was moving along the lockers toward Jordy with his hands outstretched, palms down. Will recognized him, a freshman History teacher, Mr. McCarthy. He was looking steadily at Jordy saying, "Calm down there, uh . . . son! It's over. Just put the gun down. No one else needs to get hurt. It's okay now—POW!—OH!"

Mr. McCarthy's right leg exploded in a splash of blood, and he went down.

Jordy watched Mr. McCarthy writhing on the floor and then turned back toward Will. He was muttering, "Bastard. Didn't give me a chance to make up a D. Doesn't even know my name. I've been in his class for months, and he doesn't even know my name." His words were slurred and as he spoke a waft of alcohol tinted breath reached Will.

Jordy looked at Will. "He should have remembered my name at least. He'll remember it now."

"Yeah, J-O-R-D-Y. Jordy for Jordan. Not Geordie for George. Jordan D. Willis."

Jordy just stood there staring right down Will's gaze. He straightened his arms and pushed the muzzle of the gun toward Will.

"Yeah, at least you remember." The gun was wavering unsteadily in front of him.

"Please don't shoot me."

"Oh, sorry, I wasn't paying attention." Jordy lowered the gun and then as though he had just remembered what he was supposed to be doing, turned and shot randomly into the cafeteria. POW! POW! This time there was a scream. Jordy turned back to Will, smiling, his *chiss* leaking, "GOT SOMEONE THAT TIME."

"Jordy, you should put the gun down."

Jordy lowered the gun lazily down in one hand while he wiped his nose with the heal of his other hand. Will stared at Jordy's dead-looking eyes. At the same time he became aware of a rush of fearful *chiss* all around him. He realized it was coming from reflections off the cafeteria windows. Kids must have gotten trapped in the cafeteria, hiding behind tables.

He looked Jordy in the eyes again. Jordy's *chiss* leaked out in a lazy stream, "WILL WOODS. DUMB BASTARD DOESN'T KNOW HOW GOOD HE'S GOT IT." Then he spoke out loud, "You know, this was a lot easier than I thought it would be. Just point and shoot. Bang bang bang! I could shoot you, you know." He lifted the gun with his one unsteady hand, the hole at the end of the barrel waggling at Will like the bony finger of the grim reaper.

A wave of realization poured down Will's body like a bucket of ice water—he was going to die. Why had he just stood there? What had he been thinking? He shut his eyes with the infantile hope that the act could make this go away, but when he opened them again, he didn't see a gun or Jordy. Instead, a barrage of images started flashing by like a flip book of life with a soundtrack that was just like *chiss* murmuring a commentary on every significant failure, success, trauma, and triumph. God, he was seeing his life flash in front of him. But there was something wrong. The scenes were confusing—he was seeing things he had never seen before. And then it dawned on him.

These weren't his memories. The visions suddenly stopped, and he was staring at Jordy again, his *chiss* revealing a dire reassurance. "DON'T WORRY. YOU'LL JUST HEAR A CLICK AND THEN NOTHING."

Jordy was standing stock still. His arm was no longer wavering, and the gun was steady as a rock, his arm held straight out from his body. And then he swung his arm toward his own head and made a salute with the forearm, hand, and gun completing a perfect right triangle, the gun barrel pressed firmly against his right temple.

One of the videos that went viral the next day was taken by a girl trapped in the cafeteria behind an upturned table. She had been holding up her phone like a periscope. The frantic image shook and bounced so much that it was hard to watch but it held steady just long enough and at just the right moment to show a stock-still Will standing by his locker door looking down the barrel of Jordy's gun. Then as Jordy suddenly swung the gun toward his own head and fired, Will catapulted toward him with an outstretched hand. The video made it seem as though Will himself had exploded from a gun. The two figures fell to the floor, disappearing behind an overturned table.

Will grabbed the barrel of the gun just as it went off, and the slam of the recoil tried to kick his hand off as he and Jordy fell together to the floor. The ejected shell slapped sharp and hot against Will's cheek. The gun then went off again. This time the recoil sent it flying.

Both Will and Jordy bounced hard on their sides and then came to rest on the harsh, cold linoleum floor. Will was deafened from the blast of the gun, his hearing replaced with a high pitched ringing. His hand was numb from the violent kick of the gun slide. He started to sit up and reach over to Jordy but then stopped, unsure of what he was seeing. Jordan D. Willis was writhing, his arms twisting and flopping randomly, his mouth silently jawing words from a language not of this world. A grizzly cocktail of fluid was oozing out of the side of his head, matting his hair and seeping onto the floor. The writhing gradually slowed down and then stopped like a windup doll reaching the end of its spring. Jordy's hands clenched and unclenched one last time and then he was still.

Will's stomach convulsed, spewing its contents out onto the floor. He gasped a putrid breath and stayed on all fours, panting, his head hanging. He desperately wanted the world to stop spinning and the ringing in his head to stop. His brain had come to a total halt, trying to reboot into some program that could process what had just happened, but all he could do was wait. Wait for someone to tell his body what to do. He was vaguely aware that several people had come over to him. He looked up and saw a kid he recognized but just couldn't place at the moment. The guy's mouth was moving, but Will couldn't comprehend. Then he felt hands grabbing him and helping him get up off the floor, guiding him to a cafeteria chair. He sat down, holding his head in his hands, and leaning his elbows into his knees. Staring at the floor he wondered why it was swirling and spinning as if he had just gotten off the world's most sadistic merry-go-round.

Blue resisted the urge to glance back at Will as she walked down the hall. For some reason, she wanted him to be watching her, but that was silly, she thought. Still she felt a little let down as she turned the corner out of his sight. Get a grip, she said to herself, focus on school. As she pushed her way down the hall she was aware of a distant crash and murmur of amusement behind her. It was followed with a distant chant echoing down the hallways and then a pow, like a firecracker. Some of the kids around her stopped and turned around like they wanted to go see what the excitement was about. She stopped, too, curious about who would be gutsy enough to set off a firecracker. Then there was another pow. And another. It didn't really sound quite right for a firecracker. Around her the kids had grown silent until someone said, "That was a fucking gun!" That statement hung in the air for a split second as the truth penetrated through the crowd, and then the moment it did, they shifted in unison, like a murmur of starlings, in a hurried, silent consensus away from the bangs which had suddenly trans-formed from an amusing joke into a deadly threat.

Blue stood frozen to the floor as kids jostled and pushed their way around her. Some were urging her on. "Move! Shooter! Gun! Go go go!" But she couldn't. Will was back there. She started moving against the crowd toward the cafeteria until she was suddenly yanked backward. She looked and saw tiny Miss Kendrick pulling her down the hall with a strength that was way out of proportion to her size.

"What are you thinking! Get moving and do NOT argue with me!"

Blue was so shocked by the power of Miss Kendrick's voice and grip that she didn't have a chance at countering it. She stumbled after her and nearly fell as she was shoved into a classroom just as another gunshot went off. Miss Kendrick went out into the hall and corralled kids as they went by, shoving them unceremoniously into the room until there were apparently no more to be corralled. Another gunshot. She shut the door quietly, locked it, and turned and commanded, "Everyone be SILENT! Do NOT make a sound!"

A kid whimpered in the corner and another started, "But . . ."

"SILENCE!" Miss Kendrick hissed with a ferocious look in her eye. "You," she pointed to a big kid, "help me move the desk against the door. The rest of you sit on the floor against the wall."

They moved the heavy desk over to the door and Miss Kendrick indicated with her hands for the kid to sit with the rest. She remained leaning over the desk with her ear pressed to the door. Even inside the room, they could hear two more shots. A girl started sobbing. Miss Kendrick left her post and went over to the girl and put her arms around her, shushing and rocking her. The sobbing stopped. It was dead silent—so silent that the entire room collectively gasped when two more shots went off. Then silence.

Miss Kendrick whispered, "Listen everyone, they can't get in, but they might try the door. It's important that you don't react when they do. If we are quiet, they will move on."

Blue was thinking hard. The shots hadn't gotten any louder or quieter. They must have all been in the same place—the cafeteria. Will had been there. Did he get out? Nine shots. Jesus. She realized she was shaking her head back and forth. *No, no, no, it can't be. He's got to be okay.*

She kept shaking her head trying to keep the thought of any other outcome from finding a purchase in her brain. She only stopped when she heard the distant sounds of sirens. How much time had gone by? There hadn't been any more gunshots. Kids around her started to look at each other and grow restless, sensing that whatever had happened was over, but Miss Kendrick was firm, signaling everyone to stay down and quiet.

Blue couldn't sit still any longer. She studied the window across from her and then glanced at Miss Kendrick who must have sussed out what Blue was thinking because she was glowering at her, her thoughts coming out as *chiss* practically shouting, "DON'T YOU DARE!" She respected Miss Kendrick, but she had to do what she had to do and like a lightning bolt she catapulted off the floor, unlatched a window and dropped through it before anyone could touch her. She landed hard in a prickly snow covered cedar bush, but she barely noticed the sting of the needles and icy burning of the snow as she scrambled out of the bush and ran for the front entrance. As she sprinted around the corner of the building she nearly ran right into a police officer in full riot gear, gun in hand, approaching from the other direction. She heard a short scream as she jumped out of his way. She realized the scream had come from her. The officer motioned for her to move behind him. She didn't hesitate and ran until she got to the front entrance where she was greeted with a bizarre scene of orderly chaos. Kids were everywhere but they were being herded by teachers and firemen away from the building. There were flashing lights everywhere—fire trucks, police cars, volunteer firemen, ambulances. She stopped, at a loss for where to look first. For once, she was thankful for vox, because it seemed to be the only thing that might penetrate this mess and find the only person that could hear and respond.

"WILL!" she voxed with as much power as she could muster.

No response. *"WILL!"* Nothing. She pushed her way through the mess, he had to be here. *"WILL!"*

"Blue!" She turned quickly as someone snatched her into a tight hug. "You're safe!" Her heart did an odd dance that could only be described as cardio-whiplash as it realized instantly that it wasn't Will.

She pushed away from Wu. "Where's Will?"

"We think he is still inside."

And for some reason that Blue could never explain afterward, her legs stopped doing their job and collapsed underneath her, dropping her into the wet mess that had been churned up by a hundred frantic feet, creating a salad of grass and leftover golden autumn leaves covered with an icy dressing of snow and slush.

### Friday, 11:48 am

The halls were empty, and it was deathly quiet. Chief Hannah stepped carefully along the wall past a classroom. Looking through the narrow glass window in the door, it seemed empty but there could be kids still cowering inside out of sight. The cafeteria was dead ahead and as she approached cautiously, gun extended in front of her, she could hear a sobbing echoing off the walls, amplified by the stillness. There were two kids lying on the floor in front of open locker doors down the hall across from the cafeteria. There was no motion from them, at least not detectable from where she was. She took another couple of steps forward and then spotted a gun on the floor. Ed was right behind her and she signaled for him to go forward and pick it up. While Ed took the gun and ejected the clip and the live round, she moved around him into the cafeteria scanning left to right.

Two bodies in front of the lockers, one under a table, a kid sitting in a chair bent over with his head in his hands, a kid standing next to him, his dazed stare pointed right at Chief Hannah's gun. She lowered the gun and the kid visibly relaxed.

"Shooter?" asked Chief Hannah.

The kid pointed at the floor by the lockers. The body closest to her.

"Any others?" she asked.

The kid shook his head. He pointed down the hall. "He needs help." Then he turned and pointed behind him. "She needs help, too."

Chief Hannah looked down the hall and there was a teacher on the floor crumpled, bleeding, but apparently still alive. Behind the kid she saw a girl behind some of the upturned tables. She was crouched and sobbing next to another kid who was lying in a pool of blood.

Her brain started narrating the situation as if this was a training exercise. "*You are the first on the scene and only have two officers. Do you enter the building? Once in the building do you stop to help victims before neutralizing the shooter? How do you determine the number of shooters? Can you trust the answers of the bystanders? At what point can you summon medical personnel? Example, you enter a school cafeteria, you see dead bodies, injured victims, uninjured bystanders, and a single weapon on the floor. One of the bystanders says that the only shooter is dead. What do you do?*"

In the training exercises there were endless discussions and no conclusive answers. There were always too many variables. In the end, it was up to the person of authority on the scene to decide and right here, right now, that was her.

"Ed, get the EMT's in here as fast as you can. If more officers are here, have them secure the rest of the building. You know the school, so you direct them. I'll stay here and secure this area." She looked at the shell-shocked kid. "What's your name?"

"Alex."

"Hi, Alex, I'm Chief Hannah. Who is that with you?" she pointed to the kid in the chair. He still had his face down.

"It's Will Woods," said Alex.

"Jesus, Mary, and Joseph."

**Friday, 11:55 am**

"Blue, are you okay?" Wu was crouched down next to her, a look of concern on his face. A large figure came up from behind Wu. It was Nate.

"C'mon Blue and Wu. We have to get out of here. I just talked to Pa Bill. He said to come straight to the post office."

The post office was only a few blocks away, but Blue made no move to get up. Nate stepped around Wu and crouched down by Blue. "Hey, Little Fox, everything is going to be okay. You're going to freeze if you sit in that snow. C'mon, let's get to the post office where it's warm." Nate was so massive, he radiated warmth and she suddenly felt the chill from the wetness that had penetrated her jeans. She tried her legs and realized they would support her now, but she started shivering uncontrollably. Nate put his arm around her. "There now, let's get you warmed up."

Blue gave in to Nate and his warmth and then there was a shout and suddenly she was crushed between Nate and Anna.

"Blue! Omigod! I was soooo worried about you!" Anna released her and stepped back grabbing both Blue's arms. "We have *got* to go!"

Anna's arrival just added another layer of confusion in Blue's brain. She was trying to get a grip on everything but all she could come up with was: "To the post office?"

Anna's face turned to puzzlement. "The post office? What are you talking about? Haven't you heard?"

Blue looked around at Wu and Nate who were looking just as confused as her.

"An ambulance just took Will and Mr. McCarthy to the hospital!"

Will felt a sudden urge to get out of the ambulance. The feeling of security and safety he felt when the EMT walked him out to the ambulance and strapped him into the side bench had evaporated when they rolled in the stretcher carrying the unconscious but still alive Mr. McCarthy, who clearly needed a lot more critical attention than he did. The EMT was Pete, the same one who had ridden with he and Blue last summer. Pete and another EMT that Will didn't recognize climbed in the back and closed the door.

"Let's roll, code 99," said Pete to the driver.

"Hey, Pete," said Will. "I don't really need to be here. I'm feeling okay now."

Pete looked at Will as the ambulance lurched into life and started blaring its warnings to those outside. "Yes you do. You're still in shock. You feel better because you're lying down, but trust me, you aren't ready to do jumping jacks just yet."

Will was surprised that he felt a sense of relief at Pete's words. He was right, he didn't feel right. Nothing felt right. The hearing in his left ear still hadn't fully returned which made everything seem a little off-balance. And he was exhausted. He leaned his head back on the bench and closed his eyes. This was deja-vu all over again, riding in an ambulance, only this time, he was lying where Blue had been, and McCarthy was lying where he had been. God, was his life ever going to return to normal? Was this his new normal? Was this everyone's new normal?

Will opened his eyes. "Hey, Pete, the two kids, Mike and Peter, are they . . . ?"

Pete looked at Will and paused just a moment before he shook his head slowly.

Will closed his eyes again. Jesus. It had really happened. And Jordy shot, what, two more times? Three more?

"What about the others?" He kept his eyes closed as he asked the question. He was bracing for the reply.

"One didn't make it. One is in the other ambulance," said Pete.

Jesus. He looked over at Mr. McCarthy. He had an oxygen mask and IV just like Will had last summer. "Is he going to be okay?"

Pete looked at the monitors and then back at Will. "He's stable. Remember what I told you last summer?"

"Yeah, you said the worst is over. He's going to be patched up by the best."

Pete smiled. "You got it."

Will closed his eyes again. Five victims. He could have been the sixth. Jordy had pointed the gun right at him. A wave of panic came over him again as recalled that moment of looking down the barrel of the gun, waiting for the explosion that was going to end his life, and in that brief pause, the stream of images that had come out of Jordy's head and into his. As those images replayed in his head, one came into sharp relief and wouldn't go away. Will wasn't sure he believed what he was seeing.

"Pete!"

"What's wrong?" asked Pete. He had been checking a monitor on McCarthy.

"Can you radio the police from here?"

"Yeah, if we have to."

"You have to. Tell them to check Jordy's house."

"Jordy, the shooter?"

"Yeah. I think . . ." Will paused. God, he would have to think up some explanation later, but he had to tell someone now in case there was a chance, ". . . I think he shot someone else. Not at school."

Pete's eyebrows went up. "Someone else?"

"His father."

### Friday, 12:00 noon

The blast of warm air from the dash vent wrapped around Blue like an ethereal blanket, calming the shivering but not doing a lot for her damp jeans. She was thankful, nonetheless. Jack had come out of nowhere right after Anna's news flash. All he said was "C'mon, my car's right over there," and the next instant, she and Anna were in his car, with Jack fighting through the jam of vehicles that was rapidly building up around the school. Wu and Nate had no objection. "We'll explain it all to Pa Bill," Nate had said. "Go!"

Blue looked at Jack. He seemed intent on the driving challenge at hand, but also seemed intent on avoiding any discussion. She hadn't had a single interaction with him the whole school year. Of course she'd seen him in the halls in school, but there was never a glimmer of recognition from him, not a single hint that he had any association with her or Will. Nothing, in spite of the fact that he probably saved both their lives that night. And now he drops out of nowhere exactly when they need a ride.

"Thanks," she said.

Jack glanced at her but quickly turned back to driving, saying nothing, but giving a slight nod.

From the back seat, Anna quickly caught them up on what she had heard. "Bill Edwards said he saw them. He said that Will looked okay but maybe a little unsteady. An EMT was walking with him. They wheeled Mr. McCarthy out right after."

They wouldn't have taken Will to the hospital unless there was something wrong, thought Blue. "Were there others?"

"I think so. I don't know who though," said Anna.

Blue closed her eyes. The news that Will was walking eased her mind a little but something must have happened to him. Did he fall? Was he hit with a gun? A baseball bat? Was he crazy enough to go after the shooter? She heard herself thinking out loud, "Was there more than one shooter?"

Anna said, "I don't know. There was a lot of crazy speculation going on. Some people were even saying it was Bronco coming back to town."

Blue's heart lurched. It couldn't be. The very scenario she'd suggested to Will, but here at the school? It didn't make sense. It had to be someone in the school. Who would fit that profile?

Someone who didn't fit in and had an ax to grind. And then it came to her.

"It was Jordy Willis." The words didn't come from Blue, they came from Jack. He went on, "He was alone. He's dead."

It hit Blue like a freight train. Jordy. Bam! She had seen it. It was all there in front of her. His acting weird in class, his being bullied, his introversion, all those red flags. And she saw him at his locker behind her just before she left Will standing in front of his locker. Jesus, while she was walking away Jordy had been pulling out a gun.

"How do you know?" asked Anna.

"I was in the cafeteria." Jack didn't show any emotion. He just spoke matter-of-factly. "We're almost there. I'll drop you off in front." He pulled into the hospital entrance drive and stopped. "Hey, are you okay?"

Blue turned to look at Jack. He didn't look matter-of-fact, he looked like a deeply concerned human being. "Are you okay?" he repeated.

"No, I'm not." And she jumped out of the car and ran for the entrance, not waiting for Anna.

### Friday, 12:10 pm

"This is it," said Chief Hannah. Ed pulled the cruiser in behind the ambulance that had already arrived at the Willis residence. She was happy to see that the crew had held back from entering the house at her instruction. It was a hard decision—there was a chance that the father was still alive and in need of immediate medical assistance—but she hadn't gotten enough information from Will to determine what the situation inside might be. She was just glad that the state CSST[1] crew had gotten to the high school scene quickly and she was able to turn it over to them and follow-up on Will's clue.

She and Ed moved quickly to the front door and knocked.

There was no answer, so she tried the door. It was unlocked. She opened it.

"Hello, this is Westbury Police. Is anyone . . ." she stopped suddenly as she spotted an adult male prone on the floor. He wasn't moving and there was blood. She turned and waved the EMTs over and then stepped into the house. "Is anyone here? We are coming inside." She stepped into the living room and moved toward the prone body. "Ed, you check the rest of the house." She pointed at the EMT in the doorway and then gestured to the body. He was lying between the garage entry and the open bar of the kitchen. Ed moved down the hallway off the living room. It was a small house, and it didn't take long for Ed to come back and state that it was all clear. No one else in the house.

"There's a lot for the CSST to check out from what I saw, though," said Ed as he holstered his sidearm.

"He's dead," said the EMT. "He's been dead a while. Looks like two exit wounds. I'd have to move him to confirm."

"No, don't do that," said Chief Hannah. "We'll leave it to CSST." She looked at the garage entrance door. Blood spatter. Damn. She had no doubt that if she looked she'd find a couple of 9mm shells on the floor. "You guys can go if you have to but hang here until the CSST crew shows up if you can." She said this to the EMTs and then she turned to Ed. "I hope you have some crime scene tape left in the cruiser."

"Yeah. Sure didn't think we'd ever have to use it again, though. Second time today we've had to tape off a crime scene. Third time this year. I thought this tape would grow old and die a peaceful death without ever being used."

"Very poetic, Ed. You are full of surprises." Ed knew how to get a smile out of a grim situation. "You work on that. I've got to figure out where the mother is." She pulled out her phone and was shocked to see that it was barely after noon. Jesus. Two shootings and the day wasn't even half over. She took a deep breath and searched for the number of the school district office, and as she did, noticed a couple of new messages. They were both from Rodney James. Sorry, Rodney, you're going to have to wait. I've got a few more pressing issues right now, like how to give parents the worst news of their lives and explain to the residents of Westbury how in the space of a few minutes their town was transformed from a nice, quiet, safe place into ground zero for the first major school shooting in Vermont.

She was about to punch the number for the school district office when another call came in. It was from the hospital.

"Chief Hannah," she answered. The voice on the other end of the line rattled away efficiently and ended with a question. She closed her eyes. Would this never stop? "Christ. I'll be over in ten minutes."

"What's up, Chief?" Ed had returned from the cruiser, a large roll of bright yellow tape in his hand.

"I found her," she replied.

"You mean Mrs. Willis?" asked Ed.

"In the hospital with ten stitches in her forehead and a concussion. Her husband brought her in last night. Said she fell."

"Jesus. And now he's dead on the floor. I'm guessing she didn't just fall."

Chief Hannah nodded. "Yeah. Well, let's not jump to conclusions. I gotta go over there. They are frantic because they just learned about her son and they don't know what to tell her. And now this." She gestured toward the house. "Christ, I don't even know what to tell her, but somebody has to or she's going to find out the wrong way."

Ed shook his head. "And this is when I'm glad your chief and I'm not. If it's any consolation, I think there's no better person to tell her. Hang in there, Chief."

"Thanks, Ed."

In spite of Ed's words of encouragement, she felt out of her depth. If she had a day or two to study and prepare for what lay ahead of her, that would be one thing, but that was not even a possibility. Like her academy instructor said, there are going to be some horrible incidents you can't even imagine or prepare for, but you have to deal with them whether you're ready for them or not. If you can't accept that, then don't accept the job.

"And I accepted the job," she said to no one in particular.

"What was that, Chief?" asked Ed from the driveway.

"Nothing," she replied. "I'm taking the cruiser. You'll have to find a ride."

"You're the Chief!" said Ed.

Yeah, that I am, she said to herself.

### Friday, 12:15 pm

Will sat on the edge of the exam table, the crinkly paper sheet underneath him crackling each time he moved to counter the motion of the nurse who was wiping his face more vigorously than he thought necessary with an antiseptic cloth.

"You have a little bruise under your left eye. Do you know what that's from?" She pulled back as she spoke, taking the cloth and staring at it briefly before quickly refolding it. Will picked up on her *chiss,* "*BLOOD? AND . . . OH MY GOD.*" He caught a glimpse of the cloth before she folded it. There were red and gray blotches on it.

"It was a shell from the gun," he said.

The tiniest gasp came from the nurse.

"Is it okay if I lie down?" asked Will.

"Of *course.*" Her demeanor had noticeably softened. "Can I get you some water or ginger ale or anything?"

"Yeah. Ginger ale would be great." He closed his eyes. It was blood and brains on that cloth. He was sure of it. He felt the nausea start again as the image of Jordy's oozing head and macabre motions replayed in his mind. He had asked Pete about it in the ambulance, but Pete had reassured him that it was all involuntary motion. Jordy didn't feel a thing. "It sometimes takes the rest of the body a couple of seconds to get the message," Pete had said. It sure seemed like a lot more than a couple of seconds to Will.

He could really use that ginger ale. That and a good nap, but closing his eyes just kept the replay going. He was better off staring at the ceiling. Maybe he could nap with his eyes open.

There was a clatter as a gurney festooned with tubes and wires connecting an IV and cardiac monitor rolled by his door. There was a girl on it, the other survivor besides Mr. McCarthy. He was thankful in a way that it wasn't anyone he knew. He wondered if Mr. McCarthy was in surgery now. He wondered what they did with the others, Mike and Pike, and one other kid. Jesus, he still couldn't believe it. Any hate he had felt toward them had evaporated. They didn't deserve that.

God, where's that ginger ale, he thought. He looked for where the trash basket was just in case he needed it and instead spotted a pair of blue sneakers walking through the door. He realized at that moment that if there was one person he would wish to see coming through that door it was her. Blue was carrying a cup with a straw.

"*I talked the nurse into letting me bring this. She looked upset,*" she voxed, her face set in the patented Blue stoicism. She handed Will the cup. He didn't even sit up. He suddenly felt relaxed and realized that he had been strung as tight as a guitar.

She put her hand on his arm and leaned toward him. "*Are you okay?*"

Her hand felt warm. "*I'm fine.*"

She reached up and touched his cheek where the shell had whacked him. "*You don't fucking look fine! What the hell happened?*"

Will closed his eyes at her touch. There was no Jordy replay, just the light touch of her finger brushing his face.

"Can we not talk about it right now?"

As he said this the nurse came to the door and said, "I'm sorry, you'll have to go. Will's mother is here, and we can only allow one visitor at a time."

Will glanced at Blue. Her eyes were crinkled with worry. "*Okay. For now,*" she voxed. She squeezed his hand. "*But not for long.*" She turned to go, but in a sudden panic, he gripped her hand in both of his. For some reason, he didn't want to let go of her. After an awkward moment, he released her. "Sorry. I don't know where that came from."

Blue didn't say anything in reply, but the way she stood and looked at him gave the impression that a much older, wiser person was standing there. And that person knew exactly where that came from.

## 24

## COLLATERAL DAMAGE

**Friday, 9:36 pm**

Blues eyes were focused on nothing while her nose was focused on the spicy vapors steaming out of the mug as she tipped it toward her lips and took a thoughtful sip of the hot tea. She was sitting on the couch in the rec room along with the rest of the family. They had already finished and cleaned up after a very somber dinner. Hardly anyone had spoken during the meal except for, "Please pass the salt," and a lot of early, "May I be excused, please." Afterwards, as she cleared the dishes off the table, she saw a lot of unfinished portions. The biggest unfinished portion was on her own plate.

Pa Bill had made everyone a cup of tea after dinner. One of the endearing qualities of Pa Bill was his strong belief in the healing powers of tea. He had brewed each cup separately, taking care to match the blend of tea with the individual it was for. The mug he had given Blue was a ginger and lemon blend which felt exactly right to her. It helped calm her reactions to the murmuring of *chiss* from all around her.

Pa Bill's *chiss* was a low, continuous muttering, ". . . OUGHT TO

*INVESTIGATE THE PARENTS . . . JUST TOO MANY GUNS OUT THERE . . . TOTALLY PREVENTABLE . . . THOSE POOR FAMILIES . . . DEVASTATING . . . DON'T KNOW WHAT I'D DO . . .*" Blue watched Pa Bill's gaze moving over each member of the family. She felt a flutter of intense . . . what? She searched her mind for the right word. Powerlessness? Anxiety? The best she could come up with was inability-to-protect. There was no word in her vocabulary for it. She closed her eyes and the feeling faded. She took another sip of her tea. She was afraid to hear the *chiss* from Ma Beth. She didn't need to hear it to know that she had been profoundly moved by the shooting. In the kitchen, in the dining room, after dinner, Ma Beth had moved as if in a fog except when one of the kids passed and she would impulsively embrace them in a quiet hug.

Nate was looking for answers in the open Bible on his lap. "... *HERE IT IS, ECCLESIASTES 7 'BE NOT OVER MUCH WICKED, NEITHER BE YOU FOOLISH: WHY SHOULD YOU DIE BEFORE YOUR TIME?' JORDY WASN'T WICKED, WAS HE? . . . HE WAS FOOLISH . . . AND HE TOOK OTHER'S LIVES . . . DOES THAT MAKE HIM WICKED?*" Blue hoped he could find what he needed there. She never could find much comfort in the Bible.

Wu, on the other hand, was silent. He was sitting on the couch with her, his gaze drilling into the floor, but nothing coming out of his eyes. Blue almost regretted that Will had taught him how to hide his *chiss*. It was the right thing to do, but she would give anything to know where Wu's mind was right now.

Sam was the only one that seemed to find an escape by diving into his MMO[1]. She envied him.

She closed her eyes again, focusing on the aroma of the tea realizing that Pa Bill was not wrong in his belief that tea was therapeutic. It kept her from dwelling on her own thoughts which had been dominated by guilt—guilt from why she didn't see this coming herself. She knew from the first day of school that Jordy was not in a good place. That first day in math class he came in the room and sat down shyly in the only open desk, right next to hers. It didn't take her long to recognize exactly where he was. He was like she was before she came to the O'Days. Alone. Not understood. Living his own private nightmare caused by god-only-knows what. She had befriended him, to a point. She was sympathetic, yet he represented something she had already left behind. She wasn't anxious to relive her past through someone else. Instead, she had intended to steer him toward Dr. Woods, or steer Dr. Woods toward Jordy. She had never followed through and now . . . this. She could tell yesterday morning that he was in a really bad state. She could have gone right to Dr. Woods and said something. Instead, she was more concerned about seeing Chief Hannah after school. God, if only she had, four people might be alive today. If only she had, Will would not have wound up in the emergency room—again. Once again, her obsession with Bronco steamrolled over everyone.

She pressed the still-hot cup against her cheek, it's penetrating warmth helped calm her down. She thought back to what Dr. Woods had told her about guilt. "Hindsight takes a gray situation and makes it look black and white," she had said. "It has a tendency to make you think you should have seen something when in reality, there was no way you could have seen it. Before an event, there are thousands of possible outcomes. After the event, there is only one. How can you possibly know beforehand which outcome was the right one?" Yes, she had seen that Jordy was not in good space, but how could she have seen that it would turn deadly? This thought dialed down the guilt somewhat, but not enough to erase her guilt about Will.

He was not himself and she still wasn't sure exactly why. She and Anna had been in the waiting room when Mrs. Woods walked Will out. Anna immediately grabbed him in a bear hug and he kind of patted her absent-mindedly in response.

"Are you okay?" Anna had asked.

All he said in reply was, "I'm fine."

Now Blue knew what it was to be on the other side of "I'm fine." He had practically screamed that he was not fine.

As Jack drove her and Anna home, Anna peppered Blue with

questions. "Was he hurt? What happened to him? He barely hugged me back. He looked so . . ."

"Shocked?" Blue completed the question.

"Yes!"

"I don't know. He didn't want to talk about it," said Blue.

"That's bad," said Anna. She turned to stare out the window and then suddenly turned back to Blue. "You've *got* to go to him," she said.

"What do you mean, I've got to go to him?" asked Blue

"You have got to get him to talk. To spill. To get out whatever poison is in his head!"

"He's with his mom. She'll know what to do. She's a psychiatrist. She's good."

"She's his *mother!* It's so totally different!"

"You're wrong. He'll be fine."

Anna sat back with a disgusted look. After a moment she said, "Fine." Then she swung back and looked straight at Blue and said, "You still *have* to go to him very, *very* soon."

"Why?"

"Stop being ridiculous, Blue! This is serious! You know why!" Anna actually looked angry. That got Blue's attention. And then Anna said the words.

"Because you love him, you idiot." Anna reached up and held Blue's chin, so she had to look right into her eyes. *"AND HE LOVES YOU! A LOT!"*

Blue looked at the bits of tea leaf swirling slowly in the bottom of her mug. A little wisp of steam still wafted up from the tea as she breathed out over it. Anna's words had been with her all afternoon and into the evening. They formed a neat little package that pretty much wrapped up all of the feelings that had been bouncing around loose inside her the past few months. "Go to him. You love him. You idiot." But Anna had gotten the order wrong. Blue corrected the order and recited it in her head, "You idiot, you love him. Go to him." Get the poison out of his head. Maybe she could. Maybe that would make up for something.

She sipped the last bit of liquid from her cup and stared at the tea leaves that remained in the bottom of the creamy white mug. With the loss of their watery sea, the leaves had frozen into an intricate lacy pattern. Outside, a rush of wind caused the window to rattle. The temperature had been dropping all day and it had started snowing. It would be much colder after midnight. She would have to dress warm.

### Saturday, 12:05 am

It was dark. He closed his eyes. It was just as dark. Open, closed, open, closed. Just darkness. Then the movie started replaying again. A bright, flickering square hovering in the darkness. It was like an instructional video. Here is what happened. What could you have done to improve the outcome? If you had run, would it have changed anything? No. If you had tackled Jordy right away, would it have saved people? Maybe. If you had reacted just a little sooner, could you have saved Jordy? Probably. Well, you didn't do any of those things and look what happened. The scene of Jordy's lifeless body writhing grotesquely on the floor played over and over again.

He tried to think of something else, like what he had said in the hospital, what Pete had said, what Blue and Anna had said, what his Mom had said, but he couldn't remember anything. He knew they were there. Knew that they had talked to him and that he had responded. With what? He couldn't hold on to any of it. All the words just fluttered away like dead leaves. It was just Jordy, over and over again. Gun barrel pointed at him. Scenes from Jordy's life. Vision of Jordy shooting his dad. Perfect right triangle. Shot. Hot shell. Falling. Deafness. Writhing. Blood and bits of bone and gray matter oozing. Bodies on the floor. More blood.

He craved the mindlessness of sleep and yet he was afraid that the sleeping nightmares would be worse than the waking nightmares. Darkness and wind and bodies and blood. Nothing else seemed to be in his head right now.

His mother had offered him a sedative. That much he remembered, and he had said no. He was starting to regret that. He was so tired. He was even starting to hallucinate. He started hearing a voice through the darkness and gore. It was saying "*WAKE UP...DON'T GO TO THAT DARK PLACE.*" It was Blue's vox voice. He could imagine her saying that to him, it would be just like her. Maybe she had said it to him in the hospital. Maybe he was starting to wake up—to remember things other than the endless replay of the shooting. "*WAKE UP! DAMMIT! I'M FREEZING...*" Wait, she definitely didn't say that, he thought.

"*FOR GOD'S SAKE LOOK OUT YOUR FUCKING WINDOW!*"

Will jerked upright off his back and stared blankly at his window. As he watched, a dark silhouette slowly came into focus, backed by the pale whiteness of the snow behind it.

"*THANK YOU! NOW WILL YOU LET ME IN BEFORE I FREEZE TO DEATH?*"

Will was genuinely unsure if this was real or not. It didn't make any sense. Blue would never risk being outside his window, now, on such a cold night, would she? The consequences would be serious if she was caught. But now the silhouette was jumping up and down voxing, "*PLEASE! OPEN THE WINDOW!*" Will finally found himself moving to open the window. As soon as he did, a blast of icy wind slapped his face. It was like a splash of cold water and his mind cleared a little.

"*BLUE! WHAT THE HELL? YOU SHOULDN'T BE HERE!*"

"*WOULD YOU PLEASE SHUT UP AND GET OUT OF THE WAY!*"

Blue slipped in the window as silently as only she could, even though her whole body was shaking. She plopped on the floor and hugged her knees, shivering uncontrollably. Will quickly closed the window but even that small blast sent a shiver down his back. He stared down at her in the darkness, barely able to make out her familiar form. It had been so long since the last time this had happened. A little stirring of happiness started to swell inside him somewhere.

"*Let me get you a blanket,*" he voxed.

He dragged his comforter off his bed and started to tuck it around her.

"*A body would warm me faster,*" she voxed, her teeth chattering.

He crouched down next to her and pulled the comforter around them both. She leaned into him, her shivering vibrating up and down his side. He put his arm around her and felt the cold seeping through his pajamas. He realized he was already quite warm, and the coolness actually felt good. Her shivering slowed bit-by-bit until it finally stopped, and she let out a sigh.

"*Thanks. That's better. I can't believe how cold it is. I thought I was wearing plenty.*"

"*You are crazy, you know that? Why in hell would you risk this?*"

She looked at him intently. "*Where are you?*"

"*What?*"

"*Where are you?*"

"*I'm right here. You are looking at me!*"

"*No, I mean where ARE you? Are you in a dark place?*"

God. Will realized he wasn't. He was in the real world right now. He had set aside the nightmare. For the moment.

"*No, I'm okay right now. How . . . ?*"

"*I've been there, all right? Let's leave it at that.*"

"*You've been where?*" he asked.

Blue turned and sat so she was facing Will. "*Tell me what happened. Everything.*"

He suddenly felt uncomfortable. "*I just told you, I'm all right now.*"

"*You won't be later. Tell me. Now.*"

Will didn't want to tell her. He didn't want to start that loop again. It stopped the minute she showed up and now she was asking him to start it up again? "I DON'T WANT TO TELL YOU. IT'S NOT SOMETHING THAT ANYONE WOULD WANT TO HEAR. IT'S NOT SOMETHING YOU SHOULD HEAR."

Blue's face didn't change. It wasn't angry, or sad, or judgmental. It was . . . resolute.

"I'M DETACHED," she voxed.

"WHAT? WHAT DO YOU MEAN, YOU'RE DETACHED?"

"IT MEANS THAT IT WON'T AFFECT ME. IT'S YOUR EXPERIENCE, NOT MINE."

"YOU SOUND LIKE MY MOTHER."

"HMM," was all she voxed in reply, but her gaze was unrelenting.

Will sighed and leaned his head back against the wall. He wanted to tell her, knew he should, yet even as he thought about it a knot of anxiety wrenched his gut. What was wrong with him? He stared at the dim outlines of the items that formed his room. It was familiar, yet not familiar. In the darkness of the pale moonlit night, the colors were washed out—his walls were gray, his sheets were gray, his dresser was gray. The posters on his wall were so dim he couldn't tell what they were posters of anymore. Nothing seemed right or normal anymore. The only thing that seemed right was the girl sitting across from him. Then as he watched, everything receded into darkness as a cloud passed across the moon.

If he didn't do anything, the movie was going to start again. He looked into Blue's steady eyes instead.

"I TRIED TO TACKLE HIM BEFORE THE GUN WENT OFF. I WAS TOO LATE. WE BOTH FELL TO THE FLOOR. AND I SAW HIM . . . SAW HIS . . . HIS BODY. IT DIDN'T DIE WHEN HE DID. IT KEPT MOVING. HIS MOUTH OPENED AND CLOSED LIKE HE WAS TRYING TO TALK. HIS HANDS CLENCHED AND UNCLENCHED. IT WAS SURREAL. I DIDN'T KNOW WHAT I WAS LOOKING AT. I COULDN'T HEAR ANYTHING. MY HEAD WAS RINGING FROM THE GUN, IT WAS LIKE MY HEAD EXPLODED. IT DIDN'T SEEM REAL. BUT IT WAS REAL. HIS HEAD...HIS HAIR WAS MATTED WITH BLOOD AND IT MUST HAVE BEEN BITS OF BONE AND BRAIN AND..." he found he was having trouble continuing, "AND THERE WERE OTHER PEOPLE, ON THE FLOOR, IN POOLS

OF BLOOD..." He couldn't go on. His eyes were streaming uncontrol- lably. It felt like rivers down his face. His whole body convulsed in sobs. He felt her arms surround him, her head against his shoulder. He held her and it felt like he would fall apart if he let go.

They held each other for a long time.

Slowly, gradually, he got control of himself again. He let a breath of air in and back out quickly and then released her. She leaned back.

"*I'M SORRY. I REALLY DIDN'T MEAN TO FALL APART LIKE THAT.*"

"*YOU NEEDED TO FALL APART LIKE THAT. THERE'S NO SHAME IN IT.*"

He suddenly felt exhausted. "I need to lie down," he whispered.

She moved over and let him slide down to the floor. He felt a pillow slipping under his head and then a blanket being pulled up and over them both. He sensed her head laying on the pillow next to his. He opened his eyes. The moon must have peeked through the clouds again because her features were now illuminated by a faint light. They seemed softer than he had ever seen them. And closer. He could see the detail of her iris, the very faint red outline that only their kind had. The deeply textured folds around her wide pupils.

"*YOU CAN'T STAY. YOU'LL GET IN DEEP TROUBLE.*"

"*I CAN STAY FOR A WHILE.*"

It's what he wanted her to say even though he knew he shouldn't.

"*OKAY. JUST A LITTLE WHILE.*"

He reached up and stroked her cheek, very gently. She closed her eyes. Her face relaxed. He tried to figure out what her expres- sion was. He finally decided it looked like relief. He wondered what his expression was like right now. He closed his eyes. It felt like relief, too.


**Saturday, 5:20 am**


Helen Asbury sat on the edge of her bed shaking her head

slowly. She was so tired of sleepless nights. She'd given up on the useless doctors who prescribed this and that to help her sleep. Not only did they not work, they made her sick in one way or another. A whole shelf full of sleep meds and it was all a waste. Money thrown away. At least it was Medicare money and not out of her own pocket. And if there was one night she needed sleep, it was this one. School shooting, right here in the middle of Vermont. This whole world was falling apart. There was no authority anymore. People were allowed to do whatever they wanted. Discipline was so lax kids could get guns and bring them into school and this is what happens. She'd been saying it all along, but would anyone listen? No. They sure would now.

She stood up carefully, reaching for her walker. She hated needing to have it around and she tried not to use it, but it had saved her from falling a couple of times, so she tolerated it. As she steadied herself, she noticed a movement outside her bedroom window. There was a dark shape moving. A stirring of fear troubled her for a moment but quickly subsided, replaced by curiosity. She was too old to be terrified of anything but not too old for curiosity. Some people accused her of being nosey, but they loved hearing things she discovered from being curious. She felt for her glasses on the dresser and put them on. She moved over to the window. What her eyes focused on was confirmation of what she had just been thinking and it disgusted her. No discipline, no authority in the world. There, hanging out of the window of the Woods house was the form of a girl and it appeared that she was hugging none other than Will Woods. Helen gaped in a perfect and well-practiced display of shock and indignation even though there was no one to appreciate it. She watched as the girl—it had to be that foster girl from the O'Days, she would bet her life on it—gave the boy a final hug and then dashed off into the pre-dawn darkness.

My God, maybe there are rewards to a sleepless night, she thought. The anticipation of sharing this with her circle of friends was intoxicating. She would never get to sleep now. The disgrace of it all! She'd always suspected those O'Day kids of mischief. Just that fall she had stepped out into her front yard only to find all of her precious lawn ornaments rearranged into outrageous positions. She had called the police and they came, and they appeared to listen politely, but she could tell they could care less. She suspected that they even found it amusing, though they wouldn't say as much. They had taken down all her information but never got back to her with any suspects. It was that new orphan girl for sure. She was suspicious of her from day one—with her dark hair and shifty eyes and sneaky look on her face. She was a bad influence on Will Woods, too, no doubt about it, especially after what she saw tonight. It was terrible. Will used to be such a nice, polite boy. Never any trouble at all, but now look at him. Letting that little snippet into his room at night? She probably even charmed him into helping in the lawn ornament caper. The little vandal.

She was almost giddy with excitement from the discovery of this delicious scandal. She even thought about calling the police right then and there and reporting it as a cat burglar at the Woods house. That would serve the little demon right. But that was probably too extreme. Especially after the horrible shootings that day. The police were far too busy for something like this, and she wasn't sure they'd take her seriously, anyway. No, she had several hours to think about what she should do. Plenty of time to give thoughtful consideration to exactly the proper action to take. And to help put her in the right frame of mind, she decided she needed a cup of tea.

### Saturday, 5:35 am

Blue had finally warmed up after dashing back to her house, slipping back in through the kitchen door, quietly tip-toeing up the back stairs, and up the third-floor stairs to her attic nest. This was one time when she was thankful for having the hottest room in the house. As she snuggled in her down comforter cocoon, she peeked out at the bare branches outside her window, tinged with a silver frosty outline in the dim moonlight. They didn't look real, they looked like visions. Visions are what were on her mind. She hadn't told Will.

She saw what he saw.

It was just like when she saw Bronco's father pushing his brother down the stairs in a drunken rage, his brother's body in a broken bundle at the bottom. And Bronco's revenge. This time it was watching Jordy's body writhing in its death throes. Participatio visio. How many visions like this were going to get added to her library? She didn't know. She felt like she already had too many of her own. She hardly needed the addition of other people's nightmares. Dr. Woods said sharing wouldn't burden the listener because they are detached. But she was not completely detached from Jordy. She was part of his story.

And yet, it was true, she didn't feel burdened, in fact just the opposite. The euphoria she felt with Will opening up and seeing the relief on his face after getting his story out had been intoxicating. The joy of lying with someone you cared about and comforting them stayed with her even as she hurried home through the bitterly cold pre-dawn winter landscape.

The guilt was still there, though. She couldn't run from all of it. In spite of Dr. Woods wisdom, she knew she could have made a difference. She could have gone after Jordy the other day as he ran out of school. She could have said something to Dr. Woods at one of her sessions. One simple unselfish step on her part could have changed the whole course of events. That was how she translated what Jordy's lips were mouthing in their last jawing moments. "Just one act of sympathy could have saved me, could have saved them..."

Aaugh! Fucking guilt. It infused her whole body with a sudden flush of sweat and heat. She kicked off the comforter and stared at her slanted ceiling. She closed her eyes. Think something positive, think something positive, she told herself. Remember the look on Will's face. Go back to that. Remember his face. Remember the touch of his fingers. Remember the softness of the pillow and the warmth radiating from him. Forget everything else. Forget everything. Think about nothing. Just breathe and remember his face.

Just as Will's body had warmed her up when she was freezing, these thoughts of him cooled down her guilt. She pulled her comforter back up, snuggled down into it and kept those happy thoughts going. As the slowly brightening dawn eased the last lingering darkness out of the sky, Blue eased into a deep dreamless sleep, unaware that this would be the last peaceful sleep she would have for a long time.

25

# HARRIS

**Saturday, 8:43 am, New York City**

Detective Rodney James studied the front page headline, "Five Dead in Vermont School Shooting." Below the headline was a dramatic black and white photo of a policeman cautiously approaching the corner of a brick building. His back was to the camera and his rifle was in shooting position. The image caught him in a stance that captured that moment of surprise and indecision that made you long to know what came next. The cause of his surprise was a schoolgirl rounding the corner at a full run, her image frozen by the camera with her body levitated in mid-stride, both feet floating above the snow covered ground, her face a portrait of surprise and intensity framed by a shock of dark hair splayed in a way that made you wonder if it was her speed or surprise that caused its disarray.

"That's a very dramatic photo. Iconic." Harris was sitting in a big easy chair in a very cramped and cluttered living room. It was the sort of living room that Rodney imagined Sherlock Holmes would have had. He almost expected Harris to be holding a pipe in his hand as he gestured toward the New York Times sitting in his lap.

"Fairly ironic that it happens to be a picture of our friend, Ms. DuBois. Again."

"Yes, ironic and also troubling," said Rodney. "Our other friend, Babineau, probably has this same paper on his lap this very moment."

"From what I know of Babineau, he read it long ago. He's an early riser." Harris took a sip from a large mug. The steam rising from the mug created a patch of gray fog on his glasses. The sight of it triggered a surge of longing in Rodney, a longing for the second cup of coffee he skipped in order to get over to Harris's apartment.

"You know Babineau better than me," said Rodney. "Do you think this raises the threat level? Should we be concerned about the girl?'

"Short answer: Yes," said Harris. "How big a threat? Well let's go over it from what we know and then go over it from Babineau's point of view. We know that the girl's birth certificate—Blue DuBois' birth certificate—states "unknown" for the parents and the U.S. Marshalls aren't giving you any hint on whether or not they were involved in fabricating this birth certificate."

"That's right. And they out-and-out denied fabricating the death certificate for Blue Stanton. So we're left with no hard connection between Blue DuBois and Blue Stanton except coincidental. WITSEC wouldn't even answer whether or not Blue Stanton had a younger sister. If there was one, she would have been born after the family was already in witness protection for a couple of years. The way I see it, the only way forward now is to 1) determine that the death certificate was faked and if so, by who, 2) determine when and how Blue DuBois' birth certificate and social security number were generated. Of course, we could save a lot of work if we could question the girl herself. If she just out and out said she was Blue Stanton, that would at very least be enough to elevate this case."

"And no one has asked her," said Harris.

"And she has never volunteered anything," said Rodney. "At the request of the girl's psychiatrist we've been asked not to push the question. The name Stanton doesn't appear in any of her records that we've examined so far. And after this," Rodney gestured at the paper, "I think we might want to back way off for a while. All we have is coincidental name and age connections, crickets from WITSEC, and some unanswered questions about this girl's background. Westbury PD and the Vermont State Police are way over their heads with this school massacre. We've really got nothing solid to re-open this case with. Even if we did, and even if this girl, by some long shot, is Blue Stanton, should we even be putting her at risk? I mean look at that photo. It's gone viral, for sure. It's a news orgasm. If the press got wind that she was a person of interest in an investigation, the chance of a leak is almost assured, and they would run wild with it."

Harris didn't answer right away. He looked thoughtfully out the window. After a minute he turned to Rodney and stared at him, his finger pensively tapping his lips. Rodney looked back calmly and steadily but inside he was starting to squirm. Harris was *the* guy. He set the standard in the department, and here Rodney was, second-guessing him.

Harris finally spoke. "Both families died in a home fire, correct?"

"The bodies of some of the victims were in their burned out homes, yes, but with the Stantons, as you know, there was evidence of blunt trauma on the mother and undeniably a gunshot to the head in the father. It was either murder or murder suicide. Never determined. The two girls were found in the greenhouse that was attached to the house. One was transported to a local hospital where she was declared dead and the other was flown to the burn unit in Syracuse where she died the same night. As for Blue DuBois' family, the 'unknowns,' all we have is hearsay that they were killed in a home fire. Her foster records make mention of it but have no names or any other information about the fire. Whoever created this identity left a lot of blanks, either sloppy or intential. It smacks of black market identity. Still, it is authenticated by the hospital and would probably serve Blue through her lifetime."

Harris reverted to his thoughtful pose, staring out the window. Rodney took the time to let his mind re-visit everything that had been said to that point. Harris was being persistent while Rodney was feeling like they should back off. It wasn't normal for him to back off, it was usually the other way around—others had to rescue him from his own hyper-focused obsessiveness. This case wasn't working on him that way, and it bothered him that he didn't know why.

Harris cleared his throat and then looked at Rodney. "You are right that we should reconsider how we approach this case given this new twist," he gestured at the paper, "however, I believe that this means we should do the opposite of backing off. I feel we should redouble our efforts, and this is why." He paused as he watched Rodney's eyebrow rise in surprise. He then turned back to the window but kept talking, "We haven't fully discussed the reason I brought this case up in the first place, and that is the name DuBois. Blue Stanton's actual birth name, as you know, is Belle Amélie DuBois. I think that is one of the loveliest names I have ever heard." He paused again before going on. "You have to remember that the name DuBois is how Babineau knew the family. That name is the trigger word in his brain. If he sees or hears that name, it instantly brings the Gambrel sting to mind. He lost everything—his entire growing operation, a lot of his cash, and unfortunately, his brother and nephew. But he slipped through without a conviction because, well, he is wily. He's a survivor. He knows how to obfuscate, leaving nothing tangible to tie him to any of the growing operation or the Stanton deaths. It took him a while to come back, but he has and maybe in a worse way. Instead of marijuana, he's now manufacturing a synthetic opioid—fentanyl. Unfortunately, his resources are built back up and he hates the name DuBois. Now, this very morning, he sees the same paper we have in our laps and he spots the name DuBois. What do you think is going through his mind?"

Rodney thought for a moment. He could see where Harris was going with this, but he decided to play devil's advocate. "I can see how he would be sensitive of that name, but in his mind, the DuBois family, the Stantons, are five years dead. He would just look at this reminder of the name with a sense of satisfaction, don't you think?"

Harris leaned forward in his chair for the first time in the meeting. "Initially I think he would, but there are a couple of things that you may not be aware of that would set off red flags in his head. First, is this: You didn't know the DuBois family. I got to know them quite well. André, the father, I liked very much. He was honorable, honest, but got himself into a nasty business with Babineau. His wife, Amélie Elizabeth DuBois, was beautiful and kind and strong." Harris picked up the newspaper and held it in front of him, pointing at the picture. "This girl is a dead-ringer for Amélie DuBois."

Rodney stared at the picture. He could see the resemblance to some of the file photos they had on the Stantons, but he never would have made the connection. Photos aren't always a good substitute for real life. "Okay, this is news to me. I can see how that would get his attention. But again, the Stantons are dead, This girl's name is Blue. Similar to 'Belle' I suppose, but still just coincidence. And why would anyone expose Blue by changing her name *back* to DuBois?"

"That is a very good question. In the end, that could be a very intriguing aspect to this case. At this point, I have no idea how that might have happened, but that brings me to my second point. André and Amélie were as smitten as any new parents I knew with their daughter, Belle, and like any doting parents they had a pet name for their beautiful girl. I'm sure Babineau knew of this pet name." Harris paused for an extra-long time. Rodney sensed a crux was coming and he was expected to add to the drama by begging for the answer. He had to admit, Harris had gotten to his obsessive side, so he played along.

"And the pet name was ... ?"

"Little Bluebell."

Jesus, Rodney thought. Bluebell. Blue ... Belle DuBois.

"There's more you should know about Theo Babineau. He is kind of an old-school thug. He is proud of the fact that his illegal drugs are made in America and not imported. He insists on loyalty from all his employees, and he is very rewarding to those who are loyal and ruthless to those who break that loyalty. Add to that his meticulous practice of a mob-type of accounting and you get a person who sees that DuBois, who was disloyal to him in the worst way possible, may have a survivor. And from what I know of Blue DuBois, she sounds like she is a very capable survivor. He would want to balance that account."

"I'm not sure I'm following," said Rodney.

"What I mean is that once the DuBois family was dead, Babineau felt that the account was closed because their deaths were full payment for their disloyalty, the death of his brother and nephew, and the loss of his growing operation. Like I said, this is a mob-type of accounting. He thought no more about them after that. That is, until the name DuBois bubbled up again in the news. To him, the fact that she may not have died represents a potential imbalance in the account. She should be dead and she's not. People like Theo are sociopathic—they don't see human life as being any different than money. If they feel they're owed money, they pursue getting that money. If they feel they're owed life, they pursue getting that life. And there is no statute of limitations in their mind. Add to that the fact that she could be an eyewitness that leads back to him and you can see how seriously he takes this."

"And he's not bound by law and protocol like we are," said Rodney. "So are you suggesting that he already has enough evidence from his perspective to take action?"

"I am more than suggesting it. I am certain of it. The minute I saw that picture, I didn't see Belle DuBois, I saw Amélie DuBois. I am certain he did, too."

"Shit. And with the police distracted in Westbury . . ."

"Let's just say I wouldn't waste any time. Like I said, Babineau is an early riser."

Rodney grabbed his jacket and stood up. At the same time he pulled out his phone. At minimum he had to alert Chief Hannah as soon as possible. That was the only thing he knew for certain, everything else he was going to have to figure out on the fly.

**26**

---

# OLD BUSINESS

**Saturday, 8:45 am, New York City**

The starkly trimmed narrow casement window of the eleventh-floor office window looked out over Central Park West to a view of Strawberry Fields, Central Park Lake, and Bethesda Fountains. Theo Babineau's chair was rotated away from the desk so that the morning sun streamed in over his shoulder and illuminated the crisp newsprint of the New York Times that sat in his lap. What he had just read was troubling, but only in a routine way. He had gotten so used to old problems popping up in a new way that this one was not unexpected, but it was annoying. It was one of a long line of not unexpected problems—a sea of old business that lay dormant but occasionally coughed up a threat that had to be dealt with. It was sort of like the old arcade game his kids had liked so much—whack-a-mole, or whack-a-squirrel, or something like that. The critters would stick their heads up out of a hole randomly and you whacked them with a mallet before they disappeared again. He was getting too old for whacking, but it had to be dealt with. The security of his business depended on it and his family depended on the business.

He shouted to the outer office. "Hey Jim, I need someone to listen to an old man think out loud."

A tall, lean man slipped promptly and smoothly into the room. His tailored gray suit gracefully adorned an obviously muscular frame. He lowered himself into the chair across from the desk and sat quietly but attentively. He didn't say a word. He didn't have to. This was a practiced drill, and he knew his role well. His boss needed to think out a plan of action to solve a problem, and Jim was there ready to listen and give his shrewd observations.

Babineau tapped the paper. "You remember Stanton?"

"Stanton. About four or five years ago, upstate. You sent El Segador[1]."

"Yeah, El Segador. He was a dependable man. Not a lot like him anymore."

Jim sat silently, apparently nothing to add.

"Did you read this article?" He held up the paper, pointing to the second headline on the front page. Jim leaned over for a closer look. The headline read: "Five Dead in Vermont School Shooting." Below the headline was a dramatic photo that looked like it belonged in a book of all-time great journalism photos.

"The school shooting? Yeah. It's a shame. That's a pretty amazing picture though."

Babineau felt one eyebrow rise. He wasn't used to Jim expressing himself quite so candidly. "It *is* a shame. Nothing but a waste of life. I blame the parents of the shooter. They are the ones that should go to jail. And yeah," he tapped the picture, "that is a damn good picture. Pulitzer Prize worthy if you ask me." He put the paper down and looked at Jim. "That's not the only thing that interests me about this article, though. One of the things that interests me is the town where it happened. Westbury, Vermont."

"Westbury. Sounds familiar."

"Think back a few months."

"Kidnapping?"

"That's right. Drug dealer caught this girl trying to videotape a deal and take it to the cops. He caught her and held her for a while until some kid pulled off a rescue."

"Same town. Westbury, Vermont?" asked Jim.

"Yeah, I wouldn't have noticed it except for another thing that interests me about this. I don't suppose you remember the name of the girl that was kidnapped."

Jim paused a moment and then gave his head a slight shake.

"Her name was Blue DuBois," said Babineau. "Same girl that is in this picture."

"DuBois. That was the real name of the Stantons, right?"

"Right. Now their kid's witness protection name was Blue Stanton, but her real name was Belle DuBois. Now supposedly, Belle DuBois aka Blue Stanton passed away along with her parents."

"Part of the job of El Segador?"

"That's right. He claimed he got the girl and her sister along with the parents, which is what I was paying him for, and the press releases afterward backed him up. Entire family killed in a house fire. Now you are going to think I am a crazy old man when I tell you a theory, but hear me out. The name 'Blue' doesn't grow on trees unless you are a hound dog, and neither does DuBois, unless you're Canadian."

"You're thinking Blue DuBois could be Belle Dubois, even though Belle DuBois is supposed to be dead?" asked Jim.

"I told you that you would think I was a crazy old man, but," Babineau tapped the newspaper photo, "the girl in this picture looks the right age and she looks an awful lot like the mother."

Jim sat silent for a while, which comforted Babineau, because it meant that Jim was doing some serious consideration. Finally he spoke. "Boss, you have uncanny instincts, so I'll buy that there is a possibility that Belle DuBois wasn't killed and that this girl," he gestured toward the paper, "could be Belle DuBois. If so, that would make her an orphan."

"Exactly. Guess what? This kid is with a foster family. O'Day is the name of the family. Westbury, Vermont," said Babineau.

Jim was quiet again. Babineau was patient, but he knew what the next question would be.

"Assuming this is true, why do we care about this girl? Is she a potential threat?"

"Fair question. It's possible she could identify El Segador and then El Segador could lead police back to me, but El Segador is dead. So no real worries there." Jim raised an eyebrow. Apparently, he didn't know El Segador was dead.

"So she's not really a threat then," said Jim.

Babineau tapped his chin thoughtfully and said, "That is a reasonable assessment from your point of view. However there are a couple of things that make me uncomfortable. The first is that she represents unfinished business. The second is this. This girl got kidnapped last summer because she was trying to catch this guy, Bronco. She was trying to videotape a drug deal and take it to the police. Why would this girl, who is, what, fourteen? Why would this girl go out and try and catch a drug dealer? Think about it. A kid that age—they should be thinking about boys, and school, and worrying about what clothes are in style, and make-up, and hair." He stopped, leaned over in his chair, and looked intently at Jim. "Kids don't just go out and risk their lives to trap a dangerous man. The only kids that do stuff like that are ones that are obsessed. Driven. On a mission."

"Vengeance."

"Jim," he said, "that's why I pay you as much as I do. You know how people work. Let me ask you something. Have you been following this other story at all?" He picked up the paper, turned it to the "International" section, and pointed to an article.

Jim read the headline out loud, "Dutch Teen on Last Leg of Circumnavigation."

"You follow that at all?"

"No."

"This girl is trying to be the youngest person to circumnavigate the globe solo. In a sailboat. All alone. You wanna guess how old she is?"

"Eighteen?"

"Guess again," said Babineau.

Jim paused for a moment.

"Fourteen."

"Bingo. She started when she was fourteen. Fourteen. And now, two years later, she's almost done it. The youngest person to circumnavigate the earth alone on a sailboat. Unbelievable. And get this, she wanted to start when she was thirteen, but the fucking socialist Dutch government wouldn't let her. She had to fight like hell in court for a whole year before they finally gave up and let her go. She was obsessed. She was on a mission. And on top of that, she grew into adulthood all alone on that boat. On the ocean. Everyone thought she was crazy. They thought her parents were irresponsible. They said she was going to drown. And yet here she is just a month away from doing it. I think her parents deserve a fucking medal."

"Impressive!" said Jim.

"Very impressive, but I never doubted it. She is going to make it and all those government asses are going to look like fools. You know people just don't understand what kids that age are capable of. Instead of letting them try, the government squashes it, just like they try and squash everything. But those are the years that you are free and healthy and full of energy. Those are the years you can do amazing things. You believe you can do anything and don't know any better, so you just go ahead and do it. Like avenge the death of your family."

"You really think this DuBois girl, by nailing a random drug dealer, is avenging her family's death?"

"Possibly. It's symbolic. It's a substitute. Say you don't know who killed your family, so you lash out at the next closest thing. Anyone who is involved in the drug trade. They are symbols. They're substitutes. If you had a chance at the real deal, you'd go for that."

"You think this girl is really a threat? Don't you think that's a stretch?"

"That is a fair and intelligent question. So I'll ask you. Just think about it for a minute before you answer. Imagine that I killed your family when you were ten because your father double-crossed me and killed members of my family. You were left alive. Think back to when you were fourteen and imagine you are out on the street. No real family, just a bunch of foster families. You're a loner. You've gotten tough. But you remember your family and what got taken away." He leaned over again and looked Jim in the eye. "What would you do if you recognized me on the street?"

Jim looked straight back at him and said without hesitation, "You would be dead within a week."

Babineau smiled slowly. "Exactly. But not if I got you first."

Jim sat back in his chair. He was silent.

"Now I am not saying I have anything against this girl possibly wanting to avenge her family. In fact, I admire it. However, like I said, she represents unfinished business. A detail that got missed on a job that was supposedly already finished."

"So you want to go after this girl?"

"Well let me ask you. Suppose you were a house painter, an honorable profession. Suppose you finished a job and got paid fairly. Suppose the customer calls you up a year later and says, hey, you missed a door jamb. What do you do? Do you tell this person tough luck? You do that and you never hear the end of it. It goes from one person to the next and pretty soon you have a reputation for missing details, and nobody wants to do business with you. No, you go over and paint the door jamb. No charge. It's just good business."

"So you want to paint the door jamb."

"Let's just say, I wouldn't miss an opportunity to paint the door jamb, if it needed painting."

Jim got up from his chair and straightened his shirt and tie. "When do you want me to go?"

Babineau laughed. "Jim, you are a gem. Let's just start by getting some information. First, we need to find out if this really is Belle DuBois aka Blue Stanton or if I'm just a paranoid crazy old man. You like Vermont this time of year? Well, you're going to find out I guess. Just take a couple of days, go up there, and find out what you can. Then we'll talk."

Jim turned and walked silently out. Babineau watched him go and marveled at how his head barely cleared the top of the door-way. Good man to have on his side. He thought about what he didn't point out to Jim, the one detail in the photo of the girl that Jim probably would have written off as a trick of light or a snowflake or a flaw in the newsprint. Babineau was probably one of the few people left on the planet that knew what it really was. He knew many cameras were sensitive to infrared. The tiny white dots in the girl's eyes weren't a trick of light. They were a silent scream.

He turned back to his window and looked out over the bleak winter landscape of Strawberry Fields. The bare branches of the dozens of varieties of trees—ash, locust, oak, beech, cherry, and even a deciduous redwood—stood starkly against the dull green of the bare, snowless ground. A few leftover dead leaves rattled in the bitter breeze. They all looked so lifeless now and yet every spring they all exploded with new energy, new brightness. These trees would outlive him. The only way he would outlive any of them was if they were struck down by lightning. Or man.

He turned back to his desk and opened the humidor. A delightful odor propelled by the opening lid hit his nose like a living breeze. It was amazing that this aroma was being produced by dry fingers of carefully rolled up lifeless leaves. And when burned, they were resurrected into a sweet fog that he swirled delectably through his cheeks and across his tongue.

He gently lifted a fresh cigar from the humidor and went through the comforting ritual of cutting and lighting it. After a first delicious puff, he picked up the paper and studied the picture of Blue DuBois for a moment. He took a second puff and then opened the paper to the picture of the teenage Dutch girl. She was standing calmly on the deck of her sailboat. The picture was a still life of a turbulent reality. The sea looked like it wanted to swallow the boat, but the boat seemed indifferent to the attempt. The face of the girl was turned upward. It was looking directly at the camera, which was clearly above the boat, probably on a helicopter, circling around her like a vulture. The look on her face was exactly the same as the look on the DuBois girl's face.

It was resolute.

27

——————

# RISING FROM THE ASHES

**Saturday, 9 am**

Will opened his eyes. It was bright outside. He didn't remember waking or dreaming so he must have slept straight through to late morning after Blue had left. Slept through. That in itself was a miracle and it was all because of Blue. If it weren't for her, he was sure he would have been tortured all night long by that image of Jordy.

He felt guilty, like he should be at least thinking about what happened—a school shooting, for God's sake, in their high school, four kids dead, one wounded, Jordy's dad killed, a teacher in critical condition. But he wasn't. All he could think about was Blue, next to him, her head on his shoulder, his arm around her, her shivering next to him, her lying next to him, her head on his pillow, her peaceful face. He wished she were there now. He could almost imagine it, her soft and warm body spooned against his back. It actually did feel warm against his back and he reached back expecting to find his spare pillow but instead felt something much firmer. When he grabbed it, it squeaked. He nearly jumped out of his skin as he shot out of bed. "Rose! Jeezum crow! You scared me half to death!"

"You scared me! What were you doing!"

"I thought you were a pillow!" "*What are you doing in here?*" He didn't really have to ask. He knew he had probably freaked everyone out yesterday as if they needed any more freaking out. That would have worried Rose. It wasn't the first time she snuggled with him when she was scared. "*Hey, are you okay?*"

She jumped out of bed and hugged him. "You're back! You big ugly brother! You scared us shitless yesterday!"

"Wow, that's gotta be an eleven on the scared scale. I don't think I've ever heard that word come out of your mouth before."

She looked up at him, "*Everyone is freaked out. Mom was gone early in the morning. They're holding counseling sessions all weekend. She told me to call her if you were still...sad.*" "But you're not! I'm glad."

"I'm better now." "*Sorry I freaked you out.*"

He sat down on the bed next to her. She looked up at him. "*Will, it's Thanksgiving! Things like this aren't supposed to happen!*"

He put his arm around her. "Hey, you. We'll get through this."

She put her arm around him. "You got better fast, I just hope everything is better that fast."

As she spoke, there was a distant knocking. It sounded like it came from the front door.

"Dad's here, he'll get it," said Rose, but they both stood up at the same time, walked to Will's door and looked down the hallway. They saw their dad open the door a crack and what they saw outside was an all too familiar scene.

"Damn. Here we go again. Reporters."

"Don't worry. Dad won't let them in," said Rose.

"I know, but..." he stopped. There was a buzzing on his dresser. He picked up his phone. It was Wu.

"Hey, Wu."

*"Dude, are you okay?"*

"Yeah, I'm better now. Sorry if I freaked everyone out."

*"Hey, everyone's freaked out about everything. I'm glad to hear you're okay. Are you really truly?"*

"Yeah, really truly. Just in time, too, we've got reporters knocking on our door."

*"Well, that's not a surprise. Have you seen it?"*

"Seen what?" He looked at Rose, puzzled.

"*What is it?*" she asked

"*Not sure yet,*" he replied.

Wu continued, *"It's on YouTube. It's gone totally viral. There's, like, twenty thousand hits on it already."*

"What!"

Rose tugged on his arm, "*What is it?*"

"*A YouTube video.*"

Rose let go of his arm and dashed toward her room.

Wu went on. *"Yeah. Apparently, Sue Etchells was trapped in the cafeteria behind a table. She used her phone camera like a periscope to see what was going on. It's real shaky but you can see everything. God damn it, Will! You are lucky to be alive! Why the hell did you just stand there? He had the gun pointed right at your head! You should have run, you asshole! I almost lost my best friend, again! Stop doing this shit, man! Stop being the damn hero, you jackass!"*

Wow. Wu was pissed. Will didn't say anything for a minute. He couldn't, his brain was totally rattled. A video. On YouTube. Wu saw it. Everyone is seeing it. What next?

*"Say something, dude! You're starting to freak me out again!"*

"Wu, I'm sorry, man. Really. I wasn't trying to be a hero. I just felt like . . . well, I knew he wasn't going to hurt me. I thought that maybe, since I was one of his only friends, I could talk him down." Just then, a scream from down the hall put an end to the conversation.

"Wu, I gotta go. I'll call you back." He ran to his sister's room where Rose was sitting on her bed with her laptop open. Tears were streaming down her face.

"*WHY DIDN'T YOU RUN! WHY DIDN'T YOU RUN! HIS GUN WAS POINTED RIGHT AT YOU!*" She ran to him and buried her face in his chest and wrapped her arms around him. She started sobbing uncontrollably.

He put his arms around her and started rocking back and forth. "I'm sorry, little Rose. I'm so sorry. It's okay now. I'm okay. We're all okay." Yeah, right, he thought to himself. What the hell comes next? God, he wished he could talk to his mom right now, but she was probably buried in her own hell dealing with the entire population of Westbury, and his dad was running interception on the phone and at the front door. There was just one other person that he could talk to and needed to talk to. He just hoped she had her cell phone turned on.

**Saturday, 9:15 am**

Blue sat in her bed and squinted at the bright view out her window. It was a beautiful morning. It was cold, but sunny and the sky was as blue and crisp as only a sky on a late-fall day in Vermont could be. It was so calm, too. Nothing was moving except the birds around the bird feeder and the squirrels trying to figure out a way to get at the bird feeder. Blue looked out and realized that for the rest of the world, to the plants and trees and animals and earth and sky, this was just another normal, quiet day. It was completely oblivious to the fact that inside a brick and marble building the day before a human bomb went off and rocked the very foundation of this once quiet, innocent little community.

She thought about the debris from that explosion that had littered down around her. Her collapsing at the news that Will was in an ambulance, Anna's insistent words, her freezing night escapade, Will's breakdown, an angry call from Miss Kendrick this morning condemning Blue's window exit. And now, the YouTube video. Wu flipped out when he saw it and she had overheard him as he totally unloaded on Will over the phone. She had to try and calm Wu down. The last thing Will needed was for his best friend to guilt trip him. As if there wasn't enough self-generated guilt floating around. But Wu had rounded on her, too, demanding how she could possibly think anything was all right. He came up to her room after and apologized, but she couldn't deny he had a point. Things weren't all right. Except for one thing. She had helped someone. For once she had taken a chance that she might be the one that could fix something instead of screw it up. A nudge from Anna and wisdom from Dr. Woods gave her the confidence to do that and so she did. And for the first time in her life, she experienced the rush of reaching out and bringing someone back from the brink, back to sanity. Lying next to him, watching him relax and fall asleep, at peace—it felt amazing. Amidst the wreckage of the past twenty-four hours, there was something to feel good about.

A flapping black shadow brought her attention back to the world outside. It was the big raven that liked to frequent the smurf-tree. He had become a familiar visitor since she first saw him at the beginning of the summer, always perched on the same branch, always perturbing the smaller birds and scattering the scolding squirrels. She admired how his black feathers with their iridescent purple shimmer formed a stark silhouette against the crisp blues and whites of the snow and sky. *"Hey, Mr. Raven. Wish I could hang out and then fly off whenever I wanted, like you. Being stuck in this insane human world is driving me crazy."* So crazy that sometimes I resort to voxing to ravens, she thought. She wondered why it felt good to do that—vox to critters. Maybe because they were better listeners than most humans. And as if on cue, a funny "kwa-koo" sound penetrated the window. She was sure it came from the raven. She stared intently at the raven and he seemed to be staring back. *"Was that you, raven?"* she voxed.

"Kwa-koo![1]"

She was so startled she nearly fell off her bed. It was as if he had responded to her. It had to have been coincidence, but before she could try voxing to him again, a different and familiar sound grabbed her attention. It was the rattle-buzz of her phone on top of the dresser. She checked the screen. It was Will. She looked back at the raven, but he was gone. She shook her head slightly and then flipped the phone open. "Hey."

"*Hey. I need to tell you something. Something I didn't tell you last night.*" Last night came back to her with a rush and settled over her like a warm blanket. "*It was Jordy. Participatio visio. It happened to me.*"

The warm feeling instantly evaporated, replaced by surprise. "Jordy?"

"*Yeah. Listen, I want to tell you about it but not over the phone and you can't come here, there are reporters banging down the door. It's that damned YouTube video. Can you and Wu meet me at Anna's?*"

She thought about Ma Beth and how upset she still was. Blue hated to leave her that way, but this was important. "We'll find a way," she replied and got up to go find Wu, still holding the phone to her ear.

"*That's great.*" He paused again. "*And, hey, um, thanks. For last night, I mean. It really . . . it was . . . well . . . you know . . .*"

"Hey, me, too," she said. "I'll see you soon."

"*Yeah. Soon.*"

She hung up, grabbed her jacket, and ran to track down Wu, the warm feeling completely restored, the jacket probably completely unnecessary.

<br>

**Saturday, 9:40 am**

<br>

"Jeez, Anna! I can't breathe!"

Will had barely stepped inside Anna's bedroom when she clamped him in a crushing bear hug.

"I don't care! I am just so happy you're okay!" When she finally released him she grabbed his shoulders and shook him, "Don't ever do this to us again! Twice in a year is too much! Even once in, *ever,* is too much!"

Will didn't know what to say. Everyone, not just Anna, *everyone* seemed deeply frightened—frightened of losing *him*. It felt a little embarrassing.

He looked around. "Why aren't Wu and Blue here yet?" It had taken a while for he and Rose to figure out how to get him out of his house unseen. In the end, he slipped out of the garage side door while Rose distracted the news crew by doing some antics in the front picture window (which involved some partial nudity and wagging of her rear end, he later found out).

"I don't know. I hope they get here soon, though. I've been driving myself crazy without anyone to talk to." *"AND I'M DYING TO FIND OUT IF BLUE WENT TO SEE HIM!"*

Damn, Will thought, I don't think she meant for me to hear that. "Hey, Anna. I have to tell you I just heard your *chiss*—your thought. Sorry, just want you to know," he said.

"Oh! Shoot." She frowned. "God, I have to get better at this, or I won't be able to keep any secrets."

"Yeah. I know, it was kinda of weird when Wu first learned about it, too. But he's really good at it now. You'll get the hang of it."

"How much did you hear?" Anna's eyes looked up at him from below a furrowed brow.

As his eyes met hers a flash of clarity hit him like a dash of cold water. "You told Blue she needed to help me, didn't you?"

Anna turned bright red, *"OH GOD! SHE DID! SHE MUST HAVE TOLD HIM!"* Her hands went up to her mouth, "Oh no, I did it again didn't I?"

Will didn't answer, he was trying to figure out what had just happened. His intuition of Anna's complicity with Blue had the same certainty that convinced him that Jordy wasn't going to hurt him.

"Will, you're looking freaky again, talk to me." Anna had seized both his shoulders again and he was sure she was going to start shaking him but before she could, they heard a giant clumping noise on the stairs followed by Wu bursting into the room. He stood in the doorway, his jacket steaming as he flung down a newspaper.

"You are not going to believe this! Look at the front page." He stripped off his jacket as Blue slipped into the room behind him and slumped onto the floor. "Jeez, Will, now I know what it was like with the reporters and all that crap. They're calling our house now and there's a news truck parked outside."

Anna gasped as she stared at the headline with the dramatic picture below it. "Omigod, Blue! When did this happen?" She handed the paper to Will.

It was Wu that answered. "It was Paula Derkins, that snarky friend of Wilma Watkins. I just got a text from Fred Willard. They were barricaded in a classroom with Blue and Miss Kendrick. Blue jumped out the window instead of staying in the room. Miss Kendrick was apparently ripshit about it but told everyone to keep mum. Of course, Paula blabbed to some reporter and now this picture is everywhere, and reporters are beating down our door. Fortunately," he pointed a thumb at Blue, "we were able to slip out unnoticed."

Will stared at the picture. It was so Blue. It seemed like every aspect of her fierce, intense nature was captured in detail. And the policeman in the image seemed completely transfixed by her. It was an amazing picture. He glanced at Blue. Her head was down. It was clear that she did not think it was so amazing.

"This picture is sure to go viral along with that video," said Wu. "It's probably on every front page by now."

"It's like August all over again," said Anna, "only on steroids."

"Except we're not the victims this time," said Will.

"*You* almost were! And I'm still pissed at you," said Wu as he sat on Anna's bed.

"I know, I know," said Will shaking his head. He was ready to apologize again but a glance at Blue changed his mind. She was still looking down but her words from last night echoed in his head. *Tell me, don't keep it inside.* "But it wasn't just that I *thought* he wasn't going to hurt me, I *knew* it."

Blue looked up, suddenly more attentive.

"Will, don't give us that crap," said Wu. "Are you saying Jordy leaked to you 'don't worry, Will, I'm not going to hurt you?' And even if he did, you believed him?"

Anna put her hand on Wu's shoulder to calm him down. "Is it because of the participle beesio or whatever it was you called it?"

"You mean 'participatio visio,' or 'visio' for short," he said, "and, no, I don't think so. I'm still trying to figure it out. I mean it's sort of like intuition—gut-feel—you know? Only really convincing gut-feel."

"What? Visio? Intuition? What the hell are you talking about?" asked Wu.

"Visio is when you can actually see images that another person is thinking." Will looked over at Blue who was staring at him with creased brow. "*Don't worry, I won't tell them about your visio.*"

"What? You're saying that you can hear my thoughts *and* see them? Great. Thanks for not telling me about that!" Wu was getting even more agitated.

"No, No! Wu, I haven't seen anything of yours, or anyone's until Jordy. It's never happened to me before. My dad said it only happens when the conditions are right. You have to be hyper-alert like when you get surprised or shocked."

"Like when you have a gun pointed at your face," said Anna.

"Exactly. He thinks endorphins have something to do with it. It's like it turbocharges all your senses."

"So . . . what did you see?" asked Anna.

Will took a deep breath. He felt a ghost of the panic from last night fluttering in his gut. He didn't want that to start again. He looked at Blue.

"*Start talking and that feeling will go away,*" she voxed.

He nodded and took her advice.

"It was weird. Of course. I mean just imagine having a very vivid dream when you are fully awake. Only this wasn't like any dream I've had. It was like dozens of dreams all piled on top of each other, like a pile of video clips all playing at the same time. At first, I thought it was *my* life passing before my eyes. I mean, the barrel of the gun was right *there*. But then I realized the clips—they weren't mine. They were all Jordy's. It was *his* life passing before his eyes."

Blue's jaw dropped.

"Jesus." said Wu.

Anna just shook her head slowly as she looked down at her hands.

It was dead silent in the room for a full minute when Blue broke it. "Can you remember the clips?"

"There were only a few I can remember clearly. One of them was the last one—the one where he shot his dad."

Anna gasped.

"The thing was, not only did I see it, I could *feel* how Jordy felt as he pulled the trigger. It was elation. He loathed his dad. I am sure he was abused by him." He stopped and stared at the floor.

"And shooting his dad was the only way to stop it," said Anna.

"Yeah, that's what it felt like," said Will.

"How can you say how he felt?" asked Wu. "It doesn't seem possible. I mean, vox itself is just nuts, but visions? Visions and feelings? Maybe this is like one of those synthesized memories."

Will shook his head, "I don't know. I don't think so"

"It's real," said Blue. They all turned to look at her. "What Will said, it's real. The feelings, the intuition, it's called *veraque*[2]. It's like empathy and truth at the same time. Dr. Woods told me about it. Some vox are really good at it. Dr. Woods is the best, better than anyone. And I should know." She looked at Will. "*And you are like your mom.*"

Will looked back, stunned, "*What? She calls this veraque? How come she never told me? I've never heard that word before.*"

Blue's face clearly indicated that she was as surprised as he was. And he could feel it.

"So, okay, say I buy all of this, which is pretty difficult," said Wu. "What other 'clips' did you see. Feel. Whatever?"

"Well," Will stopped. There was another scene he remembered clearly, he did not want to bring up. He dodged the question. "Nothing I really recognized—maybe his relatives, I don't know." Despite his best effort, he stole a glance at Blue.

"*IT WAS ME, WASN'T IT?*" she voxed.

Damn it, he thought. Does she have this intuition now, too?

"*SHIT.*" She turned away.

"*HEY!*" he voxed. "*<CLICK, CLICK, CLICK>.*" She looked back at him. "*HEY, DON'T DO THAT. YOU'RE NOT TO BLAME. I'LL TELL YOU EXACTLY WHAT I SAW, JUST NOT HERE, NOT NOW.*" She rolled her eyes and looked away.

Anna leaked again. "*OH, THEY'RE VOXING AGAIN. BLUE DOESN'T LOOK HAPPY.*"

Wu looked at each of them in frustration. "Would you guys stop doing that! I feel like I'm in the dark here! What's going on?"

"I'm pretty sure Jordy had a crush on me," muttered Blue, "and I didn't exactly encourage it. I wasn't always exactly . . . kind."

"*OH NO, AND JORDY SAW THAT WILL AND BLUE ARE IN LOVE, FOR SURE . . .*" Anna's *chiss* rang out loud and clear. She clapped her hand to her mouth with a smack, and then as an afterthought moved it over her eyes. "Oh God, I'm so sorry! I am really sucking at this!"

Will's ears blazed. He stared at Anna and then he swung around to Blue. Her face was wide eyed with panic, her cheeks reflecting the same scarlet hue that he was sure his ears were. Her eyes found his, and then he knew. Of course he knew. And now he knew she knew, too.

Blue leaped up, grabbed her jacket and headed for the door.

"Wait!" said Will. He jumped up and followed her.

Wu sat in stunned silence and then started hammering the bed with his hand. "What. Is. Going. On!" He started to get up, but Anna restrained him with a hand on his shoulder.

"Let them go," she said. "I'll explain. I think I know what's going on, and I think they need to talk."

"That's the whole problem, they've been 'talking' the whole time only we can't hear them. This whole vox thing is starting to irritate the crap out of me. I wish I never knew about it."

"Hey, Mr. Ben Wu. We'll figure this out together. They're our *friends*. We all need each other more than ever right now." She gave him a kiss on the cheek.

"Hey, don't do that. It's not fair," said Wu. "I want to be angry right now."

Anna laughed and mussed his hair. But her laugh was tempered by an extra dose of gravity, a gravity that seemed to be weighing down the entire world.

---

"Dammit, Blue, would you please slow down! Let's talk about this." Will tried to keep pace with her but the humps and heaves in the narrow sidewalk along with Blue's frantic pace wouldn't let them walk side-by-side. She stopped suddenly and looked at him, her face the perfect expression of confusion. She looked at him steadily but was completely silent. Will looked steadily back.

"*It's not your fault. You were kind to Jordy. You can't help that he had a crush on you,*" he voxed. "*It was entirely his dad. I could feel it. His dad crushed him.*"

Blue kept staring at him, the same strange look on her face. She started shaking her head, and then turned and took off again, at an even faster pace.

Will rolled his eyes and then ran to catch up to her. "C'mon, Blue, talk to me. Tell me what is bugging you. That was what you told me to do last night and I did, and you were right."

Blue stopped suddenly again, only looking straight ahead this time. Will followed her gaze to where there were three people standing in front of the O'Day house next to two cars emblazoned with the names of local news outlets.

"Oh shit," he said, just as Blue slammed into him sideways. Will wasn't ready for it and he stumbled and fell, landing on his side, and Blue, clearly not expecting Will to fall, tripped over his legs. He held up a hand to cushion her fall as she landed on top of him. Will saw that she had meant to push him behind a hedge that blocked them from the view of the news people. She had succeeded, they were blocked, but now he and Blue were flat on the ground. He turned to her and voxed, "WOW, THAT WAS CLOSE." Her face was almost touching his, so close that her eyes were about all he could see, eyes with an iris that was a vox-textured landscape, full of contrast and color, her pupil a deep well in the center, a well that seemed to drill into another universe. "HEY, ARE YOU O—"

Her lips suddenly pressed against his. They were soft and warm and alive, their caress sending waves of elation rippling down his skin. His lips responded with a tenderness he didn't even know they were capable of. And then there was nothing else in the world but the feeling of her body pressing down on him, her hair brushing over his face, the warmth of her face against his, her breath flowing over his cheeks like a summer wind. And her lips, her soft, warm lips.

She pushed up with a gasp, and he opened his eyes to see hers wide with amazement. At that instant, a wave of adrenaline washed across him with such heat he could feel every inch of contact with her. And more than that, he could feel his body through her. Their lips collided again in the softest of crashes and Will became lost in a warm ecstasy he never knew existed. They finally collapsed side by side breathing fast, steam rising from them like a runaway train. He couldn't take his eyes away from hers. He didn't want to lose the sensation of her sensations blended with his. It was almost more than he could stand.

A shout from down the block abruptly ended the moment. He and Blue jerked upright simultaneously. Will peaked around the shrub. Nate was on the sidewalk in front of the O'Day house and trying to move through the reporters and get to the street, but it looked like they were filming and peppering him with questions.

"We should get back to Anna's," whispered Blue.

"Yeah," he replied and turned to her. "*Why is it we never seem to get a break?*"

She answered by hugging him tightly. She whispered to him, her warm breath caressing his ear, "This *is* a break." The voices down the block got suddenly louder. "Let's go!" she said. She jumped up and pulled him off the ground. She gave him one last warm kiss, and then sprang off like a gazelle back the way they came. He chased her all the way to Anna's, not trying to catch up. He didn't want to stop watching her sinuous form as it pranced gracefully down the convoluted sidewalk, her dark hair bouncing and flinging about like a spirit set free.

### Saturday, 9:41 am, Lake Placid, NY

Bronco took a cautious sip from the chipped ceramic coffee cup. He needn't have been cautious. It was barely lukewarm, not even on the hot side of lukewarm. The tepid liquid rolled across his tongue and sent his bitterness receptors off the chart. He barely suppressed a gag as he choked it down. He glanced over at the waitress and wasn't surprised to see the stink-eye. The pot she was holding was nearly empty and stained dark brown—obviously the pot reserved in the kitchen to send a message to irritating customers. He got the message, but he wasn't going to give her the satisfaction of letting on. He'd had worse coffee. I'm going to have to find a new diner for morning coffee though, he thought.

He knew sooner or later that the waitress (damn, what was her name? Shirley?) would learn of the new hazel skinned brunette he'd picked up at the bakery. He'd only hosted Shirley at the camp once and once was enough. Way too high-maintenance and she never. Stopped. Talking. She was lucky to get back from the camp alive. Of course, this brunette—Jesse—was not exactly a choice find either.

He sighed and forced down another sip—caffeine was caffeine after all. He knew Shirley would be watching and so he made sure he put on a good act of being indifferent. He turned his attention back to the paper, which was by far more entertaining and interesting. The little demon vigilante had managed to get herself in the news again in spectacular fashion. She wasn't even the subject of the headline but there she was on a front page photo. He wondered if she knew what some girls would do to accomplish that much notoriety. Not quite shoot up a school, but damn nearly.

He studied the picture. It was surreal. She was floating above the ground as if weightless and the look on her face was that of a witch casting a spell to paralyze the cop who was clearly caught off guard. Maybe she was a witch. She could read minds, she could fly, she defied death. Was he the only one that could see it? Was he being absolutely paranoid? There were some tests he'd read about that were used to find witches. Tie them up and see if they float. Prick them and see if they bleed. Jesus. He didn't want to get sucked into that delusional fringe. But mind-reading. He knew it was real. He wondered what she was reading from the mind of that policeman—probably: "What the fuck!"

He smiled to himself. If only you knew, buddy, maybe you would've pulled the trigger. He knew he would. It would take the question out of his mind, the question that had hovered over him ever since he found out she was still alive: How much did she know and who had she told? Apparently not enough and not to anyone that had tracked him down. Yet. They'd found his Toyota, which he expected, but that was it. No warning flags from his contacts in New York. So why was he still worried about this girl? The picture in the paper told him why. This was no ordinary girl. He had no doubt he was still on her radar. She was certainly on his, though she was sure making it easy for him. It would be nearly impossible for her to move around without being recognized now.

He studied her face. She had grown since last summer and without the ashes and blood, she looked much more mature. Almost human. There was something else about her face that troubled him. Something that stirred a forgotten corner in his soul. He couldn't quite place it. You'd better, though, he thought, because if there is one thing you do not want to do it is to underestimate this girl.

He finished his coffee, put down a penny for a tip, and gathered the packages he'd picked up at UPS. With these, he had most of what he needed when the lakes thawed and got warm enough to dive. He might not even need to wait that long. He had been toying with the idea of "ice fishing" a little. He might get lucky and drill a hole in the right spot and if nothing else, it was a way to pass the winter. And it would give him time to consider this new development. It wasn't like he had anything else to do.

## 28

## OMINOUS CLOUDS

**Saturday, 3 pm**

"So now we're reduced to traffic control. In our own town." Officer Ed Simmons had just gotten off the phone and was grabbing his jacket and hat, "That was Josh LaVerdiere complaining that a news truck is causing a traffic hazard on Maple Street. Again."

"Yeah, well, it's not like we're a big city department. Even if we were, maybe I would make you chief traffic control officer." Chief Hannah tried to crack a smile as she said this, but it felt unnatural under the circumstances. Ed wasn't wrong. It felt like Westbury PD had been swept to the side of the investigation while the big boys from the State Police moved in to take over the school crime scene. In a way, it was a relief. The hard questions in the press briefings were directed at them instead of her, though there were still some damned uncomfortable ones for her. Like why didn't the police school liaison officer pick up on this? Why was there no armed security at the school? She knew the truth wasn't going to satisfy a lot of the townsfolk—that we aren't trained for this, that we'd need more officers, that we need more money for both. She had barely enough officers just to provide twenty-four hour coverage. She could imagine the heated debate that would ensue over this in the coming weeks before Town Meeting in March, with one side demanding more police presence and the other side demanding to cut their budget. And she would be right in the bulls eye of the whole debate.

If you can't take it, then don't take the job, she thought. She took the job. She could deal with it. At least for this debate she would have time to prepare.

She realized she had been drumming her fingers on the desk so hard, her nails were hurting. She stopped and closed her eyes, took in a deep breath, and let it out slowly. One foot in front of the other, Summer. One foot in front of the other. She kept repeating that to herself as she reached for her cell phone which had started buzzing almost in rhythm with her chant. Yet another traffic complaint, she supposed.

She answered the phone without even looking to see who it was. "This is Chief Hannah," she said.

"*I am so sorry about what happened there yesterday. How are you holding up?*"

The voice of Detective Rodney James was so unexpected and such a relief that her professional demeanor slipped just a bit. "Hey, Rodney. Nice to hear a voice that isn't a complaint."

A laugh that was infused with understanding and sympathy erupted from the phone. Detective James suddenly seemed like a friend rather than just a fellow professional. "*Yeah, I understand completely, sister. I've been there. But nothing like this. I really, truly am sorry for what you're going through there.*"

"Well, thanks for that. It helps to hear it from a big city guy." She realized she was smiling only this time it didn't feel unnatural. "But I also can't imagine that that is the only reason you called."

"*True, that, but I can make it the only reason if you aren't up to talking about my case right now.*"

Another laugh, only this time it was coming from Chief

Hannah, and it felt like a little breath of fresh air. "Well, thank you for that, but believe me, I am totally up to talking about your case. I need something to take my mind off all this, even if it's only a few minutes."

*"Okay then. But be warned, this is not likely to make your life simpler. Probably the opposite. I'll try to be brief and to the point. We all saw the front page photo this morning. And when I say, 'we all,' I mean everyone in New York that reads the Times or the Post, and that's a problem."*

"You're talking about the picture of Blue rounding the corner of the school? That made the New York Times?" She didn't know why she was surprised, a school shooting was always national news.

*"Yes. That photo is like crack to the newsfeeds. It's going to go far and wide and long, and the fact that the name 'Blue DuBois' got attached to it is very unfortunate. We feel that it is putting Blue at much higher risk."*

"Does that mean you've established that our Blue is your Blue?" she asked.

*"No, but that doesn't mean it hasn't triggered a reaction from the target of our investigation. To put it bluntly, these guys don't wait for confirmation. For that reason, I would like to make two requests. First, is to ask you to put in place some protective surveillance on Blue. Second, I would like to visit Westbury and talk to you and perhaps Dr. Woods face-to-face. If she approves, I would like to interview Blue and firmly establish with little doubt whether or not your Blue is our Blue."*

Protective surveillance? She wondered if he had any idea how small Westbury PD was. Protective custody, maybe, but how would she even do that?

"I don't know, Rodney. The best we could do in the short term is to ask her to stay home and hope that she would. Exactly how serious is the risk to Blue?

*"It's pretty serious. Keeping her inside the house would help a lot, but if you can spare someone to survey the locks and windows in their house, and then have a cruiser parked nearby, that would be highly advisable."*

"Jeeze, Rodney, you're scaring me. Can you be more specific about what we should be looking for?"

*"I'll send you what I can tonight, and I can show you more in person. I plan on driving up there on Monday. Will that work for you?"*

"No times a good time so it might as well be anytime, right? But you owe me a lot of information. I care about this girl a lot and I want to know what we're up against." A beep interrupted her. "Look, I've got another call. Go ahead and plan on coming up and I will give you a call after I've had a chance to talk to Dr. Woods."

*"Thanks, Summer. See you Monday."*

She flashed to the incoming call. "Westbury PD, Chief Hannah speaking."

A cranky voice started rattling on about the people trampling on her lawn across the street from the high school. Chief Hannah sighed without making a sound and nodded, saying "Yes, ma'am. No, ma'am. I agree with you, ma'am. I'll send someone over as soon as I can, ma'am." She called Ed and told him to head over to the woman's house when he was done with LaVerdiere. After she hung up, she had time to process what Rodney had told her. He wasn't wrong, this was going to complicate her life, but it was a meaningful complication. It was about protecting someone, which was really what this job was all about.

**Saturday, 4 pm**

The cramp in Jim Purcell's leg was starting to get annoying. After five hours of driving with his large muscular frame wedged inside the compact rental car, he was starting to have second thoughts about his strategy. He knew that if he had brought his sleek black Escalade, he would have stood out like a donkey riding an elephant in a little town like Westbury, but maybe he should have rented something a little bit bigger.

He was looking forward to checking into his motel and taking a hot shower to relieve the cramp, but he couldn't resist driving around the town a little bit to start familiarizing himself with the layout. It wasn't easy—the convoluted web of streets in this town was an anathema to a person accustomed to the comforting geometric patterns of the city. At least the high school was not hard to find—it was the epicenter of non-civilian vehicle activity and was adorned with fluttering police tape. A large shrine of candles, signs, flowers, and stuffed animals overwhelmed the little garden at the base of the flagpole in front of the school. The building itself looked sturdy and unfazed. He spied the corner where the famous photo must have been taken. He could almost imagine the scene, with the police, scared out of their minds and trigger happy, suddenly seeing a girl flying around that corner. It was a situation that easily could have gone very badly for the girl but didn't.

There was a slight rise of ground in front of the school. That must have been where the photographer stood. Jim could picture the whole grounds as it must have appeared from that spot, a crowd of scared confused kids and just as scared and confused adults with a handful of people that had just enough wits about them to organize the whole mess. That's the way it was with those things. A disorganized mess that spawns some leaders and reveals the rest as sheep.

He continued on past the high school and cruised around on mostly residential streets, many of them lined with old houses of elegant architecture in various degrees of decay or restoration. He secretly admired the craftsmanship and the ornate design of structures like these, generously adorned with thick trim boards framed in intricate millwork. It was something he'd never admit to anyone —this secret obsession with old architecture. It would certainly weaken his reputation as a stone-cold enforcer. And yet, he could see himself in a house like that someday, carefully chipping decades-old paint off, revealing the sound, high-quality lumber from the old days, sanding and filling it, and reviving the old craftsmanship, making it shine with new long-lasting glory.

His right leg yanked his attention away from the houses and let

him know that it had enough of the architectural tour and told him
to head for the motel. He conceded, taking a route that diverted up
the main hill in town almost to the top past the landmark he was
most interested in. There it was, the O'Day house, a big Victorian
surrounded in lilac bushes. Classic. As he approached, he saw a
couple of cars emblazoned with the logos of radio or TV stations
parked in front. A few people lounged next to the cars, chatting,
probably waiting for an opportunity for another front page photo
or quick interview. One of them was holding a camera with a huge
telephoto lens and training it on the front entrance to the house.

Jim didn't stop or even slow down, he just drove by casually,
acting like a local, giving the reporters no more than a nod as he
went by. His time was not now—that would be late in the evening
when most people were off the streets. That's when he could walk
around unobserved and get a feel for the place, scope out the
angles, check the escape routes. Those were the hours when he
would engage in some interesting and valuable conversations from
lubricated locals and visiting news crews as they made their night
pilgrimage to the two bars in town. And those were also the hours,
in the deep of the night, when some of the most interesting things
happened. Babineau had assured him of that.


### Saturday, 8 pm


Blue curled around her pillow, her arms clinging tightly to it,
her cheek cradled by its gentle cottony softness. And she felt something else cradling her—a warm glow coming from her core. It was
acting like a shield, keeping all the craziness of Westbury at arm's
length—still there, but hovering at a manageable distance. She had
never experienced a glow like this before. It was like tasting ice-
cream for the first time.

Anna knew. She had known all along, of course, and as soon as
she and Will got back to Anna's house and stepped in the front
door, Anna grabbed Blue and hugged her, whispering in her ear,

"You can't hide it now, it's all over your faces! I'm so glad." Blue was sure Anna had her own *veraque*-like power of intuition.

The four of them had spent the rest of the afternoon at Anna's, the somber atmosphere of the disaster making their normally lively banter awkward and forced. The one thing that rescued them was Anna's calm demeanor and her remarkable acuity in framing each issue in a way that gave them substance that they could grasp, like firm hand holds on a rickety bridge across a deep canyon they never thought they would have to cross. She echoed what Dr. Woods had said about hindsight and it seemed to resonate with Will and Wu, especially Wu, who seemed the most upset about everything that had happened.

But she had the additional advantage of that glow, that hot wave that still eddied around her, surrounding her, reinforced each time she glanced over at Will, sitting next to her, almost touching, but not quite, the electric potential that suddenly existed between them pulling them toward each other.

Will. She rolled on her back and closed her eyes. Will. That name, so ordinary before, felt like a mantra now. Strong-willed Will. To think that it took an accident of tripping and landing on top of him to shatter the barrier that had kept them from this. This glow. This . . . bond. It made her giddy and she realized at that moment that she had never really experienced true giddiness before.

God, she needed to see him again, just to see if it was real and not an accident, to feel what he was feeling and know for sure. The urge was so strong, she was afraid she would do something colossally stupid like try to sneak over again tonight, the first night of All-O'Day-Kids-Are-Grounded-Until-Further-Notice. A proclamation from Pa Bill and Ma Beth sprung on them a few hours ago. No explanation, but also, no-nonsense, and from what she read from their *chiss* Blue really was not going to protest. There was fear there. Real fear. She couldn't read what it was exactly, but she did know they got a call from the Westbury Police. Will's family had the same order, but Anna's didn't. She and Wu and Anna and Will had texted back and forth, speculating what it was all about. Wu was convinced that it was just to protect them from the reporters and gossip, Anna was guessing that it was because the police wanted to interview Will, but Will had a feeling that there was something more sinister behind it.

She agreed.


**Saturday, 9 pm**


"Poit!" The solitary drip from the faucet hit the surface of the bath and sent its resonant burst of sound echoing through the water and into Summer Hannah's submerged ears. It was the only sound other than the periodic hollow hiss of her breath entering her lungs like an inflating balloon. Only her face rose above the steaming surface of the scented bathwater. Every other inch of her body was immersed, isolated, secure. And behind her closed eyes, her brain sat back and sighed in the darkness and quiet.

Without the distractions of the world, her mind flipped through the events of the day without having to rush, reflecting on what each one meant and noting down on her mental checklist the next things to be done. After her call with Detective James, she contacted the O'Day and Woods' families with a request to keep all their kids at home and inside until at least Monday. She had to lie a little. She told them it was for security due to rumors of out-of-state media invading town, which was actually true, but not the real threat. The real threat was still a little bit vague even to her, but she had done the best she could with what she knew.

Next, she had made arrangements for Rodney to meet with April on Monday. April seemed very eager for an opportunity to explore more of Blue's background with Detective James. There was apparently an abundance of blank or redacted parts in Blue's medical records. This just added to the ominous possibility that

Blue really was the Blue in Rodney's case. That was not the conclusion she wanted, but at least it would be a conclusion.

She thought about the long shot—that Rodney might be able to provide some insight on her case. Since he was in New York, maybe he could help her track down the unmasked Bronco: William Farrell. An experienced detective could probably spot things that she and Ed completely overlooked. A long shot, true, but better than nothing.

Right now, though, she had to prepare for tomorrow. Ah tomorrow, she thought, as a familiar refrain ran through her head:

> Tomorrow and tomorrow and tomorrow,
> Creeps in this petty pace from day to day,
> To the last syllable of recorded time;
> And all our yesterdays have lighted fools,
> The way to dusty death.

She sighed. Tomorrow she was going to church to help heal her town. Her mere presence, she knew, was a powerful tonic for reassurance, her absence just the opposite. It had nothing to do with her skill, she wouldn't have to say a thing, thank God, it had only to do with her sound judgement of being in the right place at the right time.

She took in another nice long slow breath and let it out even slower. She felt the very last little muscles, the ones that were always the last, as they surrendered to the penetrating heat of the bath and let go. It was so peaceful. Amazing what fifteen minutes of peace can do to your body and soul, she thought, just as the sound of reality buzzed from the tub rim. She sighed as her head rose up out of the water, water flowing smoothly down her long hair. Her hand reached for the phone and a glance confirmed what she was expecting—it was a text from her DFC contact.

### Saturday, 10 pm

A knocking jolted her awake. She must have fallen asleep. Blue took a quick look at her clock—only ten o'clock—but then again she had been awake most of the previous night. Was it only the previous night? Had it only been yesterday? Another knock.

"Come in," she said.

Ma Beth opened the door and the minute Blue saw her face, she felt troubled.

"Can you come downstairs?"

At the kitchen table she sat across from Ma Beth and Pa Bill. Both had lines of concern etched across their foreheads and their eyes were pouring out whispers of *chiss* that were causing her own lines of concern to form. "*How much should we tell her?* . . . *nothing conclusive yet* . . . *did she really?* . . . *Would they really?*"

Pa Bill was the one that broke the silence. "Blue, we got a call from Chief Hannah about someone who wants to talk to you—not about the shooting—about something else . . ."

Ma Beth jumped in, "We don't know what it is about, but has to do with someone who saw your picture in the paper. It was a detective from New York City."

"New York City?" Blue pounded her brain for why anyone in New York City would be interested in her and then it dawned on her. "Does this have to do with Bronco?"

"Well, that's what we asked," said Pa Bill, "but the answer was no. It is something else. We said we'd give permission if you were okay with it, but the DFC also had to agree." Pa Bill took a deep breath and glanced over at Ma Beth. Blue thought the bomb had already dropped, but apparently they were just getting to the crux. Pa Bill looked back at Blue.

"They didn't agree?" said Blue, tentatively.

"It's more complicated than that," Pa Bill continued, "and we're telling you everything we've heard because we have always wanted to be up front with you, and Wu, and Nate, and Sam."

"Apparently," said Ma Beth, "there has been quite a debate about you already inside the DFC. We just learned that last fall there was an effort inside DFC to take you back into custody because of what happened last summer. We were told that the effort was nearly successful. And now because of this," she gestured toward the paper sitting on the table, "and this detective and . . . " Ma Beth glanced at Pa Bill before going on, ". . . another incident, they are going to have a meeting on Monday with a judge in Burlington that will rule on custody."

Blue slumped back in the chair and sagged into it as if all the bones in her body had turned to mush. Back to Burlington? Back to Brookhaven Shelter? Back into her shell? She had just started to emerge for God's sake. What were they thinking? Who at DFC would have pushed for this?

"Why?" It was the only word she could come up with. "Why would they do that? I love it here. I love *you*." She looked at each of them.

Ma Beth looked like she was on the verge of tears, "And we love you so much!" She couldn't continue.

Pa Bill did though. "Blue, they did mention an incident that was reported this morning to the DFC. I'm just going to ask you straight out, and don't be afraid to answer, I am not going to judge you on this, we just need to know. Did you go over to the Woods house early this morning. In particular, did you climb through one of their windows?"

Like an old tormentor from the past, a claw grasped her heart and squeezed it hard as she felt the sensation of being caught and could sense the long dismissed walls of bureaucracy that had lurked on the edges of her awareness as they suddenly re-asserted themselves and started pressing in on her. "*Fuck,*" she voxed to no one that could hear her, but it was clear when she looked back in their eyes that they didn't need to hear anything. It had to have been written in bold on her face.

It was a long silence, but she had to break it. "I am so sorry. I had to. Will needed my help."

"Like I said," said Pa Bill, "no judgement." That's what he said out loud, but his *chiss* said, "AND YET THE CONSEQUENCES . . ."

"Why would they take me away for that?"

Ma Beth finally found her voice again, "You see, it is a bureaucracy, and they have procedures and if an incident is filed, they have to review it. But it isn't just this incident, it is everything else added in. And this is just the straw . . ."

Blue completed the sentence, ". . . that broke the camel's back." She said it flatly because her mind was blank. It didn't want to think about it. It didn't want to think about anything. The irrational reaction, "If I don't think about it, it won't happen," came instinctively and stupidly. She wanted to go back to her room.

"Blue, it's not for sure," said Pa Bill. "We just wanted you to know everything. Ma Beth and I have a lot of say in this, so we are optimistic. Be patient, wait until Monday and we'll go from there."

Blue heard his words, but she also saw his eyes and she felt what he felt. He didn't think there was a chance. It took a great amount of effort, but she wrested her lips into a smile and hoped they didn't look as tortured as she felt. She didn't dare say anything for fear the rising lump in her throat would betray her.

Pa Bill went on, "I know this is a lot to take in, especially after all that has happened. But we will get through this. You go to bed now and rest easy and don't worry about anything."

She nodded but didn't say anything. She reinforced the sagging smile and hugged them both. They were especially long hugs, both ways.

As she trudged up the stairs, her feet wanted to drag her backwards, back toward the door, back down the street, back in that window, and do exactly what helped put her in this predicament in the first place. How could something that felt so right cause something so wrong? Her feet were almost winning her over, but a slight hum from her open door, just half a flight away, suddenly changed their mind and released her. She sprang up the steps, afraid Pa Bill or Ma Beth would hear—no phone after 10 pm or no phone was the rule. She silenced the phone and looked at the screen and was instantly glad she'd left it on.

### Saturday, 10:30 pm

Will hung up right after the second ring. He tapped his foot impatiently. He had to talk to her. She needed to know what he had just heard. He wasn't supposed to call after ten, he knew, but he should just forget the rules and let it ring. Just as he lifted the phone to dial again, it buzzed his hand.

"Hey!" he answered.

*"Hey!"* she replied.

Just hearing that one word from her was enough to trigger an image of her face floating in front of him as if she were staring back at him from his window—her soft skin, her dark eyebrows, her long dark wisps of loose hair dividing her face into a dozen wedges with her bright eyes looking through them like a wily fox through a forest of cattails. His heart beat against his chest as if it wanted to jump out and run around. It was intoxicating, this combination of sensations that he was totally unaware could exist until just hours ago, and all it took was a phone call and one word to set it off again. It caught him so off guard he almost lost track of what he had to tell her. When he remembered, he wanted to forget it again. He just wanted this sensation to go on and on.

But he had to.

"Blue," he said, "I heard about the DFC. They called my mom and I made her tell me everything." He didn't tell her exactly how much was packed behind that word "made"—that he opened up about everything. He told his mom how much better Blue had gotten because of her, how much Blue respected her, how Blue had used what she had learned from her to help him get through his nightmare—even that she'd practically spent the night with him. Before his mom could react to that, he had played his trump card— the guilt trip. Why had she not told him about *veraque*? What else were they not telling him about vox?

He felt bad about challenging his mom, but also felt liberated about coming clean about last night. And it had worked. Instead of being angry, she opened up, too. It was as if a new door had opened between them.

"They won't do it. Mom won't let them," he said.

*"Did she say that?"* she asked.

"Not exactly, but she knows the laws and the system."

*"Not like Pa Bill. He knows it better,"* she replied

Will's brow creased. "What do you mean he knows it better?"

*"Look. I've started to feel things now. A little. Not like you, not really veraque, but I know what he was thinking. I was looking right at him. He doesn't think there's a chance. And he knows the DFC better than anyone. Ma Beth, and Pa Bill, they've been doing this for, like, thirty years. Did you know I'm number fourteen?"*

Fourteen, he thought. Wow, fourteen kids have been through the O'Day's house?

"Well, even if you do, it will just be for a little while, right? And just up in Burlington, right?"

*"If until I'm eighteen is 'just a little while,' I guess so."*

"Until you're eighteen! Three years! Why? Why would they do that?"

*"Because I'm not eighteen and so I have to do what the judge says, that's why. You wanted to know me better? Well, welcome to my life."*

Will didn't say anything. He didn't know what to say. His mind was empty and spent. Two days of an unending barrage of every emotional extreme had peeled away all the layers of reason. And now this. It seemed like the last layer had ripped away and exposed all that was left: raw anger and frustration.

"I'm coming over there," he said at last.

*"Don't! We're grounded, you're grounded. You'll only make it worse for me! Did you know someone saw us last night?"*

"Yeah. Mom told me. It had to be Mrs. Asbury." That witch. She's the only one that has a direct view of his window. In the summer it's no problem but in the winter the damn lilac is bare bones and she can see right through. And now she would be watching like a hawk.

*"I gotta go,"* said Blue. *"Ma Beth and Pa Bill are coming up to the second floor. They can hear me from there."* Her voice had dropped to a whisper.

Damn the phone. Damn the grounding. "Okay, I'll figure something out. Just remember."

*"Remember what?"* she said these last words in a hurried whisper.

"Our break," he said. There was silence but Will could hear the sound of feet on stairs and Blue's last whisper, *"Damn."* And then the connection went dead. But he got an instant double buzz. A text. A heart. From Blue. The little red emoji sat glowing at him like an ember, calming the anger and frustration. It was so bright it made the entire history of Blue's monochrome texts fade, like the path of a firework obscured by the bright red flash at the end. He scrolled back but knew he wasn't going to find any other hearts. No emojis at all. This was her first. He wanted it to be just the first of many, like last night would be the first of many, like her kiss would be the first of many...

He looked out his window. The dark rectangular pupil in Mrs. Asbury's house two back yards away stared at him with its warning gaze. He was going to have to find a different way out.

29

## PERFECT STORM

**Saturday, Midnight, Upstate, NY**

The massive grey ribbon of roadway rolled out of the darkness at seventy miles per hour, emerging from the powdery black darkness that lay just beyond the reach of the headlights of the SUV as it snaked its way down the deserted interstate highway. The pristine four lane road was a stark contrast to the wilderness that surrounded it, a gash of civilization cutting through the rugged Adirondacks—mountains so ancient that the eons had worn them down from Everest-size behemoths to their current smaller, yet still formidable, forms. Even in the darkness, the SUV's driver could feel the presence of their hulking shoulders crowding around him and forcing the highway into an unending series of sharp curves and steep grades.

Rodney noted the time on his dashboard clock. Exactly midnight, three hours since he left his apartment in Queens. He was starting to wonder if this was such a good idea, traveling through this desolate and unpopulated landscape in the middle of the night. It was totally unexpected. He knew upstate New York had wilderness, but he never knew such a massive primitive area existed just a few hours north of one of the most populous cities on earth.

During the day, the scenery must have been spectacular but in the utter blackness of night with nary a glimmer of light revealing any civilized settlement and only an occasional pair of headlights sweeping past, it was a little unnerving. Maybe five cars went by in the last half hour. Maybe less. He'd never been on an interstate that was this empty and this remote.

At least there was no danger of him nodding off at the wheel. The combination of the spooky wilderness atmosphere, a bottle of ginseng energy drink, and the potential consequences of the disturbing news he received just before he left was enough to keep him awake for a couple of days, at least.

The disturbing news was about Babineau's bodyguard/tough guy, Jim Purcell. He was missing. The stakeout on Theo Babineau —started just that morning—had yielded only a report of the small-statured older gentleman going about his usual routine, doing nothing unusual, and getting no visitors, and that was the problem. He was alone. Babineau normally had his bodyguard, Jim Purcell, prominently with him wherever he went. Purcell's absence from Babineau's side was as significant as his presence.

Unless they could locate Purcell, they had very good reason to believe that he might be on the road toward Westbury. It didn't take long for Rodney, Harris, and Chief Daniels to agree that if Jim Purcell were to show up in Westbury, he was likely more than the police there could handle, and that wasn't an acceptable situation.

"It's our case, our responsibility," Chief Daniels had said, "and it is still a WITSEC concern until we get the DuBois name straightened out, so we three are the only cavalry available. Harris is retired, and you were headed up anyway so it's you, Detective James. Better move quickly and hope that he's not there already."

So here he was, the lonely cavalryman, charging through the

mountains to head off the bad guy. That was the worst case scenario, anyway. The more likely scenario was that Purcell would be spotted back in the city and Rodney would just be arriving in Westbury a day early. He hoped that was the case. He wasn't sure he was up to dealing with Purcell. Not alone, anyway. It was never ideal to do something like this alone and Daniels knew it, but what other choice did they have?

### Sunday, 1 am

Blue had given up on sleep. In its place, she had been sitting cross-legged on her bed, looking out on her private starlit landscape where the white tinged evergreens and cubes of snow-covered fields were edged by the sparkle from the few windows where people were still up late, doing up-late things. The scene was framed by her window sash like a painting in a gallery. She absorbed the image as only one who knows she'll never see it again can. The glow was faltering. The shields were falling. The inevitable was coming for her again.

She didn't bother cataloguing the factors that had stacked up against her. She wasn't going to waste her last hours obsessing about what she could have done to change this or that. It was like Dr. Woods said, and Anna had said, hindsight can drive you mad. It can make anyone feel like a fool. If you let it, it can drive you into a little hole where you never take any risks and you live your life in seeming security; but instead, just find yourself wallowing in the drain of other's mistakes.

And yet, she couldn't let go of the injustice of it. Nothing she had done was morally wrong, at least not her morality. Maybe others could challenge her concept of morality, and maybe it was flawed, but not so much that it deserved this. It was *not* wrong to try and expose a drug dealer. It was *not* wrong to escape out the school window. It was *not* wrong to help Will. Maybe it was wrong to break the rules to do those things, but whose rules were they and were they meant to prevent good things from happening? Who made the rule of when it was okay to break rules? Was it the judge's job? If so, how could the judge be the judge when Blue wasn't even allowed to present her case? Eighteen seemed a pretty arbitrary age to set for adulthood and self-representation, especially when you have no real parents. Then it's the state representing you to the state. No conflict of interest there, right? The state being mostly interested in protecting itself, of course. No one representing her to point *that* out to the judge.

And then there was this mysterious New York detective. And that stupid picture. Things that were totally outside her control. How big a role were those playing in this whole mess?

And this on a grim backdrop of four dead kids.

She punched her wall. It stung but she didn't care. It was real and it made her feel alive and in control of her own pain. She let the injustice cycle inside her, making her hot, the heat making her both angry and satisfied because it was *her* heat, *her* anger, *her* guilt. She owned it. She controlled it. It was a poor substitute for the glow, but the glow was having trouble penetrating the heat. It was hours since she talked to Will and not that many more hours until morning.

She threw herself back on her bed and stared at the ceiling. Sleep was not going to come, not with this furnace burning inside her, she was just going to have to let it burn itself out and wait. Wait until the hammer came down—unless she broke the rules again. Plan B. Why not, she thought. Was Plan B moral? It wasn't for any noble cause other than her own self-preservation. Was that noble enough? Moral enough? Did she even care at this point?

This new train of thought was interrupted by a sound. Not the normal sounds of a sleeping house in the winter, but a familiar sound to her, because she had made it many times herself. But it wasn't her making it this time.

There it was again. If she had made that sound twice she would have been pissed at herself because it risked giving away what she was doing. Someone or something was climbing the trellis. There were only three possibilities: 1) a wild critter 2) a thief 3) an idiot. She slipped quietly out of her bed and stepped silently over to her door and listened. She heard the very soft and distant rumble of the bathroom window being lifted carefully, confidently. Only the idiot knew about that window, but never would she have believed he would have been so bold. She leaned her forehead against the door jamb and pressed hard into it. He shouldn't have come here, it would make it worse if they got caught, but did she even care anymore? It was probably a done deal—but what was she really concerned about—and why was her heart beating a little faster?

Because this might be the last time you see him, you idiot, she thought. This is going to make it easier and harder at the same time. God, she hoped at the very least he could make it in without waking the whole house.

---

The trellis creaked again, and Will cursed under his breath as he eased the pressure on his left hand hoping his toes and right hand would not overwhelm the fragile structure clinging to the side of the house, attached more by the tenacity of the vines than the old rusting hardware. Blue had used this route dozens of times, but this was the first test under his weight.

He slowly moved his left hand to the sill of the bathroom window where he could feel the worn spot at the bottom of the window where he could wedge a finger in and get just enough pressure to raise the window, just as Blue had described. He was surprised that it responded with little effort, raising an inch almost instantly with only the slightest rubbing sound. He knew Blue had worked over the old window sash, smoothing it, and lubricating it with soap but he didn't really appreciate just how much difference it would make until now.

By leaning on the windowsill, he was able to take pressure off the trellis and he sighed in relief, his breath flowing past the window leaving a dash of frost behind. He knew he could make it now. He paused for a moment to listen for any commotion inside in case his creaky ascent had caused any disturbance, but there was nothing except the crisp silence of a November night.

Point of no return, Woods, he thought to himself. He closed his eyes and absorbed the moment. A year ago he would never have believed he would be that guy who had the balls to sneak over in the middle of the night to climb in the second story window of a girl's house in the middle of winter. Of course, a year ago he couldn't have imagined even half of the crazy stuff that had happened. Yet here he was, dangling in the icy breeze on the side of a house, aching to get inside and hold in his arms a girl that was there all the time, but he had denied or ignored or just plain overlooked as much as she had overlooked him. And now he was about to try and help rescue her as she had rescued him as he had rescued her in this cycle of rescue that seemed to have begun with no endpoint in sight.

He opened his eyes and studied the windowsill, planning his next moves. He leaned over and rested his left elbow on the sill so he could lever the window further up with his forearm. It slid open nearly silently, with just the slightest rumble, leaving enough of a gap that he could get his upper body inside and carefully unload the trellis, his torso dangling free for a moment while he pulled himself in over the sill and slid carefully onto the floor of the bathroom.

He stopped again and listened. Still time to get away if he had to, but there was nothing except the distant roar of the furnace in the basement and the creak of the heating pipes as they expanded under a renewed flow of hot water. Normal noises. Noises that would cover his next moves. He left the window open to facilitate a silent escape, got up slowly and walked quietly out the door and down the hall to the attic stairway.

As he stared up into the darkness, a wry vox floated into his brain. "*You're an idiot.*"

He froze in surprise and then relaxed. "*And you are an enigma,*" he replied.

Her laugh was not so much a sound as it was the feeling that she was smiling as much as he was. "*Are you going to just stand there?*"

He padded quietly up the stairs making sure his feet stayed on the edges all the way to avoid the one creaky step and he arrived on the landing where just six months ago, eons ago, he had slipped a note under her door—*Just want to be friends.* Now what were they? As if in answer, maybe it was in answer, he felt her reaching for his jacket zipper. She pulled it down and slipped her arms inside and around his back and pressed her cheek into his chest.

The pressure of her hand in the center of his back was not the pressure of a mom-hug or a man-hug, the only thing he'd experienced until now. It was something else and he nearly gasped with the sensation. His arms instinctively reciprocated, surrounding her, making the two of them a single goose-down encased sculpture swaying slowly back and forth in the darkness with the rhythm of a sailboat rocking in a peaceful anchorage. He pressed his face into her hair and inhaled the scent that was Blue.

"You're an idiot and I'm glad you came," she whispered after exactly the right amount of time. She moved her hands to his waist and stepped back, looking up at him. "*Are you okay?*"

He sighed. He didn't really want to answer. It would mean the end of the moment of peace and back to reality.

"*Yeah. Sorta. I mean I can't believe what is happening. All this crap about the DFC and detective from New York and a lockdown. Jesus, as if we didn't have enough with Jordy going berserk, I mean, when is this going to end?*"

Blue let go of him and sat on her bed. "*When I'm gone, that's when. Shit like this just seems to follow me around.*"

A flash of irritation swept away his feeling of peace. "*Blue, just*

STOP IT. STOP GOING DOWN INTO THAT HOLE. YOU ARE A GOOD PERSON. YOU ARE NOT A BRINGER OF EVIL. SHIT. JUST. HAPPENS."

She looked down, but reached out and grabbed his hand. He sat down next to her and she looked at him.

"YOU'RE RIGHT, I GO DOWN THAT HOLE A LOT BECAUSE IT IS A COMFORTABLE PLACE FOR ME." She leaned her head against his shoulder. "This is much more comfortable," she whispered, barely audible.

He put his arm around her. Way more comfortable for you and me both, he thought. He noticed a drawing on her desk and picked it up. It was a girl with her back turned, walking away across snow covered field toward a forest; the stark silhouette of bare branches forming a forbidding lattice across the sky. The girl's boots left a trail of lonely gray holes in the snow behind her.

"SOMETIMES," she voxed, "I FANTASIZE GOING BACK TO THE WOODS, LIKE WHERE I GREW UP. WE WERE HAPPY THERE. IT WAS MUCH SIMPLER. WE DIDN'T HAVE TO TRY AND FIT IN, DIDN'T HAVE TO EXPLAIN OURSELVES. IT WAS JUST US." She was looking at the picture as she voxed and the reflection off the paper gave her vox voice a distant, airy tone. "I'D BE FAR AWAY FROM ALL THIS CRAP."

"YOU'D BE FAR AWAY FROM US. FROM ME."

She looked up at him and smiled. "YOU CAN COME ALONG. WU AND ANNA, TOO."

Will thought about that for a moment. Get away from it all. Reset. Start over. Just the four of them. It was an alluring thought. Six months ago, he would have considered it ludicrous, but now it seemed almost plausible. Except . . .

"I COULD NEVER LEAVE ROSIE."

Blue looked back at the picture. "OF COURSE. I KNOW. IT'S JUST A FANTASY. IT DOESN'T MATTER. I'M GOING TO HAVE TO LEAVE YOU BEHIND ANYWAY."

"YOU KEEP SAYING THAT. WHY? WHAT MAKES YOU SO SURE?"

She looked at him, locking his gaze and a sense of inevitability seeped down into his chest giving him just a taste of the bitterness that must have been building up in Blue for years. "LIKE I TOLD YOU. WELCOME TO MY LIFE. THIS ISN'T THE FIRST TIME THIS HAS HAPPENED, IT'S LIKE WELL-WORN TERRITORY FOR ME. THIS JUDGE IN BURLINGTON? SHE'S LIKE THE WICKED WITCH TO ME. 'I'LL GET YOU, MY PRETTY!' IN HER PERFECT WORLD SHE WOULD HAVE ME UNDER CLOSE WATCH IN BURLINGTON IN BROOKHAVEN SHELTER FOR THE REST OF MY LIFE."

Will realized he wasn't going to convince her otherwise. He hoped what she said wasn't true, but he was finally getting the sense that the outlook was bleak. "LOOK, OKAY, LET'S ASSUME YOU DO GO. IT'S JUST AN HOUR AND A HALF AWAY. WE COULD COME UP AND VISIT. NATE COULD DRIVE US UP. YOU COULD TAKE A BUS DOWN AND VISIT. AND I'LL HAVE MY DRIVER'S LICENSE BY NEXT FALL."

The entire time he was voxing, Blue was shaking her head. "THIS IS HOW IT GOES, WILL. THIS IS HOW IT ALWAYS GOES. IN THREE MONTHS, SCHOOL WILL BE BACK TO ITS NORMAL DYSFUNCTIONAL SELF, KIDS WILL BE WRAPPED UP IN THEIR OWN DRAMA AND TO THEM, I'LL JUST BE 'OH YEAH, I REMEMBER HER, THEY SENT HER OFF AFTER JORDY MOWED DOWN THE CAFETERIA.' YOU'LL COME UP AND VISIT A COUPLE OF TIMES AND IT WILL BE NICE BUT THEN THINGS WILL START TO FEEL WEIRD. AND THEN IT'S OVER." She turned to the dark of her window. "It might as well be over now," she whispered, again, barely audible.

Will was stunned. "WHAT! WHAT ARE YOU TALKING ABOUT?"

"JUST THINK ABOUT IT, WILL. YOU KNOW I'M RIGHT!"

He dropped the picture and pulled away from her. He wanted to throw something, not caring about waking anyone now. And why would it matter? She'd given up, why didn't he give up?

But he couldn't. There was still a chance. He looked at her, searching for something to say, but coming up blank. Instead, a *creak* outside her door made them both jump. Blue's eyes got wide. "GET UNDER MY BED!" But it was too late. A figure leaned inside the door. A long lanky figure. It hovered in the doorway for a moment and then a faint chiss floated into Will's brain. "CAN YOU HEAR ME?"

Will nodded.

The *chiss* from Wu continued, "GOOD. YOU'RE AN IDIOT! YOU ARE

SO DAMN LUCKY *I* FOUND THAT WINDOW OPEN. WHAT IF IT WAS NATE? OR PA BILL? DON'T ANSWER! YOU CAN'T ANSWER! *I* CAN'T HEAR YOU! LUCKY ME! JUST GET OUT OF HERE! *I'LL* COVER FOR YOU. AND DON'T WORRY. ANNA AND *I* TALKED ALL ABOUT . . ." he waved his hand at the two of them sitting on the bed, ". . . ABOUT THIS. JUST GO, WE'LL TALK IN THE MORNING." And then he added, "YOU'RE STILL AN IDIOT. DID YOU HEAR ALL THAT?"

Will nodded and wondered if Wu could see his smile.

Blue got up and gave Wu a big hug and then looked up and whispered, "Thank you!" She turned to Will and voxed, *"Go!"*

Will got up and as he passed Blue to follow Wu down the stairs, he voxed, *"I HAVEN'T GIVEN UP."* He grabbed her shoulders and kissed her hard. He pulled away reluctantly and stepped through the door, wincing as Wu stepped on the creaky step. He had more to say, but there was a noise coming from somewhere on the second floor and he could see Wu gesturing frantically in the faint light of the hallway below. It would just have to wait.

**Sunday, 1:15 am**

Jim, didn't go to movies much. He didn't see the point. The few he had gone to—great reviews, very popular—were mildly entertaining but so far from reality that they were hard to take seriously. Reality was far more interesting, at least the reality he saw. His job, he knew, probably put him in much more interesting vantage points than most people had. That's why he liked it.

Right now he was finding it immensely entertaining, the show that was playing out in front of him at that very moment. Across the street and down a block and a half from where he was parked, he was gazing through his Zeiss 20x60 image stabilized binoculars as he followed a kid, must have been fifteen or sixteen, slinging himself out the second story window and scrambling down a trellis and running off up the street. This was not an awkward performance, the kid knew what he was doing. He moved smoothly with practiced form. Jim followed him with the Zeiss as far as he could. It looked like the kid dodged into a house a couple of blocks down, it was hard to tell. No matter. There was little doubt in his mind that this was the same kid that was in the YouTube video. And he could guess what he was doing in the O'Day house. There was only one girl in the family.

Something must have happened inside, at least enough of a commotion to wake people, because lights had come on. He turned his Zeiss back to the house and watched as a pair of hands closed the window where the kid had come out. He couldn't tell whose they might be. Maybe Mr. O'Day. The girl must be catching hell now, he thought. He looked up to the third story gable window where he had seen glimpses of the girl earlier. Her light wasn't on. The other lights in the house went out. Maybe she didn't catch hell. Maybe the boy got away with it. Wouldn't surprise him. Babineau wasn't wrong. Kids this age could be very sharp.

He looked back up to the gable window and watched it for a while longer but saw nothing—not even her head in the window.

It was all quiet now. The little drama was over as quickly as it had started. It was like it never happened. He lowered the Zeiss and scanned the neighborhood around him with his bare eyes. Quiet and peaceful and asleep. In a little while, it would be time for him to bed down, too. His eyes stopped on the O'Day house and he took a last long look. It was a nice house. The kind of house he imagined he should have grown up in—if only the stars had been aligned a little differently. The kind of house he would like to have if he ever settled down. He especially liked the low fence, and the bushes and the big porch. And there was a bay window on this side of the house. There were some nice houseplants arrayed in the window. He lifted the Zeiss again and saw that some were actually flowering in the late fall. I wonder what they are, he thought. It would make a nice addition to my apartment window. The Zeiss were amazing at seeing the detail, even from this distance, even at night. And then he noticed something mingled inside a tangle of philodendron leaves. A pair of eyes and they were looking directly at him. At least it seemed that way. He couldn't imagine someone would have spotted him this far away without binos, but the eyes did not move away from him. He suddenly felt uncomfortable. Babineau told him—don't underestimate this girl. Well, he thought as he locked his eyes on hers, I am impressed. I won't underestimate you again, little girl. Next time you won't even know I'm here, so get a good look now. And unless you have an $8000 pair of binos, there is no way you're going to identify me from this distance. Still, her unwavering stare was starting to spook him.

The eyes in the window faded out and were gone. Now the encounter was really over. He wouldn't see her again tonight, he was certain of it. Not exactly the way he expected things to go, but definitely more interesting than any movie plot he could think of. Now it was time for him to turn in. Tomorrow morning he would report to Babineau and then probe around and see if there were any more interesting tidbits he could troll from the locals. The way things were going, he didn't think he would be disappointed.

He started the car and rolled down the street, down the hill, into the darkest part of the night. As he drove, he shook his head. He now understood Babineau's concern. Yet half of him felt like they should just let her grow up and see how she turns out. It seemed like a fairer way to settle accounts. The other half of him knew instinctively that you should stamp out a fire before it gets out of control.

Well, it was up to Babineau. He was the boss. And Babineau was never hesitant to stomp.

---

She leaned into her doorframe, barely breathing so as to not obscure any sounds coming from below. There was no sound of footsteps—Wu and Will were doing a good job of that—there was the slight creak of the bathroom doorway—that was okay, nothing unusual about that—and then the sound of a boy peeing in the toilet—brilliant because that would obscure any sound of Will creeping out of the window—and then a moment later the creak of the trellis taking on Will's weight—she guessed nothing could be done about that—and then she heard the toilet flushing—of course, that would cover any of his moves the rest of the way. She listened as Wu left the bathroom and went back into his room without trying to stifle any of his movements. Then she heard a door shut on the opposite end of the hall and then nothing. She sighed in relief. At least this visit wouldn't add to the case against her.

She closed her eyes but didn't move from the doorway. She knew she should lie down and try and get some sleep, but there was no way. How she could feel so hopeful yet so hopeless at the same time. Everything pointed to a return to the shelter, but it *was* different this time. This time she had a family on her side and a psychiatrist on her side. And she had Will. She touched her lips with her finger, feeling the silkiness and very slight throbbing that lingered from his last kiss.

She turned and grabbed her bathrobe and slid silently down through the familiar passageways of the house and padded into the living room, sinking cross-legged into Pa Bill's big easy chair. It was all so "home" to her now. There was no corner of this house she didn't know, nowhere she felt uncomfortable, no one she had to avoid, no place she didn't feel welcome. There was no other place on the planet where she could be safer or more secure and that is what she was going to tell the judge. She was *not* going without a fight this time.

She sighed and leaned her head back into the chair, letting the gestalt of the house soak in and dispel the doubts and feelings of doom. Her eyes drifted around the room, identifying items that were familiar, yet unfamiliar when seen in the darkness, as if they were only sleepy shadows of their true selves. She studied the silhouettes of the houseplants in the bay window, backlit by the faint glow of the starlit trees and houses outside. The plants formed an intricate lacework that she thought would make an interesting abstract drawing. She started to compose the drawing in her head when she was shocked into alertness by a sudden very loud and clear *chiss*.

"... IS THAT FLOWERING, IN WINTER? *I* WONDER WHAT PLANT THAT IS ..."

It came from the window. What the hell? Someone would have to be right outside the window for a *chiss* to be that clear. There was no way it was Will. The voice was one she'd never heard before.

She eased slowly out of the chair and moved quietly over to the bay window, her eyes straining for anything that looked human outside.

"... LOOKS LIKE A PHILODENDRON ... WAIT ... ARE THOSE EYES?"

Blue nearly screamed. There should be a person practically in her face for her to hear a *chiss* like that, but there was no one. Was she asleep? Dreaming? No way, she thought. She recovered her courage and moved right to the window, keeping her face behind the plants and peering through a gap, scanning the area outside the window. There was nothing out of place outside. Nothing even moving. The only human presence she could conceive of was a car parked down the street. It was possible someone was in it, but that would not explain what she heard. And then, as if to challenge that conclusion, another *chiss*.

"... SHE'S LOOKING STRAIGHT AT ME! SHE COULDN'T POSSIBLY SEE ME, COULD SHE? SHE'D NEED AN $8000 PAIR OF BINOS LIKE THESE ..."

Binoculars! That would explain it. They magnified their eyes to her the same way they magnified her face to them. They had to be some pretty amazing binoculars for his *chiss* to be that clear. Another *chiss*...

"... BUT BABINEAU SAID NOT TO UNDERESTIMATE THIS GIRL ..."

Babineau!

She fell back from the window as if punched in the chest. A dusty door in a dark corner of her brain that had been waiting quietly for that magic word popped open and out from it danced a little girl running through the forest, giggling as she ran, behind her a deep voice followed—*Babineau, Babineau, ugly evil Babineau*—it was the start of a chant, a chant her dad used when they played Find-the-Fox.

Another *chiss* flashed into her brain from outside the window. She heard it but she couldn't process it right now. She was still reeling from the shock of that name and the memory that was trying to piece itself together.

> *Babineau, Babineau, ugly evil Babineau,*
> *He'll grab and eat you if he sees,*
> *Bright eyes flashing through the trees,*
> *Now's your chance to run away,*
> *Since Babineau is on his way!*

She was nine years old again, running through the trees to hide while her father shouted the chant, his eyes covered by his big hands, pulling them down at the end of the last stanza, and she heard him teasing her, "I'm the big bad Babineau, and I'm coming to gobble you up!" It wasn't her eyes that gave her away, it was always the way he said *gobble you up!* That sent her off into giggles and her dad would swoop in, scoop her up, and start gobble-gobbling on her belly until she couldn't breathe from laughter.

She realized she was panting, and she looked around her and saw that she had run straight back to her room. She glanced out her window and saw that the car was still there but as she watched it started up and slid down the hill and out of sight. It was real. All of it. And then she remembered the last *chiss*—". . . NEXT TIME YOU WON'T EVEN KNOW I'M THERE . . ."

Someone had been watching her. Someone serious. And the police must have been anticipating it! Why else the mysterious grounding? Both she and Will suspected it was sinister. But who? Someone who worked for a man named Babineau. Someone who didn't want to underestimate *her!* And good God, she suddenly realized he must have watched Will escape through the bathroom window! She almost tripped over herself getting down the stairs as she dashed to the bathroom where she could barely control her shaking as she worked the stiff, unused window lock and made the window fast. She stood back, almost expecting a shadow to loom into the window, but there was nothing. She made her way back up to her room with that name pounding in her head.

Babineau. Babineau. She wanted it to be coincidence, but that wise voice in her head told her it was not. Their family had been in witness protection because of her dad's testimony in a trial but her parents never, ever talked about it. She didn't know who was convicted or what the names were or even when or where it all happened.

*I'm the big bad Babineau, and I'm coming to gobble you up!* It kept ringing in her head, but she wasn't giggling now. Her parents never mentioned that name in any other context. But maybe this had been her dad's way of inoculating her, protecting her even after he was gone. Maybe he was warning her about Babineau through a game. The words were pretty clear—*So now's your chance to run away, Since Babineau is on his way!*

And then, as if a pile of rocks miraculously un-collapsed and spontaneously formed an elegant stone wall, it all un-fell together. The shooting, her picture in the national news, a detective from New York, a protective lock-down, a scary unidentified man watching the house dropping the name Babineau, and her father's game—it was all laid out in front of her. All this time she was worried it would be Bronco that might come back to get her and instead it was the man who killed her family, Babineau. Who else could it be and what other reason would Babineau have to send someone after her other than to finish the job? *You won't even know I'm there.* Jesus. Jesus Jesus. She wouldn't be safe in Burlington. She wouldn't be safe here. Nobody here would be safe—not as long as she was here.

Whispers of her old nighttime visitor started to swirl around her—she and her father playing Find-the-Fox, strangers approaching in a car at night, sounds of gunfire in the house, and then flames, and smoke, so much smoke. She could smell it even now—shit! She leapt to her door and sniffed.

No smoke.

God, Blue, you are losing it, she thought. *This is not then! Get control of yourself!*

She slumped back on her bed and pressed her hands to her face as if this could prevent her brain from spinning around and around, but nothing was stopping it now, the memories were swirling like a whirlwind. She heard her father's last words, "You have to stay hidden no matter what! Promise me this. Promise!" She hadn't. She broke her promise. Rather it was broken for her—that damn picture—a picture that wouldn't have happened if she hadn't disobeyed Miss Kendrick, if Jordy hadn't gone berserk, if she had just been a little nicer to Jordy. Will's words came back to her, "Blue, just stop it. Stop going down into that hole . . . You are not a bringer of evil. Shit. Just. Happens." God, Will, shit is happening right now, and I don't know what to do.

She let herself drop onto her back, her head thumping into her pillow. She pulled her hands away from her face and let her eyes stare into the blank, dim emptiness of her ceiling. Her hands fell to the covers, her left hand landing with a crisp slap on a sheet of pale white paper. It was the drawing that Will had looked at. She picked it up, stared at it and it stared back. She wished she could crawl into it and escape this insanity just for a moment, just for a break, or maybe forever. Get back to a simpler time, bring her friends in with her, recreate some sort of peaceful pre-Babineau, pre-shooting exis-tence. If only life was a drawing, she could control every stroke, every curve, line-by-line until it became real.

It wasn't though. She was old enough to know that now. But she was also old enough to know that she *could* control some things she couldn't when she was younger. And with that thought, the reality of what she needed to do started to form in her head. It was far from perfect, but it was the sort of plan where there was no hesitation—the sort of plan that forms when you are boxed in and the choices are few and the window of opportunity is closing fast. She just hoped it would be enough to counter the things that were now clearly out of her control.

# 30

## DINER

**Sunday, 9:14 am**

Rodney stared in wary astonishment at the layers of biscuit, sausage, cheese, and egg that he had just exposed with the first bite of his breakfast sandwich. There was something wrong here. He had been eating breakfast sandwiches for the last five years of his life because it was reliably unremarkable and satisfied his morning hunger without unduly distracting from the pure bliss of his first sip of coffee. This sandwich was not unremarkable.

"Like it?" asked the waitress. She glanced at his cup which he hadn't touched yet, her pot ready in hand.

Rodney slowly chewed and nodded. He normally would have swallowed quickly and answered politely, but he didn't want to swallow right away. He had never tasted anything like this in his life.

"It's the home-made biscuit and the local-made sausage. I make the biscuits, and the sausage is from Booth's farm just outside of town."

"It's amazing," he said, after finally swallowing. "There's something sweet in there that is just . . . just . . .'

"Oh, honey. I see this is the first time you've ever tasted real maple syrup!"

Maple syrup. So that's what it tastes like, he thought. He took another bite without thinking, realizing that he hadn't even stopped to have his first sip of coffee.

"Wait until you taste the coffee," she said, as if she could read his mind, and then she moved on to another customer.

He finished the second bite and picked up the coffee. There was something wrong there, too, because it actually smelled like fresh coffee beans rather than something you would use to clean the grease off an engine. He took a sip and swirled it in his mouth and maybe it was the lingering taste of maple syrup, but the coffee tasted as rich as the sandwich. He took two more sips before digging into the sandwich again.

"Told you," came the waitress's voice and he looked up at her. She was carrying a stack of dirty dishes. "The coffee. Right?"

He just shook his head in admiration and kept on chewing.

"You're obviously from out of state," she said.

He nodded and swallowed. "You guessed because of the maple syrup, right?"

She laughed, "Well it could be that but it's mostly because you're Black and you're not a professor at the college, and you are sitting in a diner in the Whitest state in the country. And in this town there are exactly five Black people your age that aren't professors and I'm married to one of them. He's the one that cooked that sandwich. I make the coffee. I'd never trust that man with the coffee." She topped up his cup.

"Well, I guess it's hard to hide that. My name's Rodney."

"Mona. You're law aren't you? And from New York I'm guessing. Detective?"

He smiled. "Now what gave that away?"

"I just see a lot of people from every walk of life, and you learn, you know? You just learn that people *are* who they are. You just *are* a detective."

"I'm impressed, Mona. Maybe you should take my job."

She laughed. "Never in life, honey. I just *am* a diner diva." She started to turn toward the kitchen and then stopped. "Are you here about the shooting?"

Rodney shook his head. "I'm real sorry about that, though."

Mona's bright expression turned to one of resigned sadness. "It hit this town hard. Can't tell you how shocked everyone is. We think we're immune, up here in Vermont, but we're not. We're just like anyone else. I see troubled people every day and do what I can, but you know?" She kept shaking her head. "We're normally packed this time on a Sunday morning but today? Just drive by the church parking lots and you'll see. Today is the day everyone realizes they take God for granted and they need a refresher."

Rodney could only sit and nod. Not much to say to that, he thought.

She suddenly got a thoughtful look on her face. "You know, there was another New Yorker in here this morning. Man was as big as a house. Almost had to turn sideways just to get out the door. I mean muscle big, not beer belly big. Something else going on in town drawing New Yorkers?"

Rodney felt his brow rise up in surprise. "Not that I'm aware of. He wasn't a detective, was he?"

"No, definitely a body-guard type. Somebody important in town? Wouldn't surprise me if some vulture politician was here to grab some scraps of publicity from other people's tragedy."

Rodney put his coffee down, his arm moving slowly, the gears in his mind doing just the opposite. This was not the scenario he had been hoping for. If this man was Purcell, Babineau had moved very quickly. Ominously quickly. Rodney reached into his briefcase and slid a picture out of a file folder. Mona leaned over to look at it without even being invited to.

"The guy on the right. That's him," said Mona, instantly.

Rodney stared at the picture of two men emerging from an office building. The small, wiry, gray-haired man was Babineau. His small form was made even smaller by the enormous man standing next to him on the right side of the picture. Babineau's body-guard/driver/strong-man, Jim Purcell. Damn.

The realization that Purcell was already in town sent a shot of adrenaline running through Rodney's veins. He stuffed the picture back in his briefcase, snapped up his phone and started dialing. Church or not, there was no time for decorum. He had to get hold of Chief Hannah right now. And then Chief Daniels. As he dialed, a paper bag slapped down on the table and an open hand hovered in front of him.

"Give me your business card. I'll call you if I spot him. The rest of your breakfast is in the bag. Go get 'em, Rodney."

He looked at Mona, "Damn. You *are* a diner diva," he said. He pulled a business card and a twenty out of his wallet and put them in her open hand and snatched up the bag and his briefcase. He stood up quickly and headed for the door, his phone up to his ear, urging Chief Hannah to pick up. He paused at the door and looked back at Mona. "You know, if you ever get a hankering to be a detective," he nodded at her hand, "you've got my card."

### Sunday, 9:41 am

"God bless you, Chief Hannah." The elderly parishioner held Chief Hannah's hand for longer than most. It was hard to ignore the sincerity behind it, as it was hard to ignore all the sentiments of the people filing out of Westbury Congregational Church as they passed by the pastor, then the governor (the governor!), and finally, Chief Hannah. She did her best not to mirror those sentiments because if she did, by the end of the line she would be an emotional wreck. She had to keep it together if for no other reason than she knew she had a stack of calls waiting for her response. Her phone had been humming repeatedly and insistently for at least the last twenty minutes and it took every ounce of concentration to purposely ignore it until she could gracefully bow out and find a quiet spot to check it.

She glanced to her right and saw that a gap in the line had formed thanks to an overly effusive parishioner who had a grip on the priest's hand and wouldn't let go. This was her opportunity, and she took it, nodding to the governor before she turned and slid quickly down the steps and around the base of the stairs, stepping into a basement stairwell as she pulled out her phone.

One glance showed a string of calls and text messages from both Detective James and Officer Simmons. "Christ," she said, with only a small amount of guilt. She started by dialing Rodney as it looked like he had gotten the whole avalanche started.

Rodney picked up instantly. "Here's the skinny," he said, without a hello or a moment's hesitation, "I'm here in Westbury, I got in early, and I just learned that one of my targets is in town and there is only one reason he would be here and that is the same reason I am here, Blue DuBois. This is a very real potential threat to her and those around her. I have taken the liberty of speaking to your Officer Simmons and requesting that he send someone over to monitor the O'Day house. He said he would. He also informed me that the family has been asked to stay at home since yesterday afternoon."

"That's right," replied Chief Hannah, keeping the surprise out of her voice and at the same time attempting to quell the surge of shock that was welling up in her gut. "It was the best we could do to protect Blue with our limited manpower. We asked the same of the Woods family, too, as Blue and the Woods boy, Will, are thick as thieves. There was an additional element of protection from a couple of reporters who were hanging out at the DuBois house hoping for interviews. At least as of yesterday." As she said this, a little red flag went up. "We need to be mindful of those reporters if this is a situation we want to keep confidential. Is it? How serious of a threat is this?"

There was a pause before Detective James answered. "I don't

think there is any danger if we have a presence there. It's when we're not there that the situation could become dangerous. If Officer Simmons just parks nearby and monitors the house, I think that should be sufficient for the moment. But he should definitely not reveal anything to the press at this point. I can explain why if we can meet—maybe your office would be best? And can it be now? I think the urgency is high to come up with a plan."

"I'll be there in five," said Chief Hannah, turning to head out of the stairway.

"See you there."

She hung up and started to dial Ed as she jogged toward her cruiser and then a popup message bubble stopped her dead in her tracks. Even though it looked like a routine text message from Ed, the words that populated this message screamed at her at the top of their tiny digital lungs:

*"Blue is missing."*

31

---

# DÉJÀ VU

**Sunday, 10:24 am**

The bitter air glanced off his bare arms, made impervious to the icy breeze by the hot blood pumping through his veins as he tore down the sidewalk through the dry, dead carpet of yellow-brown leaves. He was shaking, but it wasn't from the cold, it was from the adrenaline that was saturating every ounce of his body, adrenaline released by the scream of his sister who barreled into his room yelling, "No no no no no no no! Not again! Not again! This can't be happening!" She crashed into him, wrapping her arms and legs around him, sobbing uncontrollably. He calmed her down enough to hear the words that had launched him sprinting jacketless out the front door into the cold November morning headed as fast as his feet would take him to the big old Victorian house two blocks away: "Blue is missing."

He leapt up the steps and barreled through the front door without demonstrating the slightest bit of propriety, ignoring the exclamations from the knot of startled people gathered in the living room and dashing up the two flights of stairs, coming to a sudden stop in the doorway where he nearly ran into a totally unexpected blockage in the form of a medium height, but solidly built man dressed in a grey suit. Crowded in the tiny room with him was a familiar face, Chief Hannah. Will stood panting, not knowing exactly what to do or say. It had all happened so fast he hadn't even had time to process his sister's words. His whole being had just responded in a reflex action and now here he was transported to the room where only hours had passed since he had kissed Blue and promised he wouldn't give up. He peeked around the man, almost expecting Blue to be hidden behind him. All he saw was a poorly made bed. And a drawing.

Chief Hannah was the first to speak. "Will, this is detective Rodney James from the NYPD. Rodney, meet Will Woods."

Detective James held out his hand and smiled. "Glad to meet you Will. I've heard quite a bit about you."

Will looked into the smiling face, this new element just adding to the swirl of hard-to-grasp information in his head. He felt unable to respond but his hand managed to reflexively float up and grasp Detective James' hand. The handshake was firm and friendly.

Chief Hannah picked up the drawing from Blue's pillow and started speaking in a matter-of-fact but calming way. "Will, Blue left on her own." She put her hand on his shoulder and said quietly, "It wasn't like last time." She handed him the drawing. It was the one he had looked at last night. "Turn it over," she said.

He did, and there, in Blue's handwriting, he read[1]:

"Why did you give no hint that night
That quickly after the morrow's dawn,
And calmly, as if indifferent quite,
You would close your term here, up
     and be gone
Where I could not follow
With wing of swallow
To gain one glimpse of you ever anon!"

I am sorry I couldn't say goodbye.
I have to disappear for a while.
     -B


Will blinked. He read it again. And again. And each time, a mixture of anger, frustration, fear, and despair rose higher and higher, catalyzing such a conflicting set of emotions that he couldn't stand-up anymore. He leaned his back against the door jamb and slid down it until he was sitting on the floor.

Chief Hannah crouched down. "Hey, Will. I know this is sudden and upsetting. I have to ask you, though, can you think of anything that would have triggered this?"

Will looked at Chief Hannah. He knew she wasn't to blame, but the angry part of him decided that it had to get out somehow. "Isn't it obvious? She was sick of her life being run by a bunch of bureaucrats who are more concerned about their own agendas than a person's life! The DFC was going to take her away from here! This house! This family! Look around this room! This is the first place she's had a decent life since her family was ripped away from her! I'm glad she ran away." He stood up and looked at Detective James, "And what are you here for? Is there something you haven't told us that would be even more reason for her to leave? Why the lock-down? Why everything? You guys should be over at Jordy's house figuring out why the hell he went berserk instead of hanging around here and screwing up our lives just because we happen to be enjoying being kids."

He turned to get away from a room that was too crowded with people that didn't belong there. He needed to get out and breathe, but his way was blocked by Wu, who was coming up the stairs making the already overcrowded space claustrophobic.

"Dude, I kept texting you to tell you about this, but I didn't get any response," said Wu.

Will realized he had turned his phone off last night and didn't even have a chance to look at it in his hurry. He was amazed to even find it still in his pocket. He pulled it out, turned it back on and mumbled, "Sorry, Wu." He put the phone back in his pocket and started to squeeze by Wu, "I gotta get out of here." And then, as if choreographed for the moment, three phones chimed out three different ringtones in sequence. Will stopped and looked at Wu who looked back with equal surprise. Will opened his phone and Wu pulled his out and then there was silence as they read the newly arrived messages.

Wu broke the silence, "Did you get the same thing?" He held up his phone to Will.

To: benwu@westburyvt.net, annabannana@westburyvt.net, wwoods@westburyvt.net
From: waifontheroad@gmail.com
I am going to miss you all. You are the only real friends I've had. Ever. I am sorry if I was not a good friend back. I know I am messed up. I know everything is messed up right now and I have to leave. It's not just the DFC, it's something that happened last night. Chief Hannah can fill you in. I am going to miss you, but everyone will be safer this way. Please hug Rose and Sam and Nate for me. And Wu, hug MB and

PB for me and tell them I love them. A lot. Forever. You
guys, too.
-Blue

Will glanced at it and said, "Yeah." He didn't tell Wu about a
second email he had received addressed only to him. Will turned to
Chief Hanna. She was holding up her phone to Detective James.

"Well, I think that confirms it. No need to interview her now,"
said Detective James.

"Confirms what?" demanded Will.

Detective James nodded to Chief Hannah and she nodded back.

"Let's go downstairs. I think we have a lot to talk about," said
Detective James. Chief Hannah turned and held her phone up to
Will. Wu looked over Will's shoulder and they both read the
message.

To: pchannah@westburyvt.gov
From: waifontheroad@gmail.com
I'm pretty sure a man named Babineau killed my family. It
would take too long to explain why I know his name and
why I haven't talked about it before, so please just trust me
on this. One of his men was watching our house last night.
He was in a car. I am sorry I couldn't see the license, the car
was too far away. I couldn't really see him either, but I could
"hear" him. I heard enough to know that I need to disappear. I am sorry I can't help you more. Please don't try to
find me and don't worry about me. I can take care of myself.
I am sorry I waited to send this, but I wanted to make sure I
was out of reach. I am no longer in Vermont. And I am safe.
-Blue

Of all the thoughts bouncing around his head, the new one
from this message torpedoed them all, exploding in his brain and
spilling out of his mouth, "Who the *hell* is Babineau?"

### Sunday, 11:47 am

A somber silence blanketed the O'Day living room but underneath the blanket was an electric air of tense anticipation. Ma Beth, Pa Bill, Mr. and Mrs. Woods, Wu, and Will sat scattered around the room waiting for Chief Hannah and Detective James who were conferring quietly in the kitchen.

Will tapped the back of his phone impatiently as he stared intently at the screen, re-reading the last email from Blue for the nth time trying to find some solace. Instead, he felt only confusion, anger, frustration, and loss:

To: wwoods@westburyvt.net
From: waifontheroad@gmail.com
Hey. Maybe when I'm eighteen I'll reappear. I don't know.
Who knows how this is going to go. All I know is that I have
to disappear right now to stay safe and keep everyone else
safe. It's better for everyone this way. I won't be back unless
it is safe and that might be never. Please don't forget me but
please move on. This sucks but it doesn't have to suck for
you. This is my problem. You can still live a normal life.
Please do that for me. I love you and that will never change
no matter how things turn out.
-Blue

His phone buzzed, and he looked at the inbox hoping for something different to be there, but it was the same:

<waifontheroad@gmail.com>: host gmail-smtp-in.l.google.-
com[xxx.xxx.197.27] said:
xxx-5.1.1 The email account that you tried to reach has been
deleted.

The message joined the other dozen or so that had collected as he tried and tried again to contact Blue at this new, and now deleted, address, knowing each time the response would be the same. What was the definition of insanity? Doing the same thing over and over and expecting a different result? So maybe I am insane, he thought. Maybe this is what it feels like.

He scrolled through his messages. There was no response from her old email address either. No text messages. Nothing but a "not available" automated reply on his phone calls. He was sure she had turned her phone off and probably even yanked the battery so she couldn't be tracked.

He looked up at the sound of a clearing throat. Detective James and Chief Hannah had entered the living room and sat down. Detective James cleared his throat again and began. "I want to start by saying that what I am about to tell you is confidential and that I am probably breaching protocol by allowing Wu and Will to be here but given your involvement and with the permission of your parents, I am using my discretion, so please," he looked pointedly at Wu and then Will, "don't give me reason to regret it."

Will wanted to be cooperative and agreeable, but his rational, civil side had been battered down by an angry, frustrated, bitter, and decidedly uncivil anti-Will living inside him. Regardless, he gave Detective James a reluctant, sullen nod.

Detective James studied Will for a moment, his features revealing a flash of empathy. Will could sense it, and it mellowed him out a little bit.

"Okay then," said Detective James. He turned to the rest of the room and began. "The reason I am here is because the NYPD Cold Case Squad has reopened a case that I was involved in five years ago, an investigation into the deaths of a family with the last name of Stanton. The deaths occurred at their home in the Adirondacks in New York—in fact, not so very far from here. Now what most of you don't know is that Stanton is a name given to the family by the Witness Protection Program, also known as WITSEC, or Witness Security. This program is administered by the U.S. Marshalls.

What I am about to tell you is permissible only because it is presumed that the whole family was killed in this incident and hence the need for secrecy somewhat relaxed. Not entirely, just somewhat."

"Now please pay attention because this can get confusing. The WITSEC names of the victims were Samuel, Elizabeth, Heather, and Blue Stanton." He paused to let this sink in, and it didn't fail to sink into Will's brain. Heather was the name of Blue's sister. But Stanton?

Detective James continued, "However, the actual pre-WITSEC names of the victims were André, Amélie, and Belle DuBois. Heather was born after they went into WITSEC."

There was a gasp and an exchange of confused looks around the room. Wu was the first to speak, "You said *Belle* DuBois?"

"Yes," replied Chief Hannah, "aka Blue *Stanton.* Not Blue *DuBois.* It's easy to jump to the conclusion that Belle DuBois might be Blue DuBois. However, according to the case records, Belle DuBois perished with the rest of her family."

"That's right." said Detective James. "That being said, the similarity in names is actually what caused this case to be reopened. You see the incident last August that you were involved in, Will, when Blue was kidnapped, caught the eye of a retired colleague of mine and he raised a 'what if?' That 'what if' was 'what if there *was* a survivor?' What if Belle DuBois survived? It would be reasonable to surmise that the U.S. Marshalls might have covered it up and kept the survivor in witness protection."

"But wouldn't the Marshall's have told you?" asked Will.

Detective James smiled. "That's exactly what we thought, and I do believe they would have told us if that is what they had done; however, when we pressed them they claimed that as far as their records show, Belle DuBois, aka Blue Stanton, perished along with the rest of her family and the case was closed as far as they were concerned."

"That means there would be a death certificate," said Pa Bill.

"Correct, and, in fact, there is, for every member of the Stanton family," replied Detective James.

"Could someone fake a death certificate?" asked Wu.

"The U.S. Marshalls have the ability to completely re-fabricate identities and that includes issuing death certificates for people who are still living. They deny doing this for Blue, however."

"But Blue would remember if she was ever Blue Stanton, right? She would be able to explain everything," said Will.

"You would think she might have shared something like that with us," said Ma Beth, speaking almost apologetically. "But it has taken a while for her to come out of her shell. We don't push the kids. But they always open up eventually, when they're ready."

"I get it," said Detective James, "and Dr. Woods has been very helpful in explaining PTSD and repressed memories and their effect on people. Ordinarily, I wouldn't have pushed to come up and interview Blue, but recent events have made the circumstances anything but ordinary."

"Babineau," said Will. The name still had an exotic and menacing tone to it, as if it wasn't a person but a creature.

"Exactly. Babineau is a very dangerous man and the minute we saw the newspaper picture of Blue, we were sure he would make the connection. We just didn't expect him to react so fast, and to tell you the truth, I was shocked by Blue's email to Chief Hannah—that she would know or even remember the name 'Babineau' was astonishing to say the least. But that also pretty much confirms that Blue DuBois is probably Belle DuBois."

"You said 'react,'" said Pa Bill. "What do you mean by that?"

"The email Blue sent Chief Hannah said she saw someone watching the house last night. I think it is the same man that was seen at the Westbury Diner this morning—a man named Jim Purcell, Babineau's personal, um, 'assistant.'"

"You mean 'goon,'" said Will. "The real killer."

"Well, you are right in that Jim Purcell is a dangerous man, but we know for sure that he was not involved directly in the deaths of

Blue's family. We are quite sure it was a man who is referred to as El Segador. It means "the reaper." Kind of corny sounding, I know, but there is nothing corny about El Segador. He is linked to several deaths and is well known as a hit man. We suspect Babineau has used him several times, but we've never been able to positively identify him or his accomplices, that is until just recently."

"Recently?" said Wu.

"We had a DNA hit. We had some DNA evidence from the site of the Stanton murder, but at the time, we couldn't find a match. We redid the search a couple of weeks ago and got a match with a man who died. It turns out, El Segador died a natural death and wound up in the morgue and that's how we identified him."

"That's kind of crazy. But if he is dead, isn't the threat over?" said Will.

"Not at all. As you pointed out, Jim Purcell is a definite threat. And El Segador is not the only 'reaper' out there, plus there are his accomplices who are still alive, and we know a lot more about them now. It is very likely that one of them was involved in the presumed murder of the Stantons."

For the first time, Will's dad, who had sat quietly listening, spoke up. "So there is the possibility that Blue was an eye-witness to her family's murder and might be able to identify one of El Segador's accomplices and if you could apprehend them and do a plea deal, you could link Babineau to the Stanton's murder and put him in jail, which would be justice for a lot more than just the Stanton's murder. And since you now know the identity of El Segador, you have a better chance of identifying his accomplices. Am I on the mark?"

Detective James smiled and nodded appreciatively. "I saw the gears moving in your head. You are right on the mark and you are lacking only one more detail that I only recently learned of this morning from a colleague at NYPD." He held up his phone.

"You have the identity of the accomplices?" said Chief Hannah.

"I do. El Segador lived a quiet and seemingly respectable life in a small town north of New York City. He was a widower and his neighbors said he was generally friendly although he could be a little harsh with his two sons. It turns out he was grooming his sons for the family business. They were his primary accomplices. And the name 'El Segador' was a total smokescreen. This family doesn't have a speck of Spanish blood. In fact, they are as Irish as could be. El Segador's real name is Justin Farrell. His sons are William and Ethan."

Chief Hannah shot straight out of her chair and exploded, "BRONCO! JESUS CHRIST!"

The suddenness of the outburst caused every single person, and even some of the furniture, to jump. Chief Hannah looked around the astonished room until her eyes landed on Will. Her face recovered some of its professional stoicism and she turned to Ma Beth and said, "I'm sorry, I didn't mean to swear." And then, with a calm explanatory voice she turned to Detective James and said, "William Farrell, El Segador's son, is our Bronco. Bronco is William Farrell."

**Sunday, 4:37 pm**

Babineau puffed thoughtfully on his cigar, carefully considering the briefing from his body-guard and confidante, Jim Purcell.

At length he spoke, "You're sure it was Detective *Rodney* James?"

Jim sat across from Babineau. He didn't shift and didn't waver. "No doubt about it. I saw him leaving the diner not long after I was there. I had a clear shot at his face. He was in a hurry and he didn't see me. I'm guessing I was ID'ed by the waitress."

Babineau was quiet again. Another puff. "A bad break, him being there. Not your fault. It does confirm something, though."

"She's the daughter of André DuBois," said Jim.

Babineau nodded. He turned away from Jim and stared out the window into the city darkness that wasn't really that dark. It was filled with lights: neon signs, streetlights, storefronts, headlights, and something more. He saw something that no one else did. Buried in the silhouettes of the hundreds of pedestrians crowding the sidewalks in a constant flow of nightlife, he could see a constellation of very faint dots right where the silhouette's eyes would be. The glowing dots bounced in pairs to the footsteps of their owners, tiny glows, dancing like fireflies in the dark.

He turned back to Jim. "And now the girl is missing," he said.

"According to the news," said Jim. "They are reporting that she ran away because of the picture in the paper—the state was going to take her back into a group home for protection and she didn't want to go." Jim paused and then said, "You think we should try to track her down?"

Babineau leaned back in his chair and puffed thoughtfully on his cigar. Most runaways pop up again on their own, he thought. Yet this girl was not 'most runaways' by a long shot.

"Not much chance in tracking her down. There's a much better chance of netting her. A net doesn't need much tending and sometimes you get lucky. Especially if you set them in the right spots."

"Where would those be?" asked Jim.

Babineau smiled. "I'm not going to tell you *everything*. Let's just say I've got some good hunches."

"When do I go?"

Babineau laughed. "No, not you this time. For one thing this might take a long time. Second thing, I need you around here. Third thing, I have someone else that is perfect for the job. And last thing—the girl spotted you, right?"

"Right. I don't know how. I was two blocks away." Jim paused. "You know, I can't really be sure. It was likely just coincidence. She was probably staring out the window at nothing and happened to be pointed my direction." He shifted in his seat. "I have to tell you, though . . . I was genuinely spooked. Maybe I'm getting jumpy."

Babineau turned back to Jim and considered him carefully. The guy was solid. He was upfront. He'd been with him for six years and never disappointed. But this was a test Jim had never encountered before. A vox. If Jim hadn't expressed his discomfort, Babineau would have had reason to continue excluding him, but because he did, Jim had unknowingly just gained entrance into Babineau's most trusted inner circle.

"You're not jumpy. You are very perceptive. I have no doubt she did see you. Well, not exactly see you. She probably heard you." Babineau took a very satisfactory puff on the cigar as he watched Jim's face make the most imperceptible yet entertaining look of shock and surprise. Only for a moment. Babineau chuckled. "I have to apologize. I haven't been totally upfront with you about a few things."

Jim was silent, yet unable to suppress the tiniest expression of puzzlement.

"You see, DuBois inherited a certain gene that has all but disappeared from the gene pool. His wife had it, too, and hence his daughters inherited it. This gene is sort of like the gene a dog has that causes their eyes to glow—you know when you shine a light on them at night? Well, DuBois' eyes glow, only you can't see this glow because it's infrared, you see?"

He paused, watching for Jim's response. Jim nodded, the quizzical expression still on his face, but clearly following what was being said. Babineau pulled on his cigar and the end glowed fiery red.

"Sort of like the end of my cigar, only invisible."

Jim nodded again.

"The interesting thing is that a vestigial tissue still exists in most of us, so our eyes glow a little bit, too. Much dimmer, but still there. Sometimes it shows up in photography, but everyone assumes that it is red-eye reflection."

Jim nodded, but still didn't say anything.

"So what is the purpose of this glow, you ask? It's for communication, you see. Their kind call it vox oculis, or 'voice of the eyes.' They can hear each other's thoughts when they want to share them." He looked at Jim and saw that one eyebrow had popped up. "Pretty bizarre, right? Unbelievable, right?"

Jim squirmed slightly. "It is . . . a bit hard to believe."

"Let me make it a little more real to you. The vestigial tissue that we have is enough that these people can hear your thoughts in their head. The kind of thoughts that are right at the edge of your tongue, the ones you want to say out loud, but you don't. That," he took a pull on his cigar for dramatic emphasis, "is what they can hear. Like it or not, they can hear what you're thinking. If you think about it, you can understand why she reacted to you the way she did."

"Jesus."

Babineau chuckled.

"So, assuming this is true," said Jim, "I was almost two blocks away. Are you saying these people could hear my thoughts from two blocks away?"

"Well, no, probably not. They could hear each other that far because their eyes are quite bright. But yours, not so much. However, you had binoculars, right?"

"Yes, but . . ."

"Did you ever look in the other end of the binoculars?"

Jim didn't answer.

"They magnified your eyes to her. You had the Zeiss 20x60, didn't you?"

Jim nodded.

"Well, there you have it. Do you have them with you?"

Jim stepped out of the office and returned, holding the binoculars.

"Hold them up and look at me."

Jim held the binoculars to his eyes and pointed them towards Babineau.

"Now say 'fuck you, you crazy old man' in your head. Not out loud, though I know you'd like to at times." He laughed. "Don't worry about it. I certainly wouldn't blame you—and there you go! Bright as a flashlight."

Jim lowered the binoculars. "Wait, I thought you said it was invisible."

"That's right, it is. Human genetics only allows most people's eyes to see the regular light spectrum, that is unless . . ." he took another puff on his cigar, ". . . unless you happen to have a gene that I inherited from my parents."

Six years of experience with Jim was enough for Babineau to sense the slight change in posture, the crinkle of the eyebrow, the squint in the eyes, and the slight ember like glow in his retina—the cues anyone else would have missed—but revealed to Babineau, to his delight, the fact that Jim was genuinely caught by surprise.

"Now while that sinks in, allow me to explain to you a little history about *my* people…"

## 32

---

# ICE FISHING IN AMERICA

**Sunday, 4:56 pm, Eagle Lake, NY**

Bronco stared out at the wrinkled blue-green-white landscape framed in the flexible plastic windows of the fabric ice fishing hut. The image was as surreal as his mood and he was kind of digging it. He was comfortably warm, the cozy hut doing an admirable job of keeping what little icy breeze there was from reaching him. A half-empty pint of peppermint schnapps was doing a good job of stoking his inner furnace as well as his mood.

His impulse to go to the outdoor sports shop straight from the coffee shop on Saturday had yielded a complete ice fishing kit that folded itself into its own sled. Instant ice-fishing, the salesman said. Best way to try it out. "If you don't like it, bring it back within a week for a full refund." He had loaned him the ice-auger, too. "We can't take those back, so we have this loaner." An amazingly simple fishing gear package rounded things out along with the advice on the peppermint schnapps. "It's a classic," said the salesman, "but drink lots of water, too—and beer to round it out."

So now, here he was on a late fall Sunday afternoon, two brown trout sitting at his feet, a nice buzz on, and a little tingle from his saliva glands anticipating the first bite of breaded pan-fried trout tonight. It was astonishing, really. He'd never fished in his life. His intent was only to try out his metal detector but since the detector head wouldn't fit through the hole made by the auger, he decided to drop a line in and see what happened. He had his first fish within a couple of minutes, the second after a beer and two shots of schnapps. Together they made a surprisingly satisfying accomplishment for the day

A rattle of wind shook the shanty as if it was satisfied, too. Bronco looked out the window where the gust had animated the scene outside, golden brown leaves skittering across the dusty white ice, weaving through a hodge-podge of fellow ice shacks scattered about, each sheltering a fellow hermit pursuing their own personal ritual. It made him think. The town scene had gotten monotonous and the ski crowd irritating. He had burnt out on womanizing, the meagre reward being just not worth the effort. It wasn't like love was any part of it—he wasn't looking for that and neither were they. But here—it was so quiet and simple. Just a man pulling his food out of a lake. No one bothering him. He realized that this had been perhaps the best entertainment he'd had in months.

As if the universe sensed that he was getting too comfortable with that notion, the forgotten electronic tether in his pocket started buzzing. He hesitated, then took another pull on the schnapps before pulling out the phone. He looked at the name glowing on the phone's screen and swore. He did not need or want to talk to this person right now. In fact, he did not want to talk to him ever. He cursed himself for not purging that name from his contacts. Instead, it stared at him menacingly. There is no way that this guy should have been able to find the number for this phone, and the fact that he did made Bronco very uncomfortable. If he tracked down this number then he probably also knew a lot more. Far too much to be ignored. Dammit. He swiped the answer button.

*"I have a proposition for you."* The voice coming from the phone

was a few years older than the last time he heard it, but irritatingly familiar. No greeting. Straight to business.

"Fuck off, I don't owe you anything," Bronco replied.

*"Well, that's not exactly true. Your late father left an obligation behind him,"* said the voice.

"Whatever my shit-father owed you, you can take it up with him when you join him in hell."

The electronically degraded cackle that came out of the phone sounded like it was coming directly from hell. *"Well, you certainly have your dad's temper. I'll give you that. So I'll tell you what I told him when he got in a testy mood and that's this: just remember what I'm capable of."*

Bronco didn't have anything to say to that. He knew very well what this guy was capable of. He wanted this conversation to end, but he knew that he was cornered.

The voice went on, *"Look, let's get down to business. Your dad owed me way more than I'm going to ask of you. This is a simple job and after it's over you can disappear, and I'll never bother you again."*

Bullshit, thought Bronco. "Go on," he said.

*"All you have to do is sit tight until you get a phone call. And then I'll tell you when and where I want you to detain someone I need to talk to. Once that's done, the job is over."*

"That's it? Just sit here?" Bronco said it with a neutral tone, but he knew for certain there would be way more behind the job than just this.

*"Until you get a call,"* the voice replied. *"I know where you are, and you happen to be geographically located in the right place right now. Lucky you. Now during this job there will be others contacting you. You will know them because they will mention the name 'Stanton' and address you by your real name."*

Bronco froze. Using his real name. That was *not* okay, not even by this guy's standards. "You do anything to expose me and you'll regret it." Bronco realized he was squeezing his phone, hard.

*"Oh, no, no, of course not!"* said the voice. *"You misunderstand me. I*

*never betrayed your father's real name, and I won't betray your name, William Anthony Farrell. That is, as long as it goes both ways."*

I get the message, you bastard, thought Bronco. "I'd *never* rat," he said. At least not on someone who could track him down this easily.

*"No, I don't expect you would, Hijo del Segador*[1]*."*

God damn you, Theo Babineau.

## 33

## GONE

Monday dawned gray and ominous, the clouds pressing down as if the weight of the snow inside them was about to split their billowy bottoms and burst out onto the village below. By noon, the grayness had diminished surprisingly little and was broken only by the occasional patch of cobalt blue that managed to elbow its way through the shoulders of the undulating banks of cumulus as they played a non-stop slow-motion shoving match in the sky, each cloud scrambling to plow eastward and join in the blizzard that was about to envelop New England.

A lone raven hovered over the village, attempting to find a peaceful spot away from an annoying mob of crows. The crows had been hectoring him ever since he had glided a little too close to where they were congregating. He wasn't quite sure what he had done to tick these particular birds off. Maybe they had found some piece of road-kill they wanted to protect. Maybe they were just bored. Who knows? If it was road-kill, he had no interest in it, having just enjoyed a nearly intact cheeseburger that he had found in a dumpster. The previous owner of the burger had only taken a single bite and then thrown it away. The burger even still had its pickles. The raven was particularly fond of pickles.

He settled on a high branch of an immense old maple tree that was perched in a hilly section of the town. It was quieter here than in the center of the village, and it suited him perfectly now that the crows appeared to have given up and gone away.

The raven didn't come to town often. When he did, all the little winter birds seemed intent on mobbing him away from their precious bird feeders. As if he would ever get so desperate as to go down and eat that pathetic plant seed they loved so much. This tree was his favorite spot. It was quiet and he was particularly fond of the sparkly human fledgling that lived at the top of the house opposite the tree.

He didn't know why he was drawn to the humans with sparkly eyes, but they made him feel comfortable, like a mate, like a partner. And for some reason they always made him think about food.

This young sparkly flashed her eyes at him from time to time and it made him croak with pleasure. It's why he returned to the tree regularly. But today he was sad, in spite of the windfall of the hamburger. This sparkly had fledged. He knew she would someday, but he didn't know much about human behavior so some part of him hoped that she would stay in her nest even after she had fledged. But apparently they fly away. He had watched this one fly. It had been early in the morning yesterday. She had crawled out the window and he almost expected her to leap and flap her wings like a young raven, but of course their wings were poor, and they were flightless, so he was relieved to see her descend safely to the ground.

He had followed her as she scurried through the gray morning, carrying her nest materials in the strange way that humans do in bags that were made of the same material as the skins that they wore. She had then hurried down to a building where she boarded one of those long cans that he knew carried humans a long way away, faster than he could fly. They often didn't come back.

She hadn't come back. He hopped along the branch for a bit, croaking, and clucking thoughtfully. Maybe she would come back, maybe not, but he decided that for now, he would check back daily. Meanwhile, he would fly over to the other sparkly fledglings and see if he could get a flash out of the boy or the girl. Worth a try, even though they had yet to notice him, probably because he could never stay long due to the ill-tempered ancient human in the house behind theirs, who tended to shoo him away.

With a farewell "kwa-koo" to the girl's window, he pumped his powerful wings and wove his way through the trees to look for a secure perch to see if he could get a response from the other sparklies.

---

"Will . . ." Rose stood in his doorway, her shoulder pressed against the frame, her head tilted so that her hair was hanging parallel to the wall, a light brown waterfall against a mossy green cliff. Will was staring at his computer screen, his hand aching from hours of gripping the mouse and clicking deep into every search result and hoping for something he hadn't already seen. He was finding it hard to tear his eyes away from the screen, afraid he might miss something, but he did turn away. He would always turn away for his sister.

"*Hey, little meerkat.*"

"*Will,*" she repeated, "*what happens next?*"

Will looked at the floor. He didn't know. God, he had been looking for that answer from the minute Detective James and Chief Hannah had exposed the full nature of the beast yesterday afternoon straight through to now, a day-and-a-half later. It was Monday, but school was closed and would be through the Thanksgiving holiday. And while everyone outside of the O'Day and Woods households were trying to process the aftermath of the 'Westbury School Shooting' as it was now labeled and debated and discussed, inside the Woods and O'Day families it was an entirely different discussion. Where was Blue? Would she return on her own? When? How long could she last out there? What about Bronco? What about Babineau?

Yeah. What about Babineau? Will had spent half his time asking that question in every way that he could in multiple search engines. The answer was a mosaic of individual articles. Babineau was a respected businessman dealing in city landscaping. Babineau was acquitted in multiple criminal investigations. Babineau had sued multiple agencies for libel. In short, the picture, when pieced together from all the headlines, revealed Babineau as an opportunist that didn't expose much of his underbelly and was an expert at slipping through the legal forest unseen and untouched.

The other question was the one that left him depressed and frustrated. It was becoming clear to him: if someone as intelligent and resourceful as Blue wanted to disappear, there wasn't much you could do to find them. Even in this technological age, the basics hadn't changed. Unless she screws up and does something that sets a red flag in some government system, like gives out her social security number or uses her real name or gets arrested, there was nothing that Will could do short of riding out on a quest for a needle in a very large haystack.

But worse than that was the fact that he had no way of contacting her—warning her—Bronco's father was the one sent by Babineau to kill her family. Bronco may even have been an accomplice. And Bronco's real name was William Farrell. Bronco Bill Farrell. Jesus. She was out there alone, and two stone cold killers were motivated to find her and silence her.

"Will?"

He looked back up at his sister, his forehead leaning into his palm. He breathed out a long, heavy, sigh of surrender.

"*I just don't know. I don't.*"

His eyes dropped to the floor—neutral territory where he didn't have to look at worried eyes that weren't his own and would obscure the tears that were welling up. He had lost the ability to control the critical mass of emotions that churned inside of him, and he knew that was okay. Blue would have told him that. That it was okay.

Rose's arms wrapped around him. He closed the lid of his laptop, removing the harsh glow of the screen and pulled her to him. They held each other tightly as the afternoon faded into the stark grayness of a November evening. When a cold gust caused the bare branches of the trees outside to click and scrape in a macabre pantomime, Will may or may not have noticed the sound of powerful wings launching a dark-feathered observer deep into the oncoming night.

# EPILOGUE

"Two threes and a two on deck!" Flo clipped the order on the kitchen telegraph, grabbed a fresh pot from the coffee station, and made her route, scanning for any fresh customers. She had felt a blast of cold air on her back earlier, so she knew someone had come in. There she was in a booth by the window. Flo's quick, practiced glance registered a teenager, maybe sixteen, bleach blond hair (platinum, very recent), stacked bob haircut (disheveled from wearing a wool cap for too long), hasty face wash (remnants of makeup) with a small backpack and a very full, very ragged duffle bag keeping her company. Killing time before catching a bus, maybe, she thought.

"Coffee, honey?" She didn't wait for an answer, just plunked down the cup and poured. This girl looked like she needed coffee whether she drank it or not.

"Thanks," said the girl. She said it in a voice that was soft, with a tinge of fatigue, but confident.

Flo slid a menu down in front of her, "Tuesday half price special for seniors. Not high school seniors, but for today, I'll make an exception. You a senior, honey?"

"If I can get half price."

This girl is quick, thought Flo. She studied her for a second. Her clothes were neat, but clearly slept-in. The first thing that came to Flo's mind was "runaway." She knew it for sure. As soon as she thought this, though, a worried look flashed across the girl's features. It was the strangest thing. It was as if Flo had said "runaway" out loud to the girl.

"All right, sweetie, it looks like you could use a break. That's why they call it break-fast, you know." She winked at the girl and thought no more about it. She turned to the business at hand which was getting to the next table.

It was getting crowded, quick. Tuesday's were always busy with the senior crowd, and there were plenty of seniors in Malone— more than she had imagined when she first started senior Tuesdays. She didn't mind though. It was always better to be too busy than too quiet, and these were the best customers—always polite to the staff and to each other. The half-price didn't really matter because they tipped heavily. They were a close bunch, and the breakfast banter was dependably brisk with gentle old-folk humor and jabs. Of course, there were always the somber Tuesdays after someone passed, but even then, it felt good to be around people who had seen so much and were able to take everything with a perspective gained from years of experience. A couple of them were WWII veterans, for God's sake.

A shout from the kitchen turned her attention to the kitchen bar. The orders had started stacking up and food was flowing out non-stop. No time for reflection, she thought. No time for anything today. Not only was it senior Tuesday, but Becky had called in sick. Again. Sick my ass, she thought. What was it, the fourth time this month? Fifth time? Last time unless she shaped up. She grabbed the next order off the bar and glanced at the slip. The girl's order. She was lucky she got in early. The tiny diner was already full and there were people waiting in the entryway. Flo wove her way through the jammed tables over to the girl, who was poring over the local paper.

"Here you go, honey, sorry it took so long. We're short-handed. Once the holidays come, the help gets a little flakey. That's the way it is in this business." She managed a glance of the page the girl was studying. Help wanted ads. She hovered a moment and then said, "How old are you, honey?"

The girl looked up. "Eighteen?"

Flo couldn't suppress a snort. Nice try, girl, she thought. "C'mon, what's your real age."

The girl looked defeated. "Seventeen," she said and then folded the paper and turned to her breakfast. "Thanks," she added. "It looks good."

And you look famished, Flo thought. The girl was digging in with vigor. Flo watched her for a moment. She could buy seventeen. Fourteen, seventeen, something in-between—you couldn't always tell at her stage of life, but she seemed to have her act together.

Flo turned to get the next order but got held up as some customers were seating themselves at a table that hadn't been cleared yet. This was getting ridiculous. She was falling behind. It was going to be like this the rest of the day and for the next few weeks unless Becky suddenly turned reliable—or Flo did something about it.

She turned back to the girl. "What's your name, hon?"

The girl looked up from her breakfast, a fork-full of egg poised for her next bite. There was a very slight hesitation before she answered. "Sam," she said, and resumed eating.

Flo wasn't fooled, but she played along. "Sam for Samantha?"

The girl nodded. Flo kept her eyes on Sam, and Sam looked back without flinching. But you look oh so young, thought Flo at the exact moment that someone bumped her from behind. She nearly splattered a tray full of dishes across the room. Jesus, she thought, this is getting nuts. She looked back at the girl.

"You know how to wait tables, Sam?"

# ACKNOWLEDGMENTS

Eighty-eight thousand words are a lot of words to put in just the right order with just the right number of commas, semicolons, italics, quotes, double-quotes, em dashes—not to mention grammar and capitalization and on and on! I just write the story but the people in the list below make sure that story is clear, consistent, and above all, clean of all those annoying typos and bone-headed oversights. Thanks, friends, family, and colleagues, for making me look good and making *Vox Oculis: The Innocence of Westbury* readable and enjoyable for everyone else:

Collin Parker
Jessica Gang
Esther Adele Martin
Elizabeth Cady Martin

# ENDNOTES

## Prologue

1. WITSEC: Federal Witness Security program. Also known as WPP: Witness Protection Program.

## 16. Two Cases, Two Clues

1. The DFC in this story is fictional with no relationship to the Vermont Department for Children and Families (DCF).

## 23. Black Friday, November 18, 2011

1. CSST: Crime Scene Search Team

## 24. Collateral Damage

1. MMO: Massively Multiplayer Online game.

## 26. Old Business

1. El Segador: The Reaper, *Spanish*

## 27. Rising From the Ashes

1. Ravens have a remarkable capacity to mimic and create sounds. This is a raven "word" a regional flock may have developed when greeting a vox.
2. Veraque: empathy, pronounced "veh-rack," *Latin*

## 31. Déjà Vu

1.  From "The Going" by Thomas Hardy

## 32. Ice Fishing In America

1.  Hijo del Segador: Reaper's son, *Spanish*

# ABOUT THE AUTHOR

*Photo Credit: Dorothy Schnure*

Frederic Martin lives and writes in and about Vermont. He was awarded the Vermont Writer's Prize for his short story *Maybe Lake Carmi*. His first novel, *Not Alone*, was published in February, 2020. *Not Alone* is the first book in the *Vox Oculis* YA science fiction thriller trilogy. *The Innocence of Westbury* is the second novel of the trilogy. The final book, *Forest*, will be published in the summer of 2022.

www.ingramcontent.com/pod-product-compliance
Lightning Source LLC
Chambersburg PA
CBHW061322190726
48288CB00002B/619